D0475347

DROWNING PRACTICE

ALSO BY MIKE MEGINNIS

Fat Man and Little Boy (2014)

DROWNING PRACTICE

A Novel

MIKE MEGINNIS

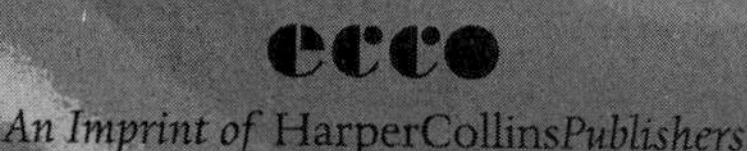

An Imprint of HarperCollins*Publishers*

This is a work of fiction. Names, characters, places, and incidents are products of the author's imagination or are used fictitiously and are not to be construed as real. Any resemblance to actual events, locales, organizations, or persons, living or dead, is entirely coincidental.

DROWNING PRACTICE. Copyright © 2022 by Mike Meginnis. All rights reserved. Printed in the United States of America. No part of this book may be used or reproduced in any manner whatsoever without written permission except in the case of brief quotations embodied in critical articles and reviews. For information, address HarperCollins Publishers, 195 Broadway, New York, NY 10007.

HarperCollins books may be purchased for educational, business, or sales promotional use. For information, please email the Special Markets Department at SPsales@harpercollins.com.

Ecco® and HarperCollins® are trademarks of HarperCollins Publishers.

FIRST EDITION

Designed by Angie Boutin
Title page image © sakura/stock.adobe.com

Library of Congress Cataloging-in-Publication Data has been applied for.

ISBN 978-0-06-307614-3

22 23 24 25 26 LSC 10 9 8 7 6 5 4 3 2 1

This one too is for Tracy, and for Mom.

DROWNING PRACTICE

MAY, MOTT

NOT EVERYONE BELIEVED THE WORLD WOULD END THAT YEAR. There remained a few optimists, agnostics, and well-meaning liars who claimed it might endure at least a few months longer, possibly even forever. Until this question was settled, however, there would be little point in spending good money to repair or replace what was broken or used up, and least of all what benefitted children, who would probably never repay such investments. Public schools stopped buying supplies. In the unlikely event that the dream about November proved wrong, they would resume their purchases in December. Taxpayers would thank them for running a surplus.

Mott attended a public middle school for reasons both financial and political, according to her mother, and though some dedicated educators now paid for necessities out of pocket, Mott's teacher was not one of these. Ms. Rooney attended class each day dressed more or less for the part, but she rarely spoke and often took naps on her desk. Her classroom was down to its last stubs of chalk. Among the dozen long, fluorescent ceiling lights that lit the children, three always flickered and one was entirely spent. These bulbs would never be replaced.

Erica Banach stood in front of the class, a piece of yellow notepaper stretched taut in her hands—it would tear if she pulled any harder. Her knees were covered in Band-Aids. They were shaking and so was her voice. "'What I Think Will Happen in November.' That's the name of my report. I think that everything will be okay. When you hear 'the end of the world,' you think about everyone dying. You can't help it, that's how you grew up. But there's another way to think. November might only mean the end of the world as we know it. Would that be so bad? Most people suffer for most of their lives. Most people live in India or China. If everything was different, some things would be better. Maybe in the new world no one will be hungry. Maybe we'll learn to be nice. In conclusion, I think that's what will happen. Thank you for your time."

A student in the front row raised his hand. Erica pointed at him, which meant that he could ask.

"What happened to your eye?"

Erica tore her paper in half. She didn't mean to do it—she only pulled a little harder.

"When you see a black eye," she said, "you think of someone being hit by her father. You can't help it. But my father is a doctor and a good man. He delivered me himself."

She gave the halves of her report to Mott and went back to her seat.

The children looked to Ms. Rooney. Her head lay on her desk and she was covering her ears.

"I'll go next," said Molly Coryell. She walked to the front of the class. "'What I Think Will Happen in November.' Everyone will fall down at the same time. If you're in the grocery store, you'll fall down in the fruits and veggies. If you're at your job, your face will fall down on your keyboard and spell a weird word. If you're at home in your bed, you won't fall down, but you won't get up either.

Everyone will make a little surprised sound, like they just checked their mailbox and inside there was a letter from their friend."

No one had any questions for Molly. She gave her paper to Mott and sat down. Ms. Rooney sobbed once.

"I'll go," said Malik Boyd. He drew a cloud on one end of the chalkboard, and on the other end a flame. "You already know what's going to happen in November. The dream was very clear. There's going to be a flood like the one in the Bible. We'll drown to death, which is supposed to be a pretty decent way to die, at least compared to all the other ways, and then we'll have to choose the cloud or the flame. My granddad died from liver failure last year. His car is still parked in our driveway. I worry all the time that it's going to be stolen. The doors are unlocked, but nobody takes it."

Malik didn't wait for questions. He erased what he'd drawn on the board and handed his paper to Mott. It was her turn. She always preferred to go last.

"'What I Think Will Happen in November,' by Mott Gabel. I have asked myself one thousand times. We all had the same dream, or close enough to the same, and we all know what the father said. The world will be over, forgotten, or maybe it's better to say never remembered again. My first memory is I am sitting on a checkered blanket in the park. My mother is scooping potato salad onto my father's plate. He keeps telling her, 'A little more, please.' Soon there's more on his plate than there is in the bowl. She's trying not to laugh. He keeps telling her, 'A little more, please. Just a little more and I'll be satisfied.' Finally she can't hold in the laughter. He says, 'A little more.' All of the potato salad is on his paper plate and my mother is dying from laughter. Someone's blue Frisbee settles on our blanket. No one ever came to claim it, so I still have the Frisbee, and that's how I know my memory is true. Becoming a person doesn't happen to you all at once. It takes months or maybe years to learn your name, and then you have to remember it every day. The world has to do the same thing. It's lucky that when we're asleep, when we've forgotten we're a world, Australia's awake to remember. They keep us alive. When November comes and the world is what it is, we'll all forget our names together. Our bodies will still exist, but we won't use them anymore. They'll use themselves."

Nobody raised a hand and no one asked. She set her paper with the others on her desk. She sat down and tidied the stack. It was quiet in the classroom. Attendance today was less than three-quarters.

The children looked to Ms. Rooney, who was sleeping or pretending.

Erica slapped herself on her own face. The children looked at their desks, most of which were badly vandalized—names scratched into their surfaces, wizards and unicorns drawn with permanent marker, wads of gum stuck there and dried. Erica's was clean.

Mott said, "I guess that's enough for today. Remember Monday is a book report. You're supposed to tell us about the best book that you've ever read and try to persuade us to read it. Your title should be 'If You Read Just One Thing Before November, Make It This.' Use evidence from your book to support your ideas. Your report should be at least one typewritten page. If you write it by hand, make it two."

"Class dismissed," said Malik. "Use your time wisely. You don't have to leave if you feel safest here."

About half the students stood, shouldered their backpacks, and shuffled out the door, mumbling goodbyes and invitations. The other half stayed where they were, played with phones, drew in notebooks, read comics, pushed earbuds in too deep, or hunched their shoulders and slumped in their chairs. Erica was one of these. She had removed one of the Band-Aids on her knee too soon. She replaced it with a fresh one from her pocket.

Mott and Malik were among those who left. First Malik put an apple on their teacher's desk beside her sleeping head.

"She doesn't deserve you," said Mott.

"I feel bad for her. She told me her mother is dead."

"She says that about everyone."

. . . . .

Mott and Malik left together because it was safer that way. The halls of the school were empty apart from a cluster of students playing cards on the floor and the girl who slept all day by her locker. Most classrooms were at least two-thirds full, but few students ever moved from one room to another: subjects and specialties were over, extra-curriculars forgotten. Each teacher gave as much instruction as they could bear in reading, writing, remedial math, and what history they remembered or saw on TV. Fridays they did an hour on personal hygiene. Children who could not sit still and keep quiet were sent to the principal's office and never came back. This is not to say they disappeared completely: they were sometimes seen wandering the school before first bell, which had been moved back one hour to accommodate the end of the busing program. Mott didn't know where the troublemakers went while she was in class. She wasn't friends with them, would never be, and so could not ask.

Mott and Malik stepped outside. The groundskeepers had all been let go a month back, and now the grass was grown enough to show seed. Butterflies searched the lawn for hidden flowers. Two condiment-colored cars had collided in the parking lot. The drivers, both middle-aged men, chose to avoid confrontation by closing their eyes and waiting for the other one to drive away.

Mott and Malik were going the same way, so they agreed to continue walking together. Mott called her mother. The phone rang twice.

"Hello love," said her mother. "I haven't looked at the clock yet, I've been feeling very anxious, I don't know the time. Did they let you out early again?"

"They said it's some kind of government holiday. Probably they made it up to get out of teaching."

"Is the weather nice? I haven't looked behind my curtains."

"It's idyllic," said Mott. "Sun is shining, moderate temperature, cotton-ball clouds, and a pleasant, aromatic breeze. There's a ladybug on my shirt's collar."

Malik searched her shirt for the bug. Mott shook her head and gestured dismissively—he needn't bother; it did not exist.

"You should come home and do educational activities with me," said her mother. "We can listen to enriching music. You can read a historically important woman's biography. I'll try to finish my work quickly so we can focus on each other once you're here."

"I need to go to the library first."

"Is there somebody with you? Somebody you trust?"

"Malik is with me. After I'm done at the library, I need to go to the grocery store. We're out of everything. But I promise then I'll come directly home."

"Don't go to the store today. It's dangerous there. You can do it tomorrow."

"It won't be any safer tomorrow," said Mott. "It could get worse."

"Maybe I could come with you though. Maybe I can find some courage by then."

Mott knew that wasn't going to happen. It hadn't happened in years.

"Are you breathing on the receiver, Mott? Honestly, it's very irritating."

"Sorry Mom, I'm not. You might be hearing yourself."

"It feels like you're doing it right on my ear."

"I'm sorry you feel anxious."

"Come home soon, okay? Don't go to the store."

"I'll come as soon as we're done at the library, but the bus might still be late or slow, so please don't worry if I take a little while, and please don't call me unless I'm very, very late and you feel too stressed out to wait anymore. I promise I'll be careful, and I'll call you if I need your help."

"You're sure that you're not breathing on the phone?"

"Yes ma'am. Try holding your breath and see if it stops."

They shared a moment of silence, each of them holding her breath. Mott stood still to keep quiet; Malik walked on ahead. Mott's mother gave a small, happy sigh.

"Did that help?" said Mott.

"I still don't think it was me. You held your breath too, so it wasn't much of a test. I'm going to get back to my typing. I want to be done by the time you get home. You know I love you more than the waves love the moon."

"Am I allowed to say I love you too?"

"You know I would rather you didn't," said her mother. "Our relationship's inherently coercive." She hung up.

Mott pocketed her phone and jogged to catch up with Malik, who was waiting for her at an intersection. He asked her, "How's your mom?"

"Still a genius," said Mott. "But sometimes she's weird."

The library was widely considered a good place for naps. Men who looked like bums and men who looked like fathers slept on all the outside benches. They covered their faces with elbows, newspapers, hats, empty bags. They rolled from side to side and scratched their bellies.

Women stayed inside, using chairs and sofas meant for readers, some with children curled against them. There was a mother sleeping upright on a small bench between the books about crafts and the ones about how to draw. Her baby fed on her left breast; the right breast was covered. Malik apologized to Mott as if the woman's nakedness was something that he'd done. He took a history of the postbellum South from a shelf. "I also need an atlas."

On the shelf under the atlases there was a small girl sleeping. She had pushed all the books out of her way, so that now they were heaped on the floor.

"This is all I needed," said Malik. "What are you getting?"

"Three novels. You should get one too. Take my mother's third and final book—it was highly underrated. Did you know that she was on a list of the best twenty women writers under forty? The order wasn't supposed to mean anything, but they did put her first on the list, and you know they wouldn't do that without thinking it over. Her picture was on the magazine's cover."

"I don't have time for fiction," said Malik, which made Mott want to slug him.

The younger librarian at the reference desk slept upright in her chair, horn-rimmed glasses hanging from a silver thread around her neck. The elder librarian was reading *Little Women*. Her white hair was thin like not enough icing.

Mott cleared her throat. "What are the best three novels ever written in English, including translations? I trust your opinion."

The elder librarian glanced up from her book. "*Little Women* is one of them," she said. "I don't know that I can say for sure about the others."

Mott clapped her hands together once, too hard. The sound filled the library. The younger librarian stirred, but her eyes remained closed. "I need you to help me," said Mott. "My mother never tells me what novels to read. She feels that it would poison our relationship, that I would not love the books she chose and that she would hate me for it. So it all comes down to you. What are the three greatest books ever written?"

"That depends on your taste."

"No it really doesn't. You can be honest. We don't have much time."

The elder librarian tore the title page from *Little Women* and wrote the names of two more books beneath that first. "Get these."

. . . . .

The woman at the checkout desk asked Mott and Malik if they would like to put the books on their cards. "You can just take them if you want," she said. "Nobody cares."

"Put mine on my card, please," said Mott.

"I'll just take mine," said Malik. "I'm not coming back."

Outside, at the bus stop, Mott asked Malik what he'd meant. He looked to the horizon. "I'm going to travel all around the country with my parents. They want me to see where I come from before the world ends."

"We were almost friends," said Mott. "We were getting so close. Now you're leaving."

"We *are* friends. You just don't know what it's like."

The bus was late. Mott imagined her mother was already starting to panic.

"I probably won't be at school on Monday," said Malik. "My mom says we're leaving first thing."

"Can I have your number?" said Mott. She looked at her feet.

"I don't have a phone, but my brother does. I'll give you his."

The bus arrived and let them on. They would ride together for three stops, and then Malik would leave. Mott would ride alone for two more.

"Do you believe in God?" said Malik.

Mott couldn't think of a not-cruel response. She shook her head.

"That's okay," said Malik. "Heaven and Hell are pretty much the same thing. I don't like to think about either."

Mott opened *Little Women* and started to read.

MAY, LYD

EARLIER THAT YEAR, ON THE NIGHT OF JANUARY 9, EVERY LIVING person on Earth had dreamed about a visitation from a man who was like a father. He said the world would end in November. Most people immediately accepted—though only a few would admit it to anyone else the next morning—that this was the truth, not only because they saw compelling evidence everywhere around them, and not only because this was the first recorded occasion of a globally unanimous dream, but because they were so tired.

A vocal minority—people for whom the current way of things was working well, who were mostly wealthy, powerful, or chemically imbalanced such that they felt good all the time—would have preferred that the world should persist forever, and largely unchanged. However, the majority discovered, though most would never speak these words aloud, that they were glad to know it wouldn't always be this way.

Lyd was the kind of person who mostly felt bad all the time. She responded to the dream by dedicating several weeks to mourning.

From the moment that Mott left for school until the moment of her scheduled return, Lyd wept relentlessly. She wept for Mott, for herself, and for the books that she had written, which were supposed to outlive her. When Mott was due home, Lyd forced herself to stop, and rubbed her face with an expired moisturizing lotion, which she believed reduced the swelling.

Lyd found some pleasure in exploring the heights and depths of her own capacity for misery, but the best thing about this dark time was that she felt entirely justified ignoring her job, disregarding every message from the boss, deleting his emails, and offering no explanation. Instead she focused on eating shortbread cookies, drinking instant lemonade, and writing long, nasty letters that she would never send to the book-club women who had asked her prying questions years before regarding her first novel and its presumed connections to her private life.

After the third week of tears, the effort of grief proved too much to sustain. Lyd began to worry she wouldn't make rent. She threw away her lotion bottle. "At least I know that I won't have to do this job forever," she said, addressing her empty apartment. It was good to have an end in sight. She returned to her work with new vigor. The days flew by.

- - - - -

Lyd consulted the wall clock that was glued to her living room window. The time was half past three. Her daughter should already be home. The sun was lost somewhere behind the clock's face.

A man in yellow pajamas stood on the roof of the hotel across the street. It was possible he did not plan to jump, but the odds were not in his favor. Lyd put her nose to the glass and squinted until she could make out what he was holding—a large, blue rotary phone. He cradled it against his stomach, advancing toward the roof's edge, peering down at the sidewalk below. He knelt and set down the phone, nudged it over, watched it fall.

Lyd drew her black curtains closed so as to hide her clock, the man in the yellow pajamas, and his exploded telephone. She focused on her breathing. She bit her thumb's knuckle and kissed the back of her own hand. She told herself to be patient and calm. Soon her daughter would be home. Everything would be much better.

Lyd resumed her seat at the dining room table, which also served her as a desk. It was centered in the dining room, which also served in her apartment as a kitchen, living room, library, and office. Her work computer hummed. She smoothed the small piece of electrical tape that covered her monitor where otherwise the time would be displayed. The ends were already curling, and every time she touched it things got worse.

She removed the black cloth draped over the webcam that watched her work. This was her way of clocking back in—when the webcam could see her, that meant she was on the job. When it could not, that meant she was at home.

She typed, *I want to be done for today.* She typed, *Mott come home.* She typed, *Nothing nothing nothing nothing nothing nothing nothing.* She typed what could have been the first sentence of a short, unpleasant story. She deleted everything she'd typed.

She gazed into the webcam. It was a gray, eye-shaped device that clipped onto the top edge of her monitor. There was a lens on the side that faced her, ringed with glowing blue, which meant the eye was watching. That blue light never turned off, and the eye never stopped. It was a security measure—mandated by the United States Congress and secret NSA policies, according to her boss.

Lyd inserted her right earbud and tucked the left inside her housecoat's collar. This way she would definitely hear the phone ring if Mott called again before she was done with her work. Using her right foot, she depressed a pedal underneath the table. There was a hiss and then her former husband David's voice, which was both deep and brittle, with a tendency to whistle slightly on sibilant sounds: "The subject grows increasingly paranoid."

Lyd typed, *The subject grows increasingly paranoid.* "She believes the government is listening to her calls. The fact she's right doesn't make it rational." His voice was slowed for her convenience—dilated, low, and strange. She lifted her foot off the pedal, depressed it again. The audio rewound two seconds, repeated itself: ". . . fact she's right doesn't make it rational." Lyd typed this too. "If you're not rational, you're wrong."

David had claimed to be a spy since the fifth year of their marriage, though he'd consistently refused to disclose which agency employed him. Supposedly he had worked his way up the ranks. Supposedly he had indirectly saved the lives of both major parties' presidential candidates some years ago. Supposedly he was now one of his agency's top men, highly valued and well compensated. Lyd worked for the government by way of David, typing documents from his dictation. Technically she was a contractor, like the people who build airplanes and long-range artillery. David mostly sent her loosely structured observations about the many people he surveilled. As Lyd understood it, these were grist for memos that would become the quasi-legal basis for further wiretaps, warrants, asset seizures, entrapments, and arrests. The work was sporadic and ethically dicey, but it paid an above-average wage, and she could do it from home. If she still wrote fiction, it would have been a perfect way to make ends meet while she worked on her books. But she didn't write anymore.

"She has no evidence," said David. "I don't allow her any. She claims to sometimes hear a third party's labored breathing on the line, a man's, and she says that this is me, or rather she says it's a government agent, but of course that's ridiculous. A phone tap doesn't go both ways. She isn't hearing anything."

Lyd typed, *She isn't hearing anything.*

"She often speaks to work acquaintances and family in what I think is meant to be a code, each word freighted with a second meaning. But no one ever understands my subject, and no one believes her." Lyd typed, *No one believes her.*

Lyd lifted her foot from the pedal. The phone was not ringing. She decided not to check the clock again just yet.

She depressed the pedal. "Last night I caught a call in progress, an old woman and a young man. I assumed she was his mother. She was begging him for money. She said that she would be evicted. He said he was sorry. She said that she was eating cat food. He said he was struggling too. At this point I realized they were strangers. She had called him by mistake, a wrong number. But he kept giving her reasons to hope that maybe he would change his mind and send some money, and so she stayed on the line, and they kept each other company that way. People are really that lonely."

Lyd typed, *People are really that lonely.*

"Sometimes I'm really that lonely," said David. "Sometimes I miss you. Sometimes I forget how impossible you made everything, and I wish that you were with me again."

Lyd lifted her foot from the pedal and looked at the phone, removing her earbud to make certain she would hear if it were ringing. Mott was smart and brave. She was careful too. There was no need for Lyd to call. If she called, the ringtone would draw attention to Mott on the bus, assuming that she was still on the bus, which any kind of person might be riding. Someone might talk to her, hurt her, or try to take her. Even if none of that happened—probably it wouldn't happen—Mott would still be annoyed, would feel that she was not being trusted, and so might not answer the next time, and if Mott ever failed to pick up then Lyd might well die from the stress. And even if she did call and Mott did answer then Lyd would be afraid for her again as soon as they hung up, just as she already was, so nothing would be changed.

Lyd promised herself, repeating it to the apartment again and again, with no way of knowing, that Mott would be safe—that very soon now, her Mott would come home.

.....

Lyd peeked behind her black curtains. The man in the yellow pajamas was seated on the hotel's roof as if poolside, dangling his feet over the edge. The clock showed quarter after four. Mott was late. The bus should not take so long.

There was half an hour left in David's recording, but Lyd couldn't hear him anymore over the thrum of her anxiety. She decided to finish tomorrow. She draped the black cloth over the government's webcam so she could be home. She turned off her monitor and tidied her work area. She cleaned the frying pan that she would use to make grilled cheese for dinner. She set the table. Though she was confident the webcam could not see her through its cloth, she avoided stepping into the theoretical cone of its vision whenever possible.

She walked a circuit of the apartment, concluding with Mott's room. She touched the back of her hand to Mott's pillow, which was pleasantly cool, and stood this way until the pillow warmed.

She bit her nails, but they were already bitten.

She yanked out one of her own hairs and turned it in the light of an end table's lamp. It was unusually fine for one of her grays, such that there were certain angles where it seemed to disappear. She needed to believe that Mott was safe. She promised herself it was true.

She needed coffee. She went to start a pot but discovered there was one already made and long gone cold. She poured it out but did not start another. The coffee maker's clock was also taped over, despite the fact that it was always wrong. She had done the same thing to the stove's clock and the microwave's, which sometimes made cooking a challenge. She stared at the phone.

She gave in and dialed Mott's number. A phone rang outside the apartment's front door.

"Mom?" said Mott, not through the phone. "I'm here."

Lyd nearly tripped on her own feet running. She unlocked the doorknob, the dead bolt, and the chain, and backed into the living room. "Come in!" she called.

Mott came inside, closed and locked the door behind her, fastened its chain. She slipped out of her shoes without undoing the laces, nudged them up against the wall. Lyd hugged her fiercely. "Sorry I'm late," said Mott. "The bus ran out of gas."

"It ran out?"

"When the driver said so, I thought she was kidding. Then she pulled over, got out of the bus, and walked away. Forever later, she came back and I guess filled up the tank, or maybe she was lying, but anyway we started moving again." Mott lay down on the couch. "It's really sunny out today. It got hot inside the bus. No one was saying anything. We all just waited. I was scared at first, and then I was just bored and tired."

"You could have called me."

"I didn't want you to freak out," said Mott. She closed her eyes. "I guess you freaked out anyway."

"Can I hold you?"

Mott sat up to make room. Lyd took the offered seat and Mott lay down across her lap. Lyd stroked her daughter's hair. Mott kissed her mother's hand.

.....

Lyd made grilled cheese while Mott drank green tea and graded essays. Lyd asked how the students were doing.

"They've stopped learning. I'm the only one who earned an A today."

Lyd set out a plate of greasy sandwiches. "Is it possible that you're not being totally objective?"

Mott shook her head. "I keep getting better. It's because I read great novels."

She tore a sandwich in two, ate half in four bites.

She said, "Do you think I could have been a writer like you used to be?"

"Maybe you should ask me that again tomorrow. Maybe you should reconsider your phrasing when you do. I'm still a writer. Some people write just one great book and everyone calls them a writer forever regardless. I wrote three good books. It's important to quit before you tarnish the work that you've already done. You know this."

"Sorry Mom," said Mott, but Lyd knew she wasn't. Mott felt for others in her own way, in her own time. When she was sorry for what she had said, she would turn on the stereo and put on an album that Lyd liked. She would make them both a peanut butter jelly. She would go outside and take pictures of things that Lyd might like to see: flowers, beetles, fire hydrants, bus stops, trees, anything that looked like a face. She would email the pictures to Lyd as she took them.

Lyd used to tell herself that someday her daughter would learn how not to hurt people without meaning to. First Mott would move out on her own. She would make friends and drink at parties. She would say some bad opinions just a little bit too loud. She would love someone who didn't deserve it. She would work a grinding job, surrounded by human mediocrities and slackers. She would spend whole weeks not speaking to her mother. These things would make her softer.

Lyd couldn't believe anymore. There wasn't time enough for Mott to change or learn or grow. Who she was now was all she would be.

Lyd pushed Mott's hair aside and kissed her forehead. This was the girl she had made. This was the girl she loved.

. . . . .

That night Lyd dreamed that Mott's bedroom door refused to let her inside. In the dream it was not clear whether Mott was actually in the room. That didn't seem to matter. Outraged by the door's intransigence, Lyd built a fire in the hall.

She woke with a burning throat and an ugly, bitter flavor in her mouth—the results of stomach acid. The hour was both small and dark. She went to the kitchen and mixed a glass of instant lemonade with twice the recommended powder. This helped a little with the taste.

Lyd knew that she would be incapable of sleep for at least the next two hours, and that the time would pass more quickly if she put it to practical use. Seeing as she was, per Mott, no longer a writer, that left her day job. She sat down at the table that was also her desk. She took the black cloth off the government's webcam. She inserted her right earbud, tucking the left inside her housecoat's collar so that she would definitely hear if Mott came out of her room.

Lyd depressed the pedal. Soon there was a sound she recognized as David sucking on a joint. Like Lyd, David was the kind of person who mostly felt bad all the time, but he aspired to always feel good, and so he daily engineered a different chemical imbalance. He coughed into the microphone, thumped his chest, and cleared his throat. "Sorry Lydia," he said.

She sighed and lifted her foot from the pedal. Once he spoke her name, it meant that he was finished working. Everything else in the audio file would be him speaking directly to her, saying things he wanted her to know. It was Lyd's firm policy that these were not love letters but professional dictations. She would type each word, including each promise, each tearful confession, each lecture on quantum mechanics, every sexual reminiscence, and all in the same fixed-width government font, and all in the government's template, each page watermarked *CLASSIFIED*. She would show him his own words exactly as spoken, and the spirit of total indifference in which they had been received. She would gaze into the webcam intermittently as she worked, dry-eyed and utterly bored, so that David could see, when he reviewed the footage, that she was not afraid of him, that she was not ashamed of anything he said, or of the fact that she took his money to listen. Then she would bill him for her time.

She depressed the pedal. "Speaking of lonely. Have I ever told you about gravity? The eggheads don't know how it works. It seems that astral bodies, even small ones, have a native desire to be close to one another. Recent photos by the Hubble Telescope show that all the stars are being slowly pulled together, all toward one point in space. One infinitely dense, slowly growing black hole. Sometimes it's scary, falling in love."

Another sucking sound, an exhalation, as he filled himself with smoke and blew it out. "I remember I was scared when I met you. This beautiful young woman, and smarter than me, and all I wanted was your attention, was to look at you all the time and talk to you all the time. Were you ever scared of me like that? Or scared of me at all?"

Lyd typed, *Or scared of me at all.*

"You never needed to be scared," said David. "I was taking care of you. Right now I bet that you're rehearsing some long-clutched grievance of yours. Maybe you're thinking about when I held you down, or when you say I did, which I don't remember the same way that you do, so I can't see it the way that you do, so I can't feel sorry, because the way I remember I did nothing wrong. And there's nothing that I can do about that—about the way that I remember what you say I did to you. And I could never hurt you, because you are so strong. Nothing ever happens to anyone that they don't want to happen. That's something that I learned from God, who as we both know is a woman."

Is a woman, typed Lyd.

David continued in this vein for some time, explaining to Lyd how powerful she was, how jealous he was of her beauty, and how he wished his body could be half as wonderful as hers, which was a gateway, which gave birth and took love, which his could not and never would. His voice grew smaller, slower, slurred. She typed until he talked himself to sleep. She typed, *[Voluble snoring.]* She took out her earbud and covered the government's webcam.

She parted her black curtains. The clock reported it was past her bedtime. The moon was lost somewhere behind it. She sipped her lemonade.

The man in the yellow pajamas stood on the roof of the hotel across the street. He cradled another large rotary phone, this one fire-truck red. He approached the roof's edge, peering down at the sidewalk below. He knelt and set down the phone, nudged it over, watched it fall. As his eyes drifted back upward, they appeared to settle on Lyd—there was no knowing at this distance. He hopped to his feet, his whole body lit with surprise. He threw both arms into the air and waved, bouncing up and down. Lyd smiled at him and waved back. It was possible he did not plan to jump, but in the long term, the odds were not in anybody's favor.

MAY, MOTT

A YOUNG GIRL WOKE EARLY. FOR A MOMENT SHE WAS NO ONE, BLANK and calm and only breathing. For lack of a better idea, she opened her eyes. This was her first mistake of the day. Mott remembered her name, what kind of person she was, and what would happen in November. She whimpered once and beat the mattress with her fists, but there was nothing she could do—this really was her life. She climbed down from her top-bunk bed and changed into fresh socks.

Mott's bedroom ceiling lamp was on because she couldn't sleep without it anymore. Her mother said that too much light kept the body from resting. Mott was usually tired, so she tended to agree. Bad sleep was better than no sleep, however.

The ceiling lamp outside her room was also on. That used to be enough for her—to look at her door and see what glow leaked in around it. Her mother still left it on for her every night.

Lyd was snoring loud enough to be heard from the hall. She used to only snore when she drank, which was most of the time, but now she never got to drink and still snored every night.

The downstairs neighbor was watching church TV with the volume turned up far too loud. The sermon was about November, which was the only word that came through the floor's muffle clearly—"NoVEMber," shouted with that kind of lilt, "NoVEMber," and the congregation's applause rising after every invocation, and their hallelujahs, which they must be screaming, but which reached Mott's ears as raspy murmurs. Her mother's work computer hummed and popped, thinking secret government thoughts.

Mott ate a bowl of cereal, drank the sugary milk. That was the end of the cereal, and that was the last of their milk. She really needed to go to the store.

When Lyd was asleep, the apartment seemed intolerably small. There were four rooms: the master bedroom, the bath, Mott's bedroom, and the living room/office/dining room/library/kitchen. Along the equator of this latter room's walls, Lyd had pasted up a fantastic skyline, an impossible amalgam of the world's great cities, made of buildings razored from glossy ads and magazine covers. The Taj Mahal appeared three times in this series, the Sears Tower once, the St. Louis arch twice. Above this architecture hovered the heads, shoulders, and occasional face-clutching hands of major intellectuals, artists, and historical figures (no living musicians, no filmmakers but Kurosawa and Miyazaki, no actors at all), these also cut from magazines or printed from the Internet before the color printer broke. Given sufficient light, this visual cacophony might have been cheerful, but the lamps in the room were all dim, and the black curtains that covered the living room's sole window allowed no sun inside. The paper skyline and great thinkers were a dark, oppressive swirl. So too were the dirty dishes that crowded the kitchen counters, sometimes overflowing to the dinner table, and the cleaning supplies lined up on the floor beside the sink, which were meant as a reminder to handle the mess.

"NoVEMber!"

Perhaps worst of all were the piles of books that littered the dinner table, coffee table, end tables, couch, and floor, their corners pointing in every direction, all multiply bookmarked, many bookmarking one another—books nestled in books. It had been about four years since Lyd finished writing a novel and may have been just as long since she finished reading one. Mott had learned not to ask what her mother thought of anything she was reading, as this made her defensive about her slow progress. "I used to read very quickly," she would say, "when I was young, and didn't pay any attention. Now I'm old and slow, so I see everything."

The downstairs congregation dissolved into a hissing white-noise wall of applause.

Mott had dreamed the night before about a book with infinite pages. No matter how much she read, there was always more to go, and she had grown old searching for the end. Everyone said she would be better off seeing the movie, but she didn't want to see the movie—she wanted to finish her book. The last thing she remembered was turning to the index to see if she could get some sense of where the final chapter was, but the index was infinite also, so that once she looked at it, she couldn't even get back to the story.

It occurred to Mott now that the ending, had she ever found it, would have been unspeakably sad.

Mott sat down at her mother's work computer. The password was written on a coaster on the desk. Mott lifted the black cloth from the webcam because she knew that was the rule, although of course it was also a rule that she should never use this computer at all.

She made a new document, a blank page. She typed the title of her weekend homework: *If You Read Just One Thing Before November, Make It This, by Mott Gabel.* If Lyd found her using the computer, this would be her alibi. She would say her laptop wasn't working correctly, that the word-processing program was running too slow. Lyd wouldn't believe this—she never believed that anything was wrong with any computer, and always assumed human error—but she might take the lie as an excuse to not punish Mott.

Lyd's email account was left open. The inbox was bereft of anything but spam, but there were four unfinished drafts, all of them addressed to Lyd's editor.

Mott read the first. The subject line was *just checking in.*

Hi Gerrard,
I know my royalty statement isn't due until June, but I've been wondering about my book. Is it moving again? Will there be a second printing? Do you need anything from me in terms of promo matter? We'll keep the old photo, I was prettier then.

Lyd was referring here to her third and final novel, *Failure,* which was a book about the end of the world. It argued—persuasively, Mott felt—that everyone would be better off dead, and that Earth would be a better place without people. Critics had liked it, but not quite as much as her previous books. Sales had been mediocre, verging on poor.

Mott read the second draft email. The subject line was *Numbers.* The body was empty apart from one comma.

Mott read the third draft. There was no subject line this time.

Gerrard!
We should brainstorm ways to promote *Failure.* Not to be crass about the apocalypse, but we have an opportunity to die rich. Some people are calling my novel prophetic. They're saying that I saw November coming. Maybe so and maybe not (ha! ha!) but I think some readers might find comfort. [something about afflicting the comfortable, comforting the afflicted, etc.]

Mott read the fourth draft, which also had no subject.

Gerrard,
If there has been no resurgence of interest in the most critically successful apocalypse novel of the last five years in

light of November, I will eat my fucking hat. Call me? [ask about his children; recall their ailments, ages, names.]

Mott closed the browser. She opened the document her mother had been working on the night before. Noting the *CLASSIFIED* watermark, she weighed the odds she would be prosecuted were she to read what was written inside. Certainly, given the webcam, the government would know what she had done if they cared to. Considering her legal status as a minor, and given that the materials in question had been entrusted to her mother, herself no officer of the law, in fact a self-confessed juvenile delinquent and former frequent user of illegal substances, and considering the fact that Mott's father never wrote and rarely called, surely Mott would be forgiven, or, if she was not, then her sentence would be lenient. Her father's transcribed dictations would represent the first time he had spoken to her, however indirectly, in more than seven weeks. In fact, considered in this light, the document essentially belonged to her. She was entitled to its contents, just as all children are entitled to the fruits of their parents' labor (money, milk, grain, fiction, government secrets: whatever they make).

Lyd touched Mott's shoulder. "I'm up."

"Mom! I was just—"

Mott opened the document that was supposed to be her homework.

"Is there something wrong with your laptop?"

"Yes," said Mott. Lyd glared at her. "No."

Lyd draped the webcam with its black cloth. "Do I need to punish you?"

"I'll punish myself. I'll look you in the eyes for five minutes and know I was wrong."

Mott set her phone to chime in five minutes. They sat together on the couch and looked into each other's eyes. Lyd's eyes were not unkind, but neither were they stupid, dull, or blind. She blinked less often than she should. Mott made her face defiant at first, but by the end of her punishment she was crying into her own mouth.

Lyd wiped a tear from Mott's cheek. "That's good, honey. Next time you feel like being a sneak, you'll remember how this feels."

- - - - -

Lyd worked while Mott read *Little Women*. They lunched on leftover grilled cheese. Mott turned on the stereo and put in Debussy because she knew Lyd loved him. Lyd read the newspaper. Each time she turned the page she snapped the paper tight. Mott read her book, flipping the pages pointedly so that Lyd would notice how loud she was being with the newspaper.

"You're reading too quickly," said Lyd. "We've talked about this. Ideally we would read each book twice. If we must read only once, we should do so with care."

"I have a book report due Monday," said Mott. "It's about the best book that I ever read. I have to read fast, in case this is it."

"My second book is your favorite."

This had long been a point of contention between them: Lyd felt her second book was her weakest, and that Mott's favorite should be her third. Mott didn't feel like talking about that again. She asked, "How old was Alcott when she wrote this?"

"I don't remember," said Lyd. "An adult, if that's what you're asking. I think middle thirties."

"How many pages is a novel?"

"It's not pages—it's words."

"How many?"

"That depends who you ask."

"What do most people say?"

"At least sixty thousand."

"How long was your first book?"

"About a hundred thousand. Too long, really. What do you want for lunch? I'm going to make pasta. Do you want tomato sauce or alfredo?"

"Do we really still have both?"

Lyd checked a cabinet. "We have alfredo." She filled a pot with water and turned the stove's most functional burner to high.

Mott said, "I want to talk about writing a book, because I'm going to actually do it and I want your advice."

Lyd salted the water. She broke a handful of dry spaghetti noodles in half.

Mott said, "You don't want to talk about writing a book because you don't think I have time before November. Or you think it will be terrible and I'll die disappointed. Books make you feel bad, so you think they'll be the same for me. But when I was small you thought that maybe I was stupid. You made me see specialists. I could have been enriching myself with cultural activities and reading biographies of historically important women, but instead I took remedial tests with flash cards that said *kitten* and *triangle*. Now you admit you were wrong, that I'm the smartest girl in my class, maybe even my school."

"I never said that about your class or school." Lyd tossed the noodles into the pot. She peeled the electric tape from the stove's clock and set the timer, then covered it again.

"If I did write a novel and you thought it was good, would you show it to your editor?"

"Gerrard doesn't care about me."

"Would you take me to New York and try to get a meeting?"

"Even if I did, there isn't time. They wouldn't be able to publish it if they wanted, which they wouldn't, because even the smartest girl in her school will fail to write a great novel if she is thirteen."

"Well. I think I'll do it anyway. I just need to have a really great idea."

She tried to think of one.

For the duration of their meal, the downstairs neighbor thumped their floor (his ceiling) with what sounded like the handle of a broom, even though they were being so quiet. Mott didn't see how she could ever hope to have a really great idea for a novel while someone was thumping their floor, but Lyd forbade her to stomp or otherwise respond.

After dinner, they curled up on the couch and listened to "Clair de Lune" on repeat. Lyd told Mott she loved her. Mott wasn't allowed to say anything back. Because the lights were on, Mott was capable of sleeping here. She felt herself drift. Sleep was the same thing as death. She remembered the dream about November. She remembered the snow and the smell of the father.

. . . . .

The dream had come four months before, on January 9. This was the last night Mott slept with her light off, the last night that Lyd didn't snore. Mott woke when it was over, all cold sweat and gasping for air. She went directly to her mother's room. She believed she had a really great idea.

She opened Lyd's door without knocking, taking care to keep the knob from squealing. She was greeted by a sharp, familiar mildew smell that felt to her like motherhood. She stepped inside and onto the layer of discarded clothing that had accumulated on the floor like a second carpet. The only light was her mother's alarm clock—the time was 4:43. Lyd rolled onto her other side but did not wake. Mott made her way to the foot of the bed and slipped beneath the covers and the sheet, worm-wriggled up to the pillow end.

"Mom." She stroked her mother's shin with her toes.

Lyd hissed. "Your feet are so cold."

"I had a bad dream." Mott pressed her back against her mother. Lyd wrapped an arm around her.

"Me too." Lyd kissed Mott's head.

"I think that maybe it could be a book. I could write it down and publish it."

"Do you want to tell me?"

Mott put her hand over her mother's. She felt the knuckle wrinkles, the dry skin around her nails, and picked at the cuticles as she spoke. "I woke up in a hospital. We were there for Grandma Jean. She was hooked up to all those machines. They were sucking out her blood and putting in medicine. You could see it happen through the tubes. We were in the chairs beside her bed and you were still asleep. We were sharing a hospital blanket. And then this dad came into the room. He had a clipboard under his arm."

"This was your father?"

"Someone else's. He was wearing office pants and a blue shirt with the sleeves rolled up. He smelled like cold coffee. He said, 'Oh good, you're awake,' and smiled at me like I was his favorite. Then he pulled the blanket off me. You still didn't wake up. He said, 'Can we talk?' I was wearing just my nightgown. He put my sneakers on for me and tied them, double knots. I asked him was it cold outside. He said it only looked that way."

"Did you go outside then?"

"Yeah, we went out. There wasn't any parking or buildings nearby. The stars were out and there was lots of snow. The hospital was alone in the middle of this thick, dark forest of—what are Christmas trees called?"

"There are different kinds."

"He led me through the woods. His hand was soft like a hamburger bun. He said, 'We want you to know, first and foremost, this isn't your fault.' I asked him what he meant. He said, 'There's a process. We consulted every stakeholder. No stone was left unturned. There were countless factors to consider.' He asked me—"

"He asked, 'Do you ever think about death?'"

"Yeah exactly! It was just like one of your stories. Is that how you guessed?"

Lyd did not acknowledge the question, which, in the dark, made it seem not to have happened.

"Well, anyway, I told him Grandma Jean died years ago. He

asked me did I miss my grandma. I said I didn't like the hospital. He said, 'So you were glad when her suffering ended.' And I said, 'Not at all.' So did I want her to suffer forever? I said that wasn't right either."

"But he got distracted," said Lyd. "He was doing something else."

"Um," said Mott. "Yeah, he was. He was fishing in his pockets. He found a stick of spearmint gum and gave it to me, and he said, 'Again, we want to emphasize that this is not your fault. There was a vote. The world is going to end this year. We didn't know if we should tell you.'"

"And you asked him why."

"I did. But how come you know that?"

"But he said, 'November. It happens in November.' And you wondered was he even listening at all. And he led you onto a lake. It must have been frozen, but at the time you didn't see it that way. And somehow the water was both very clear and quite dark. And he said, 'Death isn't like what you think. Practically nothing is.' He rubbed his hands and blew in them to make them warm."

"Really, Mom. Come on. How come you know?"

"You reminded him he'd promised that it only looked cold out. But he didn't answer. He kept saying he was sorry. He kept saying—"

"He kept saying, 'The fault isn't yours, the fault isn't yours,'" said Mott. "So I asked him whose it was. But he couldn't say."

"And I knew it really was my fault what's going to happen," said Lyd. "And he didn't save me from the water when I fell into the lake. He said, 'You're not really drowning. We thought that you could use some practice.'"

Mott's eyes had adjusted by now to the room. She could see the fear in her mother's expression, and the way that Lyd, remembering the water, held her breath.

Mott said, "Did we have the same dream?"

Lyd nodded.

"What does it mean?"

Lyd thought for what felt like a long time before answering.

"It doesn't mean anything. These things happen all the time.

There was an essay in *N Plus One* about it. I'll find it for you tomorrow."

"Okay. Do you think you can sleep?"

"No," said Lyd. But they both tried.

Over the next several days, it emerged that everyone on Earth had dreamed the same thing that night—or, in the case of people on the far side of the International Date Line, the night before. There were minor variations from one dream to the next, and these were quickly catalogued online. The hospital was sometimes a nursing home, sometimes a church, sometimes a hospice, and sometimes the home of a loved one—though in the latter case, the home was always cavernous and strange, with high ceilings and many unexpected rooms. The lake was sometimes frozen, sometimes not.

The dying family member was not always a woman, was sometimes only a family friend. Sometimes they were a character from TV. The family member who slept beside the dreamer, apparently there to help them watch the dying family member pass, was usually the person to whom they felt closest—in Lyd's case it was Mott, in Mott's case it was Lyd, and for most people it was a mother or daughter or sibling or partner or wife, sometimes a husband, only rarely a father or son. Sometimes this person too was a character from TV.

The trees were not always healthy. The dreamer did not always see the stars. The gum was sometimes cinnamon. These minor differences seemed to many people as if they must be quite significant, but no one could be sure of what they meant; the dreamers who saw stars were not obviously different, as a set, from those who saw empty night.

Some things about the dream were always exactly the same. The father's hand was always soft. He never seemed to hear the dreamer quite correctly, never answered their questions directly, always promised the world would end in November, and always let the dreamer practice drowning. He always apologized. He always said November was nobody's fault. Or if it was somebody's fault—if the father ever did, in anybody's dream, lay blame—then the guilty party never publicly came clean.

MAY, DAVID

LYD'S FORMER HUSBAND DAVID LIVED IN A PALATIAL THREE-STORY home in a well-to-do Virginia suburb forty-five minutes out from Washington, DC, where he hadn't gone since the November dream. The Agency allowed him to telecommute both because he was a star and because they hated dealing with him at the office, which might have hurt his feelings if it weren't so convenient.

David's home was precious to him, and it looked exactly the way that he wanted it to. It had blue exterior walls, white trim, and white fascia, with gingerbread-brown shingles and a never-used chimney. The yard was poorly maintained, patchy and slick, which irritated the neighbors, who mainly left their homes these days to tend their lawns. There were typically at least seven cars parked all jumbled in David's driveway and against the curb, sometimes blocking the mailbox, often trapping one another, which was completely fine with David, as he would prefer that nobody leave. The cars belonged to beautiful young people.

The interior walls of the home were butter yellow with brown trim. The floors in the living room, kitchen, bathrooms, and first-floor hallway were orange tile, which helped with cleanup after parties and other mistakes. There were nine frameless paintings scattered throughout the home, six inches wide by six inches tall, each depicting a planet: Mars, Venus, etcetera, small, distant, surrounded by no stars. The walls of the communal areas were otherwise bare.

David worked, or sometimes simulated working, in an office on the first floor of his home. It was a dim, windowless room occupied by six buzzing computer towers and an unknown number of oscillating fans. Mounted on the smoke-damaged walls were twelve large screens, which were connected to the computers, which were wired to many button-sized or smaller cameras secreted throughout the home. If anyone made love or quarreled, or talked about David when he wasn't there, or smoked without him, or finished his favorite chips, or hosted a party without telling him, or even did nothing of interest, he knew it and watched or could watch if he wanted. They didn't talk about him much. Young people can be self-absorbed.

David's office had a mini-fridge, one framed *Yellow Submarine* record sleeve nailed to the wall, and one toy mini basketball hoop on the door. There were rolling papers and several plastic baggies full of weed on his desk, each labeled with permanent marker. The rolling papers had Zen koans written on them in lemon juice, which worked like invisible ink, only appearing when the joint's burning had warmed them sufficiently, by which point they were practically gone. David was smoking one now. He wasn't high yet, but it was early in the day and he planned to try his best.

The kitchen, living room, laundry room, breakfast nook, and soundproofed meditation room were also on this floor. The second floor was where David slept, and where many of the beautiful young people who lived with him slept. On the third floor there were even more people who chose to live with him, who loved him and accepted his love in return, though there were also several empty rooms that no one slept inside, which David found unnerving, so he never went to the third floor, and only saw what happened there through his cameras, which exclusively recorded rooms with living things inside, so that his home always seemed to be completely full and entirely used. About nineteen young people were present on average at any given time in May. Most of them lived there, and David knew most of their names. He never charged anyone rent. That way they had one less thing to worry about.

David's favorite tenant was a dog, a Newfoundland named Laverne, who weighed about one hundred fifty pounds. She wanted to cuddle him always, so she didn't get to be with him when he was working, as that would be a big distraction, and he distracted himself enough as it was. She used to bark at new people; now she wore a shock collar. Every time she opened her mouth, she remembered the pain and thought better. She was leaned against the other side of his office door, resting, waiting for him to come out. He could hear her breathing, the periodic shifting of her weight as she drifted to sleep or to waking—as she pined. When his work was done for the day, they could snuggle. Dogs were supposed to be happy. He didn't like denying her or anyone. He knew how much that hurt.

One screen in David's office was devoted to surveilling Lyd and Mott. Its largest window displayed the current feed from Lyd's webcam, blown up to twice the size it should have been. The light in the apartment was poor, so that Lyd always looked dismal, her life without David hollow and chintzy. Presently this feed was all black, however, as Lyd was not working today—was probably not even up. There was also a waveform display that visualized the sound captured by the webcam's microphone, so that if there was an unusual noise in Lyd's apartment, David would see it right away, even if he were listening to something else. Currently the only sounds were the AC and the fridge's constant buzz. In another window, this screen also cycled randomly through old photos of Lyd, and video clips from the last several years, such as moments where she'd cracked a smile or walked past the camera in a state of partial undress. A warning message would flash on the screen if she made a phone call. His computer would assume, correctly, that he wanted to hear.

There were three screens devoted to David's actual, official work. On these, he observed his assigned suspicious persons—tracking their movements, listening in on their lives through microphone malware installed on their phones and assorted devices, reading their emails and social media inboxes, and watching them through a mix of cameras in public places and cameras that he or other Agency employees had, under one pretext or another, installed in their homes, offices, and vehicles. He was currently responsible for closely tracking seven individuals and occasionally checking in on fifteen more. With enough time and attention, he could have observed or inferred every moment of their daily lives. Unfortunately they were mostly quite boring—this was part of what made them suspicious—and so their surveillance was a chore. Presently the Pensacola-based unmarried Muslim man that David watched was seated on his living room couch, laptop balanced on his knees, researching water softeners and their benefits. The Black math teacher who lived in Miami was writing a suicide note in her breakfast nook, which was something she did over cinnamon tea every week. She always threw away the notes when she was done, crumpling the paper but leaving it in good enough condition that her husband could, if he were ever curious, take them out of the trash, smooth them, and read. The white teenage boy in Stapleton, Nebraska, who had sent violent anonymous threats to his high school was drawing tattoos that he would maybe like to get before the world ended. The Senegalese immigrant, recently divorced and living out of his car, was driving as directed by an app, delivering food from various restaurants to scattered middle-class Richmond homes. David's other assigned suspicious persons were asleep or watching TV, as was their general habit. They had been more interesting before the November dream, or at least they had changed up their routines more often.

Somebody rang the doorbell twice. The sound did not reach David in his office, but the presence of a person at the front step did activate the relevant camera. The visitor was a young man, probably Latino, soft of cheek, head shaved clean, wearing a new, ill-fitting black suit—loose around the wrists and tight across his chest. The young man itched his nose, smoothed his shirt, attempted to tuck it in better, and straightened his tie. This was the assistant that David had been requesting for months, the shadow who would clean the home's common areas, recycle bills and other mail, tip pizza delivery people, and do grocery shopping, among other chores. He looked twenty-four.

David pushed a button that let him speak through the doorbell. "I thought you weren't coming till Sunday," he said.

The kid startled, realized where the voice was coming from, recognized that he was being watched, and nervously saluted the door. "It is Sunday," he said.

"Oh, well that's perfect. Hold on a minute bud, I'll be right out." David sucked the last spark out of his joint, tossed it on the floor, locked his office behind him, and made his way through the house, Laverne the dog at his side, rubbing her flank against his, shedding hair on his tweed suit coat, marking him as hers.

There were two beautiful young people necking on the living room couch, listening to Pink Floyd. David asked them to take it elsewhere. "We have a guest. Let's be polite for like a minute." The couple ultimately chose to cooperate, heading upstairs with hands in each other's back pockets. David turned off the speakers but let the record go on turning. He didn't feel like lifting the needle right now.

As David opened the front door, Laverne shoved past him and out into the open air, nearly knocking over the kid with the shaved head and new suit. "Sorry," said David. "That bouncing ball on the horizon is Laverne. She loves me, and she loves freedom."

The kid ran his hand backward over his scalp. "No, that's fine, but I'm sorry—"

"Not a problem, kid, it happens all the time. She always finds her way back. Come on in. Leave the door open or she might knock it down."

"My name is Alejandro. The Agency sent me to help with your work. Is this a bad time? It looks like you maybe have guests?"

"Those cars all belong to my big, loving family. I'll introduce you later. First let me give you the tour."

"Do you want to see my Agency ID?" The kid reached for his wallet.

"Nah, man, it's no problem. I'll look you up later."

David showed the kid the living room, kitchen, paintings, meditation room, and first-floor bathroom. "Close the door when you're done using it, or Laverne will drink from the toilet."

The kid smoothed his shirt for what must have been the thirteenth time since he arrived. David decided to put him at ease. "Hey, you know what Alex? I like you. I like your suit. I can tell that you're anxious." He patted the kid's heart. "This is a time bomb, my friend. You have to take care of it. Every animal lives for one billion heartbeats. Some of us have faster hearts than others. Consider the rat and the blue whale. The rat gets stressed out because he's so small."

"Oh," said Alex, who was already shaping up to be a real drip.

"You seem like a diligent worker. I bet that you'll feel better in my office."

As David unlocked and opened his office door, he remembered that he had neglected to close the programs that showed the video feeds from throughout the house. "Don't tell anybody what you see in here," he said. "It's all very top secret."

Alex nodded. He would have a midlevel government security clearance, would understand about secrets. His face lit up red as they entered the room and he saw David's screens. It was a sleepy afternoon. Many of the cameras showed young people unconscious—holding each other, or alone with open books on their chests, or listening to earbuds, or facedown on top of their covers, naked and pink, backs dotted with hours of sweat. Others were smoking, ashing cigarettes into paper bowls, drinking soda. The couple who'd been going at it in the living room were cheerfully rutting in the bedroom they shared.

"These are some of the cool, kind people who live with me in my house," said David. "More and more are moving in since the November dream. They feel safe and loved and wanted here. I keep an eye on them because I need to know what happens under my roof." He turned off any screen with naked bodies so as to help the kid relax.

"Of course," said Alex. He ran his hand over his scalp.

"These screens are where I watch my assigned people," said David. "They haven't been much fun since the November dream. I think they're depressed. That dream by the way is just nonsense. I want you to know that. The world ends when we end it. The whole thing is just a trick by the Russians, Israelis, Chinese, or some combination. Someone wants us confused."

"Yeah, I think so too. I don't feel like I'm going to die this year. Things are just getting started. It wouldn't make sense."

"I don't even really remember the dream," said David. This was a lie. "Hey, look at my girls." He pointed to the screen that featured Lyd and Mott. There was an image of Mott from the previous day, when she had briefly used the computer to snoop on Lyd's email inbox. There was an older image of Lyd walking through her living room in a towel. There was a years-old picture of Lyd stirring a whiskey cocktail with a plastic butter knife. There was a picture of Mott reading from a book while she wandered the apartment.

"That's my wife, Lydia, and that's our daughter, Mott. She's a brilliant little girl."

"That's great," said Alex. "They're beautiful," he ventured.

"We're banana splits right now. It's partly my fault, but I don't think we'll stay that way forever."

"I'll look forward to meeting them, then."

"Yeah. They're pretty far away." David sat down in his wheelie office chair and gazed up at the ceiling. "So here is the thing. I feel tired all the time. Between my work, watching over my girls, and managing the house, I can barely keep up with anything else. That's why I need you to help me out. If you pick up some chores, I can focus better on my work."

"Okay, sir. Whatever you need."

"You sound disappointed."

"When I got this assignment, they made it sound like I would get to help you with surveillance. Like you would maybe teach me how you do what you do."

David sighed, made his chair turn in circles. "I've already told everyone how I work, but nobody listens. The suits think I'm a full-of-shit hippie. They don't believe in anything but algorithms and upskirt photographs. Did they tell you about how I saved the republic?"

"They said you would probably tell me, even though I'm not cleared to know."

"And I bet they said you shouldn't believe me," said David, twisting his beard. "But here's the God's honest. I have a dialer program. Every day, I use it to tap at least one random phone call above and beyond my assignments. In the long run, if I listen well, the universe gives me what I need to hear. One day five years back, sitting at my standard-issue workstation in my anonymous Agency cube, using this method, I randomly tapped a call wherein the parties were finalizing a credible plot to assassinate both major parties' presidential candidates at a future debate. They were using coded language, but I immediately understood what I was hearing, and we were able to arrest them before they could hurt anyone. Even now the bosses don't know what they want to think really happened. Sometimes they say it was a dumb coincidence, or they insist I'm lying, that I couldn't possibly do my work in the way that their own records show them I do. But I get results." He kicked his feet up on his desk. "Honestly, anyone who cared to could do what I do. The world, like a beautiful woman, wants to be seen. I'll demonstrate."

David pushed off with his feet, rolling away from his workstation, gestured that Alex should take over, and talked him through the process of tapping a random phone call. "This will be revealing," he said, closing his eyes and making his chair spin again. "I feel very connected to all of creation right now. If we let it, if we open ourselves to its love, the cosmic metaconsciousness will show us something we need to see. Turn up those speakers. Make sure we're recording."

The first two random calls were telemarketers selling life insurance policies. David rolled a joint (the kid pretended not to notice) and breathed it in. "Marketing doesn't count," he said. "It's just noise. The way I work, I dial till I find something else."

Alex tried a third time. The sound of human breathing filled the room, and telephonic pop and fizz. One end of the call was a cell phone in Rhode Island. The other one, the breathing end, was a landline in Kentucky. "I'm sorry," said the Rhode Island caller. "Lo siento. Je suis désolée. Jeg beklager." They paused between each word, planning the next.

The Kentucky landline's owner tried to break in. "What all are you saying? Who is this?"

The Rhode Island caller pressed on. "Es tut mir leid. Prosti menya." Their voice was more tone than air, their pronunciation both perfect and wrong, melodic and mechanical.

"Ma'am, or, I'm sorry, sir? You have the wrong number."

"Maf kijiye. Duìbuqǐ. Gomenasai."

The Kentucky landline hung up.

"You see?" said David. "I don't know how yet, but I'm certain that will prove important and useful. You hit the record button, right?"

Alex played it back to show that he had. He asked, "Do you think it's a code?"

"Must be," said David. He cracked his knuckles in a way that was supposed to announce he was going to do some serious government work. "Buddy, I need you to leave me alone for a while. Go upstairs, introduce yourself to the other kids. Maybe you'll meet a nice girl."

"You sure you don't need anything else?"

"Nah, man," said David. "I'm good. Go on and close the door behind you. I'll see you first thing Monday, whenever I get up."

The kid left the room. David rolled a new joint, breathed it in, and went to work. He still wasn't fully high, not quite yet, but he was getting close.

The Rhode Island number belonged to a woman who worked at an outlet mall and lived in an apartment above a dry cleaner. He read her last forty emails, found nothing of interest. She was planning a trip to visit her parents before the world ended. She had recently sent her girlfriend instructions for how to take care of her cats.

The Kentucky landline was a car wash. The voice on that end of the call might have been any one of seven men who worked there.

David searched the Internet for words he believed the caller had said, spelling as best he could guess them. In several cases he could not find a spelling that returned any useful results. For those he could find, the translations were all some version of "I'm sorry," each in a different language.

David felt that the apology must somehow be about November, though if anyone had asked him to justify that belief, he would have struggled to explain. The caller was at fault for the dream, or believed that they were, or that they knew who was. "It's about the dream," he said, testing how it felt to say. It felt right and true—as if the universe were speaking through him again. "It's about the dream," he repeated, his voice firmer this time, more commanding.

This was all very exciting, but he had no idea where to go with it next. He decided to focus on his usual routine, trusting that the process would lead him to new insights and avenues of investigation. As he observed his assigned suspicious persons, he spoke into a digital recorder, making words for Lyd to type. At some point he mentioned that Laverne had got out again. He said he was sure that she would come back. He talked at length about the personal failings of the people he was watching, highlighting flaws that Lyd shared, with the hope that she would see them in herself, learn from the experience, grow as a person, and become a better wife. Technically an ex-wife, but he didn't like to think of her that way.

The white teenage boy was drawing on himself with a permanent marker, looking at his body in the mirror; what had begun as practice for future tattoos was now a brutal self-critique, the boy drawing circles and arrows indicating his worst features, everything that made him ugly and bad. In his dictation, David focused on the kid's self-loathing, which he hoped would help Lyd to think about hers. The unmarried Muslim man was hand-washing dishes. He didn't listen to anything while he worked. David emphasized his unnecessary isolation, how empty his life was alone, which he hoped would remind Lyd that she was alone, that her life was empty.

While he worked, David also watched Friday footage of Lyd typing, which he had not yet taken the time to fully review. He pretended, as he often did, that she was transcribing what he said in real time, typing the words he spoke now. Though he knew it was impossible, he tried to make her laugh.

He periodically checked in on his own home's cameras also, making sure that everything was what it should be. He watched Alex introduce himself to other young people on the second floor, watched him stammer and reach for handshakes not forthcoming. He watched Alex discover that the record in the living room was still turning, lift the needle, turn off the turntable, and put the record away. At some point quite late in the day, Alex went home without a word to anyone.

David watched the beautiful young people cuddle, reheat pizza, read comic books, and look at their phones. He watched himself wander through the footage, a lost-looking man in a tweed suit jacket and gray slacks, eyes barely open, increasingly gray in his long, braided, black hair and overgrown beard. The day was already over. There were stars and half a moon on the screen that showed the sky. David rolled a joint and closed his eyes. Later he woke to the sound of Laverne the dog lying down against his door. Then her breathing, the periodic shifting of her weight as she drifted toward sleep, pleasantly exhausted from her run. He had known that she would come back. Everyone always wants to come home.

MAY, MOTT

MOTT'S TEACHER WAS NOT CRYING OR EVEN ASLEEP WHEN THE BELL rang. This was a worrying development but not in itself a disaster; she'd had good days before. There had been one whole week wherein she appeared to forget November entirely, indeed refused to recognize the word, and when the children alluded to the world's end she pretended not to understand. When they named the month, she had cupped her ears and asked them to speak up, enunciate, say what they meant. On the fifth day, Mott shouted with such volume and clarity that no one could fail to hear, and on that day Ms. Rooney froze and blinked until Malik changed the subject by asking her to show him where Italy was on the class globe. "Of course," she said, all smiles, but she sniffled twice while her finger searched Europe, and the following week she was back to her old, bad self, collapsed and inconsolable, only speaking up to name the dead: her parents, her brothers, her boyfriend, her cats, her turtle, her students.

This time was different. This time she brought animal crackers in boxes that looked like miniature circus cars. Each desk got its own box, including those long abandoned—Ms. Rooney hadn't noticed how poor attendance was now. Mott wordlessly claimed the box from Malik's empty desk as her own and opened it first so nobody could object. Several students followed her example with their adjacent empty desks, but most were too awed by the sight of Ms. Rooney upright, shampooed and trimmed, eyes bright and kind. Her cardigan wasn't even covered in cat hair. She wasn't even coughing her constant fake cough.

"My therapist and I agreed that I owe you an apology. My calling is your care and education. No one ever promised me you would all live to see adulthood. That's not why I do what I do. We need to get back on task. Raise your hand if you remember your last assignment."

Mott raised her hand and also stood so Ms. Rooney would be forced to call on her.

"We were supposed to write a book report. It's supposed to be called 'If You Read Just One Thing Before November, Make It This,' and it's one typewritten page, or two if by hand."

Mott sat down.

"I don't think that's right," said Ms. Rooney. "I know it's been a little while, but I'm fairly certain that your last assignment was to interview a parent. You had a list of five suggested questions. I know I've let things slide, but you've all had more than enough time."

Mott raised her hand and stood up. "Excuse me ma'am, we did that assignment a long time ago, you refused to accept it, and so I graded it for you. The class did pretty well, especially Malik, who interviewed his grandmother about his dead granddad."

"Ms. Gabel, I appreciate your enthusiasm, but you need to wait your turn to speak. Now do you have the assignment for me, or do you need more time? We can discuss an extension."

Mott opened her mouth, but Ms. Rooney rudely interrupted: "Everyone, please raise your hand if you have the assignment."

But nobody did. It was already turned in, marked, returned, and trashed.

Mott said, "If you like I can bring in my grade book and show you how they did."

This made Ms. Rooney blush. "We can move on to our next lesson," she said.

Mott stood up again. "Who wants to read their paper first? I'm sure that everyone worked hard. We can do your lesson tomorrow, Ms. Rooney."

Ms. Rooney wrote on the blackboard in perfect, fussy cursive: *Mott, please be quiet.*

"Fine," said Mott. "I'll start." She walked to the head of the class, essay in hand.

Ms. Rooney wrote: *Mott, this is your last chance.*

"If I had finished *Little Women* then I might have chosen that," shouted Mott.

The teacher threw a chalkboard eraser at the ground beside Mott's feet. It coughed white powder on her shoes and the cuffs of her jeans. Nobody in the room dared breathe.

Mott folded her essay in half and halved it again. She put it in her pocket.

Ms. Rooney wrote on the board in quick, vicious strokes. Mott turned around to see.

Mott, you may report to the principal.

Mott Gabel, by far the smartest girl in her class and possibly the school, the best behaved, the most promising writer, soon to die though she was very young, no great beauty yet but possibly she would have been someday—Mott Gabel was being ejected from class.

She shouldered her backpack, overturned her desk and chair, and left.

.....

Mott went to the restroom. She peed and did not flush—a punishment for the school. She rinsed her shaking hands in cold water and dried them on her pants (the soap and paper towel dispensers long empty). She went out into the hall and sat on the floor, resting her back against somebody else's locker. There were other children here, some sleeping, others playing games on phones.

She had never been sent to the principal's office. Even before the November dream, she would have been afraid to go. Now it was worse. Now she knew that today had been her last day of school—her last day this year, her last day forever. And this was all she knew. She did not know what would happen next. Most students sent to the principal's office were never seen again. Some were occasionally glimpsed in the hallways before school, though never after. If she went home now, then she would be safe, and would not disappear. Or it was possible that this was what happened to most of the punished and disappeared students: they went to the toilet, did not flush, rinsed their hands in cold water, and decided not to risk it, to leave and never return.

If she left then she would have to tell her mother why, and her mother would not understand the answer. There were many things that Mott had not told Lyd about the way the world was now. The fact that bad kids disappeared was one.

There was chalk dust still on the cuffs of Mott's jeans. Ms. Rooney had practically assaulted her. Everyone in class had seen. Mott decided to go to the principal, show him the chalk, and tell him her side.

The principal was not in his office. His assistant sent him a text. "He'll be here shortly," she said. "Pop a squat."

Mott waited in the lobby. The principal's assistant cheated at solitaire on her desk with an actual deck of red Bicycle playing cards. There was nobody else in the office—not the vice principal, who had recently swallowed a bad pill in his childhood home, and no other punished children. Mott kicked her feet together sideways. She played a puzzle game on her phone.

The principal swept into the lobby and sat next to Mott. Every inch of him was a wrinkle. He was like a used-up sock collapsed around somebody's bony ankle.

"Sharon told me it was you, Ms. Gabel, but I couldn't believe it. You've always been so well-behaved."

"Do you maybe want to go into your office?"

"I don't see the need." He smelled like butter.

"I would be more comfortable."

"You were disruptive in your class. That's fine, Mott. It's a challenging time for all children. You feel confused and afraid."

"I'm not confused. She threw her eraser at me for no reason. See?" Mott pointed at the chalk on her cuffs.

"You're the only student who has a problem with Ms. Rooney."

"She hasn't taught in months. I led the class with Malik while she cried on her desk."

"It sounds like she had the situation under control, then, in a way that worked for her, and now she's decided to shift her approach to better suit the needs of her other students, who after all outnumber you and need more help. Do you like movies?"

"I would rather talk about this in your office."

"Please come with me. I'm missing my favorite part."

"Your favorite part?"

"We're going to Kids' Club." He grabbed her by the wrist, yanked her up, and led her out the door.

"I don't want to go!"

"Right now you're being punished, so it doesn't matter what you want. You will report to Kids' Club every day from now until the school year's end. What's your favorite movie genre?"

"I'm not allowed to watch them." She jerked her arm. He squeezed. They turned a corner in the hall.

"My favorite films are black and white, but we don't watch those at Kids' Club."

Mott tried to stomp his foot but all she got was empty shoe.

"My second-favorite kind of film is thrillers." His hand twisted and made the skin hot. Now her arm would definitely bruise.

"Here we are." The auditorium's blue doors. The principal pushed her inside. Horizontal strands of light hung high in the dark and the dust, painting a projection screen suspended from the ceiling over the stage. There was a movie on that looked like a western. Somebody was gut shot, but he didn't seem to mind. He was talking to his buddy, who wouldn't stop touching his face. That was what bothered him—not the pain, but that his buddy kept touching his face.

"Goddamn it, I missed it," whispered the principal. "Choose a seat."

Mott considered her options. Most kids were clustered toward the front rows, with a few hanging back to fondle each other and whisper. All of them were really bad. They were the ones who used coarse language, who smoked in the bathroom, who fought in the halls, who left gum and snot on the undersides of their desks, who knew about sex, who pretended to know. She couldn't sit beside them; they would eat her alive. The principal tapped the back of her head. She waded into the deepest, darkest section of seating available, where she would be nearly alone. The nearest boy had a face that was shaped like the moon and shone with borrowed light.

The bad children ate popcorn from loud paper bags. Most were already finished—they worked patiently on bare kernels, sucking salt, risking their teeth to break shells. A woman's hand appeared over Mott's shoulder and offered her a popcorn bag of her own, three-quarters full. The hand patted her shoulder, her head, and glided away.

The gut-shot man was dead. His buddy was digging a hole in red sand. The sun was burying itself. The music was too loud for thought. Mott settled in and closed her eyes.

.....

Mott woke to find the moon-faced boy eating from her popcorn bag. He didn't notice she was watching and so chewed the way he would were he alone—mouth open, eyes drooping, heavy with the sublimity of his total boredom.

Mott slapped him on his forehead (which left her hand damp).

He recoiled and skittered backward, showing her his teeth. Then he froze—he'd realized what Mott was going to do next. She gave him her bag, which she didn't want anymore. He moved several seats away and hunched over his prize, apparently gravely concerned she might take it back.

Meanwhile, the credits were rolling and the music had finally calmed.

It wasn't fair. Mott was not supposed to be with these bad kids. Her school had failed her—not only today, and not only this year, but each day since she started middle school. She was supposed to be a big success. There should have been an essay contest so she could win the grand prize and read her winning essay for all the other students. The teachers were supposed to tell her mother how fortunate they felt to have her in their classes. They were supposed to love her very much. No teacher had singled her out for praise since fifth grade. They gave her high marks because she gave them no choice. They hated her for being so good.

Now it was her last day of school forever, and she hadn't even known that it would be, and she had worn a shabby and un-special outfit, and she had never made friends with practically anyone in her class, and she would never finish eighth grade, and all the delinquents were getting to stay. It was as if the school were really meant for them. She decided they could have it.

Mott left the auditorium through the doors that led directly to the parking lot. Nobody tried to stop her. Someone shouted, "Close the door behind you!" But the door would close itself.

The world was blinding white at first. Mott felt her own heartbeat in her temples as the color poured back in—a chalky blue into the sky, green into the trees, and breath into her lungs. An orange crop-duster airplane dragged a long, white banner slowly across the sky: 170 DAYS TILL THE END. GET $$$ FAST: LASTCHANCEPAWNSHOP.COM.

There were only a handful of cars in the lot, and most of these were parked across two spots or more, luxuriating like cats in the sun, their doors and fenders scratched and dented where they had drifted into other cars. Neglectful people ran this school—people without hopes or plans.

The time was three p.m. Mott called her mother. The phone rang four times.

Lyd said, "Is everything okay?"

"No," said Mott. "I'm dropping out."

MAY, LYD

SOMETIME IN THE PAST THREE YEARS—SHE COULDN'T NAME THE day—Lyd had stopped leaving her apartment. She knew it was close to three years because that was how long it had been since her flight to DC for the background check that cleared her to type government secrets. (There was proof of that date on her dresser: two boarding passes marked her places in two books.) She didn't know the last thing she had done outside, but she suspected it was groceries. She had been finding it increasingly difficult to face the shoppers and their gray, crowded teeth. She would have insisted that Mott come along. She would have said it was for Mott's sake, that she couldn't risk leaving her daughter alone with the stove, steak knives, and electrical outlets. She would have held Mott's hand whenever possible until they were back home, would have mixed herself a cocktail in her bedroom, would have gone to sleep and woken up in small hours, tasting snot and sour milk. It must have been something like that.

The phone rang but she did not hear.

Sometime in the past three years—possibly after she gave up

leaving home—Lyd had stopped checking her bank account's balance. There came a point (after the flight to DC, after David's first dictation, and after two months in which the account maintained a positive trend) where she allowed herself to trust that she would make rent, and she could keep her daughter warm and fed, so long as she was careful. It was simpler not to look, it was better, she didn't have to watch the browser load her information, she didn't have to wait with a yucky heart for the numbers to appear.

The phone rang but she did not hear.

Sometime in the past four years—it was impossible to say when; this wasn't something that happened to a person all at once, was rarely even a decision, was more like falling out of love—Lyd had given up on writing fiction. Three books was enough. That wasn't the reason, and literally no one ever asked, not even her editor, not even her agent, not even Mott, but had they asked she would have said it anyway. "Three books is enough." She would have changed the subject, stirring her drink until the ice cubes disappeared.

Lyd was curled up on the couch, eyes closed, black curtain drawn, the lights all switched off, an open book on her face, a hardback book, one with yellow pages for smelling. She was listening to *Nixon in China* through the bulky noise-canceling headphones Mott had bought her as a birthday gift. The phone rang and she finally heard it. She rolled from the couch and crawled toward the relevant end table, overturning several stacks of unfinished books and an empty glass.

The phone rang and Lyd picked it up. "Is everything okay?" She found a light switch with her fingers.

Mott said, "No. I'm dropping out."

"Honey, you can't do that."

"I could be an actual genius and we'll never find out because they're wasting my time."

"But you love to help the other students learn. We agreed that was very enriching."

"All they do now is show movies."

"You know that I need my alone time. I have to read and do my typing."

"Mom, am I allowed to watch TV? Did you change your rule? Because I am telling you, when I go to school from now on they will only let me sit still in a dark room watching movies."

"Honey."

"The principal bruised my arm."

"You can show me a bruise?"

"For God's sake."

"Come home and show me your bruise."

"That's what I'm already doing. You're like three steps behind."

Mott was breathing on the receiver. Lyd knew that if she told her to stop then Mott would deny it. The sound was hot on Lyd's ear; it made her want to hang up.

"We'll talk."

"You can homeschool me. Homeschool kids are smart."

"Mott, just come home."

"Promise you won't make me go back."

"I won't. We'll do something else. Come home and I'll make you a sandwich."

"Crunchy peanut butter?"

"Crunchy peanut butter," said Lyd. "It might be all we have left anyway." Her daughter hung up.

Her daughter hung up, but the call didn't end, and neither did the breathing.

"Lydia," said David's voice.

Lyd hung up the phone.

It had been fourteen years since Lyd squeezed a trigger. David had insisted that she learn. He explained that soon he would be a hot target for covert Russians, and she might find herself in the cross fire. He was going places in the Agency, and it was better safe than sorry. She didn't believe him—he was not, in her eyes, a serious person. In the long run he still got his way. He tricked her like he always did. First, he got her high (the first step in most of his devious plans), and then he said that he would take her out for hamburgers and a movie. When she asked him what movie, he said, "Whatever looks like fun to you, pretty," because he used to say that was her name, would go whole weeks without calling her what she liked to be called, which was charming to a point. She was ravenous for movies then, the dumber the better. Her favorite Saturday was to go to the theater and watch whatever everyone was watching. Riding in cars made her sleepy even when she was sober, and after using any kind of substance she was guaranteed to pass out at the first red light. When she woke up they were parked outside the gun store. David was shaking a box of loose bullets next to her ear. It would have been a fight if she refused. She couldn't fight with him in public. He was not afraid to make a scene. He taught her how to use the gun, told her what the parts were called and what they did. He made her try several models. She chose a Smith & Wesson .38 Special revolver because it was simple. It lived in their bedroom closet, in a shoebox on a high shelf, for several years. Later, when they were nearly finished, Lyd would sometimes take the gun out of its box while he was away and think about how it would feel to hold it until he came home. He never saw her do this that she knew of, though his cameras must have seen. One day her gun disappeared.

The phone rang and Lyd heard, but she didn't answer.

The phone rang again. Lyd realized it might be Mott calling. She answered.

"Lydia," said David. "Honey it's so good to hear your voice."

"I'm not talking."

"Okay. That's fine and cool. It's just, I was listening to your call with our little matzoh ball, and I'm concerned about your decision. It seems like Mott should finish the school year."

"You've been listening to our calls for how long?"

"Ever since you got her a phone. I sort of thought you knew.

Like, I didn't say it, but I figured that you would assume, because you know that we can do that, and you seemed to hear me breathing. But that's not the thing. The thing is this homeschool decision. You have to realize that's a bad fit for our daughter. She needs to learn to deal with other people. The two of you at home alone for the next five years is no one's recipe for a well-adjusted social butterfly."

"David, we don't have five years. We probably have like six months. Not even six."

David sighed. "The world is not ending. That was a dream."

"It was a dream that we all had, everybody on Earth, together. Don't talk to me like I'm crazy for thinking what basically everyone thinks. It's real. It's probably real."

"It's a psyop, babe. Total nonsense. Somebody put it in your head."

Lyd hung up the phone.

It rang again. She did not want to answer.

It rang again. She carried the phone's receiver to her workstation, removed the black cloth that draped David's webcam, and answered.

"Lydia," said David.

"Fuck you." She flipped off the webcam. "I'm not letting them waste what's left of her life on TV."

"Do you know how many times folks have thought the world was ending? Remember Y2K? People pulled their kids from school then too. They bought portable generators and hoarded green beans."

"You're ridiculous."

"You only think that because you don't see me clearly. Let me tell you about quantum physics."

"Oh my God not again."

"No, I think you'll like this. Quantum physics means that the apparent laws of nature don't apply to very small objects, like particles and light photons. They behave irrationally. So why do the big things made out of those little pieces—like people, chocolate bars, and moons—behave rationally, following the laws of Newtonian physics? How come a bowling ball falls when you drop it? You might say, 'because it's heavy.' Thing is, those little pieces, the particles and photons, they only break the law when they're alone. When you put a bunch of them together—billions and billions—they get highly predictable. All their weirdness averages out to normal. That's the world, honey. It averages out. It's not going to end. Not for a very long time."

Lyd couldn't think of a retort. He could sound so reasonable when he wanted to.

David said, "Can we maybe compromise? Mott's school sucks now, cool, I get it. Let's try it this way. You both come back home and live with me. I've got a nice, big house with loads of rooms. You can have your own bed—it's not about that. I've always known that you would come back."

Lyd hung up the phone. It rang. She punched a wall and answered.

"Now I am going to talk and you are going to hear me," said David, his voice an icy snarl. Lyd's stomach twisted; her legs all but folded beneath her. She tilted back onto the couch, weighed down with a dread and impotence she hadn't felt since the end of their marriage. He shouldn't be able to do this to her anymore. "You will make Mott finish out the year or you will come live with me now so I can see my daughter and protect her from the foolish things that people do when they believe the world is ending. I was going to call for you in the summer, this was always the plan, so you're not disrupting my life and I'm not disrupting yours. It's fine. You'll be safe and you won't feel afraid anymore. I know how to help you relax. Mott will be loved—we'll do a family game night. You can meet all my friends. Darling you must have been lonely. I've been very generous about this whole divorce experiment. You've played it out now and you know where it leads. Everyone has a path like planets have orbits. I've watched you sit and type and scratch your face red between keystrokes. You're so miserable and alone. You're afraid that I'm going to hurt you. But I could never hurt you if you didn't want me to. You're far too strong. I'm the one who is afraid. Have a drink if you still have a bottle. Tell our Mott the joyous news. Wait for me where you are. Lover, I will gladly come to you."

Lyd knew what he wanted to hear. One good thing about David was he always made it known exactly what he wanted. She said, "Okay."

"Do you mind if I tell you I love you?"

"You can if you want."

"It's not—it's nothing about how you feel. That's a separate issue. I wouldn't pressure you to feel a certain way. You're responsible for your heart and I am for mine."

"Sure."

"So you don't have to say that you love me."

She didn't answer.

"I love you, Lydia. I'll be there with you soon."

He ended the call.

It had been about three years since she'd left the apartment. About four since she'd given up writing. Fourteen since she'd fired a gun. Mott would be home in half an hour.

Lyd's hand shook as she reached for the front door. She was wearing her housecoat and slippers. That was no excuse. If she didn't go now, then she wouldn't. She and Mott would live with David in his home. They would get high together. She would watch her daughter blow smoke out her nose and giggle and dig in the cupboard for chips. If she didn't open the door, then David would get everything he wanted from now until the end of the world. He would touch her if he wanted to. He would hold her down and say he never did. He would tell her how repressed she was—how out of touch with her own body. He would put his ear between her legs and claim that he heard her heart beating.

She turned the knob. The door opened easily. She took her car keys from the peg on the wall where they had hung for so long. She stepped out into the hallway. It hadn't changed at all.

. . . . .

Of course the car would not start. Lyd must have known it wouldn't. The engine barely tried. She climbed out to appraise its condition. The car, a red sedan, was parked in its assigned spot in the apartment complex lot. The tires had gone flat at some point, and the license plate's sticker was three colors old. The passenger-side mirror had vanished—an exposed wire hung from the hole it left behind. She lifted the hood but didn't really know what ought to be inside a car. It looked, if anything, as if there were too many parts.

For years Lyd had thought of herself as a person who owned a car but chose not to use it. Now she knew the truth.

Fifteen minutes till Mott was due home. That was long enough for a bad shower and a thoughtless change of clothes. David would arrive before the night was out. He would have a gun, a pair of handcuffs, and substances that they could use together—substances that she would really like to use. First a bottle. Then whatever. He would rub her shoulders and her neck. The tension would just melt away. He would call her by a name that was not hers. He would repeat the name until she knew that when he spoke it that meant she should listen.

She ran upstairs and slammed the apartment's door closed.

She didn't know how to turn off David's webcam. The cord that plugged it into the computer workstation was not a USB connection, which would have been easily yanked, but a thick, black cord that fed directly into that larger machine—through the case and into its guts. Lyd had searched for screws that she could turn to open the computer, but there were none visible; it appeared to be one smooth piece. If she unplugged it from the wall, David would know something was wrong. If she unplugged the ethernet cable, he would know. If she broke the webcam, he would know. All she could do was leave its hood on. She would have to remember not to talk to herself until it was done.

It had been almost three years since last she checked her bank account balance. She navigated to her bank's website and tried three times before she got her password right. Her balance was $23,149.52. This could last until November. For years Lyd had thought of herself as a person whose lax spending and bad judgment had led her to the edge of financial ruin. Now she knew the truth: she had been frugal.

WHAT IT WAS LIKE LIVING WITH DAVID

THE DREAM ABOUT NOVEMBER CAME ONLY ONCE. THOUGH MOST people were haunted in following nights by certain elements—the idea of drowning, the texture of the father's hand, the forest path they had walked, the father's clipboard, the lake that must have been frozen—no one ever saw the whole of it again.

There was another common dream that did recur often, but that the dreamers typically failed to recall. This one had many variations. In Lyd's version, she was visiting a man's home. He was out on his deck, seated at a plastic hexagonal picnic table with three benches: one for him, one for her, and one for nobody. It was a nice, warm day, and the leaves of the trees in the yard seemed to glitter in the sun. He had a lemonade pitcher and two glasses, all full. He had a notebook and a silver pen. He looked like someone she could trust.

Sometimes Lyd began the dream in his kitchen. Sometimes she began it in his sunroom, looking at him through the picture windows. Sometimes she was parking her car in his driveway. She always made her way to the deck, sat down at the plastic table, sipped her lemonade, and waited for him to ask what he wanted to know.

In the course of this dream's repetitions, he asked about her childhood, her mother and father, elementary school, high school, college. He asked when she first had the thought that she hated herself. He asked when she first thought she wanted to die. He wrote down everything she said in his notebook. He reviewed it with her again and again.

He asked her, "Have you ever been married?"

Lyd felt herself blush. "Yes. My husband was named David. We're not together now."

"Please tell me about life with your husband."

.....

Twenty-three years ago, David introduced himself to Lyd by handing her a disposable camera. "My friend and I are about to do something charming. Can you do us a solid and capture this moment on film?" He pointed at a heavy kid in a novelty tuxedo T-shirt and a rubber Chewbacca mask. David was dressed as Luke Skywalker. He wore a white bathrobe, brown jogging pants, black snow boots, and a toy lightsaber tucked into the robe's belt. Lyd wasn't wearing a costume. When people asked her who she was supposed to be, she had been telling them, "In the long run, and assuming I don't kill myself first, a very famous author."

She turned the camera in her hands, examining its orange-and-yellow cardboard shell. "I didn't know they still made these."

"That's okay," said David. "There's a lot of things that I don't know myself. The button is here on the top." He showed her with his finger, which required that his hand touch hers. She noted that he smelled like weed, which was at the time her favorite cologne.

"Tell me when you're being charming," said Lyd. She centered him in the viewfinder.

David sidled up to Tuxedo Chewbacca, who held a square of

silky black fabric up in front of himself at arm's length. They each gripped one of the square's corners and tugged, unfurling a black banner four feet wide by three feet tall. The cloth was decorated with white stars, shining sequins, and a message, also white: GIRL, YOU LIGHT UP THE NIGHT SKY.

Lyd snorted, snapped the picture, and returned the camera. Tuxedo Chewbacca wordlessly folded the cloth, stowed it in his pocket, and disappeared into the Halloween party.

"Thanks." David put the camera too close to her face, pressed the button. She smiled for him despite herself. The flash bruised her vision. "I'm David like the Bible king, and I would love to kiss your hand hello."

"I bet you would," said Lyd.

"Based on the fist you just made, I bet that if I try it you'll sock me."

He was thin, even delicate, pretty, maybe two inches taller than her, with sleepy eyes and long lashes. He wore his hair in a thick, black braid. She wanted to untwist it and see how far down his back it fell.

They left together half an hour later. They took her car to a chain diner, smoked some of David's weed outside, and shared two heaping plates of chili cheese fries plus one chocolate milkshake. He told her everything he knew about quantum physics, returning frequently to the theme of the field's spiritual implications. "If consciousness determines the state and behavior of matter, then reality is our collective property." The words weren't interesting, but his voice was easy listening. She told him an idea that she had for a novel, which she claimed had no implications, absolutely none of any kind for anything at all—a book that was only itself and would contain itself completely. He said he would read anything she wrote for the rest of his life.

When she felt near enough to sober, she drove him home. He talked about how repressed people were, how estranged from their own bodies—especially women. "Women have been socialized not to ask for what they want, and never to demand it," he said.

"I told you what I wanted," said Lyd. She had wanted his weed, the chili cheese fries, the milkshake. He was literally along for the ride.

"Sure. But most people don't, because they're afraid or embarrassed."

"Or maybe they just don't like you," said Lyd. But the fact was she did. He had seemed to listen to her closely when she spoke, had looked at her as if enchanted, had let her talk as if she were an actual writer. And he really was good-looking. In his apartment complex parking lot, before dropping him off, she asked him for his number. He used a pen from her cup holder to write it on her hand, which she also allowed him to kiss.

.....

Lyd was twenty-one, a junior at the University of Houston. David was twenty-three, a fifth-year senior. They never officially declared themselves a couple, but he made his claim known by holding her hand whenever they were together in public, and fussing often with her hair, and saying "us" and "we" when "I" would suffice, and being slightly too affectionate at parties.

She studied writing not because she believed it would make her better but because there was nothing else that she liked enough. He studied languages because that was supposed to be his shortest path into the CIA or any of its sister agencies. He had no natural facility with anything but English and struggled to memorize words. When she asked him why he wanted to be a spy, he said it was the only job he'd ever wanted ever since he was a kid. He asked her what else he should want. He said, "They get to know all the secrets." She told him the whole concept was ridiculous. He said, "No more ridiculous than being a writer."

They liked swimming in the campus pool together. They liked drinks with plastic bric-a-brac. David liked to talk about ideas; Lyd liked to pretend she was paying attention, slipping into his voice like a warm, thick sock. They liked eating greasy food. They liked fooling around with their friends, liked watching each other. They took an art class together. They tried cocaine once but agreed not to do it again. They liked skipping class. They watched hundreds of movies. Lyd sometimes read to him from books she admired. He asked when she would write hers. She said she didn't know, or said that she would start that summer, or said it was his fault she hadn't already—he was a distraction she couldn't afford. She said she would never write one, would die having accomplished nothing.

They were never a truly great couple, and Lyd would never have said she was happy with him or with anyone else, but it soon became impossible to imagine life without David. He was, in his way, the most reliable, predictable person she had ever known, and if he wasn't actually interesting, at least he was interested in her.

The day that David proposed, he took Lyd on an hours-long walk in Hermann Park, holding her left hand, rubbing her fingers, feeding her weed gummi bears. He'd spent the previous week researching the plants in the gardens, learning the names of the trees and the flowers, and taught these to her now, guiding her hand to each one, urging her to touch it as he spoke its name. She would repeat the name and forget it, no matter how beautiful. It was the most words she ever forgot in one day. She wanted to ask him why he could remember the plants' names when he couldn't recall that *biblioteca* meant *library*. She wanted to ask if he had ever considered being a florist. He guided her hand to a rose. There was an engagement ring on her finger—a braid of white gold with small sapphires embedded in the gaps between its strands. She had grown so accustomed to the feeling of him rubbing her hand that she hadn't noticed him putting it on her. She was crying.

"Old Blush China Rose," he said, because that was the name of the bloom. "Marry me. I can make you happy."

"Nothing's ever going to make me happy. But yes, I'll marry you."

As they kissed, she continued to weep, stroking and bruising the rose.

.....

They graduated together—her fourth year, his sixth. They moved into an apartment with thin walls and linoleum floors. Lyd introduced him to her mother, who was still angry that Lyd had left home. Their engagement dragged on for more than a year; they fought often. They tried substances that were supposed to subdue the ego. When Lyd was alone in their home, she cried and thought about how she was and would die a failure, and cried and watched the clocks tick, and cried and asked herself why she couldn't write a great novel when so many others had done it before. They were married in a large and mostly empty church, said vows they had written together. In sickness and in health, whether rich or poor, in good times and bad, they would care for each other. They would be kind.

In the moment between "I do" and the kiss, Lyd was struck by the arbitrariness of it all—how strange it was that anyone should choose to commit to anyone else, that she was with David, that he was with her, that they were the people they were, and if all went according to plan it would be that way until they were buried. Even supposing they were right for each other, and even assuming that they stayed in love, what were the odds of that? Why should anybody be so lucky?

.....

Fourteen months into their marriage, David said that he would like to try filming their sex. "Lots of healthy, loving couples do this," he said. Lyd couldn't think of a good reason not to. This was the first time he had ever sounded even a little bit timid asking her for anything, which made her feel that he must really be requesting something else, something more, and probably something to which she would never agree if it were explicit, but she couldn't think of a way to explain this that he would choose to understand.

"Okay," she said. "We can try it."

He ordered a tripod for the digital camera they already owned. Lyd spent the next week wondering when it would arrive, and then, once he had it, when he would next announce that he was in the mood. (She bought herself time by not wearing his favorite outfits, by avoiding eye contact in their bedroom, and by dressing quickly after morning showers.) He waited three days to broach the subject, which he did by wrapping his hand in her hair and kissing the base of her neck. Her stomach clenched painfully. If she told him no now, the fight would be the rest of their evening. He would guilt her about the money he'd spent on the tripod based on his reasonable understanding that she was on board. He would tell her that he only wanted to get close to her, to please her and make her feel happy. He would say that he would never do anything to her that she didn't want. By that point she would be softening her opposition, would be saying maybe they should try it after all. It might not be so bad—might not be what she imagined. He would sulk and tell her it was time to drop the subject. The only way to end his fit would be for her to beg him to record their sex after all. Then and only then would their evening proceed exactly as he had planned it, and she would be tired, and would have to get off anyway, or persuasively fake it, because if she couldn't come that would be an hours-long argument too. So what was the point of any of that. She led him to bed by the hand.

David opened the tripod, set the camera on top, and turned it in circles until it was firmly affixed. "We can stop if you don't like it," he said. "No problem at all."

"How do we know if it's aimed right?"

"I'll lie down on the bed. Just point it at me. If I'm on-screen, you will be too."

David pressed the record button. A red light beside the lens blinked on. He removed his paisley lounge pants and lay down. Lyd centered him in the viewfinder and paused to consider him as an image—his skinny legs all spread for her, his ribs exposed and thin and very breakable. There was a bug bite on his hip, swollen and luridly pink. She stepped between him and the camera and took off her clothes one piece at a time, swaying to the rhythm of the next apartment's mariachi music. He said that was perfect. She asked him now what next.

"You look beautiful when you put me in your mouth. Please make eye contact with the camera while you do it. Don't feel like you're being judged—you never will be."

Lyd pushed him flat on his back, straddled his chest, faced the camera, and stared into its gaping eye. She became aware that she was breathing, and could see in her mind's eye how her breathing would appear on-screen, and could feel David's breathing beneath her. They were not breathing at the same rate in the same way, so they were not together, and she was alone.

"You can start whenever you want," said David. "Maybe drink a beer if that will help you chill."

"No, I don't like this. I'm turning it off. It makes me feel like someone else." She climbed off.

"Lydia, I swear on my life that I don't want to change you—it's the opposite. I'm preserving you for the ages."

"But it does change me." She rubbed her arms to make them warm. "I feel changed."

"Go ahead and turn it off, then. We'll try again next time."

Lyd went to the kitchen, poured a beer. Someone had left a motorcycle running in the parking lot outside. Someone was hammering a nail into a shared wall.

David wrapped his arms around her as she swallowed the last foam of her drink. He kissed her cheek, her shoulder, the back of her ear. She relaxed into his arms. She felt foolish. It wasn't like she'd ever have to see the video. It wasn't like she hated the thought of him watching her later. David asked her, "Would you feel better if you couldn't see the camera?"

This was what he'd wanted all along.

.....

The following weekend, David installed a hidden camera somewhere in their bedroom. It took him three hours; Lyd watched three episodes of *M*A*S*H* in their living room while he worked. When he was done, nothing had visibly changed, and yet the room was entirely different. It now existed in two distinct but overlapping versions: the physical space and its image. The air was heavier. Lyd felt every breath twice.

David put his hand inside her hair and twisted. He kissed the back of her neck. "Does this help?"

"Yes," she said, though she wasn't sure. He pulled her back against himself, laid a hand across her collarbone. She glanced nervously at the place where she thought the camera was most likely hidden—at a high point in the corner, ideally positioned to capture her side of the bed. He leaned his knee against the back of hers, adjusting her stance, spreading her legs just a bit. He must have thought she'd look better that way.

.....

Lyd made a list of rules for David and his camera.

First, he should not use the camera unless they were together, making love. She did not want to be recorded trimming her nails, sleeping, or doing whatever she did in their room when she was alone. Secondly, he should not tell her when he used the camera and when he did not. She didn't want to know when she was performing and when she was being a person alive.

She required constant access to the footage. David must always save his recordings to the same folder on his computer, and he must always allow her to view them whenever she wanted. He could delete anything that he didn't like. She was allowed the same privilege, up to and including deleting all of the files at any time and for any reason.

Another rule was that she could make new and unreasonable rules any time she wanted, and these would not be subject to discussion, and she would not be subject to reproach.

She emailed these rules to David. He replied right away despite being at work: "Okay."

"Don't write emails on this topic using your office computer," wrote Lyd.

"Okay," wrote David.

He was working in IT at the time. His employer, a private company that provided procurement support to the air force, had recently fired nearly all their staff and rehired most of the top performers as independent contractors. He was an underqualified replacement for one of the employees who had refused to accept the new structure. As best Lyd could tell, he spent most of his time snooping through coworkers' email accounts and Internet browser histories; he frequently told her who was having an affair, who was surfing porn during the lunch hour, and who was secretly in trouble with the boss. The whole point of his taking the IT job was that spy agencies supposedly liked to see that sort of thing on a CV. He saw his surveillance as practice. She assumed he was also reading her email. Sometimes she wrote lists of irritating things he had recently done and saved them to her drafts folder in case he was looking. That was his punishment—and it also happened that he often stopped the irritating behaviors soon afterward, so there were practical benefits too.

The first rule David broke regarding his camera was he left it turned on all the time. Lyd didn't notice for months—she was not in the habit of checking the folder where he kept his footage—but one morning she felt an urgent need to delete any records of the previous night, wherein she had been both sloshed and horny and had said some foolish, shameful things that she didn't mean about what her body was for. When she opened the most recent file, she found it began three mornings before, with her asleep and David brushing his teeth, pacing in and out of the room as he worked, now looking down at her on the bed, now stroking the blanket beside her, now spitting somewhere off-screen, now rooting around in the clothes that lay piled on the floor, searching for workable socks. He left and the footage continued. She skipped forward two hours—the footage continued, showing now the empty room and the bed that neither had made. There was a fly on her pillow. She skipped forward a day. She was sleeping in bed with a book that she'd meant to read. It was open on her face, was hiding her a little.

She skipped forward a day and some hours, found the shame she had planned to erase, and deleted the file.

There were weeks of similar recordings, all made in violation of her rules. She didn't touch these. She did not raise the issue with David.

Having accepted this violation, Lyd found it easiest to continue feigning ignorance when David installed more hidden cameras without consulting her, and without making any announcement, while she was not at home to see him do it. He started with a second in the bedroom, this time in the opposite corner, which was arguably well within the spirit of their original agreement. Next he added one in the living room, which showed what was on the TV, and then another that showed how Lyd looked on the couch while she watched the TV. Next he added one in the kitchen, then the bathroom, and then the hall that joined them. Then, somehow, inside the fridge, documenting what she ate and when. All these devices saved to the same folder on David's computer as the first camera, so that Lyd knew they were being installed more or less as it happened, though David never acknowledged what he was doing. He wanted her to know, and he wanted not to discuss it. Just the thought of raising the topic herself—of developing a principled objection to the new cameras when she had already allowed the first, and of articulating that objection with a clarity and calmness that would force David to actually hear her—caused bone-deep exhaustion. Lyd could not find the energy to ask him to stop, and so she was silent. But this was never consent. It was only giving in.

There seemed to be an algorithm running the cameras, so that whichever one saw the most motion was the one that wrote to the hard drive. This meant the videos followed Lyd throughout the house when she was home alone, and split the difference when David was there in some other room, alternating back and forth between them. (He did not appear to mind the cameras at all, never paused to glance at any of their hiding places, never seemed to hesitate to do something unflattering because it might be seen, used the toilet freely, ate all he wanted, and hummed out of tune.) There were many times that Lyd and David passed out together drunk or high or both at home, and consequently moved so little that the recording cut to a bug in some other room, seemingly that same fly from before, and watched it climb the walls or buzz around a plate of food half-finished, cutting back to Lyd and David when one rolled or moaned or scratched, or when the fly was motionless too long or dead too long, so that David and Lyd seemed to be parts of a whole that included the fly and its death. And when there was no motion anywhere in the apartment, the video cut at six-second intervals from one angle to the next, so that when David and Lyd were asleep and there were no flies they seemed to be already dead, equivalent to empty rooms.

When Lyd was home alone crying, she tried to be as still as possible so the cameras would not watch. *I will die having accomplished nothing*, she mouthed to herself, and watched the clocks tick.

Each morning Lyd woke to the knowledge her waking might later be watched. She dressed for the cameras, imagining what they might see as she consulted the mirror, perceiving herself from within and above, both now and in the future, through her own eyes and through David's. Crossing a room had become an ordeal—she had to navigate so many versions of the floor plan. It felt like walking one path seven times. A delay developed between impulse and physical action: before every movement, her body consulted the cameras, hesitating to do anything that might later look strange or affected. Her limbs felt stiff and numb, stupid—weird. She banged her shins on every piece of furniture, each time barely resisting the urge to turn and stare accusingly at the nearest hidden lens.

When David was home, it only meant he was watching her twice, both now and then later. She spoke simply and directly, avoiding any sentence that might be perceived on review as ambiguous, ungenerous, impatient, or even potentially cruel. "Good morning." "Do you want an egg?" "I liked my lunch." "What are you watching?" "Is the volume okay?" "Do you want to cuddle?" "You look nice in that shirt." "What do you want for dinner?" "Can you please tuck me in?" "Good night. Don't stay up too late."

It was better when she drank. It was better when she watched TV. It was better when she closed her eyes, though even then the image of the room persisted, and indeed her own image persisted, and in fact she seemed to grow larger with each passing second, or possibly rose toward the ceiling.

Her job was clerical and only part-time. She called in sick one day in four.

She found it difficult to eat. She wrote nothing at all.

If she killed herself, she wondered, when David found her body, would he pause to cover her or close her sightless eyes before he went to watch his record of her death?

When she finally chose to confront him, she did it by digging his cameras out of their walls while he was at work. She used a hammer and chisel. Some she found on the first try. Others took several attempts. She never found the one in the fridge.

When he got home, they argued. She broke his nose. It wasn't the first time she'd hit him, but it was the first time that she did it sober, and in earnest hope of causing lasting harm.

They moved out the next day. The landlord called to let them know their deposit was forfeit. "I should sue you but my doctor says I got a melanoma. It isn't worth the time."

Lyd quit her job and made David work enough to pay for everything. She started a new novel that she believed would be her breakthrough. It was all she thought about for months. David's nose healed straight. He apologized to her between kisses, after meals, at red lights, during movie trailers, and while credits rolled. The novel never ended. Her interest in writing it did.

MAY, MOTT

MOTT FOUND HER MOTHER WAITING IN THE HALL BESIDE THEIR front door, wild-eyed and recently showered. Lyd was seated on the floor, legs crossed, hair dripping on the yellow carpet. "Shoot," she said, "I'm sorry. I forgot your crunchy peanut butter sandwich."

"You left the apartment?"

"I didn't go far."

"Is everything okay?"

Lyd swallowed in the way that meant she was about to lie. It looked like she was trying to force a live bird down her throat.

"It's fine."

"I don't believe you."

"Of course you don't. Nothing is fine. When November comes, we're probably dead. But that's what I realized. I had an epiphany. It came to me as a question." She took Mott's hand in her own shaking hands. "Mott, my love, what's the one thing that you most want to do before you die?"

Though she had not expected the question, Mott knew her answer right away. "My novel," she said. "I have to write one."

Lyd kissed Mott's hand and let it go. "I thought so," she said. "As for me, what I want most of all is to read this book that you're going to write."

Lyd stood and smoothed her housecoat. "I'm giving in to you completely. I'm taking you out of school, and I will help you write your novel, but I think that you should brace yourself for disappointment, though I hope you won't be disappointed, it's just that novels are hard."

Lyd was keeping her voice low, almost a whisper. Mott decided she would do the same.

"Thank you," she said. "I'll do my best. But I'm still confused." She nudged the apartment door with her toe and peered inside. There was no fire. "How come you're out here?"

"Because once I got out, I had to stay out, and we need to buy a new car. Ours is broken."

"What do we need a car for?"

"Because you need to see the world." Now she really did whisper: "We're going to leave and never come back. And we're going to get groceries."

Mott peered into her mother's eyes. "You're being weird and it's making me nervous."

"Oh." Lyd clicked her tongue. "There's that bruise you promised."

Mott turned her wrist to show her purple bracelet's full circumference. "The principal did it. He was missing his favorite part of the movie."

"I'm sorry, love. You can tell me on the way."

Mott hugged her mother. Lyd pulled the door closed.

.....

They held hands on the bus that took them to the dealership; Lyd squeezed too tight. She kept scanning all the passengers' faces. For the last three years, the only people she had seen up close were Mott, a handful of delivery boys, and one apparently mute plumber who had listened to talk radio for the duration of her visit. By comparison, the dozen riders on this bus were a swarm, and none of them looked happy. The air smelled like tennis shoe rubber and corroded pocket change.

There was a thin man with badly chapped lips sitting opposite them, constantly rubbing his eyes. There was an old woman holding and watching a muted portable TV, which was attached to a lanyard she wore as a necklace. There were identical twin sisters sleeping together upright, their heads tilting to make a steeple.

Mott pulled the bus cord one block north of the like-new dealership. The driver stopped too soon—almost immediately—so that Mott and Lyd were forced to walk the road's broken shoulder until it became sidewalk. A yellow inflatable tube man convulsed manically beside a sign that promised everything was priced to move. NO CREDIT CHECKS, NO QUESTIONS ASKED. START A LIKE-NEW LIFE WITH YOUR LIKE-NEW CAR.

Although most of the country's money movers (like most people in general) believed the world would likely end before the year was out, they were still happy to make any loan that would have profited them in the long term, preferring theoretical future wealth and climbing line graphs to actual money on hand. There was a kind of mania among the banks to issue debt, and interest rates had reached record lows. However, potential borrowers had not so far provided similar demand. They focused on repaying what they owed, in many cases liquidating everything they owned—reducing vehicles, homes, movie disc collections, digital ownership rights, furniture, tools, family heirlooms, sports memorabilia, collectible dolls, and even medical devices to cash.

This left most salespeople idle, listless, and disoriented. There were in fact three salesmen waiting motionless in the like-new dealership's lot: one stood and two sat on the hoods of two white cars, sweating like lemonade glasses. The standing man saw Lyd and Mott approaching. He checked his palms, right and then left. When the seated men saw, they checked their palms too. The answer was not there.

The standing man apologized. "It's been so long since we sold one, I don't remember how this goes. Would you like to shake my hand?"

Forty minutes later, Lyd drove Mott away in a newborn-looking car, financed with a generous loan. She planned to never make a payment, and practically told the salesmen as much as they neared the transaction's end, but they didn't care. They were all three of them so happy to be useful. Everything was easy, and all of it happened so quickly.

.....

Next Lyd and Mott went to the grocery store, which was the kind that also sold everything else. Lyd drove there without any guidance from Mott, as if she had made the trip often over the past several years. She had to park at the far edge of the lot because of how full it already was. "Is this a busy time for them?" asked Lyd.

"It doesn't really get busy," said Mott. "It's more that some people don't leave."

Many cars were in advanced states of decay, rusting and peeled, wounded, windows shattered, plastic bags taped up in their stead. There was a truck with all its tires stolen. There was a van rolled over on its side.

Lyd asked about the smell. Mott led her to the nearest car and pointed through its window. There was a man asleep in the passenger seat, most of him covered by a thin Big Bird blanket. There was a sun-bleached ball cap on his face. The driver's seat beside him was piled high with candy bar wrappers and empty beer cans.

The whole lot was scattered with sleepers both living and not. Some lay in their cars and others in their open trunks. Some were folded up in shopping carts. For every person or body there was at minimum one garbage pile: empty pretzel bags, two-liter bottles, rewritable CDs, saltine sleeves, plastic cars, deflated footballs, white bread, bags of liquid Fun Pops. There was a girl about Mott's age standing in an overflowing cart corral and rapping under her breath, eyes closed, one earbud in her ear and the other swinging free so she could hear herself rhyme. There was a dead man with bare feet seated by the entrance, propped against the wall. He held a bagged betta fish—haggard but still swimming, probing the plastic membrane for a weakness.

The automatic doors slid open and welcomed them in. Lyd paused here and held Mott back. The doors hissed closed again. Lyd said, "How long has it been like this?"

Mott sighed. "It didn't happen all at once. Every time I come back, things are a little bit worse." The doors parted again and waited for them.

The air inside was cold and dry. Lyd chose the best of four remaining carts, which stood out from the rest by virtue of having the usual number of wheels.

"Don't be afraid of the greeter," said Mott. "Just stay out of his reach."

The greeter was an old man on a stool. He was missing both his legs up to the knees. His body was shaped like a hammer—he had a long, thin torso and a large, heavy head. He kept his balance by clutching his seat. He leered at them with total hate as they entered the store.

"He bit me once," said Mott, while they might still be within his hearing. "It didn't break the skin, but it stung."

"When did that happen? I didn't know that happened."

Of course she didn't: for the next two weeks, Mott had worn only long sleeves. "March, I think. I didn't want to tell you, you were crying all the time back then."

"You shouldn't have to worry about me."

"Maybe," said Mott. "You don't give me much choice."

The lights above were flickering or they were out. Here and

there were puddles of liquid from ruptured bottles and cartons, were nibbled-on slices of bread, were smashed bananas, were discarded scraps of packaging and used plastic forks. There was music people used to think they liked on the loudspeaker. There were prerecorded public service announcements about healthful eating. Some aisles were more shadow than visible product: the one with flour and instant pancakes, the one with pasta and red sauce, the one with all the soup.

Lyd said they could buy whatever food Mott wanted. Mott knew this was a test. If she were good then she would ask for mostly healthy things. She led her mother to the canned fruits and veggies. The shelves had many gaps. Mott wanted black beans, but there were none in evidence. She wanted pineapple rings canned with juice, but there was only the syrup kind. They settled for pinto beans and pineapple tidbits, which did have the juice.

"It's strange to see so much missing," said Lyd. Mott had told her many times about the absent products, but Lyd never remembered, and frequently included things that didn't exist anymore in her shopping lists.

Mott said, "I feel more weirded out by all the stuff that's still here. They know about November in the Cheerios factory, the people who run the machines. Why do they still go to work? They should stay home and write novels."

"Most people can't write a novel, and almost nobody can eat one. Most of us don't have anything better to do than make Cheerios. It's elitist to assume that the people who make what we eat are unhappy because they do manual labor."

"Maybe," said Mott. "Or maybe it's worse to assume that they aren't."

In fact, people mostly went to work for the same reasons they always had: first, it was what others expected of them, and second, no one seemed to have a better idea.

Lyd and Mott heard footsteps in adjacent aisles. They glimpsed sleepy, roaming shoppers. They saw an elderly couple comparing incomparable products: a tube of kosher salt and a box of chocolate chip cookies. The husband wanted the cookies. The wife argued that salt was both cheaper and better.

Lyd promised Mott that it was fine to have some treats. Mott chose three bags of kettle chips, two boxes of sour fruit snacks, a pack of peanut butter crackers, a cylinder of cashews, and two mixed assortments of dehydrated fruit. With Lyd's encouragement, she took one box of every kind of Little Debbie. Mott asked for cinnamon cereal, but there was none left.

Next were the office supplies. Mott chose a bag of ballpoint pens and one dozen yellow legal pads. There was a man asleep on the floor. Someone had tied his shoes together. His feet leaned away from one another, pulling the laces taut.

Lyd turned a corner into dairy. There was a lifeless child on the floor, twelve at the oldest, encircled by bloody footprints. Lyd made a small sound and covered her own eyes—not Mott's.

Mott had seen eight dead people in public for sure since the November dream, not counting the ones in the cars parked outside, which she'd never looked at closely enough to be certain they weren't sleeping. This one was by far the worst. She turned away, walked to the next aisle, and waited for Lyd to catch up.

Soon, but not soon enough, Lyd put a hand on Mott's shoulder. "I'm sorry," she said. "I knew it was bad, but I didn't know it was scary like this. I wouldn't have let you shop on your own."

"It's okay," said Mott, though she wasn't sure that it was. "I've been trying not to let you know."

.....

They went to the gun counter. The man behind was peeing in a vodka bottle. He opened his eyes and saw that he was not alone. "Christ," he said, "I'm sorry. Can't stop, I'll try to be quick." He covered it as best he could and turned his back to them. Lyd sighed pointedly. The man (fortysomething, troubled skin, sky-blue hat, employee vest, untucked T-shirt, ratty jeans) finished, screwed the bottle's cap back on, stowed it by his feet, closed his pants, and turned to face them again. He reiterated how terribly sorry he was.

"It's fine," said Lyd. "She's seen one before."

Mott couldn't think of when. Never her father's. Did her mother count textbook drawings, anatomical cross sections? Did she count tasteful European painted nudes? Not that it mattered. Mott didn't care about anyone's penis.

Lyd told him she wanted a Smith & Wesson .38 Special like the one she used to have. He confirmed that there was one in stock. There would be no waiting period, and licensure was not an issue. Guns were going to be a Christian family's last defense come November. He expressed dismay that so few were buying protection in these trying times. The government, he noted, would certainly be ready. He suggested Lyd should also buy a gun for Mott. "Something little. Just a cutie." There was a law against it, but the constitution was in favor.

Mott imagined herself with a gun.

"No thank you," said Lyd. She bought six boxes of ammo. She told him to remind her how it loaded.

Lyd said she needed one more thing. She asked Mott to lead her to the liquor aisle. The most direct route would take them past electronics and therefore the big TV wall. Instead Mott led her through purses, backpacks, pajamas, and seasonal clothes. They heard the TV wall's buzz but avoided its glow and onlookers.

Now here were several yards of shelves of shining bottles. Here was gin and whiskey and vodka and all. Everything was stocked at minimum three bottles deep, not because nobody bought them but because the nation's distilleries recognized continuous production was their civic duty.

Lyd reached for a bottle and lowered her hand.

She reached for a bottle and lowered her hand.

There was a woman in the aisle. She had dirty cheeks and a yellow raincoat. When first Lyd and Mott approached, this raincoat woman had been trapped in the same loop as Lyd, continually lifting and dropping her hand as she re- and reconsidered the best drink to buy. Now she openly gawked at Lyd's waist. Lyd had taken a holster that went inside her waistband and positioned this so that her new gun's handle protruded. She was clearly a dangerous person.

Lyd reached for a bottle and lowered her hand. She said, "I don't remember what I like."

"I don't think you're picky," said Mott.

"Maybe I like gin." Lyd looked to Mott for memory, but Mott did not recall and did not want to see her mother buy a bottle. "Honey, don't fret. I won't have any today, we'll travel first, but when it's bedtime I will need some help relaxing. It's hard for me to be outside."

"Excuse me miss." The raincoat woman raised her hand.

"I think that I like whiskey better."

"Excuse me." The raincoat woman touched Lyd's elbow and tried to make her warmest smile, drawing tight the many tender strings in her thin neck.

Lyd jerked her arm away. "We don't know you."

The woman dropped her hand as if startled to learn that she had one. "Can you shoot?"

Lyd said, "It isn't hard."

"Perfect. You can kill me then. Let's work something out." The raincoat woman pulled a bottle of tequila off the bottom shelf and hoisted it for closer study. "What do you think about doing it here? This is a place I really like."

"We're leaving now. Don't follow."

The raincoat woman followed. She walked with what looked like a counterfeit limp.

There was only one cashier working; the rest were huddled in the electronics section, gawping at the big TV wall. It took him a long time to scan what they'd chosen. The raincoat woman waited. Lyd paid with her card and withdrew as much cash as the store would allow.

When their purchases were bagged, they left quickly.

The raincoat woman overpaid for her tequila. "Keep the change 'cause I don't need it." She followed them out, limping with the other leg now. The greeter clicked his teeth.

The sun had gone down while they were inside. The lights were all in perfect condition, brighter than ever; the stars were no contest.

"Do you want to know my name before you do it?" said the raincoat woman.

"No to both," said Lyd. "To your name, and to the other thing."

The woman unscrewed her bottom-shelf tequila's cap and took a pull that made her cough and spit onto the pavement. "You gotta do it or I'll hurt your little girl."

Lyd turned and drew the gun. She patted Mott's shoulder in a way that meant *Stay here with the cart.* She closed the distance between her and the woman, grabbed her by her hair, and pressed the gun against her jaw. "Tell me how you'll hurt my daughter." Mott could not see her mother's face and could not see the raincoat woman's. She only saw her mother's back.

"I'll get her," hissed the woman. "I'll use the bottle."

"It's plastic."

"I'll choke her and hit her head on the street. You don't know what I can do, I'm mean and bad inside from all my pain."

Lyd pushed her away. "You won't."

The raincoat woman tipped back her tequila again. It ran down her face on both sides. She let the bottle swing low, wiped her mouth. "I'm so tired of waiting."

"You won't have to wait long. Better to do it with a bottle than a bullet. At least this way you'll have some fun."

The raincoat woman lay down on the asphalt. "I'm not having fun anymore."

MAY, LYD

LYD AND MOTT RETURNED HOME AND PACKED WHAT THEY NEEDED, but that wasn't much. They needed some music. They needed shoes. They needed pillows, blankets, and pens. They needed antacid tablets, sunblock, painkillers, rubbing alcohol, Band-Aids, and chewable vitamins. Toilet paper, pads, toothbrushes, sandwich baggies, Q-tips toothpicks floss.

Lyd told Mott to speak as little as possible while they packed. She refused to explain why. She had wrapped the webcam and its black hood in a dozen layers of duct tape to keep it from hearing them work.

They needed some clothes, so they packed their best seven days. Lyd struggled to determine what counted as "best." It seemed that each garment was faded, discolored, shrunken, worn through, or stained. Mott had ruined many of these in the washers and dryers downstairs, where Lyd had been too cowardly to go for years.

Mott also packed both of her swimsuits. She didn't say anything about them explicitly, but made sure that Lyd saw—she hadn't been allowed to swim since Lyd stopped leaving the apartment, and missed it very much.

They needed to eat. All the groceries they had fit into just two of the many eighteen-by-twelve-by-twelve-inch cardboard boxes that had carried their books when they moved in. The one refrigerator photo coming along for the trip was Mott as a baby, which Lyd tucked into the hardback *Anna Karenina* she was using to carry certain necessary paper artifacts. In this photo, Mott was standing for the first time. She faced away from the camera, holding herself upright with the help of a top-heavy pile of books. She wore a diaper ringed with cartoon dinosaurs around its waist and a pile of dark, curly hair on her head. Lyd remembered telling Mott how big she was, how strong and tall—but now, on reflection, she wasn't entirely certain whether she had said these things aloud or only thought them to herself as she twisted and focused the lens.

Soon, maybe in as few as thirty minutes, David would arrive at the apartment complex. It would be his first time visiting in person. He would climb out of a yellow cab, which was the only kind he ever patronized because he loved the way they looked just like the taxis on TV. His right foot would snag on the curb and he would stumble, nearly fall. He would curse, look around to check if anyone had seen, then resume his habitual posture of slouching, militant chill. He would peer up at the complex, leaning back to see it all, and find their apartment's windows—he surely knew which ones were theirs. He would see that the curtains were open and yet it was dark. In this moment, he would know that Lyd and Mott were gone. He would briefly grasp that Lyd had left because she didn't want to be with him now or ever again. This would injure both his feelings and his sense of himself as a man, and so he would smother the thought in its crib.

If he wasn't currently smoking a joint, he would roll one where he stood. He would light it with his Jimi Hendrix lighter. He would enter the complex, call down the elevator, and hum to himself while he waited. As the elevator doors closed, he would watch the halves of his reflection slide into place. He would gaze into the image of his own red eyes and weep unblinkingly, and tell himself it was because the weed was so good and strong—and not because he knew he would be leaving the building alone.

Mott asked why they couldn't wait to leave until morning. She proposed making a checklist of necessities and then using it the following day to confirm that they were ready. She pointed out that if they took more time and care, they could fit more things inside the car. She had taken several trips out to load it, depositing bags and boxes, and she said the back seat was already full.

"I asked you not to talk," said Lyd. "And besides, I already waited too long. I don't need more excuses to stay here. If I sleep another night in this apartment, I will never get away." She was taking dirty dishes off the counters and putting them in the cupboards as if they had been cleaned. She shouldn't care what David would see when he arrived, and it was far too late to fix anything now, but she did care, and wished that there were time enough to fix it all. She felt so ashamed.

"Are you going to tell Dad where we're going?" whispered Mott.

"I wrote him a letter that explains everything."

"Who's gonna do his typing?"

"Probably nobody will. He doesn't really need it. He's just addicted to my attention. Go to the car, Mott. I'll turn the lights off and follow."

Mott closed the door behind her. Lyd took the tape off all the clocks and opened the black curtains. She tried for a moment to pull the clock that was glued to the window free from the glass but found it would take her too long. She tried half-heartedly to sweep the tiled portion of the floor. Old bits of scabbed tomato sauce and maple syrup clung such that the broom could not dislodge them. She could get down on her knees and use her nails, or use a sponge, or leave things as they were forever. She chose the latter. It was long past time she left.

Lyd backed out of the apartment and peered in through the doorway one last time. It had been a fine home once. She was the one who made it bad, who glued too many wonders to the walls, who turned the air sour, who dripped wine on the carpet and neglected the fixtures, who never cleaned out the bugs that died in the lights. This apartment deserved better.

She closed the door but did not lock it. She wanted David to feel welcome. He would bring flowers, she could see that clearly now. The bouquet would be red, white, and blue—roses, lilacs, and lilies. A ridiculous arrangement, and the florist would tell him as much, or was telling him now, or already had, but he would insist. He would say, "If it's good enough for Old Glory."

David would knock before coming in. He would still be pretending at this point that someone might be inside. "Lydia, it's me," he would say to the door. "Mott," he would say. "Is your mother awake? It's your father."

The apartment would not answer.

"I'm here for you now. It's going to be okay. The moon likes the sun very much. They have a certain relationship. We're restoring our balance. Come be my moon and use my light. You can even eclipse me." He would say some nonsense like that.

"Please," he would say. "I came all this way on the government's dime. At least hear me out." He would finger the gun he wore strapped to his side, under his blazer. Or possibly he would draw the gun and show it to the peephole. Or perhaps he would have already drawn it and used it to knock.

He would lay down his flowers and open the door. He would lock the knob, dead bolt, and chain behind him as he traipsed inside their home. He would not remove his shoes. He would see the plastic grocery bags that lay beneath the dinner table. The unread magazines piled next to the couch in the order of their arrival. The discarded twist ties on the countertops. Everything on the walls. The unopened minor bills, each several months old. He would find most of their books—overflowing the shelves, piled on the floor and every other surface, sorted by size if sorted at all. He would say something unkind beneath his breath. He would pour a glass of water, failing to notice until it was too late that the glass had already been used. Those were Lyd's partial fingerprints on the rim: thumb, index, and pointer.

"Lydia?" he would say. "Are you anywhere in here?"

She was riding the elevator down to ground level. She was exiting the lobby, spilling out into the night, gasping at what she had done and all she would do. She was avoiding the cracks in the sidewalk. She was waiting for the walking white stick figure that meant she could cross. She was finding her like-new sedan in the parking garage. She could not remember its color, and so held its fob in the air, pressing the button that sounded the horn, working her way toward the sound. Finally Mott came to her, told her to "please for God's sake stop," and led her to the car.

"You scared me!" said Mott. "I didn't know why it was honking. I tried to make it stop, but all I could do was make it honk more."

"I can't believe we're actually leaving," said Lyd. She backed out of her space, nearly colliding with some stranger's parked Jeep. The rearview was mostly full of things from their apartment—boxes, blankets, backpacks they had owned for years.

"I guess it's an adventure," said Mott.

"I just hope it isn't too exciting," said Lyd. She merged into traffic. There were hardly any cars out—there was nowhere good to go or be.

Soon David would find the letter Lyd had left him on the dinner table. He would sniff the envelope and sniff the letter too. He would lie down on the couch to read it, first sweeping every book that was piled there onto the floor.

Dear David. You expected to find me waiting for you. You expected our daughter. You believed she would be delighted, and I will concede that she might have been. You believed that you would lift her up in your arms. You wouldn't have. You forget that she's grown. You forget that you've grown older. Just because you're still pretty, that doesn't mean you're healthy or strong.

You're disappointed and I understand the feeling. I'm disappointed with me too. I haven't always been kind to our daughter. I've encouraged her to live in books, and often she's chosen my own sorry efforts, and I have not corrected her. I soak up all her love and admiration like a sponge. I haven't nurtured her writing. I haven't shown her the world, or even this country, or anything worth seeing.

You're going to think I'm kidding you, that I'm running away. You're going to think this is a cover story. I recognize that a certain amount of paranoia comes with what you do. But this is real, David, this is important, so I'm going to give you one more cause for suspicion: I'm going to do my best to hide us as we travel. I won't turn on my phone again, and I'm leaving your computer. I have no doubt that you can find us if you choose. I know that you have resources; I know that you are a serious man. All I can say is that I dearly hope you won't. Though we may often disagree about how best to raise her, I know you love our daughter. I know that you love me. Your best quality has always been your generosity. You were never jealous, even when I strayed.

You say the world won't end, and I'm trying to believe you. Go home, please, and wait for me. I'll come to you. Mott too. Just wait till October. Be patient. Good things will happen again.

He would crumple the paper and stuff it in the inch between the couch and the wall like smearing a booger.

Or he would light the paper's corner and let it ash on his face.

Or he would fold it into an airplane and throw it at the stove.

Then he would go into her bedroom and take what comfort he could find. He would lie down in her bed and smell the pillows that she'd left behind, kiss the sheets, ransack her dresser drawers, examine her abandoned socks and underwear, search for any evidence of how she'd changed since their divorce, check the tags on her clothes to see what sizes she now wore. He would eat the years-old fun-sized candy bars that were hidden in her closet—would fail and fail to find anything that made him feel anything but bereft, abandoned, unwanted, inadequate, unlovable, unloved.

"You're breathing really fast," said Mott.

"Very quickly," said Lyd. "It's better to say that I am breathing 'very quickly.'"

They merged onto the highway. It was practically empty, and many of the lights had failed. The sky was big and cloudless, and Lyd could see what seemed like miles down the road, even in the dark. Anything might happen next, and there was no end but November, assuming November was really the end. The apocalypse felt, for a moment, impossible. Lyd was free. She might stay that way forever. She already felt the next thing coming: a crushing need for four walls she could trust.

WHAT IT WAS LIKE LIVING WITH DAVID

ANOTHER NIGHT IN SOME HOTEL ROOM, AND THEN ANOTHER NIGHT and another, Lyd dreamed again of the trustworthy man seated at the plastic picnic table on the deck of his good home. She was in his kitchen. He was waiting for her to come outside and be with him. She was studying his spice rack. It had everything it should.

He called to her. She went out to the deck, sat down on her bench, and sipped her glass of lemonade. He lifted the pitcher (she marveled at the steadiness of his hand) and topped her off again. "Thank you," she said.

He opened his notebook and tested his pen by drawing a quick circle in its margin. "Okay," he said. "Let's continue where we left off."

.....

David received a tentative job offer from a government agency, or possibly a contractor. He refused to say which one, and neither could he tell Lyd what he had done in the interview process or in his career so far to distinguish himself. She suspected that they were impressed by the way he'd surveilled her—perhaps he had sent them a tape. To be hired, he would need a security clearance, which would mean he had official permission to make and know government secrets. This required that two men in charcoal suits and matching, lacquered haircuts fly all the way to Houston to ask Lyd invasive questions designed to establish whether David was trustworthy, whether he could be blackmailed, and whether his wife would be trouble. David said she had to be totally honest. She hoped that she could blow it somehow, both for her sake and for his.

The interviewers asked her whether David ever lied to her. She said yes, perhaps often, but she rarely caught him in it. They asked for some examples. She told them about the cameras—that he had said they were gone, that he had promised never to watch her without her permission again, but every now and then she found another, or some listening device, or a log where he tracked her diet, or other data compiled for data's own sake as best she could tell, and they had the same fight over again, and he promised again he was done. The charcoal suits nodded, typed notes on their matching laptops. They asked if she had family outside the country. She said no, not to her knowledge. They asked if she or David had money trouble. She said not really, not lately—she was working again, typing pricey documents at a law firm downtown.

They asked about David's politics. She said she didn't know. When they first met, she'd thought herself too smart to vote, but had since developed many strongly held opinions, and sometimes shared these with David, who appeared to agree but never quite made himself clear, preferring to reply exclusively in cosmic terms: discussions of "heavenly bodies," of light, of reincarnation, of the love that holds atoms together. "He's kind of a hippie, aesthetically speaking," she said. They nodded and wrote it down.

Did David have a history of illicit drug use? Yes, she said, a long one. She told them what all he had done. Had he had any affairs? No, he had not, though they had occasionally fooled around with friends when they were younger. Had she slept with anyone other than him since their marriage? Yes, several times. Did he know about each one? Yes. She had more or less asked his permission. He had always answered, "You know that I am not a jealous man."

Did anybody have pictures of her, of her body, or evidence of her affairs? Anything embarrassing, that she or David wouldn't want other people to see?

"No," she said. "Only David."

. . . . .

David got the job. They moved to Washington, DC, and leased an apartment in a neighborhood full of bright young government employees. The money was enough, so Lyd focused exclusively on trying again to write her first novel. It was another story without implications—something only beautiful and sad, at least in its intent. This time it happened. She reached the manuscript's end before she could hate it enough to delete it. She found a reputable agent, a supportive editor, a generous contract. The book sold well by literary standards. She was warmly received by audiences on her reading tour. Critics wrote superlative praise. David said he liked it too, though he couldn't say much about why. Lyd was now in line to become a major author. Her publisher asked her to please write something else soon, sent an advance to help motivate her. They wanted it out before readers forgot she existed.

She started a new manuscript, talked drunkenly to David every night about what she hoped it would be, wrote ten thousand words in ten days, then gave up and deleted it all. She started another and gave that one up after nine thousand words. She started another, spent three months researching the history of professional figure skating, wrote six thousand words, and gave up again. There were many more like these, each one potentially perfect until it was shit. David listened patiently while she told him where she had gone wrong with her latest and how she hoped to make the next better—or, in her words, "worth fucking anything to anyone, good God, Jesus Christ."

"I will love you even if you never publish again," said David. He repeated it each time she started over, and with increasing frequency between.

"Probably I never will," answered Lyd. "Instead I will probably die."

She tried to focus on reading. She hated every beautiful book for being better than hers was or could be. She searched the apartment for cameras. She slept in late, ordered groceries online, cooked ill-considered meals for herself and David, smoked weed when he was away, smoked weed with him when he was home, ordered pizzas, watched cable television, ate sour candy. She cried and watched the clocks tick. To die having published just one book might be worse than dying without even one. All of the decent ideas were already taken. She spent months on a draft before realizing she was rewriting *Strangers on a Train* almost verbatim. Things were easier when she drank. Maybe she just wanted to drink. She didn't leave the house for two weeks. David rubbed her comprehensively with soothing lotions. He went down on her for what felt like hours. He knew that it was possible to make her feel good. She needed to change.

"Get a job," he said. "Learn an instrument. Clearly books make you unhappy. Stop throwing good after bad. Surrender to the universe. Meditate. Tell me anything you want. I can get it for you, or if you ask the world the world can do it."

Lyd stopped taking birth control without telling David. (Odds were decent that he knew—that he regularly checked the pack to see how many were missing.) They had never seriously discussed children; one time, during their engagement, when her period was late, he had refused to speak to her for two days, until she was bleeding as she ought to be. But now, when she told him she was pregnant, he said that it was joyous news. He asked her if it was a boy or a girl. Lyd had no idea. "A girl," she said. She stopped drinking, stopped using substances, stopped leaving the house all together, and stopped feeling bad about failing to work on her book. Eight months later, Mott was born. David let Lyd name her. He talked for years afterward about the horrors of cutting the umbilical cord. "It felt like I'd severed their connection forever. Like somehow I'd cut one person in two."

Lyd had known that motherhood would not make her happy. Her own mother had wept frequently when Lyd was a child, often in plain view of the rest of the family, sometimes for no stated reason, and sometimes explicitly because of something her children had done. Lyd had believed, however, that she would love her daughter at first sight, and with a violent urgency that would reset her heart and mind, allowing her one final chance to become the woman and writer she wanted to be. None of that happened. Hers was not that kind of love. It was careful, thoughtful—slow.

Lyd accepted that it would take years for her to love Mott the way she deserved and would take at least as long to write a second book.

Readers mostly forgot about her. She wrote one hundred words per day. She read at least two books per week. She stopped finding David's cameras—not because they weren't there, she supposed, but because he learned to hide them better. They gave of themselves to each other freely. It was the easiest that being married ever was. They made friends who visited often. The friends thought Lyd was funny. They laughed when she talked about dying.

Mott learned to read. She carried Lyd's first novel everywhere. Lyd finally finished her second so Mott would have something new to carry.

Her reputable agent was shocked by its beauty. Her supportive editor said he was glad she had taken her time. The publisher gave her a little more money. In the months before her second book was out, Lyd was the closest to happy she knew how to be. Mott carried a galley and then the hardback. Whenever she felt blue, she asked Lyd to sign it again.

. . . . .

Lyd's mother fell ill and died. The death took a long time. Lyd spent most of the money her second book made to move this process to a Virginia hospital where she could watch it all happen up close. Her brother visited once near the beginning and once more at the very end. During the first visit, he used a digital audio recorder to capture the sounds of the room, their mother's body, and the many machines that kept it alive. He said that he would sample it and use it in his music. On the second visit he let Lyd listen to what he had made so far, but they were in that same room, among the sounds that he had used to build the music, and so it sounded like nothing but more of the room.

For seven months and three weeks, Lyd went to the hospital every day she didn't believe she had something contagious. She brought her laptop, a flask, a book she hoped to one day read, and a blanket. Sometimes she also brought Mott, who was seven years old at the start and not quite eight years old at the end. Mott didn't like it but tried to behave. She asked all the time about what Lyd was writing. The answer was typically nothing. Lyd sometimes did a few meaningless keystrokes into her word processor software so Mott wouldn't worry. Sometimes she took her laptop to the bathroom, sat on the toilet, peed or didn't pee, typed twenty-five actual words. When she went back to the room she found Mott laid out on the floor, breathing in time with the thing that breathed for her mother, or found Mott seated outside the room, mouthing the words as she read from her book. It was difficult being with Grandma alone.

Lyd's mother's words didn't work anymore. The nurses promised Lyd her mother wasn't cold, that her gown and blankets were more than enough. No one asked Lyd if she wanted them to pull the plug. She kept expecting them to ask.

Lyd found it difficult to eat. (When Mott came along, she also missed meals.)

Lyd did not want to be touched. (Mott cuddled a doll that she got God knows where, and which she would make sure to lose right away when her grandma was dead.)

Lyd did not like David's voice. (He was always too loud in the room, which made him seem quiet at home, but the problem was really he refused to modulate.)

Her mouth was painfully dry. No amount of water helped. David told her to drink more and more. He said by definition you could never have too much. Her stomach sloshed. She held on to her mother's hand, rubbed the knuckles.

David visited with Lyd on Sundays unless he had a conflict or was too tired from work or too stoned. On many other days he bought some combination of yogurt, trail mix, smoked salmon, baby carrots, sushi, hamburgers, beef jerky, chicken nuggets, cheese singles, sliced bread, and peanuts, heaped these on the dining room table, and demanded that Lyd eat something when she came home. "You need protein. You need fat. Starving isn't helping anyone."

It wasn't supposed to help anyone. A mother's death should never be productive. No one should recover.

"Everybody has needs," said David. "It's nobody's fault."

When Lyd gave in and ate, she was always glad.

He made her go to bed by midnight. He told her to listen to music. He told her that she needed pot. They mostly smoked where Mott couldn't see. He told her that she needed sex. "Babies die if you don't touch them. People need affection. They need to feel connected. Your mother doesn't want you to die. I don't want to die from not touching you. Let me hold you. I can make you feel good. You need to let me." He rubbed her back and stroked her cheeks and tidied her hair. He put his hands under her shirt or sweater, touched her hips and sides. His hands were colder now than when he was young. His skin was different—she could swear she felt his fingerprints.

Most of the time she said no and he let her be. When she did give in, it wasn't like dinner, and she was never glad. Sometimes calmed, sometimes spent in a way that was mildly pleasant, sometimes blank, but never grateful. She blacked out afterward, woke up at small hours. She tried to work on her book, or sat outside Mott's room, curled up in the dark hallway, listening for her daughter's breathing.

. . . . .

One night Lyd came home from her vigil and David loudly announced that he had been secretly honored for a top-secret accomplishment at work. He gave her some time to ask what it was, but she didn't ask. He told her that he couldn't say anyway. She said that she was proud of him. She said, "I'm sorry I don't have the energy to celebrate with you right now." He said that was fine. He told her that she had to eat, so she did. There were twelve-dollar hamburgers on the table. He told her that she had to drink, so she drank. There were chocolate milkshakes and cans of red wine. He told her she looked much better already. He told her to watch some TV, so she did—two episodes of *Star Trek*. Mott lay in her lap and gazed up at her, completely in love. "It's so beautiful, seeing my girls together like this. You're looking better and better," said David. "I just had a thought, Lydia. Your mother's situation is a reminder for all of us. We need to take care of our bodies. There is no cause for shame in being a person with limits and needs. Your mother has reached an important limit. We still have our needs." He kissed her ear. He told her she needed to go to their bedroom.

"I don't need to right now," said Lyd. "I've already done a lot of things that you said I needed to do. Now I want to do nothing for a while."

David sent Mott to bed early. He told her to listen to music if she couldn't sleep.

He kissed Lyd's shoulder. "You need rest too. You need affection." He touched her face under her eyes.

"I'll go to our room if you let me just sleep. We can cuddle if you want, by which I mean actually cuddle, not sex."

David looked at her as if he had no idea what she meant. "Of course you can sleep. Would you like a backrub?"

"No thank you. You can hold me until I get warm."

David led her to their room. He watched her change into her nightgown, stripped down to his underwear. She crawled into the bed and he pushed the covers up to her chin. She rolled to face the wall. He tucked himself against her, kissed her cheek beside her ear. He held her until she was warm.

"I feel like I can sleep now," said Lyd. "I want to get up early."

David pressed against her back.

"Good job at work today," she said. "We should celebrate this weekend. Maybe we could get a nice meal. You should think about where you'd like to go." She said, "I'm too warm." David kicked off their covers, put his hand between her legs.

"Maybe tomorrow," she said. "We can get a wine bottle, send Mott to bed early again."

David pushed up the hem of her nightgown. He kissed her belly. He said, "We are all of us tethered by invisible threads. Even when our loved ones die, those threads remain, connecting us to them through the veil as a fishing line connects us to the swimming trout."

Lyd tried to close her legs. His shoulder was wedged up between them. He was breathing her in; there was nothing to breathe. "I feel too warm," she said. "Maybe when we wake up."

"Sweating helps us expel toxins." David pinned her legs apart with his, gripped her wrists. He held her down and entered her. It was too dark to see his face.

"People need this," he said.

She pushed back enough to make sure he would know he was holding her down. She did not push enough to get free. If she got free, then she would hit him. If she hit him once, she might not stop.

"I hope that I'm not hurting you," he said.

Truly, he wasn't. She wasn't fighting back enough to make him hurt her. There was some discomfort—a pinching inside.

"I don't want this," said Lyd.

David would later claim that she had never said anything of the kind, or that if she had, then he hadn't heard. "You can't blame me for what I didn't hear. You always whisper when we're making love. You have to speak up for yourself if you're not being heard," he would say.

Now he said, "It's okay if you can't come. I know you're tired."

"I'm tired."

"I know."

Later, when they fought about what happened (David's position being that nothing had happened at all), she would demand that he let her see his recording, and he would insist there was none, that he was done with all of that. He would offer to install the cameras again if she wanted, if she needed an impartial record, if that was the only way she'd feel safe.

When he was done, she counted down from forty, exhaled, and said, "I have to pee."

Lyd used the restroom. She went to the kitchen, mixed a glass of instant lemonade, diluted it with vodka. She did not want to sit beside Mott's door. She would save it for a better night.

She mixed another glass and sat down at the dinner table, in the chair that David liked. She considered how she would choose to remember what David had done. There had been other nights that he didn't care what she wanted. In each case up to now there had been some possibility of miscommunication. She had been drunk, or high, or he had been, or she had changed her mind too late for him to want to listen, or he had guilted her until she pretended. This was the first time he had definitely held her down, the first time there were no possible confounding factors. If she chose to let it go as she had done before, then he would continue misunderstanding her whenever he wanted, and there would be no point in trying to correct him, and there would be no point in telling him what she did or did not want. He would know that he could do whatever.

Lyd decided that she would remember her husband had raped

her, though she would never say the word *rape* to him, as this would give him an opportunity to respond as if terribly wounded. She would only say he held her down.

Lyd decided furthermore that after her mother had finished the long and difficult project of dying, she would find a way to separate from David. This would be a lengthy project too. She wrote *I will never change my mind* one hundred times on a yellow piece of college-ruled legal-sized notepad paper. She pinned the paper to the fridge with alphabet magnets to make sure that David would see it. When she woke up the next day, having slept on the couch, the paper was gone—not in any of the trash cans, and not in the document shredder, simply vanished from their home. But Lyd never did change her mind.

After the divorce was final, Lyd hoped to be reset by the scale of the change in her life, just as she had previously hoped would happen when her daughter was born. She moved with Mott to a new city, rented a new apartment, started a new diet, eating meat at most two days per week. She gave up weed, allowing herself only spirits and wine. She bought a new wardrobe, bought an account on a website designed to help her exercise routinely, bought free weights and resistance bands. She started to write a new novel. Mott went to a new school. They read to each other daily. For several months they slept together, and held each other, and they were never too warm, and never could be.

Lyd almost changed. There were several mornings that she woke without the old, familiar feeling of having lost something important by the act of surviving the night. She no longer felt she was wasting her life, and so it was possible for her to look at a clock without her heart lurching. The book came to her quickly, as she found that she had much to say regarding its subject: the many benefits of the end of the world.

Lyd refused alimony. David's child support and fifty percent of their savings account were enough to cover the rent and essentials until she published again.

Lyd didn't know this book would be her last, but rather hoped that it would be a new beginning—her definitive arrival as a critical darling and reliable commercial performer. It reviewed well enough and sold fine, but the money wasn't enough to change anything. Her promotional readings were poorly attended, but Mott did sit in the front at each one. Lyd sometimes remembered to take a picture of the audience (therefore Mott) and sometimes forgot.

After a New York event, an interviewer from a literary website asked Lyd if she believed her own book's thesis: "Would everyone really be better off dead?"

"Absolutely," said Lyd. She glanced at Mott, who was browsing the bookshelves nearby. "I would, anyway."

The tour ended. Readers mostly forgot about Lyd and the book. Within half a year, it was moving six copies or fewer per week. Mott read it several times, and had Lyd sign it after each, but found she still preferred Lyd's second book.

Lyd saw less and less reason to leave the apartment. She drank anything in their home until there was nothing to drink, then waited as long as she could to buy more. The checking account asymptotically approached nothing. She applied for any decent-sounding job listed online, but there weren't many—sometimes she accidentally submitted for the same position two or three times in one week. If she had stayed in school longer, they might let her teach writing, but she felt there was no going back.

She interviewed for a position at the public library. She was not qualified, though the librarians were great fans of her work, and asked her to sign their personal copies.

She tried to teach a writing class online. Mott said the reason nobody signed up was they were too intimidated by her genius.

Methodically, systematically, and beyond question, Lyd proved that she could never hold down any kind of ordinary job. Clocks became unbearable again. She cried every day. When she decided to leave David, she had hoped that she would find her worst habits were caused by living with him and his cameras, his drugs, his incessant monologues. She had hoped that everything she hated about life was at root or in some way his fault. And certainly some of it had been. But she was still, even without him, very much herself, with everything that entailed.

On the day of his first phone call to her since their divorce, she was throbbingly sober. He asked how Mott was doing. "Wonderful," she said. "I'm doing well too." He asked her about money. She said, "I'm working on finding a way."

He said, "You can work for me." He needed a typist. All she had to do was let the men in charcoal suits and matching, lacquered haircuts interrogate her for as long as was needed, and on any topic they judged relevant, so she could have a security clearance. This time she would have to come to Washington for the interview. She would also have to accept a special government computer into her home. It would come with a government webcam, which she had to let watch her whenever she worked.

At least she would know when the camera was watching. At least she would know where it was at all times. At least she wouldn't have to live with David. At least he would never touch her again. "Okay," she said. "Thank you."

The security clearance interview was held in a hotel room. The suits asked her many of the same questions they had asked before. Had she had any affairs. Was she seeing anyone. Did she have any family living abroad. Had she used any drugs? Did anyone have compromising pictures or video of her? "Have you ever been sexually assaulted by a stranger or a loved one?"

That question was new. The man who'd asked it looked away, at the hotel TV, which was currently turned off. The other concentrated on the laptop where he was typing his notes. They were seated side by side on the hotel room's bed, their feet not quite touching the floor. Lyd had the armchair. She waited to answer until both men were looking at her eyes again.

"Yes," she said. "Several times. Only by my husband. We're not together anymore."

. . . . .

David stopped sending Lyd child support. He felt the job he'd given her was charity enough.

She heard his voice every day. It was easy, familiar, and pleasantly disabling, like a warm bath and a dose of mild poison. The webcam's gaze was like coming home too.

Three years passed quickly. She stopped leaving the apartment, which meant that she couldn't buy liquor, which meant she couldn't drink herself to death. Maybe that had always been the point of staying in. She wanted to see Mott grow up. There would be plenty of time for killing herself once her daughter was established, safe, and self-sufficient.

JUNE, MOTT

IN THE DAYS THAT FOLLOWED THE NOVEMBER DREAM, MANY PEOPLE believed that they would live better, more satisfying lives until the end—that they would spend their nine remaining months doing all the things they had put off, reconnecting with loved ones and old friends, learning to play the piano, watching all the best movies, going abroad, tasting new food, taking big risks, making major moves.

There were a few who really lived this way, but suicide was far more common, and the most common choice of all was to continue living almost exactly as before. The typical person commuted to work, spent nine hours on the job including their lunch break, commuted home again, watched some television, microwaved dinner, interacted minimally with family, and crawled into bed. The biggest change for this crowd was that they slept longer—the average number of hours unconscious per person per day rose from six to ten. Many struggled to stay awake even when the sun was out, frequently napping over lunch, succumbing to sleep in unfortunate places, curling up for days at a time in government buildings, retail outlets, and publicly owned spaces. Some of the heaviest sleepers said they were depressed about November. Others explained that they couldn't wait for the world's end, and that their naps were meant to make the year go faster. Still others said it was simpler than that; they were tired.

Mott could sympathize. Whenever Lyd left her alone in a hotel room, the idea was that she would use this time to work on her book. But she was always tempted to lie down in the king-sized bed, forget her name and what she was like, and dream until Lyd came back.

Five weeks had passed since they left home. In that time, they had slept in many rented rooms, and Lyd had established many rules, some of which were true in every state and city, and some of which were only true in certain places, for example their current dingy motel.

They were presently in Arizona, and Mott was alone, which meant that she was not allowed to leave the room, unlock the door, or open the blinds. The sun was too much, so it didn't matter about rules; she never would have gone outside, would never have opened the blinds. They let too much in as it was: the opposite wall was all lit up with skewed, gappy stripes. Mott sat cross-legged on the queen-sized bed, where she was not allowed to eat. There was an empty chocolate cupcake wrapper on the bedside table. There was frosting on the wrapper, frosting on the corner of Mott's lip. If she did eat on the bed, then she must be careful to avoid leaving crumbs. If she did leave crumbs, then later she would have to eat them. But Mott didn't worry. She was certain she never made crumbs.

One final rule, the most routinely broken, was that Mott was not allowed to write in bed. Her mother said that sleep was fiction's natural enemy, every writer's constant temptation. Mott agreed in principle but nonetheless struggled. The motel was so quiet, equal parts empty and dreaming. She wanted to be quiet too.

She was writing in a legal pad. Today so far she had about two hundred words. Most of these described an arena. Her novel was about a young girl who traveled back in time to ancient Rome or possibly Greece. (The girl would not have known the difference, and so Mott reasoned that she did not have to choose.) The girl didn't time-travel on purpose—it was just a thing that happened, like a car accident or falling in love. The trouble was that the emperor had decided he would spend the year watching one thing of every kind die, and was presently working his way through the alphabet. He had seen an aardvark die in his arena, had watched a bear bite and tear until it was gutted, had cheered as a cartwright was quartered, had wept at the sight of his own dog's demise, had applauded an elephant's sudden beheading, and had tittered while his gladiators stomped ribbitty frogs, among many other creatures and people *A* through *F*. Now he was on *G* as in *girl*. It was time for him to see one die, but he didn't want to alienate any of his courtiers by taking their daughters, so the protagonist's appearance was timely.

The motel had wireless Internet, and so Mott was not allowed the use of her laptop, which was duct-taped closed and sealed away inside a messenger bag under the bed. The sugar soda was also kept there. She had removed one can of grape so far today. There was a little bit left in the can, not quite enough to bother with, still fizzing on the desk, weighing down the pizza coupons that had come with the room.

Writing longhand was difficult. Mott hated that she had to count the words herself to know how many she had written. It was less than four months till the end of the world. At this rate there would be no novel. There would only be a dead *G* for *girl*, unaccomplished, forgettable, indeed forgotten—not yet beautiful or even anything.

Mott's phone was turned off but not duct-taped. She was only allowed to use it in the case of an emergency, and the only thing that counted was somebody trying to hurt her or take her away. Loneliness did not count. Inexplicable fear did not count. Bouts of weeping on the toilet did not count. These things would pass. She was not allowed to panic.

She was not allowed to write her father a letter until she had seen enough of the world to tell him something that he didn't know, and it seemed that he knew everything. Mott asked her mother at each stop on their zigzagging tour: Has he really had Chicago-style pizza? But has he eaten Ethiopian before? But has he seen Shakespeare in the park? Has he really seen this massive ball of twine? I can't believe it. When did that happen? Was he just passing through? Did he make a special trip? Just for this twine? So then what about this museum? He's been to this museum too? So what about this bench? I mean *this* bench. I like how it's orange. He never sat on it, did he? No, I guess you're right. He probably knows about benches.

He wouldn't write back anyway. Lyd was probably just protecting Mott's feelings.

The motel TV screen was covered with duct tape and so were the dials. The cord was unplugged. The outlet was covered with duct tape. Mott was not allowed.

She gave in and lay down. Lyd had been awake for most of the previous night—mostly silent, mostly still, but unmistakably awake, pretending to sleep for Mott's comfort. Mott pretended also, rolling over once per hour—once was all she would allow herself; she used the alarm clock to keep track. It was the analog kind with physical numbers that rolled upward as time passed, so that in general the rightmost digit was not properly the minute but rather the nothing shape between itself and the next: not 8, but the bottom of 8 and the top half of 9.

If she napped now, then she would sleep too long and wake up with a headache. She might as well nap anyway. Today she would accomplish nothing.

Lyd opened the door and swept into the room, stepping out of her shoes and nudging them against the wall. Mott sat upright and made herself look alert. She didn't bother trying to hide the other broken rules in the room: her work on the bed, the soda can, the cupcake wrapper.

Lyd saw them but she didn't care. She asked, "Do you want to see the Grand Canyon?"

Mott shook her head. She played the role of an author nose-deep in her work. She chewed her lip and read through what she'd done so far, and crossed a sentence out from end to end. Lyd sat down at the desk and spun the chair to face the room. She leaned forward, elbows on knees, as if to meet Mott at her level—when in fact her head was now much lower. "Honey, you want to see the Grand Canyon. This will literally be your only chance."

"I don't care about that."

"Okay, I hear you and I understand, and I never thought that I would care about it either, but I'm telling you it's gorgeous. And the beauty is it doesn't matter if you care. The canyon doesn't need your love, or even know that you exist." She tossed her hat onto the bed. "It's perfect with or without you."

"I hate my book."

"I would be worried if you didn't."

"It's boring. It doesn't have any ideas or feelings. No one would ever read it."

"Honey, I'll read it."

Mott crossed out another sentence. "You'll pretend to read it. Or you'll think that you're reading it, but when you're done you'll realize you didn't understand a word, or you understood but didn't care, and it's all fallen out of your head. I'll ask you what you think, and you'll tell me a lie to make me feel better. You'll lie, but you're not a good liar."

"If I ever lie to you about your book I promise I'll make it convincing."

Mott tossed away the legal pad and lay down. She pulled up the covers over her head. She knew she was being a child. She didn't have time to be anything else.

.....

Mott woke to the unfamiliar sound of her mother's laughter. Her eyes were still covered. She felt strange in her stomach, then everywhere. At first she felt certain she was wetting the bed, and then she realized that Lyd was tickling her. Mott laughed painfully, without sound.

"Stop it! Stop it stop it stop it!" Mott milled her feet, tangling them in the sheet and the blanket. "Mom please!"

"Not until you get out of bed!"

Mott wrenched herself free and stood with her back to the wall that the sun striped, eyes drying, hands balled into fists.

"We have to use the ATM," said Lyd.

"You never used to tickle me."

"We're having an adventure."

Mott wiped her nose and found there was a trail of snot already on her upper lip. She went to the bathroom and put the gross where it belonged. Here was the mirror. Her hair was a mess: she was not allowed professional cuts anymore. Her mother would not trust a stranger with scissors.

"You need sunblock," said Lyd. "Take off your shirt so I can get you properly."

"It makes me feel greasy."

"You're a teenager, you're always greasy. Get in here."

Mott did as she was told. She stood rigid in front of her mother, arms crossed over her chest, flinching with each contact of the cold lotion.

"Don't shrug. I can't do your shoulders that way."

Mott refused to let her mother's touch be a comfort, refused to relax.

Lyd pulled one shoulder and pushed on the other. Mott turned to face her. Lyd tugged gently at her crossed wrists. "Hold out your arms."

Mott obeyed. "Do you think I need a training bra?"

Lyd stifled a laugh. It settled on her face as a charmed smile instead. "Not yet, love."

"Not ever."

"Not yet," said Lyd. She rubbed the lotion into Mott's arms and hands. Their fingers tickled in the lotion.

"It's like I'm still a little kid. I don't even need deodorant."

"You can use some if you want. Honestly it wouldn't hurt. Especially when we're driving. You could smell like baby powder and lilacs all day. Wouldn't that be something?"

"I don't want to pretend just to feel like a grown-up."

"Love, I didn't want to make you feel bad, but a little deodorant would not be pretending at all. Congrats, little lady: you stink."

Mott raised her arm and breathed in her own smell.

"We'll get some while we're out. Now do me." Lyd peeled her shirt and pushed her bra straps off her shoulders.

Her shoulder skin looked weird and itchy. There were several black and curly hairs. She flinched also for the lotion's cold. There were purple stretch marks where her breasts began. There were pale, shiny marks like watermelon stripes on her belly. There were moles on her that Mott could not remember ever seeing.

"You've gotten older," said Mott.

"I know."

"Your belly looks bigger to me."

"It does to me too."

They rubbed sunblock on their own faces. Mott put too much on her ears. Lyd dabbed the excess away with a tissue.

"Maybe my book should be about a mother and daughter," said Mott.

"You shouldn't start over again. You won't have time to finish." Lyd put on her straw hat. "You have to wear yours too."

"It looks dumb. I don't want to wear it."

She didn't want to, but that was the rule.

.....

Theirs was the cheap motel nearest the Grand Canyon. The ATM nearest the cheap motel nearest the Grand Canyon was embedded in a small, plastic kiosk in a neglected bowling alley, between the crane game and the men's room door. The alley also had one dozen lanes, a teenage boy who rented shoes, and a thirtysomething man who sold candy, potato chips, soft drinks, beer, prefab submarine sandwiches, and microwave pizza on crust that looked and tasted like a big, soft cracker. Mott had come here with her mother three times before, and during each visit the only people bowling had been three Native American women old enough to be grandmothers, all of them smoking cigarettes and eating corn chips with mostly untouched nacho cheese cups on the side. Mott assumed that they had come here every day before the dream about November, and would continue bowling right up to the end, either because it was something they liked or because any given habit is as good as any other—a way and a reason to keep the body moving.

Lyd asked Mott if she wanted to play the crane game. She asked this every time because she always caught Mott looking at the stuffed fish in the prize tank. It had a cute, stupid face, transparent fins far too small, and a little golden crown. Mott wanted it, but the fact of wanting it made her feel like a dumb baby.

"Okay," said Mott. Lyd dumped a pile of quarters in her hands. Mott fed the crane game. The quarters were enough for three attempts.

Meanwhile Lyd worked the ATM. She would make the maximum withdrawal, pocket the funds, and lament the exorbitant fee. There was a backpack full of cash beneath their motel bed. Mott was not allowed to open the backpack, count the cash, or ask how much there was inside. Lyd said that it would only make her anxious.

Mott's claw missed the king fish. One of the grandmothers bowled a strike. The others congratulated her by cursing her out.

"Where should we go next, when we leave the canyon?" said Lyd.

"Somewhere quiet." The claw caressed the king fish plushie's cheek. He shifted on the other toys. There was another fish behind him that looked even harder to get.

"Do you need more quarters?" said Lyd. "I could get a water, break one of these bills."

"No thank you. This can be my last try."

The claw gripped the king fish's crown and hoisted him an inch, but he slipped free.

"That's okay," said Mott. She kicked the crane machine.

Lyd let her choose a bottle of sweet tea. It was always the same guy selling concessions—sleepy, soft face; unflattering red T-shirt; eating candy. Today his hair was clipped down to fuzz. Before it had been past his shoulders. He was eating from a bag of M&M's.

"Do you pay for what you eat, or do you just take it?" said Mott.

"Huh? Oh right, I get you. Let me show you how it goes. See that?" He pointed at a camera that hung from the ceiling. "That feeds a TV in a building in Connecticut. They're called Loss Prevention. They got a bunch of TVs over there, and all these guys are watching the TVs, which are plugged into VCRs that record at all hours. So here's what I do. Gimme that bar there, please."

Mott handed him a Hershey's. He showed it to the camera. He scanned the chocolate's barcode and chose cash. The register opened. He took his wallet out and showed it to the camera, then took two dollars from the wallet. He showed the dollars to the camera. Taking care not to obstruct the camera's view of the cash tray, he put his two dollars inside. He took his change, took his receipt, and closed the register. He showed his receipt to the camera, blew a kiss. He opened the Hershey's.

"And I gotta keep the receipt basically forever," he said. "They can ask you for it anytime, and you gotta have it or there's a fine. I had to sign my life away to get this job. It's minimum wage, but when there's no customers I can read magazines."

"Do you think the guys in Connecticut are really still watching the screens?" said Mott.

"I don't know. You'd think they would stay home and enjoy life a little. But look at me, I have a daughter and a super-pretty girlfriend, and yet I still show up for work."

Lyd said, "Will you be fired if I cheat that claw machine?"

"Naw. The camera that watches that part of the alley is busted."

"Then I'll be just a second."

Lyd set her straw hat on the counter and stalked away toward the machine.

"Your mom seems intense," said the clerk.

Mott blushed. "She's incredibly weird."

Mott and her mother drove away with two hundred dollars and a king fish with fins far too small. Mott held him in her lap and looked into his eyes. She didn't have it in her to pretend she wasn't smitten.

As they approached the Grand Canyon, they passed a roadside billboard, which read:

121 DAYS TILL THE END. LIQUIDATE YOUR BELONGINGS, BE FREE. GO TO LASTCHANCEPAWNSHOP.COM TODAY

Someone had climbed the billboard and vandalized it twice. First they had crossed out the 121 with red spray paint, and painted a correction above it—120. They had done the same thing the following day, so that now it said 119. Mott did a little math. She would need to write more than four hundred words per day to finish her novel before November, and faster still if she wanted Lyd to have some time to read it.

She wanted to go back to their hotel room.

.....

They stood on a horseshoe-shaped walkway that projected from the canyon's edge, hanging on the empty air like a mispronounced word. It had a glass floor, glass walls almost Mott's height, and a metal guard rail. No one had cleaned the glass in weeks. Either the park employees who managed the canyon and the Native Americans who owned the walkway had abandoned their stewardship, or they were pursuing it more completely: they were, Lyd said, probably wandering the park, saying goodbye to their favorite parts. "It must be nice to care about nature."

"I've tried several times," said Mott. "And I can't. But you're right, the canyon is nice."

"It isn't nice," said Lyd. "That's what I like about it."

"It's indifferent?"

"I'm not sure that's right either. People are indifferent. The land isn't. It's not even land. It's just us looking at the Earth that makes it real."

"You sound a lot like Dad right now."

"I'm much smarter than your father." A note of genuine hurt crept into Lyd's voice and made a home there. "Most of the time so are you."

"Dad may not be as smart as us, but he isn't mean like we are."

"You were very young when we divorced."

"Has Dad ever been here? Could I write him a letter about it?"

"Of course he's been here."

Mott jumped up in the air, using the rail to push herself higher. It was scary coming back down, but she trusted that the glass would catch her.

"Did he ever jump off this walkway?"

"It wasn't built yet. We couldn't make glass that was strong enough then."

"I keep trying to find a way to say I miss Dad without saying it, but I've run out of ideas."

"It's his own fault he never calls."

"We turned off our phones. I don't understand why."

"It makes us harder for bad people to find. But even before, he practically never called."

"He knew about me though. He knew everything I was doing. So we didn't need to talk."

"I thought you were intelligent enough to see through your father."

"If you mean he was a bad husband, I believe it."

"That's not what I mean."

"You're saying that he's a bad person."

"He isn't a good one."

Lyd spit off the walkway, over the railing. Mott laughed. She spat too. Lyd did it again. Mott tried and failed, blowing raspberries instead. Lyd giggled.

Mott wiped her mouth dry. "We shouldn't do that, Mom."

"Why not?"

"Because there are people down there. Dead bodies, I mean."

"I can't see them at all."

"You're not missing much."

The wind was picking up. Every cloud was shaped like a forbidden object. There was a cupcake. There was a sugar soda can. There was a TV trailing its cord.

"I hate writing," said Mott. "Books are great but I'm bad at making one."

Lyd didn't say anything, but that was okay. Mott didn't know what she wanted to hear.

"Would you stop me if I tried to jump?"

"It would depend on your reason," said Lyd.

"So you would let me."

"If you had a good reason. It's your life. You're a person."

"What's a bad reason?"

"Writing. Your father. Me. Anger. To get a reaction."

"What's a good reason?"

Lyd gazed down at where the bodies were, unseeing. She had to hold down her big straw hat to keep it from blowing away in the wind. "Taking control. Choosing your moment. Fear."

"What do you think it's going to be like, when the world ends, if it does?"

"Really scary."

"I want to go somewhere nice and quiet, Mom. A place where I can work."

Lyd pulled Mott close and covered her eyes. "We can do that."

Mott's straw hat jostled loose and blew away. Her mother caught it.

JUNE, LYD

YOU COULDN'T HIDE THINGS FROM DAVID. NOT REALLY—NOT LONG. What you had to do was show them to him in a way he would enjoy misunderstanding.

For example: Say you were running away. You couldn't actually leave his sight. If you did that he would rouse himself to find you. Once he found you he would never let you go. (He would get you stumbling drunk. He would lie to you. He would make you too angry to leave. He wouldn't plan to be violent, but he wouldn't rule it out. He would maybe hold you down. He would pretend not to hear when you said that you wanted to go.) What you had to do was eat his favorite foods from the fridge and pretend you didn't know. You had to flush all his pot and tell him you smoked it without him. You had to make him believe that you slept with his friends while he traveled. You had to watch TV with the volume too high when he wanted to tell you his day. You had to laugh at him in an almost-affectionate way while he undressed for bed. You had to buy expensive gifts for other people. You had to get him the wrong birthday cake.

You had to let him catch you picking your nose and scraping it off on his favorite chair. You had to make him tell you that he wanted out. You had to play dumb. You had to ask why. You had to plead with him to let you stay, to please reconsider, to let you make it up to him, to let you show him you could be a better person. You had to be abject. You had to hint you would be waiting for him if he ever changed his mind.

He had to believe that he was the one getting free.

Later he would see it clearly, would understand what you had done. He would revise the story slowly—would accept that you had wanted out, would maybe glimpse some fragment of why. Might even say sorry one night, drunk and high and alone in his very large house, over a phone line, all but unconscious, the curly cord wound around his finger and his throat. He would call the divorce "your experiment." He would not ask you to come back. Asking would risk fresh rejection. He could accept that he had been rejected at some time in the past. (The pain was past too.) He would never risk it happening *now*. (Would never risk pain that he could foresee.)

Or so Lyd had thought. David was not obligated to follow his own rules. He believed a man could change. Now he was come to collect on the implicit promise, standing offer, second chance—his wife restored, his daughter a daughter again, and David a husband, a father.

If Lyd hoped to escape him again, she had to move slowly. She had to make him feel he knew exactly where she was, where she was going, what she would do when she got there, and why. She had to make him feel comfortable, like she was already sorted, his in all but name (and even in name; she had never taken back her own, preferring that her personal documents and ID match the spines of her novels), and would come to him when he called.

David could be managed. All you had to be was careful one hundred percent of the time. All you had to do was think about him always.

Lyd had told him in her letter that she was not running, that she only wanted to travel with Mott. She had told him they were seeing the sights. So the ATMs that she used had to agree with that story. They needed to be close to landmarks and aquariums, museums in notable cities. She had to use her debit card at each stop. She had to buy Mott special treats: pastries, T-shirts, prints of famous paintings. Sometimes there were no treats to buy; sometimes every wanted thing was all sold out or looted. Sometimes a town was already rotten—the decent people chased out weeks or months before, replaced by other kinds of people, or by other, lesser versions of themselves, hungry and ready to hurt someone else for a meal. Sometimes the buildings were burning already, and all they could do was drive past. Sometimes the streets were flooded despite lack of rain. Sometimes the electric company failed for hours every day, or flickered in and out at random, so that entire towns turned alternately bright and dark at night. Sometimes there was an unfathomable smell, the product of a factory that made budget dog food or industrial plastics. More than once Lyd and Mott spent several days holed up in some nameless, mostly empty motel, Lyd ordering pizzas and Chinese chicken that she didn't want so her card would show the right kind of activity. She never answered the door in such places. If the delivery person left the food (already paid for, already tipped) in the hall, then she left it there too. Someone else would have to find a use for it. (Someone else always did.)

Roughly once per two weeks, Lyd had to buy one bottle of liquor and drink the whole thing and never go outside for forty-eight hours or more. David would see the purchase on her card, would be glad to see she was still weak in the ways he remembered. He would trust her not to go too far too quickly.

When Lyd was drinking or recovering from drinking, Mott knew not to ask about writing, make any loud noises, mention the time of day, uncover the alarm clock, or turn off the TV set. Lyd was trying to catch up on current events. It would be election season soon. The candidates had been selected. They were already running ads. "When we're gone, our choices will be all that remains to define us. Make the right choice. Make your voice heard. Vote for decency. Vote before November first."

Mott was allowed to use the hotel pool (if there was a hotel pool) if Lyd was incapacitated by alcohol and if it looked safe and if there was no one else swimming and if Lyd couldn't stop her anyway. Mott was allowed if Lyd would not see her and would not therefore have to think about the November dream and would not therefore have to imagine Mott drowning.

If you were driving cross-country to avoid seeing David's face even once before the world's end, and if you had some money saved, and if you needed that money to keep you alive while you ran, it would be natural to fear that he would freeze or worse seize your account. He could do that with a phone call. You would need to withdraw the money, but you couldn't do it all at once. That would be too obvious. You had to take it out in chunks. If you did this the right way, then he would make excuses for you. He would tell himself that you were afraid of a bank run. (And he would be right: Lyd *was* afraid of a bank run.) This would buy you time in which to plan your disappearance, to take new license plates from an abandoned sedan in Illinois—abandoned but not empty, in fact full of buzzing bees—and time to teach your daughter safe habits. Time to live without David. Without but not wholly free.

Now, in the last week of June, seven weeks into their journey, less than five months till the promised end of the world, Lyd had sufficient cash in her backpack—not all that there was but enough. Now she would give up the lie.

She took Mott west to California. They drove an hour past the state line, ate cheeseburgers and curly fries in a diner attached to a gas station. Lyd put it on the debit card. When the meal was done, she filled the tank and bought a bottle of bottom-shelf gin and a pair of scissors meant for trimming beards. Mott and the cashier watched as Lyd cut her card into thumbnail-sized triangles, swept the triangles off the counter and into her hand, and threw them away in two separate trash cans. She wiped her hands clean on her skirt, although they were already clean. Mott asked why she did that to the card. Lyd said it was because of something she'd heard on the radio news in the car on the highway while Mott was asleep. "There are people getting hurt or worse because of these. There's a scam that junkies pull in places just like this where they get all your info and then they take the card and steal your identity. They give you their info and make you steal their identity too, and then you can't go to the cops. It's complicated how they do it, but the bottom line is I don't want the card anymore." The truth was that she only didn't want the temptation. It had to be cash from now on.

"Okay," said Mott. Her king fish was under her arm. She had tried to leave him in the car but changed her mind as soon as the door closed.

"You should talk to me instead of falling asleep while I drive," said Lyd. "Then I wouldn't have to listen to the news and get so worked up."

"The car is so boring. I'm just a kid, I can't stay awake. Where are we going now?"

"Somewhere you can write, like you wanted. We'll stay put for a while."

"Thank you, Mom. But I really want to start my book over, okay?"

"If you do, this has to be the last time."

"I understand." Mott hugged her king fish and hid her nose inside his crown.

The gas station parking lot was littered with abandoned cars. Some of these were stripped for parts—their hoods popped open, guts removed, partly laid out on the pavement, partly taken, or doors appropriated for other cars or purposes, or hubcaps or tires detached. A man in white overalls pruned trees across the street. Their branches were hanging too low—were interfering with traffic. When he cut them they fell on the road, where they were driven over and broken.

Lyd drove east, back across the Arizona border. David wouldn't know about the debit card yet, would assume that she and Mott were still in California. The gin's purchase would explain their apparent lack of movement for the next several days. But soon thereafter, David would realize that something was changed. He would come looking. Probably he would find them. Probably he knew a way. It would be traffic cameras or spy satellites. It would be a buzzing helicopter drone. She didn't know. She could not imagine what she could not imagine, and when she tried she couldn't breathe.

Mott announced that she had a great new idea for a book. This would really be the one, she said—she was sure.

"Do you want to tell me about it?" asked Lyd.

"It's about a mom and daughter. They're on a camping trip and there's a really bad storm that blows away their tent while they're gathering wood for a fire. So they find a cave to sleep in. And it's this really old cave with dinosaur bones in the walls and weird, glowing moss. They have to sleep real close together for warmth. They have this dream. It's sort of like the one about November, but it's about them, not the world. And something weird happens while they sleep, so when they wake up, they've switched bodies."

"With each other?"

"Yeah, they trade. That's what the book is about. How they live in each other's bodies."

"Like in that Jodie Foster movie?"

Mott huffed, crossed her arms, and closed her eyes.

Lyd waited for an answer. Mott appeared to go to sleep. Lyd turned on the radio. All stations were weak signals. There is every sound in static. She drove past an overturned semi. There were two mangy cows asleep in its shadow. They looked to be at peace.

When David finally accepted that Lyd was truly running away, not merely keeping her distance, he would get very high. He would call his elderly mother and ask her if she was okay. She would say she was fine. She would complain about his father's behavior. She would not ask him how he felt. David would feel disappointed. At some point he would lose patience. He would say that he had something in the oven and then he would pretend to realize dinner was burning. He would say he had to go. He would smoke another joint to make sure he was as high as he could be. He would look at naked girls online. The websites would claim that all the girls were eighteen years or older. They would be "amateurs." Most amateurs were women who never consented to the sharing of their pictures—were women who'd trusted a man. They offered themselves to the camera. They were not afraid.

If he was alone in the house, then he would fall asleep at his desk. If there was a woman in the house who had ever even just once said she loved him, then he would go to her and ask for sex. "Can I? Do you want to? Should we?"

Lyd wished she knew who that woman would be. She could give her some useful advice:

If David wanted to have sex and you did not, then you needed to get high with him. You needed to imply that this would make the love better. You had to touch him through his pants. You had to kiss him on his neck but not his mouth. If you kissed him on his mouth, then he would become fascinated, impossible to redirect. You had to show him parts of your body. You had to do this from far enough away that he could not reach. You had to do this while he was seated, when he would not try to stand. You had to keep him talking. If he smoked enough and spoke enough, then he would fall asleep. It helped if you could make him drink. He didn't really like to drink; it made him feel sad. If you poured it in his soda, then that was dishonest. If you changed your mind and slept with him later, having spiked his drink without his knowledge, then you would hate yourself the next day. It was always an option, however. David trusted food and drink absolutely and would swallow whatever you gave him.

The risk of getting high with David as a means of putting off sex was that getting high might make you want to have sex. It was important to remember you did not want to have sex with David. That was the truth, and if it changed while you were smoking, then that was a lie, a scam the drug was running on your body. It was important to remember that even if you changed your mind you must resist the urge until you were sober and could know your own true feelings. If you still wanted him, you could do it then. He would always pick up on the slightest sign that he was desired.

He credited himself with understanding people, especially women. He credited himself with knowing what they wanted.

It wasn't that he didn't know. It was that he made your wanting about him—about the fact he knew. Every act a demonstration of his special knowledge. Every question rhetorical. "Like this?" He only asked what he already knew.

You had to talk about his body. You had to tell him how it was. You had to come.

It was possible to survive David, or even escape him, or even live with him in his home. All you had to be was careful. All you had to do was think of him always.

After he accepted that Lyd had run away, and after he had called his mother, and after she had failed to comfort him, and after he had looked at amateurs online, and after he had slept with the woman who lived in his home (if there was a woman who lived in his home), he would spend two days mourning his loss. He would, for the first time in years, fully feel the pain of Lyd's absence. And then he would collect himself. And he would come looking for her.

JUNE, DAVID

DAVID CONTEMPLATED HIS ASSIGNED SUSPICIOUS PERSONS. THE white math teacher in Baltimore who had written a disturbing manifesto was lifting weights in his garage, listening to the music of his youth. His wife was in their living room alone, watching *Wheel of Fortune*. The Chinese engineer in Bellevue was writing and deleting texts to her adult children, who read everything she sent but never replied. She was trying every strategy to provoke them. The unmarried Muslim man was filling out an online dating profile.

The day's theme was abandonment. The ones who were supposed to care for them were not in evidence, were not helping. The white teenage boy who had sent anonymous threats to his high school was home without his parents. They had been missing for days. The boy had not yet found his father's gun, but it wouldn't be long: his forays into the master bedroom were growing longer and more probing. The Senegalese immigrant was delivering meals for a smartphone app eighteen hours per day, frantically saving for no obvious purchase—David watched him nearly drift off the road twice in ten minutes.

He might work less and sleep more if he still had a wife to love him when he was at home.

There was no reason David's people should have to be alone, just as there was no reason that he should have to be—there was nothing wrong with him, and no reason he should feel like someone bad just because his wife was choosing not to be with him in this moment, and in fact there was no reason anyone should ever feel sorrow, pain, or shame. Given the limited time people were granted to live on this Earth, and given their capacities for sensory and spiritual joy and sublimity, pleasure was the only rational response to any given stimulus or situation. Everything should feel good; everything *was* good if correctly received.

David asked the universe for guidance. He breathed smoke out of his mouth and nose. Laverne the dog rested against his door. He breathed at the same pace that she did.

Over the past several days, as he accepted that Lyd was truly attempting a permanent disappearance, David had behaved exactly as she expected, except for the part about sleeping with someone. Among the many beautiful young people who lived with him or frequented his home, there were a handful of girls who would, under the right circumstances, permit him to touch them, and who might touch him back, and who might even say that they loved him if he applied the right pressure, but none of these youths were much comfort to him—they were supposed to be his friends and children. It was enough to watch them love each other from the safety of his office, and this had the added benefit that he never risked the pain of disappointing them with his older, less beautiful body.

Half the screens in his office were now devoted to Lyd. He had tracked her as she traveled—collecting video from traffic light cameras, gas stations, ATMs, even satellites when orbits lined up as required. The satellites didn't work out as often as he would have liked, as their network was degrading, with some sky eyes colliding, others going offline, and still others falling to Earth for no obvious reason. There were problems with the traffic cams as well, blind spots where equipment had failed or where the local electric company couldn't keep up with demand. Now, having lost track of Lyd's car, David worried he might never find her again. Presumably she would have changed her license plate, which made traffic cams close to useless, and she had stopped using her debit card.

There was a screen that displayed the state of Lyd's bank account, her practically empty email sent folder, and her disused social media account. These things didn't change anymore. There was the still-blank video feed from Lyd's webcam. He had left her work computer in her apartment and the webcam all taped up, and all her mess and garbage as it was, and only taken things that she and Mott would want to have again when they moved in with him, and these were boxed and stacked in his garage. They had taken their best things with them, had left him with only the dregs. He should have known what Lyd was doing. It all seemed so obvious now.

He woke up from an accidental nap. His joint had fallen to the floor and burned itself out, leaving a small, black mark on the carpet. If he didn't accomplish something today, he might start to feel a little bit depressed. He had promised himself that if he waited and trusted the universe, if he only did his job, he would be rewarded, and he would find Lyd. He scooted his chair up to his desk, rolled a new joint, and played back his recording of the puzzling Rhode Island–to-Kentucky call. "I'm sorry. Lo siento. Je suis désolée. Jeg beklager. Es tut mir leid. Prosti menya. Maf kijiye. Duìbuqǐ. Gomenasai."

The voice seemed at times to be obviously synthetic or mechanical, a computer creation. At times he felt certain that it was a woman. Running voiceprint samples against Agency databases turned up nothing useable—a couple in-flight safety video narrators, a fictional video-game robot, a recording of a Bach flute sonata.

Concerning the call's content, it seemed plausible that the apologies might be a code. There were many ways the chosen apology words could carry hidden information intended either for the recipient or for some third party listening in. Since the meaning of the words did not vary significantly, perhaps the sequence of the languages spoken was the key—beginning the cycle of apologies with English might mean one thing, for example, and ending with it might mean another. This would not be a data-rich method, but most codes don't need to be. All they need to say is *wait, go, lie low, they're onto you, come home, do it now, you're on your own*. There might also be information encoded in the pauses between words, with minor differences in length working something like Morse code. This would be challenging for a human speaker to perform, but a recording on a soundboard could do the job fine. That would be consistent with the voice's uncanny quality and cadence as well.

David spoke into a digital recorder, dictating for his new assistant, Alex, as he used to do for Lyd. "Suppose there is no code," he said. "Suppose some unknown person hijacked the number of that girl in Rhode Island, called a perfect stranger, and earnestly begged his forgiveness. You can tell the guy who answered has no idea what's going on. So what is the caller sorry about? What does anyone have to be sorry about?"

He played back the call for what must have been at least the thousandth time. He tried to speak the words as did the voice, but there were too many he couldn't pronounce. He felt stupid. "Probably this is nothing," he said.

He was dangerously close to being actually high now. He rolled another joint. He breathed it in and emptied himself of desire. The way he did this was he said aloud that he felt no desire. He said, addressing the universe, "I don't want anything at all but what you want for me. I'm yours, all my everything, and I'll move as you move me, and learn what you want me to know." He breathed in. "Please want me to find my wife. Don't you want me to be happy?"

He opened a random email inbox, the first one he happened to type without thinking, which as luck would have it was Lyd's. He opened her most recent personal email. It was a weeks-old message from her brother, whom Lyd never spoke to or mentioned. The subject line was *please don't delete this.* The text of the message was *I am thinking of killing myself. Should I do it? Looking forward to your response.*

David opened the brother's email account. He had sent several similar messages the same night, each one to a woman—a coworker, a high school acquaintance, and someone he'd met through a dating website. Nobody had replied. David opened each woman's email account. None of them had ever mentioned Lyd, which was the arbitrary search term that he happened to try first, nor had they mentioned a "Lydia" or anyone named "Mott" or "Gabel," which were some other random words he tried. The high school acquaintance had recently received an email from her boyfriend, a Peoria police lieutenant. The subject line read, *Feeling weird.*

> I keep having this dream. I'm wearing my uniform, and the sleeves feel too short, so I keep tugging them, trying to make them fit. A boss calls me into his office. (Not my actual boss, but I can tell that's what he is in the dream.) He's typing something really fast. He says something like, "You are a tool that's being misused. You want to be good, but you can't do it alone. You need to be used better." Then he turns his screen to show me what he's writing. I can't ever read the screen. He says it's a new law. I tell him that it's good, or has my vote, but I'm only trying to impress him, I don't know what it says. He puts his hand on my hand on the desk and holds me still. His palms are weirdly soft. He tells me to keep looking, and I do, and I still can't read it, but I keep nodding as if I understand, and it feels as if I'm learning something, but I don't know what. Please call me when you get the chance.

David closed the useless email. He turned on jazz music and tried to want nothing. He wanted Lyd. He asked the universe to please be kind. He tapped a random call.

His random number program chose a phone-sex line.

". . . jeans, not too tight or too loose, a T-shirt with a logo on the chest, it's a polo T-shirt, the kind with a collar."

"Ooh baby, sounds like you had a long day at work. Let me take off those shoes."

"Uh, sure. Is that something people like to talk about? Their shoes?"

"We can do whatever you want. I'm slowly taking off your shoes and rubbing your feet."

"Do people sometimes ever tell their dreams?"

"Only the hot ones. I'm sucking your toes."

"Uh, okay. I manage an Olympic-sized swimming pool. Last night I had a dream that I went in to catch up on work after hours. But there were people swimming in the pool, I think three or four, probably teenagers, even though it was closed. I was yelling at them to get out, but they wouldn't listen, they were doing horseplay."

"You don't want to get off, do you sir."

"I can't concentrate. Can we just talk about my dream first?"

"It's your money."

"So, I'm a strong swimmer. But one of them started drowning. And he was pulling down another one, his friend, so both of them were drowning. I should have gone in and saved them, and I wanted to help, but it was like my legs wouldn't move. Or it was like I didn't actually want to help. What I felt like was, these people broke the rules, they aren't supposed to be here, so it's okay to let them drown. So I watched and did nothing. It seemed to take hours, like it felt like normal, waking time. When I woke up, my bed was wet and I'd overslept. I was late to work today. I don't think that anyone noticed."

"Do you believe that dreams are prophetic?" said the phone-sex operator. "Or do you subscribe to a more rationalist, psychological model?"

"I, uh, I hadn't thought about it before."

"When people have a bad dream, they often imagine it means

something is wrong. Either in the future, in their body, or in their character. But the relationship is rarely that direct. Consider tarot cards. By now I think most people know the Death card isn't necessarily bad news. It's the same with your pool dream. Maybe you're trying to tell yourself something, or maybe it's nothing at all. Are you stroking your big cock for me?"

"Yes ma'am."

"It makes me so happy to hear that."

David hung up on the call. "There's nothing worse than people talking about dreams," he said to his recorder. He told himself he wanted nothing. He tapped another random call.

"I'm sorry," said the caller, a voice he recognized. "Lo siento. Je suis désolée."

"This again?" said the call's recipient. "Really?"

"Jeg beklager. Es tut mir leid. Prosti menya."

"I don't understand what you're saying or why you keep saying it."

"Maf kijiye. Duìbuqǐ. Gomenasai."

The call's recipient hung up. David stayed on the line. He unmuted himself but didn't say anything—only breathed into his microphone enough to let the caller know that someone was still there and listening. They continued: "I'm sorry. Lo siento. Je suis désolée."

David watched his new assistant on various screens as he listened to the voice. Alex was sweeping up pieces of a broken glass on the kitchen floor. "Jeg beklager. Es tut mir leid. Prosti menya."

The kid was sweeping the floor in his suit. He wore it every day. A young, beautiful person walked through the kitchen and emptied his pockets onto the floor, scattering wax paper candy wrappers and shredded receipts. Alex did not object, and began to sweep this up also. The other boy walked away.

"I'm sorry. Lo siento. Je suis désolée." The voice would never stop. It would continue as long as David would listen. "Jeg beklager. Es tut mir leid. Prosti menya." Lyd was the one who ought to be sorry. She was the one who had lied. "Maf kijiye. Duìbuqǐ. Gomenasai."

Outside the office, leaning against the door, Laverne's breathing slowed. David's did too.

- - - - -

David opened his eyes. The call had ended while he slept—he'd hung up by accident. Alex was long finished sweeping the floor, was seated at the kitchen table, using his laptop, listening to something in his headphones (probably some of yesterday's dictation), typing as quickly as he knew how.

An email chime sounded. David had received a message from the man who was above him on the agency's org chart—technically speaking, and solely for administrative purposes, his boss. The subject line was *Glad to have you on board.*

> We are glad to see you working the November question. Of course we have a team assigned already, and arguably this lies far outside your own remit, and I would be within my rights to reprimand you, and this option remains on the table, but we are impressed by the speed with which you alone have already repeated so much of our collective research, though I should emphasize that this is all you've accomplished so far: you have learned things we already know.
>
> In order to save you some time and potentially advance your efforts, I will tell you a number of secrets. You have heard two calls from the "Apologizing Woman." (There is some controversy in our offices about her gender; many say they clearly hear a man.) You will have noticed she disguises her signal as a cell phone call from some ordinary other person's number. I will tell you that it's flatly impossible to trace her. We've tried everything.
>
> If there's a pattern to the sort of person the Apologizing Woman calls, we haven't found it. She's contacting folks

of all kinds and classes all over the globe. Her use of many languages suggests she may not herself know to whom she is speaking or where they are. Her refusal to acknowledge any interruption suggests she cannot hear the recipients or has no interest in what they say. Possibly she hears but does not understand. We do not believe her to be a recording: there are minor variations in the rhythm and intonations of her message that suggest a thinking person. Some analysts are certain that they hear her breathing. I would be glad for any insights you can share. We need to know whether she breathes.

You have read or overheard several people describing unusual dreams. This has become a theme in our research as well, with certain key images and ideas repeating across state borders and time. Some experts believe humanity shares a collective unconscious populated by universal structures and archetypes. Some even hold that we unknowingly communicate by quasi-telepathic means—that our brains are somehow networked. Some of our agency's more imaginative analysts have long speculated about the potential of tapping such a network, or even manipulating its contents so as to eliminate malignant structures/concepts. Some have argued the November dream represents an attack on our collective unconscious by sophisticated operators—possibly a Chinese project. R&D is currently exploring competing in this space. However, our efforts will almost certainly fail to bear fruit before November, which, if it does end the world, will likely also end our labors, assuming the government ends with the world.

For now, we only know what people share about their dreams over the phone and online. Thankfully this is a rich data set; people love to talk about their dreams (especially women, ha ha, if you'll forgive a humorous generalization).

We have found that citizens in certain professions seem to be especially affected. Law enforcement officers, private security guards, and military personnel, for example, describe repeated encounters with a so-called boss, which often culminate in the unveiling of an illegible new law. Many lifeguards, swim instructors, dolphin trainers, and other aquatic professionals dream about watching people drown. Others describe a series of dreams about answering questions. An apparently trustworthy figure asks the dreamer about his or her personal biography. The dreamer supplies what he or she can, apologizing obsequiously for any forgotten information, and the trustworthy figure writes it all down. This dream often feels endless. (I will tell you I've had it myself.)

The commonalities, which only grow more common, appear to my inexpert eye malignant, but my psychologist assures me it's rarely that simple, that an apparently straightforward image or concept (drowning, for instance, which seems obviously negative in every regard) may contain its opposite. Some dreams are even meaningless.

We have a working consensus that these and other phenomena relate to the November problem. We are not confident that we know how. We hope you will share your insights as they emerge. Please continue to report on your assigned people, who may grow desperate as 11/1 approaches. We are watching every second of your work. We wish you the best in finding your wife.

JULY, MOTT

IT WAS THE FIRST WEEK OF JULY. A RADIO ADVERTISEMENT HELPfully reminded Mott and Lyd that there were 107 days left to save big money on auto insurance. They were presently driving east through Texas on a highway surrounded by nothing but rust-colored dirt, thirsty weeds, and billboards for steak restaurants. Lyd had so far refused to tell Mott where they were going. All she would say was, "You're going to like it, you're going to be happy."

Mott still felt injured by the way that Lyd had compared her book idea to the Jodie Foster movie. She said, "I haven't been happy all year. I'm not going to start now."

"You may need to reconsider how you define being happy. I have personally seen you smile several times this month alone. Weren't you happy when I gave you your king fish?"

"It didn't last long."

"Does it have to last long to be real?"

"There's feeling happy and there's being happy. Feeling happy ends quickly, and it doesn't really matter. *Being* happy takes longer, weeks or even months. I think you only really know on Christmas whether you've been happy that year. That's why the holidays are so hard for so many people."

Lyd loudly sipped her extra-large fast-food lemonade cup, got nothing but ice. She chewed on the straw. "Maybe."

They passed several dozen wind turbines barely turning, their whiteness unreal in the dusk. Mott had read they caused a lot of noise pollution, but she had never heard one make a sound. She asked her mother why that was.

"They're farther away than they look."

Mott resolved to put one in her novel, if possible as the centerpiece of a pivotal scene. She so rarely got to write about something she'd seen for herself.

They took the next city exit, bought fast-food chicken sandwiches and new lemonade for Lyd, this time without ice. Mott fiddled with the radio's dial, caught a bit of sleepy jazz. They drove past a small moving truck that had been pulled over by the police. One of the cops was inside the back of the truck, holding a clipboard and pen, taking inventory of everything inside—a plush, new-looking sofa; a washing machine and a dryer; several colorful floor lamps; a clothing rack on wheels; and two TVs (boxed). A woman in blue jeans and a pink tank top watched with her hands in her pockets, shifting from foot to foot. The other cop was seated in the truck's cab, warming its engine, adjusting the mirrors.

Mott asked her mother what the police were doing.

"They're playing repo men, taking back things that haven't been paid for. I heard about this on the news. Most of it goes to a big, open lot like a landfill, where I guess it will wait till November."

They pulled back onto the highway. Mott asked again where they were going.

Lyd tapped the steering wheel. "You're going to like it. You're going to be happy."

Mott gently thumped the console between them with her fist. "Actually, I don't want to be happy. I am trying to compose the greatest novel ever written by a thirteen-year-old, so I need to suffer all the time like you do, so I can make beautiful art."

"Like I used to," Lyd corrected her. "I'm doing much better since we left home."

"You've been crying in your sleep. Muttering too."

"Sometimes I have bad dreams."

"I keep dreaming that I'm late for school."

Lyd smiled. "You're going to like it where we're going. You're going to be happy."

.....

Before the dream about November, Mott had lived for the idea of college. "It will be so different to feel challenged," she would say, "and so refreshing to be recognized." She anticipated earning a 4.0 GPA, extensive merit scholarship support, departmental honors, a thesis award, and at least one devoted lifelong mentor ("a woman of course, though I am sure there will be several decent male professors"). She also believed, despite her mother's oblique warnings to the contrary, that she would be popular in college, winning many friends, intimates, and admirers, perhaps including—this part would come down to luck—several she could proudly call her peers.

She planned to attend the University of Houston as her mother had done. She would also study writing—would even, to the extent that she could without Lyd commenting, pursue the same courses, taught by the same professors, and in the same sequence.

Mott did not plan to replicate every particular of her mother's higher education. She would, for example, experiment with substances (alcohol, marijuana, and mushrooms were on the list) but would steer clear of psychedelic excesses, addictive opiates, and anything injected or snorted. She would also strive to avoid falling in love, which had been her mother's big mistake.

After the November dream, Mott had stopped talking about the future, except to lament all the things that she would never get to do.

She would never fall in love, never have her first kiss, never travel to Europe, never host a dinner party, never have a daughter of her own, never win an award, own a home, grow old, have a terminal disease, go to hospice, would never go to college, would never earn her degree.

A road sign promised thirty miles to Houston. "Close your eyes and cover them please," said Lyd. "I'll tell you when you can look."

Mott closed her eyes. The radio's fuzz resolved into a popular song about how wonderful it is to be young. She thought about how quickly the turbines must be turning now, how loud they must be to those who could hear them.

The car stopped. "You can open your eyes," said Lyd.

They were at an empty intersection. All the lights were blinking red. A blocky seven-story building the color of sand stood to their left, surrounded by a mostly vacant parking lot. The building looked familiar. Each of its faces was dotted by a series of small, square windows, regular as a chessboard. Most of these were dark.

"Where are we?" said Mott. She could feel her mother's expectations buzzing.

"It's the University of Houston," said Lyd. "This was my dorm for three semesters."

Mott startled herself by weeping. Lyd gently squeezed her arm.

"I'm sorry," said Mott. "This is very nice of you."

"That's all right, honey. Let's go and get ourselves a room." Lyd turned left, nudged the car forward—then hit the brakes hard. A white limousine with one working headlight blazed through the intersection, nearly clipping their like-new sedan.

"Careful!" said Mott. The limo's back end swayed like a snake's tail as it receded in their mirrors.

"It's okay," said her mother. "I saw them, don't worry. We're fine."

- - - - -

The dormitory's lobby had two elevators on each side, two potted plants, four wooden chairs with pink cushions, white-and-silver tiled floor, and a wide, shallow table against the far wall, burdened with magazines, pamphlets, outdated announcements, missing cat fliers, and a pair of microwave ovens. A paper sign on the left microwave read DO NOT USE THE POPCORN BUTTON. A sign on the right microwave read DON'T USE THIS ONE AT ALL.

There was a young woman seated at the front desk watching TV on her phone without apparent pleasure. The phone was propped up by a tall, silver thermos, uncapped, filled with chicken noodle soup. The young woman was exceedingly thin, with long fingers, sharp elbows, pale skin, and stringy yellow center-parted hair that hung past her shoulders. She supported her head with her hands, rubbing painful-looking zits on her temples. There was one tattoo on the back of each hand—a pair of asymmetric eyes, large and poorly drawn, with long, thick eyelashes. They were a shade of green that suggested she might have done them herself. She glanced furtively at Mott and Lyd twice, then forcefully redirected her attention to her show.

Mott skipped to the desk and cheerfully drummed on its surface. "Hello!" she said. "We just got here. Sorry it's late—I recognize that's probably inconvenient for a person in your position."

The young woman raised an eyebrow, suppressed a smile. "Hey kiddo."

"We'd like a room," said Mott. "Or two?"

"One is enough," said Lyd. "We can pay."

The young woman took a binder off a shelf behind her, flipped through plastic-sheathed pages. "How long are you staying?"

"We don't know for sure. At least a month."

"Hopefully longer," said Mott. "I'm trying to become a great writer."

The young woman nodded. "Third floor work for you?"

"It's perfect," said Lyd. "That's where I stayed when I was a student here."

"No kidding." The young woman pocketed her phone without pausing her show, so that studio laughter issued at odd intervals from her jeans. She opened a metal box that was fastened to the wall, revealing many hooks and hanging keys, and cross-referenced these with the page that she'd extracted from the binder. Once she found what she was looking for, she dragged a blue highlighter across the page twice and set two keys on the desk. "These are for you."

Mott said, "Do you need our names or transcript information? I'm Mott Gabel. If I were old enough to have a major it would be English with a concentration in creative writing. I got pretty much straight As in school. My mom is a kind of famous writer, she was a finalist for all kinds of awards. Maybe you've read her before, she writes under the name Lydia, last name Gabel like me."

The young woman smirked, but there was some warmth behind it. "I believe you, 'cause nobody would bother to lie about any of that, but I don't recognize that name, but I don't read a lot. I'll show you how to get to your room." She came out from behind the desk, pocket laughing all the way. She wore canvas tennis shoes, skinny jeans with catastrophic holes, and a T-shirt advertising a band. Mott saw now that this woman was really a girl—a teenager—and had the ungenerous thought that she was probably stupid. There was a dullness in her eyes, and the tattoos on her hands were an obvious, silly mistake.

"My name is Meredith," said the girl. "I never got As, but I'm glad you did. You seem nice."

"She *is* nice," said Lyd. There was a warning in her tone Mott did not fully understand.

Meredith led them to an elevator and then to their room, which said 308 on the door. A grasshopper in the hallway leapt aside to let them through. The other doors were closed and quiet.

"It's a pretty nice place," said Meredith. She opened the room and showed them inside. "You've got a window. They told me to warn people it's cold in the winter, but I don't see why. We don't have that long. The deposit is two hundred dollars." She held out her hand.

Lyd opened her wallet and counted out cash.

Meredith tucked the money under a red rubber LIVE WRONG bracelet she wore on her left wrist. She said, "I don't really work here, and I don't go to this school, but they let me rent the rooms out because their student workers left, and I'm street smart, and I have a knife." She took the knife out of her pocket and showed it to them like they ought to be impressed. It was a switchblade, closed for the moment, with a marble grip and white gold details. She stowed it again with her phone. "Also I think they forgot that I'm here."

"Nice knife," said Lyd, who clearly didn't care. "Maybe don't get that out around my daughter again."

Meredith's eyes rolled a little. "This dorm has three rules that I care about. Don't do anything weird that could get me in trouble. Don't burn shit in the microwaves. And if you do anything fun, like have a party or order some food, it'd be cool if you would include me."

"We'll behave," said Lyd, crossing her heart.

"How old are you?" said Mott.

"Almost eighteen. How old are you?"

"Fourteen in October," said Mott.

Meredith tucked some hair behind one of her ears, where it didn't seem to belong. She said, "So thirteen then. You act old for your age, but you look really young."

"I'm just short, and I don't wear makeup."

Meredith didn't either, and neither did Lyd, but they still looked like adults.

"Maybe you should go back to the desk now," said Lyd.

"Yeah." Meredith tried to tuck her hair again. "Guess so." She backed a couple steps out of the apartment, peered in from the hallway. "Sorry there's no blankets. I don't know where they keep them."

"That's okay," said Mott. "We brought our own."

Meredith's pocket played a bleach commercial as she walked away.

.....

Mott and Lyd's room came with two beds, two desks, two cheap wooden chairs, two small dressers, two electrical outlets, one window, no curtains, one ceiling lamp, one David Bowie poster puttied to the wall, no wastebaskets, no fridge or means of cooking food, no thermostat, and one large square of purple carpet covering most but not all of the floor, which was brown tile. They made several trips to their car and back, stacking their belongings in a corner of their room. They emptied one of their book boxes and designated it the trash can. Mott transferred her clothes to her dresser and enthroned her king fish on top. Lyd plugged in their travel-sized stereo, shuffled through the CDs they had brought, and finally settled on silence. She gave Mott permission to drink a sugar soda. They were celebrating because Mott was happy, just as Lyd had promised. Mott asked how long they could stay.

"As long as you like, or until it's not safe, whichever comes first."

"Do you think that I could take some classes?"

"We can try. The summer schedule here was light even when it wasn't the end of the world. But there may be something in creative writing you can audit. We'll need the professor's permission, but they'll have to say yes to an excellent student like you."

Mott nodded gravely. She agreed they would have to say yes.

Lyd opened her gas station gin and poured it into a red picnic cup, then added several shakes of bottled lime juice. She swirled the cup until the cloud of juice dispersed and the gin turned a milky shade of clear.

"What are you doing?" said Mott.

"It's called a gimlet. It's not a great cocktail, not even a good one, but it certainly has gin and lime juice, and sometimes that's all that you can ask."

"Can I try some?"

Lyd grinned. "Actually, this one's for you."

Mott accepted the cup with both hands. Lyd mixed herself another.

Mott considered the gimlet and its familiar citrus scent. There was an unaccountable nostalgia—a rare, intoxicating feeling at Mott's age. She must have seen her mother drink one years before or smelled it on her breath. Yet still she was afraid to swallow any.

"Don't worry," said Lyd. "I made it extra weak for you."

Mott smiled, she suspected unpersuasively, and drank. It would have been better if it had been cold, if she had been older, if she could have sneaked it alone, and felt what she was feeling now alone.

"To near-death experiences," said Lyd, "and white limousines." They toasted their cups.

"I thought you saw it coming."

"I did!" Lyd sipped her gimlet and sighed. "But that's not why it missed us."

"So how come it did?"

Lyd mimed shooting herself in the head. "Dumb luck."

JULY, LYD

THE DAY AFTER THEIR ARRIVAL, MOTT ASKED LYD FOR THE CURRENT list of rules. They were in a new place, so it followed there would be new restrictions. Lyd told her she must never leave the dorm room unaccompanied, except to use the shared bathroom, and even this should be done with Lyd's escort whenever possible. Mott must never answer the door for anyone but Lyd. Mott was still forbidden her phone, her laptop, and all Internet-connectable devices, and she still was not allowed to send her father any letters without Lyd's permission. "And you must write every morning," said Lyd. "Try to get as close to one thousand words a day as you can. It's the only way you'll finish your novel in time." They had less than four months to live.

"Yes ma'am," said Mott. "And am I allowed to drink cocktails, even though I'm a kid?"

Lyd followed Mott's gaze to the empty gin bottle that lay on the floor between their beds. She must have had the rest herself. She never would have let Mott drink more than one. Indeed, she could barely believe that she had allowed—had *suggested*—even that much. What had given her the idea in the first place? She couldn't remember. Her eyes hurt.

"No," said Lyd. "You're not allowed. That was a special occasion."

"What was it like for you the first time you drank?"

"You know how there are deep-sea fish with so much pressure inside them, they need the whole ocean crushing down on them just to keep from exploding?" Lyd popped the tab on a can of grape soda. "Back then it was like I was the opposite, a shallow water fish who had gone too low, like I was about to implode. My first drink gave me some of the pressure inside me I needed. I felt weightless, like I was in balance with my environment."

"Sounds like it was nice."

"I loved it. I couldn't stop laughing. And then I threw up."

Mott smiled. "Me too." She pointed at the garbage box. "Sorry."

.....

Lyd and Mott's first full day in Houston established what would become their new routine. Mott wrote until noon. This involved a lot of staring at bare walls. Lyd suspected it would be easier if she were not there but could think of nowhere else that she wanted to be. She said she might try writing something too, just to see how it felt, which made Mott very happy, so Lyd sat at her desk also, pen in hand, but never managed more than a pronoun.

Lyd made turkey-and-cheese sandwiches with mayonnaise for lunch. "Another rule is you have to stop and eat lunch when it's time, even if your work is going well." She poured water from a liter jug into a plastic cup and set this on Mott's desk. "You can have a sugar soda if you finish this first." She poured herself gin.

After lunch they showered. There were hardly any other people in the dorm, so they had the bathroom to themselves. In the stall beside the one Lyd used, a biology textbook lay on the drain, the thickness of its pages tripled by water, its hard cover flaked and curling. Interlocking rings of black and purple ink stains spiraled outward from the textbook on the tile.

The next thing was leaving the dorm. "We have to go somewhere outside every day," said Lyd. "It enriches your fiction and helps you keep sane. We always have to use sunblock, and we always have to wear our hats."

Meredith was working the front desk when they left. She waved hello at them in a way that suggested she would like to talk, but Lyd pretended not to notice, and Mott followed her lead. Mott didn't need a friend with bad tattoos and a knife.

They went first to the campus bookstore, which was open but not staffed, fully lit and half-stocked with leftover books from the spring semester. "You can have any book you want," said Lyd, "even if you don't plan to finish it. Just pick whatever looks interesting."

"I'm still reading *Little Women*," said Mott. It had been days since Lyd last saw her open that book—she often held it in her lap while they drove, but it was always closed.

Lyd chose several books for herself, all novels she had been meaning to read for some time, and which she thought that Mott might also enjoy. They left without paying. There were no employees present to operate the register, which Lyd took to mean that nobody cared.

Mott said she wanted coffee, which seemed like the essence of college to her, so they found a café. The barista was a young woman with a French braid, and a small, silver nose ring. She behaved as if this were all routine for her, as if people still visited every day, which it was possible they did, but there were no other customers in evidence, and half the lights were dead, and there were no pastries in the display case, and the café was running short on cups, lids, napkins, and straws. The whole scene made Lyd nervous. She and Mott took their coffee outside. Mott drank from her cup and scrunched up her face. "I want to learn to like this," she said.

Lyd said that liking coffee was beside the point. The pleasure was in needing it, in having something to do, in holding the warm cardboard cup. The pleasure was that the café had outdoor seating, mismatched wicker chairs and glass-top tables shaded by variously colored umbrellas, with bamboo wind chimes hanging from all corners of the building, and the tables were that perfect size where each person had a little elbow room to herself, but not too much. Mott took an hour to finish her cup.

They got hamburgers for dinner, picking them up from a fast-food restaurant on their way back to the dorm. When they returned, books and greasy paper bags in hand, Meredith was still at the desk, watching TV on her phone. "Welcome back," she said. "Did you bring me any?"

"No," said Lyd. "Were we supposed to?"

"Not if you don't want to. But it sucks to eat alone, so I'd rather eat with you."

"Sorry," said Mott. "Next time we'll remember."

"We can count it against your rent if you want," said Meredith. "If that would make you happy."

"It would," said Lyd.

Lyd and Mott went back to their room and Mott wrote again, achieving far less than she'd managed that morning, and at the cost of much more effort. Lyd sat at her own desk or on her bed and listened to music, and itched and thought and wished that she were writing too. She filled a lime-green flask she had bought at a California gas station and drank from it experimentally. Someone on the third floor had their television set too loud—the shouting preacher and his congregation again, "NoVEMber." There were more grasshoppers in the halls.

- - - - -

This was how they lived at the University of Houston. First writing, then lunch, then showers, then sunblock and going outside, often to the café or campus bookstore. When there was a cashier present, Lyd paid for the books that she chose. When there wasn't, she took more. Then hot takeout dinner or delivery and Meredith working the desk at the dorm, waiting for her share of their meal, and she would hint that she wanted to eat with them in their room, but the most Lyd would allow was for Mott to eat and talk with Meredith a little in the lobby. They tried to keep their visits with her brief. Then more writing for Mott, though less was accomplished. At some point in the evening Lyd would become too anxious to stay in the room. She would refill her flask, check her gun, and take a night walk.

Sometimes, not according to any schedule that Lyd could understand, Meredith would say the rent was due. Lyd would give her some money—whatever was handy was always enough. Lyd started to carry less cash. The next time she saw them after a payment, Meredith would show Lyd and Mott some new purchase: a bracelet, peace sign earrings, a collectible band T-shirt, a pair of headphones, a DVD of some movie she remembered fondly from when she was a little girl.

Once, one perfect day at the café, there was a nice breeze, and the cups were still warm in their hands, and Mott had just said something clever, and they were seated with their elbows touching, and the sun was veiled by clouds so that the sky had turned a pleasant gray, and Lyd felt serenity in her heart, and kissed her dear Mott's forehead, and Mott laughed and wiped the kiss dry, and Lyd nearly wept. It was a good life, even if it was scheduled to end soon.

Lyd sometimes wished Houston could be actually beautiful. For several years now the Atlantic had been seeping into several nearby coastal cities—La Porte, Seabrook, Channelview, and parts of Pasadena—flooding basements and foundations, eating low-lying buildings and waterfront homes ankles first. When the wind blew inland it carried smells of seawater and swollen, ruptured wood. Even on campus, the air was constantly damp, so that patches of mold grew on any untended surface, paint peeled prematurely, and wild weeds flourished in all public soils. Every building seemed to sweat.

The campus was largely empty. Barely more than one thousand

students had lingered for the summer sessions. No one was sure how many faculty remained, but the course offerings were officially unchanged. The abandoned students who bothered to show up continued to meet on their own, reading and discussing what they supposed the assigned texts would have been, imagining syllabi far more demanding than any their teachers would dare. They graded one another. Their rubrics were elusive, developmental, and infinitely complex, though mostly it came down to love—the students that cared for one another tended to determine that their colleagues had earned As, while those who were indifferent made efforts to maintain a standard bell curve.

An ethic of accelerated consumption prevailed among the community: the school and all its elements were theirs to use and use up. The technology-enabled classrooms were for screening movies. The computer labs were for games, masturbation, and unlimited free printing. The planetarium was for getting high, group sex, and occasional stargazing. The cafeteria was still for eating. Everywhere was for sleeping. Anything that had no other use was fuel. Every day there was a fire. The optometry library was reduced to ash in late June.

Facilities staff struggled silently to assert their ownership of the buildings. They mopped and vacuumed floors, wiped fixtures and mirrors, painted over graffiti, refilled printer paper trays, fought fires, woke public sleepers, bleached or cut blood from the carpets, and did what they could for the windows.

Life was mostly peaceful at the university, not because the people there were naturally gentle but because they were so few, with so many useful things gathered to them—a concentration of culture, capital, concrete, and cafeteria chicken tenders so dense that it would easily see them all through to the end of the world, or at least the fall semester.

Lyd and Mott were safe or something like it.

On their third full day in Houston, during Lyd's second night walk alone with her lime-green flask, she visited her former mentor's office in the building English shared with foreign languages and history. The office door was closed, and as Lyd knocked she realized that she was drunk. A stranger answered. "I'm sorry," said Lyd. She screwed the cap back onto her flask.

"Don't be," said the stranger. "Let me clear a chair for you." She was a woman some ten inches shorter than Lyd and about her same age, whose frizzy gray-brown hair had been cut into a punky style several months ago (shaved sides, asymmetric bangs, cropped close in the back) but had since grown in and gone a bit wild. She transferred a large stack of books from one of the visitor chairs in her office to the other, then resumed her own seat and turned off her computer monitor to show that Lyd would have her full attention. The books that lined the walls loomed over her and seemed to threaten falling.

Lyd checked the nameplate on the door to confirm that she had the right one. "Obviously that's not me," said the stranger. "Come on inside, Lyd. Tell me how it's been."

Lyd pocketed her flask and took a seat. The room was dark, lit only by a desk lamp.

"Now I recognize you," said Lyd. "Teresa, right?"

"Te-ray-sa," said the woman, correcting her pronunciation. "We studied under Laura together. I was two years behind you I think."

"Did she retire?"

"She died."

"I thought that she was in remission."

"She was. She killed herself. Overdosed on heroin."

"I didn't know she used," said Lyd. She rubbed her arms warm.

"Nobody knew, but her house is full of paraphernalia. I'm taking care of it now."

"I guess you're taking care of her office then too."

"I've unofficially assumed her course load. It's sort of my tribute, and sort of a principle thing. I felt a woman of color should continue to sit in this chair."

Lyd squinted at Teresa, searching her for color.

"I'm Mexican."

"Oh sure," said Lyd. She blushed. "Of course." She extracted her flask from her pocket, twisted the cap, took a pull, and offered one to Teresa, who graciously accepted.

"I've read your books," said Teresa. "I didn't love them, but I understood why other people did. They're impressive."

Lyd nodded, shook her head. "I came here because of my daughter. I was going to ask Laura to teach her. She's thirteen, she's brilliant, and she wants to write a novel before November. She always wanted to study here."

"She can still take the class if she'd like. I would love to have her."

"Hm," said Lyd. She took another pull.

"You're thinking that you haven't heard of me since college. You're wondering what I've published and whether I'm any good. I never sold a book. I got an MFA here, wrote some stories, and published them in magazines nobody reads. Then I got my PhD. That took seven years. After that I had what was supposed to be a novel. No one liked it. I stripped it for parts, spun those into stories, and published the best in the same magazines. I got a secretary job in the neuroscience department, scheduling flights and arranging conference hotel rooms, answering phones. Nobody cared if I wrote during work hours. Nobody read the results. I applied for every opening in the English department, professional or academic, and I was never interviewed. I hung around and went to all the readings and reading after-parties and drank and waited more and then Laura died. Now I've taken her job and her home. What I've learned from all this is that you can have exactly whatever you want. You just have to wait till nobody else wants it."

Lyd was sleepy from her liquor. She said, "Okay. Mott would like to take your class."

"Thank you for your vote of confidence. You can't attend with her if you want her to learn anything. You'd be a terrible distraction."

Lyd's flask was empty now. "How come you wanted this job so bad?"

"The heart is dumb." Teresa made a heart shape with her thumbs and pointer fingers. "I loved my professors." Lyd looked at her through the heart she had made.

After their meeting's completion, on her walk back from the building English shared with foreign languages and history, Lyd encountered six young women who stood in a circle outside the library, warming their hands over piled burning books. They wore stripes of pastel paint on their cheeks, foreheads, and noses. Lyd approached them, asked what they were burning.

"Patriarchy," said the one nearest her. "Any book by any fascist, rapist, colonizer, slaver, killer, pornographer, labor thief, or carnivore. Any book that corrodes the reader's moral instincts, anything that is not beautiful, and everything that has no kind or loving use."

"It's not too late to save America," said another. Lyd wanted to kiss her forehead.

"Is there anything you wanna burn?" said the first.

"That's okay. It seems like you're doing the work."

Lyd lingered at the edges of their circle and their strident conversation, keeping all of her thoughts to herself. There were so many things in her that should be thrown onto that fire.

JULY, MOTT

IN MOTT'S NOVEL, THE DAUGHTER AND HER MOTHER TRADED BODies. It began with a dream. In the dream they were together in a hospital. The mother was the mother. The daughter was the baby in her womb. They could talk to each other. The daughter said, "I'm afraid of being born into this world." The mother said, "I'm afraid to let you go." The daughter said, "I want to stay with you forever." The mother said, "You'll be okay, I'll keep you safe." The daughter said, "I don't believe you."

In the dream, when the mother said she would not let her daughter go, the doctor put her small, cold hands inside and pulled out the baby. The mother dreamed of birthing herself—emerging from her own body, extracted by the doctor—and the daughter dreamed of abandoning her baby body to stay in the womb, where she was warm and safe. And the mother wept in her sleep. And the daughter slept more deeply.

And when they woke, they were holding each other on the floor of the magic cave, whose walls were coated with many colors and intensities of luminescent moss and embedded with dinosaur bones. Because they were so thoroughly entangled—the mother's arms around the daughter (one arm still asleep, all numb and deadweight), the daughter's arms around the mother (one arm waking, pins and needles)—it took them a weirdly long time to realize that they had switched bodies.

They sat side by side, at rest against a glowing cave wall.

"Does it always feel like this, being you?" said the mother. "Did I feel like this when I was young?"

"My leg hurts," said the daughter. "I mean, your leg does."

"It always hurts," said the mother. "I forgot." She rubbed her body's achy leg.

The rain had stopped. They made their way out of the cave.

. . . . .

Mott usually woke half an hour before Lyd, when the small square of sunlight their window allowed them was highest on their door. She began her days by tidying—throwing away her mother's picnic cups, her own soda cans, and any empty potato chip bags or cupcake wrappers. She screwed the caps back onto open liquor bottles and returned them to the dresser drawer where they were kept. Any empties were lined up against the wall under the window. She sorted their growing collection of never-read books, pushing these against the wall on either side of the door. The books all looked so beautiful, with such interesting covers, and must all be so much better than what she was writing, whatever it was. She was barely halfway through *Little Women*. It was less than four months till November, and she would never have the time to read these others at this rate, would never surpass them, would be completely forgotten.

Lyd usually woke just as Mott's mood reached its nadir. Mott would ask her, "Do you really want me to finish my book?"

"I do."

"Are you really going to read it?"

"I really will."

"Are you looking forward to it, Mom?"

Lyd would smile then. "It's keeping me alive."

.....

In Mott's novel, the mother quickly adjusted to living in her daughter's body. She found that school was easy and made As in every subject. Her teachers praised her as a genius. They said she demonstrated both maturity and leadership. They confided secrets in her about their failing marriages and organs.

The mother was also well-liked by her classmates, who appreciated her new wit and social grace. She was not cowed by teenagers as her daughter had been; no matter how pretty they were, no matter how cruel or wealthy, they were still children in her eyes, and therefore must defer to her experience. They respected her because she required it of them.

Perhaps most important to the mother's success (among both the adults and the children) was the obvious, effortless pleasure with which she wore and used her daughter's body. Intoxicated by her sudden youth, the mother seemed to invite the whole world's admiration with each twitch of her muscles, every lingering smile, each snap of her fingers, and every weightless step. She smelled herself often. She played with her hair. She flirted with the mirror when she thought no one could see. She walked around the house in her underwear. "I always told you it's important to let your skin breathe."

.....

According to the course catalog, Mott's writing class was scheduled to meet three times a week. The professor, who preferred to be addressed by her first name, demanded that the class meet every weekday afternoon. There was no time to waste, she said, if they hoped to make great art before the world ended. The other students were devoted, scribbling notes each time Teresa spoke. She often told them what their stories were really about. "This is really about how straight men negotiate their love and erotic desire for one another." "This is really about what people do when they think that nobody is looking." "This is really about the fear of being discovered as a fraud. I think if you revise with that in mind, you'll see how to align its events and its form to create a startling and beautiful effect."

She would look up from the story, adjust her glasses, smile nervously. "Does that help?"

They met on the third floor of an aging building whose walls looked like pale gingerbread. There were seats enough for thirty-six students. Mott was disappointed by how much the facilities resembled her middle school, from the fluorescent lights to the desks, which were fastened to red, plastic chairs. She was largely satisfied with the class, though it was nothing like what she'd imagined. She only wished that Teresa would treat her as a full participant. Whereas the other students regularly turned in stories for critique, bringing copies for their teacher and one another, Mott was not allowed to bring her own writing, and supposedly never would be.

"It wouldn't help," said Teresa. "You're too young. The most important thing is you keep writing. A lot of people give up after their first workshop. I won't risk that with you."

"I'm not going to quit."

Teresa touched Mott's hair. "You almost quit every day."

Mott glared at her. "Just because I'm a kid it doesn't mean you get to touch me."

"Sorry. You're right. But we still won't be reading your stories."

"My novel."

"Have your mother read it," said Teresa. "It's her job to spare your feelings."

Teresa recommended two or more books to her each time the class met. Mott dutifully recorded each in her notes. It was another futile list, not even a thwarted ambition: an impossibility memorialized. A failure from birth.

.....

In Mott's novel, the daughter struggled to live well inside her mother's body.

The problem was not with the body itself, though its myriad complaints did not raise her spirits, and neither did the stunning array of medications she was required to swallow each morning (calcium and other supplements, omeprazole, statins, birth control, antidepressants, Saint-John's-wort). The trouble was her job.

The mother was—had been—an executive assistant to the VP of marketing at a large company that made soaps, toilet cleaners, laundry detergent, personal hygiene products, and, under a different name, low-quality chocolates. Her work involved scheduling the VP's flights and hotel rooms, answering his calls and emails (often in the latter case pretending to be him), and looking up things on the Internet for which he could easily have searched himself (e.g., "funny jokes to start a speech," "what happened to that one kid actor," and "the diameter of the Earth"). He also had no sense of smell, and so often called her into his office to sniff new products and describe their scents or odors. ("In every case," wrote Mott, "whether it was chemical or chocolate, the item stank of orange peels, lavender, or lemon.")

The VP was a gentle, understanding man, respectful and courteous in all things. He had come to rely on the mother completely, and followed her every instruction without question. He went where she told him to go. He slept where she told him to sleep. He ate what she had delivered to his hotel room. If nothing was delivered, then nothing was all that he ate.

The mother did her best to explain to the daughter how plane tickets could be purchased and entered into the corporate expense-tracking system, how to get the best hotel rooms at a discount, and how to feed the VP without running afoul of his many and various food allergies, but her explanations would never be adequate. More than anything else, her work required practical experience of the world—a sort of highly advanced, finely tuned common sense. The daughter did not understand the world. She did not know what grown-ups knew.

(Many of the details in this chapter were gleaned from conversations with Lyd about the sort of problems a woman might face at work and with her body.)

And so the marketing VP was subjected to an escalating series of catastrophes, each one clearly the fault of his assistant, up to and including a nearly fatal allergic reaction, and every time he blamed himself, apologizing to the daughter for misunderstanding her instructions, for forgetting what she'd never told him, for being such an absentminded ass. He was befuddled by his own capacity for error. "I don't know what's happened to my mind!"

"You're doing fine," said the mother. "It's fine. He'd never fire you."

But the daughter could not sleep for all her fear that she would lose her mother's job. Soon she developed an ulcer. Unsustainable amounts of hair fell out of her head in the shower. There was a new rash on her feet. Her body was increasingly the problem.

. . . . .

One night three weeks into July, Lyd came home from her regular walk with a boxed 13.3-inch TV set in her arms. "Sorry I'm late," she said. "There was a sale."

She plugged it in and turned it on. A news program anchor was interviewing a movie star. How did it feel to know this film would probably be the last he ever made? The actor laughed. "I don't think that's true at all. There's got to be movies in Heaven! Otherwise they couldn't call it that."

Mott said, "For someone who doesn't like TV, you sure do watch a lot sometimes."

There was a commercial for a company that would give you a funeral while you were still alive. Your friends and family would come in Sunday dress and speak and weep about you while you lay with your arms crossed in the coffin. The company would help your mourners write and revise their eulogies for maximum beauty. They would also rent and decorate the church, choose flowers, build a slideshow, provide a minister, organize the potluck, tailor your suit or dress, and make you up to look like death. All you had to bring was your body.

Lyd changed the channel.

"Liquidate your heirlooms! Turn your fixtures into cash. There's gold in things you'd never think to check. Your broken VCR has gold in it. Your phone has gold in it. Your car has gold in it—both the antilock brakes and the airbag inflation system's computer chips have gold. Many old reading glasses have gold. There's gold in photographic toners. There's gold in some fancy desserts. There's gold in your high-end CDs. There's gold in your china. There's gold in your scrapbook. There's gold in your teeth, and the teeth of your children."

"Gold," said Mott.

"Apparently," said Lyd.

"Maybe you could use your headphones. I think I can write some more before bed."

Lyd muted the TV, mixed a drink, gave Mott a sugar soda and a cupcake, and plugged in her noise-canceling headphones. She turned the screen to minimize its presence in Mott's vision. There was a presidential candidate on-screen, who touted the virtues of voting by mail.

Mott crossed out the sentence that she had most recently written. She tried to think of something better.

In Mott's novel, the mother and the daughter sought help with their condition.

They searched for relevant scientific journal articles. There were none.

They read Internet forums belonging to people who believed that they were trapped in the wrong bodies—that they were really cats, really dragons, really cartoon characters, really angels, really historical persons—but never found a thread discussing body swaps.

They searched for information on the magic cave where they had made their exchange. There was no record or legend that any such cave had ever existed. They emailed regional geological experts, who told them they must be mistaken. They wrote to scientists who studied bioluminescent moss, who could name no species that matched their description of the bright and many-splendored glow that grew on the magic cave's walls. They wrote to paleontologists, who said that so many dinosaur bones would never be found intact in one place.

They asked their librarian for literature relating to out-of-body experiences. She furnished them with books on mysticism, meditation, and reincarnation. None of this was what they wanted. They checked out most of the books anyway so as not to hurt the librarian's feelings. They failed to return these on time, and so the late fees quickly mounted. They renewed the books and let them lapse again; the fees doubled.

They visited a fortune-teller, who read their palms and promised them riches and thrilling romantic adventures. The daughter asked when she would die. The fortune-teller said she never answered that question. "It's supposed to be a surprise."

"Then show me where my lifeline is. I'll judge it for myself."

- - - - -

Later, another night, while Mott was wrestling with her novel and Lyd was half-asleep in front of her little TV, Meredith knocked on the door. "It's me," she said. "Can I visit?"

"Mott's busy right now," said Lyd. She took off her headphones, then unplugged them, so that the TV's sound filled her corner of the room.

"It's just the pizza delivery guy dropped your dinner off with me at the desk. He was in a rush and he said he didn't want to come upstairs. And also, he made me pay." Meredith's voice hitched as she spoke in a way that made Mott confident she was lying. Clearly, she had commandeered the delivery as an excuse to come up and see them. Mott felt a sudden surge of guilt and pity. They should be nicer to this girl. Lyd sighed and opened the door.

Meredith held two grease-spotted pizza boxes, cradling them awkwardly against her stomach. "Two larges," she said. "One is pepperoni and the other's a supreme."

Lyd sighed. "Are you hungry?"

Meredith's face lit up like a night-light. "It's weird 'cause I just ate, but yeah I am actually starving."

"You can come in. We're out of paper plates right now, so just eat it out of the box."

Lyd traded Meredith two twenty-dollar bills for the pizzas and set them out on her bed, then took out a slice of supreme and sat down on the floor. Mott and Meredith helped themselves to pepperoni. There was a story on the news about California wildfires. Much of the state had been burning for days.

"Do you drink?" asked Lyd.

"Yeah," said Meredith, "sometimes I do. My parents drank a lot and made bad mistakes all the time, but I know how to handle it. They didn't."

"I'll make you a gimlet," said Lyd.

"What's in that?"

Mott said, "Gin, or sometimes it's vodka, and lime juice. They taste okay."

Meredith was impressed. "Cool. That sounds good. I usually drink a white Russian."

"Gross," said Lyd. She gave Meredith the promised gimlet and set to mixing one for herself. Meredith smacked her lips obnoxiously after each sip. Mott wondered why no one had ever told her not to do that.

There was a story on the TV about a missing girl named Margot Gravel. She had been kidnapped by her mother. She was thirteen years old, would soon be fourteen. She had, at last sighting, a thick nest of curly brown hair. There was a portrait of the girl. She looked a lot like someone that Mott used to know, whose name Mott couldn't remember. "Law enforcement officials tell us Margot's mother may have changed her hair, or otherwise disguised her appearance, in order to avoid detection." The girl's hair turned blonde. Then it was short. Then it was pink. Then she had big sunglasses. Then she had the glasses and a baseball cap. Then her skin turned tan. It was at this point—when the photo's resemblance was weakest—that Mott recognized herself on the screen. The portrait's backdrop was the apartment that she and Lyd had abandoned. It was recent. Mott forced herself to swallow the bite in her mouth. There was no reason she should be on the news. Her name was not Margot. She was never kidnapped.

"Hey," said Meredith, pointing at the screen. "Isn't that you?"

Lyd said, "Be quiet for a second please." She lunged for the volume, turned it up too high.

"The mother, Linda Gravel, is forty-three years old. She has a history of mental instability and substance abuse, although the father says he had believed her habits were under control." There was a photograph of Lyd from eight years or so back. She was gesturing with a lit cigarette, grinning at the camera, flirting with the entity behind the lens. Her hair was longer then. Now the photo changed and it was shorter. The photo changed again and it was blonde. Now she wore a baseball cap, and now sunglasses. It changed again and she was tanned.

The program interviewed the missing girl's father. He was a handsome, wholesome-looking mustached man wearing a gray T-shirt and an open red flannel with the sleeves rolled up. His name, they said, was David Gravel. "I know that Linda believes she's somehow protecting Margot by taking her away from me, but she's confused."

He addressed the camera directly: "Honey, you need to come home. We need to be together this November, to see it through as a family. Whatever's coming next, you don't want to face it alone."

The anchors asked their viewers to call the special tip line number on the bottom of their screen if they had any useful information. There was, they said, a cash reward.

"I thought your name was Lyd," said Meredith.

"It is!" said Mott. "And mine's really Mott! That was so weird—they must have got the wrong photos somehow. That guy wasn't Dad. Everything about that was wrong."

Meredith hastily set down her half-drunk cup on Lyd's desk and stood up too fast, stumbling backward toward the door. She put her hand in her pocket—felt her knife to make sure it was there. "Lady, are you a kidnapper? I told you that you're not allowed to get me in trouble."

"She's my mom," said Mott. "You won't get in trouble. I don't think anybody even knows we live here except you."

"That's right," said Lyd. "So if you told anyone that we're here, if you ever called that line, I would know it was you." She made a fist, reaching unconsciously for the gun holstered under her clothing.

"Fuck this," said Meredith. She opened the door, backed out, and closed it. "I would never call that tip line," she said through the door, "but lots of other people saw that story, and they could see you anywhere on campus. So if you ever do get caught you should know it was them. And by the way, I always have my knife, which I used to kill my parents earlier this year, so don't think you can scare me or push me around."

Mott, startled, looked to Lyd for guidance.

"There's no way she's ever touched anyone with that knife," said Lyd. "She's just trying to sound tough."

Meredith's footsteps receded down the hall.

Mott rubbed her own eyes too hard. "Mom? What happened? Who was that man on TV?"

"I don't know," said Lyd. She was setting down her newly empty cup, eyeing the one that Meredith had left behind half-drunk. "God, I don't know. All I know is that your father did it."

"What? Why would he want to do that?"

Lyd downed Meredith's gimlet. "He's trying to scare us and make us come home."

Mott wished she could rewind the broadcast and watch it again. She wanted to know for sure it had happened. "I didn't like how it felt being on the TV," she said. She didn't like being called the wrong name.

.....

Lyd drank herself unconscious that night. Mott didn't have that option, and Lyd's snoring made sleep harder still. Come eleven, Mott gave up and opened her eyes, slipped her feet into thick socks, and left the room as quietly as she could. She found Meredith at the front desk, plugging her phone into a power strip on the floor. The way Meredith bent in her chair made her T-shirt ride up in the back, revealing what seemed to be the ends of several scars—raised, pink skin.

"Don't be startled when you sit up," said Mott. "I'm here."

"Knew I heard someone," said Meredith. "Isn't it past your bedtime?"

"I snuck out."

"Nice. Did your mom ever calm down?"

"Not really."

"There's another chair back here behind the desk if you want to sit."

"Okay," said Mott. The second chair had orange-brown cushions and metal arms and legs. It was against the wall, between two shelves loaded with years-old binders and DVDs.

"I searched around online for Mott and Linda Gravel," said

Meredith. “There was an online version of the story. You can see it on my phone if you want.”

“I’m not allowed to use the Internet,” said Mott. “My mom thinks people will find us or something if I do. I thought that she was being paranoid, but now I feel paranoid too. She says my dad is trying to scare us. She says that he’s the one who put our pictures on TV.”

“Is your dad a bad person?”

“Maybe. I never thought so. You won’t believe me probably, but he’s a spy.”

“Why wouldn’t I believe that?”

“Because it’s stupid,” said Mott. “Nobody believes it. I don’t even always believe it.”

“Parents are assholes.” Meredith was digging the tip of her knife into the desk’s surface and twisting, gouging little holes. “Would you want to be friends? I want to look out for you. I’m very protective.”

Mott scratched her right heel through her sock by rubbing it against the corner of her chair’s metal leg. “I haven’t had a lot of friends. Maybe none. I don’t think I know how.”

“Oh. It’s not supposed to be super hard.”

“Did you really kill your parents?”

Meredith shrugged, pushed her knife deep enough into the desk to stand unassisted. “I thought about it a lot.”

“My mom is never going to be intimidated by you, so there’s no point in making stuff up. She carries a gun.” Mott leaned forward, touched Meredith’s back. “She literally has a gun.”

“Yikes Margot.” Meredith laughed. “I hear you, I get it. I’ll be careful.”

“Don’t call me Margot. That’s not funny.”

“I know, I’m sorry. I get why you wouldn’t want to be friends.”

“It’s not that I don’t want to.” Mott rubbed her upper arms warm. “I’m sorry if I made you feel hurt. It’s just I’m extremely stressed right now. I guess I’ll go to bed.”

"Have a good night," said Meredith. "Don't worry, I promise I won't call your dad. And we don't have to be official friends, but maybe we can hang out sometimes."

"Absolutely," said Mott. "But next time we do, please be nice to my mom. You need to know she's my favorite person."

JULY, LYD

THE TELEVISED MAN WHO CLAIMED TO BE MARRIED TO LYD, AND who said she was a kidnapper, quickly became a minor celebrity. He toured news programs and talk shows, sharing stories of their life together, telling sympathetic hosts what a wonderful wife Lyd had been (when she wasn't using), how kind a mother she was (when she wasn't drunk), how beautiful she had been on their wedding day (she was clean for forty-eight hours), how much she had enjoyed her hobbies (she wrote "little stories"), how strange it was to live in his big and beautiful home without her. He also spoke for other lonely fathers and sons who had been abandoned by their wives, children, and mothers, and who had written him letters or called his tip line to share their suffering. "I'm learning there's a loneliness epidemic," he said. "November's become an all-purpose excuse. Nobody wants to waste what's left of their time on this Earth with anyone at all imperfect. If a woman doesn't like the man in her life, or if he annoys her or acts out a little, she just disappears. If a mother's disappointed in her son, she stops taking his calls. And maybe we deserve it. But I don't think it's very generous or kind."

Lyd spent most of each day watching TV, searching channels for his next appearance, taking notes through all his segments, diagramming inconsistencies and factual errors, proving to herself what she already knew: this man was not her husband and never had been.

Although he called her Linda Gravel, and though he called their daughter Margot, the man identified himself as David. He was much more classically handsome than the real thing—his broad face as smooth and untroubled as a cloud until he smiled, which scribbled many soft, friendly lines on his skin. His salt-and-pepper hair was pleasantly shaggy—just long enough to pull. In the course of each appearance, he would inevitably look directly at the camera, address Lyd ("my wonderful Linda"), and beg her to come back. "I'm waiting for you in our beautiful home," he would say. "The sunsets have been lovely lately. I haven't watched any of our shows since you left. We've fallen so far behind."

Lyd imagined kissing him. His mustache would tickle, would probably go up her nose. He had an actor's gym-built body, which had never been her type, but there was undeniable appeal in the idea of squeezing his sides, pushing her fingernails into his meat—just deep enough to leave two parallel columns of small, white crescent moons.

The hosts implored their viewers to call the tip line if they knew anything that might help.

News networks ran melancholy trend pieces on the plague of lonely men the false David was doing so much to promote. They interviewed other husbands left behind, sons abandoned in twice-mortgaged homes, brothers forgotten by caretaker sisters. Lyd was skeptical of every story, but she would have freely admitted, if anyone asked, that she could not imagine loving any of these creatures—that she would have left them too.

She could afford to drink while she watched, as the majority of what she saw did not require her attention. The day after the first news segment about her supposed kidnapping of Mott, Lyd had gone to the nearest pharmacy and purchased, in the course of three trips, twenty bottles of gin and ten whiskeys, as well as a bag of five dozen disposable cups. The bottles lay on their sides beneath her bed, stacked in neat pyramids. The cups were in her dresser's top drawer.

Lyd felt that it was now unsafe for her and Mott to be seen together in public. Separately, they were easy to miss; as a pair, they were quite obviously the mother and the kidnapped girl from TV. They stopped leaving the dorm room for frivolous things like coffee and dinner. Instead they ordered in. Meredith helpfully intercepted every meal in the lobby, so that the delivery people never saw Lyd or Mott. All she required in exchange was that she be allowed to eat with them more often—most dinners and many lunches. It wore on Lyd's nerves the way Meredith rarely finished her food.

They stopped visiting the bookstore. Lyd tried to read what she already had. She did so seated at her desk, with one headphone on and one off, so that when the false David was on TV she would hear him and know it was time to take notes. It was hard to concentrate. She read the same paragraphs over and over. None of the books were what she wanted.

Lyd stopped walking Mott to writing class. Meredith chaperoned her instead—she had cheerfully volunteered for the task. "If anyone bad tries to get Mott, I'll use my knife," she said. She probably wouldn't.

When they left the dorm room, Meredith always led, nudging the door open wider for Mott as she passed but not holding it, walking briskly as if she felt Lyd fighting the urge to declare that Mott couldn't leave after all. After the door closed, as the girls walked away, Lyd imagined Meredith slowing to walk beside Mott, very close, down the hall. It was even possible that they held hands. Lyd didn't want to know. It was childish, but she felt so jealous. It should be *her* walking Mott to the class.

When Mott came back, she had to let Lyd hold her close and look at her a little while. It was a new rule.

. . . . .

When she was in middle and high school, Lyd listened to her best-of Cyndi Lauper album so often that she could hear "Girls Just Want to Have Fun" beginning to end whenever she wanted. All she had to do was not concentrate on anything else. It was there for her over breakfast, on the school bus, in any class that didn't hold her interest, at the dinner table, and while she made her way (haltingly, and with some effort) toward sleep.

In her last six months alive, Lyd didn't think about the song once. That part of her mind was now devoted to simulating David—predicting his movements, hungers, and whims. When she failed to concentrate on anything else, she saw him in his home, eating from a bag of baby spinach with his hands, or watching classic *Cheers* episodes, or rolling a joint, or searching for her, always encircled by a thick ring of smoke.

She imagined him having the idea of the false David. He would have been watching TV when it happened, perhaps a late-night talk show, pretending that he was the interview subject, thinking of what he would say if he had the chance. In addition to the spiritual implications of quantum physics, his ideas about love, and the importance of feeling good all the time, he would have talked about Lyd and how much he missed her. But he wasn't allowed to be on TV. Not being seen was part of his job.

A false David would be different. He could be on the news without any problems.

Lyd imagined him flipping through books of actors' headshots, searching for a man who had the perfect look to make her feel like an idiot child: someone manly and dependable, sexy and paternal, stern and sweet and soft and patient.

After the first broadcast, there would have been a flurry of activity as he prepared for Lyd and Mott's incipient arrival—party supplies purchased, paper plates and fancy whiskey, cake mix, corn chips and candy, fruit punch, whatever was still in stock at the grocery store nearest his home. He would have searched the house for his missing guitar. He would have told everyone how much he looked forward to having her back, and how it had been his decision to split in the first place. They would laugh at him behind his back, and he would see as much with his cameras, but he wouldn't know how to stop.

As it became clear that the plan was not going to work quickly, as the first week passed and the tip line received only useless calls, mostly from other men searching for their own escaped wives, David would get that old sinking feeling. He would spend more time asleep, though rarely in his bed. He would get so high that hours of his memory never had the chance to form. He would record long, weepy dictations for whoever had replaced her in the role of typist, would eat and drink the things he had purchased for her welcome-home party, and this would make him feel like shit. He wouldn't bathe unless he had to, wouldn't care for himself, wouldn't see any point. He would work, and he would search for her, and he would wait, and want, and though his hope of finding her would slowly wither, his desire never would. She imagined him in his kitchen, scrambling eggs, hands shaking. She imagined him in his office, looking at pictures of women. She imagined him looking at old, embarrassing pictures of her body, and him all shivering with a hatred that he would call lust.

. . . . .

On the last day of July, Lyd and Mott woke to the sound of rain coming down like a hammer. They went to the dorm lobby and microwaved four leftover pizza slices: one for Lyd, two for Mott, and one for Meredith. They would leave the latter on Meredith's desk, for her to find if she came in. Presently she was elsewhere—Lyd chose to imagine her trapped under the partial shelter of a tree, afraid to face the full downpour unprotected, and so being slowly drenched instead.

As they watched the last plate turn, Mott asked a question that Lyd had been dreading.

"You said Dad hired that man to talk about us on TV. You said that it's his way of trying to make us come home. But why does he have to do something so weird? If he can get a person on TV, then why doesn't he go on himself and just talk to us?"

The microwave sounded. Lyd extracted Mott's slices and checked with her fingers to be sure that the cheese would not burn her.

"He's afraid," said Lyd. "If he came out and said what he wants, then we could reject him. This way we can't hurt his feelings."

"I see," said Mott. They went back to their room and ate pizza for breakfast. Mott tried to work on her book. Lyd lay in bed and brewed a headache. Hours passed.

"Okay," said Mott, resuming their previous conversation as if it had never been dropped. "But how come the fake Dad calls us by names that aren't ours?"

"Your father doesn't call people what they like to be called. He calls them whatever he wants. It makes him feel like he's in charge."

"I see," said Mott. She returned to her novel. They didn't bother with lunch. Lyd dozed and woke and poured some whiskey. The rain had not abated even slightly. She looked out their little window; the streets that she could see flowed like rivers. A red cooler drifted by on the water, and so did a recycling bin, and so did clothes that looked like bodies, or possibly those were bodies.

"Okay," said Mott, who was sitting in her bed, holding *Little Women* in her lap. "But won't people recognize your pictures? You were a pretty famous writer once. Won't they say, 'I know who that is, and her name is not Linda Gravel'?"

Lyd couldn't hold back her laughter. "Oh honey. That's sweet. But nobody knows who I am anymore, and barely anybody ever did. Come here and let me kiss your cheeks."

"I think I should skip class today," said Mott. She presented her cheeks.

"You're right. I'm sure it's canceled for the weather anyway."

They watched a TV movie, then another. When the night grew cold, they shared a blanket. At some point the rain did stop. It would be days before that water fully drained. There would be stories on the news about some people lost in the course of the storm, but there would be no estimated numbers. No one was all that worried.

. . . . .

The next morning, Mott asked if she could go to the restroom alone. Lyd said no she could not. They went together, occupied adjacent stalls, though Lyd did not have to go.

"I was wondering," said Mott. "Does Dad know where we are?"

Lyd sighed. "He hasn't known since California."

"You said you sent him a note that explained."

"I lied to him. I promised that we would come home if he waited. Then, once I'd pulled enough money from our account, I did my best to hide us. He's using that liar on the TV because he doesn't know how to find us."

"It feels like you lied to me too."

"Not directly. I would agree I've been dishonest. There are things that I can tell you as your mother and other things I can't. Trust me when I say that David is a bad man, and if we lived with him he would hurt me, diminish me, and diminish you too."

Mott slapped her stall's toilet paper roll in frustration. It lowered a long strand of itself to the floor, where it coiled and piled. "What can you tell me to prove that he's bad?"

"I'm not sure. Some of it is too yucky. Give me until the end of the day."

Mott tapped her untied tennis shoes on the floor. "Mom," she said. "I have to poop, okay? Can you please get out of earshot? Go watch the door or something. You're killing me here."

Lyd flushed her own toilet, which she hadn't used, and washed her hands so Mott would do the same. She stepped outside and waited.

Soon Meredith took Mott to class.

If Lyd's task for the day's remainder was memory, then she

shouldn't drink. She did anyway, mixing gin and instant lemonade. She hunched over her notepad, listing candidate memories as she recalled them: shopping list, broken door, broken cup, restaurant fight, overdraft fee, police intervention, broken television, email snooping, jealous fit, stolen bank card, vegan phase. She couldn't tell Mott about the night that ended their marriage. What she needed was to find another story that clearly implied David's capacity for doing harm—a way of telling Mott he was an abuser and a rapist without making her think too much about abuse or rape.

The false David was making another TV appearance, this time as one segment in a two-hour special on people searching for people they loved. It occurred to Lyd for the first time how happy this actor must be: the past several weeks almost certainly represented more combined airtime than he had managed in his entire career to that point—had he been successful, ergo recognizable, David never would have used him. This perhaps explained the manic, gleeful undertones in his performance, which Lyd had previously taken for malice. He wasn't a sadist. He was only glad to finally be seen. Lyd was overcome with pity. She thought how lucky she was to have been recognized, however fleetingly, for her work. Most people were never admired by anyone else, never praised for anything they made or did or were. This would be the liar's only moment in the sun.

"Linda can be very absentminded," he said. "Margot isn't safe with her alone. One time about eight years ago—Margot would have been five—we took our daughter to the art museum. They had a special exhibit by this big-time woman artist, Jenny Saville, who paints these massive, naked ladies." The TV showed a painting of a woman's back, wide and fat and blotchy. Lyd didn't recognize the image, though she'd seen others like it before. "Linda thought it would be enriching for Margot to see them. Now as far as I know she was sober that day. But she had this tendency to get totally absorbed by any halfway decent painting. She would start out twenty feet away, far enough back to see these big canvases, but then she would lean forward to see better. And her balance would shift, you see, so she would take a step forward. And then she would notice some new detail, and lean farther forward, and this would mean she had to take another step. And it would go on like this until she was basically nose-deep in the paint."

He sipped a bottled water. "So maybe it was my mistake, but after half an hour of this I went to the restroom for maybe two minutes. When I came out I found Linda inching toward this picture of a naked mother on a stool, holding her naked kids. I asked Linda where our daughter was. I said, 'Where's Margot?' And Linda looked at me, and she said, 'Who's Margot?'"

The interviewer inhaled sharply. The false David turned his gaze to the camera. "Of course our Margot was in the next exhibit, looking at glass sculptures, and Linda would say that she always knew. But I never believed it. So I need to find them as soon as I can. I love her more than words can say, but I learned long ago that Linda's not responsible for everything she does."

The actor settled back in his chair and fought to keep from smiling. He was so proud of his performance—of the range and reality he brought to his role.

- - - - -

Dinner that night was fried rice and egg drop soup. Mott might have told Meredith she expected to have a serious conversation with Lyd—Meredith didn't even hint about staying to eat.

"I've decided what I should tell you," said Lyd, "to prove I'm right about your dad."

Lyd told the story the actor had told, correcting the facts where he was mistaken. Mott had been seven, not five. The painting Lyd had found so fascinating did not depict a mother and her children on a stool but a woman alone on a chair. Lyd was never too close to the canvas. She had known where Mott was the whole time. David had been in the bathroom for more than two minutes before his return, had been useless all day, straying constantly to study anything that caught his eye, so that Lyd felt solely responsible for their daughter, and that was one more reason why she would never have lost Mott, because she knew she couldn't count on him to help. And furthermore (she said, distantly aware that her voice was rising), when she said "Who's Mott?" that was clearly a joke. She was being clever and self-deprecating by implicitly admitting that maybe she had spaced out for a moment and forgotten where she was. The woman in the painting looked so sad. And this had been when Mott was still too young to talk about art or interesting things, so it was only natural that Lyd's attention would drift from her occasionally in a building full of overwhelming artifacts made to fascinate, *but regardless*, the point was David knew she was joking when she said "Who's Mott." He pretended not to know. He'd seen a weakness in her. She was afraid of being a bad mother, was insecure about the idea that loving art too much might cause her to neglect Mott. That had been the subject of her joke. And the joke had been—"Like any of its kind between any husband and wife!" said Lyd, all but shouting—a request for reassurance, which he coldly denied, and twisted and wielded against her, quoting her to herself for year upon year—"Who's Mott?"—never forgetting, never admitting that he understood, that he knew Lyd loved their daughter more than anything on Earth.

"I feel like there's something I'm missing," said Mott. "Some of this story seems kind of mean to me, so maybe that's distracting me from the point that you're trying to make."

"I'm not saying he was always a bad father," said Lyd. "I'm saying that he was a terrible husband. You need to understand that marriage isn't about being kind. It's a step beyond kindness. It requires constant, active mercy." She tried to make her hands speak. "But your father couldn't handle that. He held everything against me, saw everything, recorded it all. He was never merciful with me."

While her mother spoke, Mott made a game of bending her plastic spoon's handle as far as she could without making it snap.

"You look like you have a question," said Lyd.

"I'm just wondering." Mott broke the spoon. "Were you ever merciful with him?"

Lyd wanted to say, *More times than I can tell you.*

She wanted to explain that living with David was managing him all the time, was endlessly holding back. It was letting him hurt her. It was willing forgiveness. It was sparing his feelings at all costs, always being gentle. It was the nicest thing she'd ever done, and she would never have the energy again, and if they had to live together she would definitely kill him.

What Lyd actually said was this: "You don't know anything about it, Mott. With any luck, you never will."

AUGUST, DAVID

DAVID WOKE IN HIS OFFICE. HIS CHAIR TURNED IN SLOW CIRCLES; THE world was revolving around him again. He put his foot down, made the world stop. The nearest screen showed the actor who played him on TV. The video, which he did not remember opening, was paused on a frame that happened to make the actor look one modicum less handsome.

A manila folder slid into the room through the gap under his door, pushed by someone on the other side. He glanced at the relevant video feed, saw Alex walking away, Laverne the dog beside him, rubbing her flank against his thigh. There was a pink sticky note on the front of the folder: *You asked me to remind you that we have to be at your other office before 2 PM.*

David pocketed the note and opened the folder. Alex had typed his latest dictation:

> Good morning, kiddo. Is it morning for you when you listen to this? Can you see the sun rising? I hope so. I have a camera on the roof so I can always watch the sky.

First I want to work on the next script for David. It should be a video package about him searching for "Linda" in all their old haunts. We see him driving down a Virginia highway, listening to country music. Voice-over: "I wake up alone every day. Most of the time I stay home, waiting for her to come back, but sometimes I go out and look for her." David parks across the street from a bar, goes inside, sits down in a booth, orders whiskey on rocks. It's a nice place but basically empty. He's isolated from everyone else, even though there's nothing wrong with him. "Linda loved this place," he says. "It's a short walk from our old apartment." The waitress is beautiful. He glances at her longingly, repeatedly.

The dictation went on like this for twelve pages. None of it was useable. None of it would work.

David glanced at his cameras to see if the path to his bedroom and bathroom was clear. He didn't want to talk with anyone. Several young, beautiful people sat in various rooms, drinking Everclear and grape Kool-Aid, playing solitaire games on their phones, reading trashy paperback books. Some of these children wore rubber animal masks—one girl wore a bear's face, another a horse. This was a recent trend in the house. It seemed to help them manage stress.

There was an opening for David. If he moved decisively, he could get to the shower without being seen.

It might have been as many as five days since he'd last cleaned himself and changed clothes. His teeth and gums hurt. He rinsed and lathered, repeated, and dried. He applied cologne with notes of sandalwood and bourbon. He dressed in houndstooth and tweed, leather elbow patches, argyle socks and moccasin shoes. He looked like a trustworthy person.

He went out to his car and sat in the passenger's seat. He sent his assistant a text: *Alex come drive me to the Arlington office.* A moment later, *Please and thank you.*

The kid came out with Laverne at his side. David noted that she did not strain the leash as Alex guided her to the back seat, opened the door, and gestured for her to climb in.

The roads they drove to Arlington were largely empty; people had mostly stopped going outside when it could possibly be avoided.

Alex parked David's car in a reserved space in front of a squat, orange building barely south of the Potomac, constructed in the shadow of a Marriott hotel. "I didn't think up anything cool or productive for you to do while I work," said David. "Laverne seems to like the car. Maybe drive her around for a while?"

Alex made a little salute and reversed out of the parking space.

David almost lost himself inside the building, this being only his third visit since signing the lease for his office within. There was a nameplate beside the door, yellow printer paper in a cheap wooden frame: "THIN BLUE LINE" LAW ENFORCEMENT OFFICER COUNSELING SERVICES—PETER DOUGLAS WARFORD-CAMPBELL, MS, LPC, ADC-II, CSAC. That was him. For the next two hours and change, he would need to remember to answer to Peter. It had been at least that long since he'd smoked a joint or used anything else to help lighten the load. He was currently at the point, always short-lived, where his sobriety itself felt like a different kind of high—jittery and lightheaded like hunger, like the pleasant part of need.

• • • • •

David's first client arrived at two p.m. sharp. He came in full uniform, cuffs and gun and radio. David welcomed the officer. "Have a seat, Sam. Settle in. How's it been since our last session? Are you sleeping any better?"

Sam sank into the couch. His eyes were too small for his head, but his face was otherwise pleasant, with a lukewarm, open expression and a neat mustache. The way that David had connected with him—the way that he had won Sam as his first patient in this fraudulent practice—was he had placed several ads online, promoting himself as a counselor specializing in helping law enforcement professionals face November and sleep through the night. What David wanted was a more direct form of surveillance, a new way to study the November problem. He couldn't record people's dreams, but a counselor could get unlimited description from his patients, and police were his top priority, as they seemed to have the most ominous dreams.

"I'm tired," said Sam. "I mentioned before, I've been drinking to help get to sleep. This week it stopped working. I get drunk, but I don't get tired."

David scribbled something on his notepad. "Alcohol has a mixed record as a sleep aid," he said. "Do you feel sad this afternoon?"

"I feel burnt out."

"Why do you think that is?" David had never visited with a counselor in his life, but he had eavesdropped on a few sessions, and understood this to be the usual rhythm.

Sam took off his navy-blue ACPD baseball cap and held it in both hands, between his knees, bending the sides of the bill a little bit inward, looking into the hat as if it were a mirror. "I never had a real dream of my own, like a personal goal, so, what I like is protecting other people, so they can do their dreams safely. But lately nobody calls us for help, or if they do, dispatch doesn't tell us. They give us lists of things to seize instead. We go take stuff from people and take it to storage. It's like I'm just a repo man, a jerk with a hand truck and work gloves."

"It sounds like your life isn't what you thought it would be. You're not the person you planned on becoming."

"No," said Sam. "I'm not."

"I'm guessing you feel that you don't have a lot of time left. I don't want to put words in your mouth. Have you been keeping up with your dream journal?"

"I write down as much as I can remember as soon as I wake up."

"That's perfect. I admire your dedication. Most patients struggle with homework."

"Last night's dream was bad, but it's not gonna sound that bad to you. I was in my car alone, parked on the highway, using my radar gun. A voice like my father's came out of my radio. Said something like, 'You have to take care of your people. That's what you're for. They need you at the start, when they're small little babies, and they need you at the end, when it's time to go back to the warmth and the dark.'"

"How did you feel when the voice said that?"

"I felt scared. He said something like, 'All units drive to the big hole A-S-A-P.' But I didn't know where that was. He said, 'It's any place a person can go when they're finished. Any place they can dive in. You have to take care of your people. They're afraid but you've always been brave.' It's like, sometimes when you're in your car alone or your partner is asleep and you're driving or the car is idling and you haven't slept enough, it feels like you could hear anything through the radio, just by accident, like you're going to pick up a weird signal. That's something I worry about."

"You're right that I don't entirely understand why this dream was so unpleasant for you."

Sam put his cap back on. "My dreams keep telling me what I'm for, and there's a part of me that accepts it, like their version of me is more real than mine. I feel myself changing, and what I want changing, a little bit more every night."

"I want you to try embracing this process," said David. "Have you ever heard of lucid dreaming? It's where you take control of your dreams. The first step is you have to recognize that you're dreaming. There are many useful methods you can use to figure this out. Make a habit of pausing to read something every now and then, like documents or the back of a cereal box. When we're in dreams, we can't read, so if you try to read something and find that you can't, this is a sign that you're dreaming."

"Okay," said the officer.

"When you recognize that you're dreaming, this gives you the power to change your dream and make it better suit your personal needs. People often choose to fly. In your case, I would suggest you take the opportunity to demand an explanation from these authority figures who keep bossing you around. What are they doing? What do they want from you really?"

"Will they answer?" said the officer.

"They will if you make them," said David. "Can you commit to really trying?"

"For sure, absolutely. If you think it will help. You're the expert."

"Make sure to journal your results."

They talked about Sam's father for the remainder of their session. David kept himself awake by doodling on his notepad. When they were done, Sam went out to his car, retrieved his dream journal, tore each page that he'd used loose, and handed them to David, who reassured him that everything that they shared with each other was confidential as a matter of law. They scheduled their next appointment. Sam went back on patrol.

Several minutes later, his next patient arrived, sat down on the couch, sank deep into the cushions, and opened a seaweed snack pack. She also wore her uniform. Her name was Rebecca. She was an officer in the DC Metropolitan Police Department, two years on the job and four months pregnant—the baby was due in January of the next year. Like Sam, she struggled with sleep. As had happened during their previous session, she described a dream substantially identical to Sam's.

Rebecca asked what she should do. "It's bad for the baby, me missing sleep."

"When my wife was pregnant with our daughter, she also had terrible dreams," said David. "Life on Earth isn't normal right now, but trust me, you are. Have you heard of lucid dreaming?"

No, she had not. She was willing to try anything.

David collected her dreams from her journal, scheduled their next appointment, and sent her home with a reminder to dream lucidly if she could. He texted Alex: *Please come get me & take me home.*

David ate weed gummies while he waited. The kid showed up

with fast-food combo meals: chicken sandwiches, French fries, diet soda. The car smelled fantastic. They didn't see anyone else on the road their entire drive home. The whole world was for them—more proof that it couldn't be ending. "The signs are everywhere," said David. Alex rolled down the rear passenger-side window. Laverne put her head outside, in the wind, and opened her mouth.

AUGUST, MOTT

THE CHEMISTRY BUILDING BURNED DOWN WITH A SPEED AND VIOlence its arsonists never intended. Their fire started small—a half gallon of gasoline sprinkled here and there on the ground floor, a burning candle overturned—but it proved to be more than enough. The blaze was punctuated by a series of muffled explosions, which shattered the windows and sent lab supplies flying out onto the pavement: sensitive instruments reduced to scrap and wire, melted circuit boards, foaming machines. A plume of black smoke rose from the building's remainder. For the rest of the day, there would be no escaping the stench. Even in the dormitory, Mott's nostrils and throat burned. Her eyes produced a continuous protective film of tears, which, when she was outside with Meredith, walking to her writing class, reacted with the ruined air, becoming a vapor, which rose from her face in white strands. Meredith's eyes made the same kind of steam.

.....

Mott's professor ran her fingers down the surface of a student's writing, smoothing it against her desk. The paper was wrinkled by her heavy application of multiple highlighter markers and red ballpoint pen. It peeled where she touched it the hardest, making white and Day-Glo twists of pulp that recalled the thin, black strings of gunk that Mott could generate by rubbing her hands together when she was sweating.

Teresa asked her students what the story was really about. Nobody volunteered an answer. One of the boys exhaled impatiently. Mott turned and glared at him. "I think it's about fear," said Teresa. "The protagonist understands from the outset that he needs to move in with the father character and nurse him through his decline. The story claims that Matthew is afraid to move home because the father was abusive in his childhood, but the father is hardly a physical threat to our protagonist, who is described as healthy and strong. What scares Matthew is the same thing that frightens the author, I think—the fact, the sight, and the smells of his father's body. The father's physicality is never described. We know his health is failing him, but we never see this in the narration. Turn to page four—"

A boy coughed pointedly, interrupting Mott's professor. "I personally think it's good the way it is," he said.

Teresa adjusted her glasses. "I didn't say it was bad. We're here to help the author."

"The author will be dead in three months," said a girl in the front row.

"We don't have to talk about this anymore," said Teresa. "In fact, we can call it a day."

The students were already zipping their backpacks and passing their marked manuscripts to the author, who thanked everyone for their help. "This is a lot to think about," he said. "I have a call with an agent tomorrow. We're going to discuss whether he would have represented me if there were any time left for him to sell my book."

"Congratulations," said Teresa. "Hypothetical representation is more than I got."

All the students filed out. Mott glimpsed Meredith through the doorway as it swung closed—she was seated on a bench in the hall, flipping through a comic book she'd brought to pass the time.

"God," said Mott. "I'm sorry that they were so rude."

Teresa rolled up her copy of the day's story and slid it inside the cloth grocery bag that carried her things. "That's okay. I don't take it personal. It isn't me they're angry with."

"Did you have time to read my sample?"

"I said I wasn't going to."

"But did you?"

Teresa nodded. "Do you like coffee?"

"I'm not allowed to go there anymore," said Mott. "Mom says it's too public."

"Lyd's probably right to be cautious, the way people are acting. Let's go to my office."

They left the classroom together. Meredith stood from her seat in the hall as they did so, more than ready to leave, tucking her comic book under her arm. Mott asked her to please wait a little bit longer. Meredith sighed, plopped back down, started reading again.

Mott noticed the nameplate on her professor's office door as they passed through it. "Who's Laura Hova?" she said.

"This used to be her office," said Teresa. "She was a great writer. She died recently."

"That's where I recognize her from. I think my mom had a few of her books."

"I would guess that she had all of them. Laura only wrote three."

They sat down on opposite sides of the heavy wooden desk that dominated the office. Teresa laid out the handwritten sample that Mott had prepared and smoothed it with one of her forearms. Mott noted that there were no highlights and no written comments.

"Did you like it?" said Mott.

"I'm not your ideal reader."

"You didn't like it."

"If I didn't, would you quit?"

Mott touched what she had written. "Maybe. The whole premise seems dumb to me now. Did you ever see the movie *Freaky Friday*? I never did, but I guess that it's basically that."

Teresa removed her glasses and set them down on the paper. "I actually think it's very interesting. This is really a horror story about an inversion of the natural order. A mother is supposed to give nourishment to her daughter—to feed her milk, love, and money until the daughter's strong enough to get her own. In your story, the mother extracts from her daughter what nature demands that she give."

"Oh," said Mott. She supposed that was true. "It's not about my mom."

"Of course not. Lyd is a nurturing woman who would do anything within her power to make your life better. We're only talking about the character in your book."

Mott nodded.

"Our parents do sometimes see themselves in our work despite our best efforts. If your mother's going to read this when it's done, you should know the structure of your novel implies the mother character is monstrous. Children your age have a strong sense of justice. There is a feeling in your prose that what the mother does is wrong. But there are many kinds of animals, each with its own nature, including a few who devour their young. Have you considered that the mother may be justified? That she might need more than her daughter does?"

"No," said Mott. "Not really."

"I'm not saying that's the case. But remember that readers are judgmental creatures. They'll take any excuse to stop caring. The cognitive load of empathizing with so many imaginary people is unbearable, especially given the ceaseless demands of the real. Unless you want your readers—your reader, that is—to hate the mother character, you should try to study her more objectively, and withhold your own judgments as much as you can."

Teresa lifted her glasses, breathed moisture onto the lenses, wiped them clean as she could with the hem of her shirt, and slipped them back on. Her eyes seemed to grow.

"Thanks for sharing this with me, and for listening when I teach. I'm not sure how many meetings we have left."

.....

Mott asked Lyd's permission for Meredith to stay through dinner and after. The reason she gave was that she didn't feel she could write more this evening after what had been an emotionally trying class. The reason that she didn't give was that Lyd was clearly drunk, was fixated on her TV, and was consequently unappealing company, as she had been since that first newscast with the fake father. "I promise to write extra tomorrow," said Mott. Lyd said that would be fine.

Meredith asked if they could change the channel to something fun. Lyd said they could not. Meredith asked if she could choose what they ordered for dinner. Lyd said that would be fine. Meredith selected a nominally Greek place that made gyro sandwiches, then complained when the food took too long to arrive, and again when the delivery boy called her to demand that she meet him in the lobby. As they ate, she complained that it was too salty.

"Yeah," said Mott. "You're being kind of rude though."

Meredith winced. "Sorry. I was raised by no-class people with outdoors manners."

Lyd cursed at the TV, which wasn't showing her what she wanted to see. She poured another drink and turned off the screen. She lay down in bed with a book she was trying to read.

Mott asked Meredith why she liked Superman.

"When I was a kid, whenever I tried something new, if I was good at it at all, I used to get really excited, like, 'Maybe this is my superpower. Maybe I'm just naturally great at basketball,' or keyboard or whatever. But it never worked out. Nobody ever asks Superman why he's alive. It's obvious why. He's just totally great. I wish it was obvious for me too."

Mott wanted the same.

It was late. Lyd lay on her side, hugging her book, marking her place in it with a thumb. Her eyes were closed. "Hey," whispered Meredith. "I think she's asleep."

"Yeah," said Mott.

"We should sneak out."

"We already went outside today," said Mott. "It smelled awful."

"Yeah, but that was daytime, and you had permission, so it wasn't a cool adventure. Now it would be."

Mott was surprised by how persuasive she found that line of reasoning.

"Come on," said Meredith. "I wanna show you some stuff."

. . . . .

Meredith played with her knife while they walked. She slashed the night air, showed Mott her best moves, carved quick letter *M*s into each bench they passed. "*M* for Mott and for Meredith. If someone tried to get you, I would cut his throat. Even your weird TV dad if you wanted." She demonstrated how.

The smell of the chemistry building's combustion had diminished, but it wasn't done. The sky was hung with many pink cobwebs—fumes that had condensed into loosely woven pastel threads. Most of the lamps that lit the sidewalks were dead, but those that remained had become blinding balls of light, amplified and distorted by lingering gases.

"There are signs of the apocalypse everywhere if you know how to look," said Meredith. "Polar bears are starving, everybody's starving. Do you want some music?" She fiddled with her phone until it beeped and burped electronic music, then pocketed it and turned up the volume.

"Here's a sign," she said. There was a star-shaped fountain in the shadow of the arts building. The water hadn't run in months. What was there was stagnant rain. "Look how much money's inside." It must have been hundreds of dollars in change. "But nobody wants it."

Mott dipped her hand in the fountain. The water left an oily feeling on her skin. They moved on. The night was colder than it should be.

"Here's another sign," said Meredith. There was a series of bicycle racks on the sidewalk, each overflowing with left-behind bikes, few secured by locks, nearly all of them rusting and ruined: flat wheels, broken chains, stolen seats. Some lay on the ground like dead things. Mott felt an urge to bring another bike and leave it here to comfort the others.

They walked a little farther, held hands as they crossed the street. They turned a corner into a large, open green space of the kind where college students used to lay out on blankets, throw Frisbees, and run lines for auditions. The grass here was thirsty and haggard. There was a bonfire at the center, on a paved circle, burning painfully bright. "Here's another sign," said Meredith. "This one I've never seen before." As they walked a little closer to the fire, three dark smudges at its edge revealed themselves as young women dressed in torn sorority T-shirts and blue jeans streaked with ash. They wore stripes of paint on their cheeks, foreheads, and noses, and their heads were crowned with wreaths of plastic Christmas tree branches and ribbons. The girls were engulfed by the light—as were three figures who stood on the fire's opposite side.

"What're you burning?" said Meredith, gesturing at the blaze with her knife.

"We began with unforgivable texts," said the nearest sorority girl. "Now we're burning anything that we don't love."

"We're letting ourselves be selfish about it," said a shape on the fire's far side. "When we were little girls, there were already millions of books. Soon there's going to be a whole new world. We have to make room for its culture." She took a fat paperback from a canvas tote bag at her feet and tossed it into the fire.

"I feel like this is wrong," said Mott, though it did have a certain appeal.

"Did you burn down the chemistry building?" said Meredith.

The sorority girls glanced at each other. "Yeah," they said. "That was totally us."

"Did you burn the optometry library?"

They nodded. "We just wanted to."

"That's not fair," said Meredith. "You have to leave some for the rest of us."

"We don't have to do anything," said one of the shapes on the fire's far side.

Meredith said, "Whatever, let's go. I don't like these geeks."

"Okay," said Mott, "but wait one minute please. I was just getting warm."

- - - - -

The journey back to the dorm was brief and easy. They had been walking outward in a spiral, so that their return was as simple as turning their backs on the moon and crossing two streets. Meredith declared that she would show Mott her room, which it turned out was on the first floor.

"It's been a little while since I gave it a deep clean," she said. "Don't judge me too hard." She unlocked the door and touched Mott's shoulder, urging her inside.

"Wow," said Mott.

The room was a trailer-trash dragon's hoard. The floor was heaped with distressed jeans, band T-shirts, matchless holiday socks, opened packs of batteries, and still-boxed tennis shoes. The walls were hung with many overlapping posters, which advertised movies from before Mott's time, sports cars, superheroes, and mega-famous athletes even she recognized. On one dresser there were many candy bracelets and necklaces, some half-eaten or reduced to string, others still packaged in plastic bags. There was a microwave on a TV tray. On one desk there were breath mints, chewing gum, a toothbrush, and a stack of Dixie cups. On the other there were many plastic-sleeved comic books, a few romance paperbacks, and several punk-rock box sets, plus a tub of mixed plasticware. There was a bedazzled I HEART NY ball cap Mott had never seen Meredith wear. There was a Superman logo beach towel slung over the back of her chair. One bed was missing. The other was piled with blankets and pillows, all apparently borrowed from other dorm rooms.

Mott had just begun to wade in when Meredith slammed the door closed, stubbing Mott's toe. "Jeez!" said Mott.

Meredith backed away. "Sorry. I got embarrassed. I don't know why I thought you'd like to see that stuff. It's just a bunch of garbage, I guess."

"I mean, it's messy, but so is our room a lot of the time. I liked your posters."

Meredith leaned back against the wall and slid until she was seated. "Thanks. I used to be better with money."

Mott sat against the opposite wall, rubbed her eyes. They were still irritated from the fumes and the fire.

Meredith touched Mott's toe with her own. "Thanks for hanging out with me," she said. "Do you think we're friends yet?"

"We must be by now," said Mott. There was no way around it. A part of her wished that her first real friend could have been someone smarter, prettier, or otherwise more impressive—somebody like her mom. But here Mott was now, in this dormitory hallway, watching Meredith fight tears of gratitude. Everything was so embarrassing. Everything was stupid. Mott had to stay with her friend. They had to bear it together—the shame of Meredith's desperation, and the shame of the miserly way that Mott granted what should have been easy to give.

.....

Mott went back to the room she shared with her mother and opened the door as quietly as she could. The lights were still on. Lyd lay in bed on top of the covers, muttering to her dreams. At first it appeared she had slept the whole time Mott was gone, but there was a new picnic cup on the floor beside her bed, emptied but dewy inside, and the book that she'd been reading was relocated to her desk. She must have woken up while she was alone, then drunk herself to calmness and finally sleep. Tomorrow, she would pretend not to know that Mott had gone outside without permission. She would pretend that she hadn't panicked.

Lyd's muttering grew louder, more insistent. "I understand," she said. "It's no problem. It's fine. I'll start over, I'll go slower. What I wanted to be when I grew up was I wanted to be a musician. I think I wanted to play the piano, I'm sorry I'm not sure. I wanted to be an actress, not in movies but in plays. I practiced making faces in the mirror because I thought that was how people learned. I wanted to be some kind of farmer for a little while. I wanted to own a bookstore or a bar, like Sammy in *Cheers.* I wanted to direct. I'm not sure that I know when I realized I wanted to write. I'm sorry, I'm not sure. I'm really sorry. Maybe I was twelve or so. I read a lot that year. I used to imagine the characters were me and my friends. I'm sorry I don't remember which friends. I didn't really have friends, I was lying. They were just other kids that I wished liked me. But I don't remember which ones." She was crying. "I'm sorry that I don't remember more."

AUGUST, LYD

JUST AS THERE WERE THOSE WHO STAYED ON CAMPUS THROUGH the summer because they had no better ideas for what would likely be their last year alive, there were thousands of students who had enrolled that spring for lack of clear end-of-life plans. Put-upon teenagers accompanied by anxious parents began to move into the dorm where Lyd and Mott lived on August eleventh, one full week early. Mothers brandished letters of acceptance at Meredith like royal writs, demanding preferential treatment for their children—for example, given the smallness of the incoming class, surely they should have their own rooms. Lyd and Mott occasionally encountered these families in the halls, carrying lamps, rugs, beanbags, desktop computers, speaker systems, and bedside tables, arguing about lunch, searching for bathrooms and vending machines. Lyd told Mott to avoid eye contact at all costs. "These people absolutely watch TV," she said. "They've probably seen our faces."

The newcomers arrived in small groups. They started out loud but grew quiet as the work of moving in absorbed them and their energies. The building sublimated every occupant, sorted them into rooms, and forgot them.

Mott continued to attend her writing class, and Meredith continued walking her there. They often laughed in the hallway, both coming and going, but they didn't sneak out at nighttime again. Lyd passed the time that Mott was gone drinking gin-spiked triple-strength lemonade and watching TV, scanning channels for the false David. He wasn't enjoying his role anymore. A regional accent that he had suppressed for the job was creeping back in; he was, it seemed, from New England. When Mott was in the room and working on her novel, Lyd still passed her time with lemonade and news. She wanted to talk but wasn't sure how.

On the afternoon of August eighteenth, the official move-in day, a man in a yellow suit knocked on Lyd and Mott's door. Lyd wouldn't have answered, but she was returning from the restroom and so encountered him in the hallway. She was carrying the biology book that had lain rotting on the shower floor for months, which she'd been compelled to pick up by a mix of nostalgia and pity: soon some responsible person would throw it away. When she saw the man at their door, she hugged the book closer. A sharp mold odor rose. She approached the man, who was now examining a familiar copper-colored key. "Excuse me? Can I help you?"

"It doesn't work," he said. "I'm sure she said this was the room."

"Couldn't be," said Lyd. "This one is my daughter's. Maybe you're next door."

The man glanced up at her for the first time. There may have been a spark of recognition. "My kid's a freshman," he said. "He didn't want to come. He's scared of being alone in November. I told him he's being ridiculous. No offense meant if you're a believer."

"I'm not," said Lyd, who thought he meant God.

"My hobby is investment. Even in a downturn, you hold on to your stocks, because in the long run it tends to pay off. I figure there's no point in betting on death."

Lyd produced a laugh designed to end the conversation.

"Do I know you from somewhere?" asked the man. "I feel like I've seen you before."

"I promise you haven't." Lyd pushed her room key into the doorknob. She wanted him to feel ashamed when it fit perfectly, as his key had not.

"What's your name?"

"I'm a very private person." Lyd opened the door just enough to slip through and closed it hard behind her. Mott peeked out from under her bed, where Lyd had told her to hide if anyone tried to come in. *Don't say anything*, mouthed Lyd. *Stay there.*

The man knocked on their door. "Excuse me miss?" He jostled the knob. "Can we talk for a minute?"

"I don't know who you think I am, why you think I'd want to talk to you, or why you think that you can touch my young daughter's door."

"How old is your daughter? Have you ever been on TV?"

Lyd ignored him. She set the rotten book on her desk.

He knocked three more times before giving up and walking away. The next door opened with one twist of his key. "You were right," he said through the wall the rooms shared. "Our kids are going to be neighbors. Maybe we'll see each other again."

He called his wife and they talked for some time. Lyd put a cup to the wall and listened, but nothing of interest was said. Mott fell asleep under the bed.

.....

When Mott woke and crawled out of her hiding spot, Lyd presented her with a new list of rules written on a notepad.

The first rule was, *We are no longer speaking out loud.* The second one was, *We are no longer leaving the room.* Third, *There are two exceptions to the second rule. We may leave to defecate once per day. We may also leave to shower, but only if it's absolutely necessary to keep our minds working so we can continue our projects. In either case you must ask my permission. I will listen closely to the goings-on in this building, maintaining a detailed activity log, so that I can identify the safest times to leave the room, when other people will not see us. We'll shift our schedule so our waking hours overlap as little as possible with those of the students.*

The fourth rule was, *When Meredith comes over, she must only talk to you using a notepad, like this. She has to be quiet if she wants to be here.* Fifth and finally, *Understand that I am only trying to protect you. That man almost recognized me, I'm sure, and I was so scared. Please write any comments or questions on the following page.*

Lyd handed Mott a pen and knelt on the floor across from her so that their knees were touching. Mott turned the page. She wrote, *Meredith will not like using the pad. It will make her feel stupid.*

Lyd wrote, *I think she will do it if it means that you two can keep talking.*

You're just mad because we're best friends now.

I didn't know you had become so close.

That's not the point. I don't want to live this way.

Lyd wrote, *It's almost September. There's probably just a smidge more than two months left. We won't have to do this for long.*

Mott wrote, *I want to go to my class.*

You need to focus on actual writing. You're as good now as you ever will be.

I don't want to be here anymore if this is what it's like.

There's nowhere else that's any safer. Travel is the most dangerous thing we could do.

Lyd and Mott knelt together, leaning against each other, foreheads and knees touching, holding the notepad between them—a notepad that nobody wrote on for hours thereafter.

.....

Meredith visited three times in the three days that followed. She and Mott communed at the room's center much as Mott and Lyd had done, sharing a notepad, writing things they wished that they could say out loud. Sometimes they would laugh, which wasn't in the spirit of the rules, but Lyd had not explicitly forbade it.

Lyd made a show of never interfering in these conversations. She recused herself by plugging her headphones into her TV, placing her TV on her bed, propping it against the wall, and lying down facing the screen, comforter pulled up around her head to block her peripheral vision. When they were done, Mott would hug Lyd and mouth a silent thank-you, which made Lyd almost glad to have Meredith over.

Lyd woke all three nights with an overfull bladder. Though it caused her considerable guilt, she would go to the restroom (a direct violation of her own rules), bring the notepad, and read what the girls had written. On the first day:

We're not allowed to talk out loud?

We need to not be noticed anymore.

Because of the TV tip line thing?

Because of my dad. The fake one but also the real one. Mom says someone recognized us.

This stinks out loud

I hate it. I want to go away.

Where would you go

I don't know. Mom says there's nowhere safe.

Could I go with you

Maybe, I don't think she'd let you. And then, on the next line, but in Mott's same perfect handwriting, *Would you want to?*

I don't know I'm just joking

And so on. They talked about weird people Meredith had checked into the dorm recently, what Mott would like to eat the next day, and whether there would be more fires.

On the second day:

What would you do right now if it wasn't for Nov. and you knew for sure that you were gonna get to grow up

I would ask for a vacation. I want to be somewhere with nice weather. And I want to write or not write in my book when I want. And I want to rest, and sleep as much as I want, and not be afraid, and play games and have fun, and I want to swim and to float.

I can teach you poker if you want, and then, on the next line, still in Meredith's childish handwriting, *We can play that pretty quiet if we don't get too worked up*

On the third day, Meredith brought a deck of playing cards, in addition to the food that she brought every day (gas station sandwiches, or delivery pizza, or microwave Chinese—whatever it was would be all they ate for twenty-four hours). The notepad conversation was mostly tedious definitions of various poker hands. There was also this:

Mott, I was wondering about your Dad. And then, on the next line, in Meredith's same sloppy handwriting, *say he found you.* And then, on the next line, *like found you here. Because you got recognized*

okay

What do you think would happen

And then an empty line, which seemed to signify Mott thinking.

Mott wrote, *I think that he would try to catch us. And we would try to run away.*

If you do ever run I want to come with you

Okay, we can try

I don't like it here anymore either there's too many people

I'm sorry

I want to swim and float and stuff too

.....

August twenty-first was the first official day of class. Most new students stayed in their rooms. They listened to sad, stupid music with the volume just high enough to be heard through their doors. They texted summer friends that they had left behind. Young couples lay together on their sheets, too warm for sex. Those who had substances used them.

Meredith knocked on Lyd and Mott's door. It was eight in the morning, which was earlier than she had ever visited before. The only thing that kept Lyd from panicking—from assuming it was David come to get them—was that Meredith had devised and adopted, without forewarning or explanation, what she clearly thought of as her personal "secret knock." It began with three quick taps, then there were two slow ones, and then she snapped her fingers, which was perhaps the most secret part. Lyd wordlessly ushered Meredith in. Mott was at her desk writing a letter.

"Hey," whispered Meredith. She glanced over her shoulder as the door closed behind her.

Lyd wrote *Hello* on a notepad and handed it to Meredith, along with a pen.

Sorry, wrote Meredith.

Mott is busy writing a goodbye to her teacher, since she can't go to her class anymore.

Meredith reached for the notepad again, but Lyd kept it close and wrote something more: *Actually, we were hoping you could deliver the letter for us.*

Meredith read the message, took the notepad, and quickly wrote: *YOU HEARD ABOUT THE BUILDING?*

This perplexed and startled Lyd. She wrote, *What building*

The English one. It burned down.

"It burned down?" said Lyd. This was the first time she'd spoken in days.

"That's what I came to tell you. The English building burned down," said Meredith.

Mott stood up so forcefully her chair fell on its side and spun several degrees on the floor.

Meredith said, "I'm sorry. It happened last night. I don't think too many people were hurt. I don't know about your teacher."

Mott grabbed Lyd by her sweater sleeves. "We need to go check on Teresa. She's in that building all the time."

"Okay, yes," said Lyd. "We can risk it."

Mott, who had been wearing cloud-patterned pajamas, was dressed and ready to go in less than three minutes. Lyd, four days deep into her current jeans and wearing an unnecessarily thick flannel shirt, used the time to fill her flask. There was a little funnel that she needed to get the drink inside. No matter how careful she was, some would always drizzle down the side, and she would wipe it dry with her fingers, and any little cuts or abrasions on those fingers would sting. Today there were more than expected.

When they left, Lyd assumed that Meredith would follow, as she generally took any excuse to be with them. Instead she peeled off at the lobby. This was a surprise, but Lyd didn't have time to give it much thought, as Mott was pulling her out the building's front door.

.....

Much of the stone exterior of the building English shared with foreign languages and history still stood, however blackened, ashing on the breeze. Several college kids played Frisbee on the lawn nearby, pausing periodically to gawp at the ruins they were pretending to find unimpressive. Teresa sat on the steps that led to the building's main entrance, reading a novel and sipping a bottle of sugarless tea. As Lyd and Mott approached her, she uncapped a pink highlighter marker and dragged it across the book's interior. Lyd recognized it as her own second novel.

Mott jogged up to Teresa, put a hand on her shoulder. "I'm so glad that you're okay. Were you here for the fire?"

"I was home. I stayed up late last night rereading your mother's book. Hi Lyd."

"Isn't it beautiful?" said Mott.

"I'd like to have her sign it if I could." She offered Lyd her book and highlighter. It would have been rude to refuse.

"I don't know what to put in the inscription," said Lyd.

"Tell me that I should have gotten three books too."

Lyd wrote that on the title page and made her name in pink below. The whole book smelled of marker ink. Lyd flipped through the pages, noting marked passages and stars drawn in the margins.

"I wrote you a letter about how I can't go to your class anymore," said Mott. "But when I heard about the fire I panicked, and then I forgot it at home."

"That's all right," said Teresa. "The building is gone, and no one was coming to class anymore anyway, so I'm going to leave. Assuming I can think of somewhere I want to go. Otherwise I'll kill myself, I haven't decided."

"Oh," said Mott. "It's up to you I guess."

Lyd returned her book. It occurred to her that this would almost certainly be her last-ever signing. "Is your mother still alive?"

"She's in Denver. I don't know if she'd want to see me now though."

"Did you ever tell her that you're a professor?"

Teresa blushed. "I haven't. I do think that she'd like to hear it. When I got my master's degree, she wrote me a letter about how sorry she was for underestimating me—for not believing when I said that I was going to make a career for myself as a writer and teacher. It wasn't that I lacked the talent, she said, it was that the deck was stacked against me. I had too many negatives: my sex, my color, my personal style and manners. She hadn't even believed that my program would let me graduate. Now she believed that I could do anything, could have any career that I wanted, and would soon have my own office, a living wage, and generous health insurance. I spent the next twenty years of my life proving she had been right the first time, but I never wrote her a letter about it. I wanted to make her idea of me true. When it finally happened, when I took Laura's position, it felt like the wrong way, and maybe it was. But I can tell you now that my office was beautiful, it smelled perfect, and I'm so glad that it was mine a little while, insofar as anything is anyone's."

Mott said, "I want to hug you, but it wouldn't be appropriate."

Teresa stood. "A teacher and her student may shake hands."

Lyd had to look away. She pretended the smoke was hurting her eyes and made herself cough. Soon, though, like anything pretended long enough, the tears and the coughing were real.

AUGUST, MOTT

MEREDITH WAS WAITING OUTSIDE THE DORM, CRADLING MOTT'S king fish against her belly, when Lyd and Mott returned. Seeing them, she ran to meet them, holding out the fish. Mott asked her what was wrong.

Meredith had been chewing the chap of her lips. The skin was pink or bloody red. "Your dad is here," she said. "I got your fish." She pushed it forward with both hands.

Mott accepted the king fish, automatically kissing its forehead, and tucked it under her arm. "Thank you."

Lyd grabbed Meredith by the collar of her T-shirt. Meredith reached instinctively for the knife in her pocket—Lyd seized Meredith's wrist and twisted it until she squealed.

"We're going to my car right now," said Lyd. "Don't say anything until we're inside."

"Mom!" said Mott, but she didn't know what to say next. There was no way to get anything that she wanted. It was only going to get worse.

Lyd led Meredith deep into the parking lot, toward the car, tugging her carelessly, squeezing too tight. Meredith did not struggle, focused on staying upright, watching her own feet through downcast eyes, maintaining practiced silence. She had been handled like this before. Mott followed close behind. The car was on the far side of a blue minivan, where it was supposed to be partially hidden from view. Lyd opened a rear door and pushed Meredith inside, diving in after. Mott closed the door that they had used and entered through the front passenger-side door.

"Please be nice," said Mott.

"How do you know it was him?" asked Lyd.

Meredith did not look to Mott for help or comfort—she seemed to feel she was alone. "He asked for you, and he knew your name and Mott's. He said that he was here to take you home." Meredith watched Lyd's face as she spoke, waiting to see how each clause was received before she embarked on the next.

"What did he look like?"

"There were two of them. A young guy with a shaved head and suit and tie, and an older guy, I guess about your age but maybe even older, with a long braid and a kind of nasty-looking beard. He was wearing a suit too, but his shirt was untucked and half-open."

"What did you tell him?" asked Lyd.

"I was scared. I didn't know that he would be like that."

"Does he know where we are?"

"I tried to pretend not to know who he meant. I acted really dumb so he would believe it. And I looked through my binder, and checked all my keys, and I was thinking maybe I could say you were dead or moved out, but he looked so angry, a lot like you now, and all I could think of to say was you did have a room, and I told him which one, and then took him there. He didn't even knock, just made me unlock it, and he was talking to you as I opened the door, and as he checked under the beds, and when he finally believed you weren't there he got in under your covers and talked to himself, and said that he could be patient. So I think that he's still up there waiting. And I didn't ask permission to go. I just left and took Mott's fish."

Mott kissed her king fish again.

Lyd sucked air through her teeth. She sat upright, leaned back from Meredith, opened her flask, took a drink. "So we're fucked then. We can't go back up. He'll be there for hours. Almost all of our money's up there."

"All our books," added Mott.

Meredith pulled herself to a sitting position, her back against the door.

"Oh no," croaked Mott. "My book is up there. All my notepads. They're in our room."

"I don't know what I can do about that," said Lyd. She was crying.

"We have to get it," said Mott.

"If I go there then your father will make me go home."

"You have a gun. Tell him you won't go. I'll tell him too. He's not allowed to kidnap you. You're stronger than him. I can't leave without my book or you'll never get to read it and my life will be ruined and wasted. It was the only thing I wanted. You asked me, and I told you, and you promised I could do it—could write one."

Lyd dried her eyes, wiped her cheeks. "You'll just have to summarize the first part for me. The second half will still be great."

Mott turned around, sank into her seat, and squeezed her king fish so hard it made her feel guilty. "If I lose what I have written of my book just because you're scared to talk to Dad, then I am going to quit for real, and I won't write it, so you'll never get to read it."

There was the sound of Lyd unscrewing her flask's little cap. Mott tried to remember how many times that would make in the last sixty minutes.

"You don't mean to be as cruel as you are right now," said Lyd. "You don't understand how scared I am. You don't know what it would be like living with him in his house. Meredith, get out of the car. We're leaving."

"Ma'am, you've been drinking," said Meredith. "You just drank. You can't drive the way you are right now. You could hurt Mott."

Lyd appeared to notice the flask in her hands for the first time. "Oh God."

"It's okay," said Meredith. "I can help. Give me the keys. Tell me where to go. Put your heads down." She scrambled awkwardly forward into the driver's seat, nearly kicking both Lyd and Mott in the process.

Lyd said, "I'm probably fine to drive. You should go. I can't take care of you both."

"Mom," said Mott, "I want her to come. I don't want to be alone."

Lyd swallowed, shook her head. "You wouldn't be."

Meredith held out her hand for the keys.

Lyd said, "If you go with us, you can't ever come back, and you can't ever leave us. He'd find out somehow; he'd catch you. You'll have to hide until November too."

"That's okay. I believe you that he's dangerous. I want to keep Mott safe."

"Throw your phone out the window if you mean it."

Meredith rolled down the window, kissed her phone on its screen, and tossed it outside. This was the second- or third-coolest thing that Mott had ever seen anyone do. Mott remembered all the treasures Meredith would also be leaving behind in her room.

Lyd gave her the keys. Meredith turned on the car, buckled in, pulled out of their spot. Mott lowered herself to the floorboard and squatted there.

"Goodbye," said Lyd. She lay down across the back seat. "Goodbye to all my liquor, books, and music. Goodbye to most of what's left of our cash. Goodbye to Mott's novel. I'm sorry, Mott. Goodbye, alma mater. Fuck you, David."

Lyd began to open the flask, then twisted its cap closed again without drinking.

Mott raised her head enough to see out the window as Meredith drove around the dorm and swung toward the parking lot's exit.

A young man with a soft body and a shaved head in a black suit stepped out of the front entrance and leaned against the wall, scanning the sidewalk for wives and daughters. This must be the one who worked with her father. He didn't look like anyone to her.

Meredith asked, "Left or right?"

"Left," said Lyd. "Then take the third right. Don't go too slow or fast."

Meredith neglected her signals but was otherwise a skilled and careful driver.

.....

Lyd had planned for David's appearance. About one-fifth of the cash she'd withdrawn was stored in the car, bound by rubber bands, sealed in sandwich baggies, taped to the undersides of the seats. There was one bottle of emergency vodka in the trunk, as well as two boxes of ammo, three dozen summer-warmed water bottles, and eight protein bars. She had even already decided where they would go first and how they would get there. It was a parking ramp at the edge of a swollen brown river, leaning subtly toward the water as if considering a swim.

The air inside the ramp was damp and relatively cool. One in five spaces were full. Lyd directed Meredith to the third level, where they parked on the side overlooking the river. The floor's angle made Mott worry that the car would slide out of the building if she fell asleep.

"We'll spend the day here," said Lyd. "We can leave again when it's darkest." She explained that David had access to satellite cameras. Since he knew about the dorm, he would be able to study old pictures of its parking lot and figure out which car was hers. He might even be able to find footage of the moment where they drove away, and where they went from there. He would also use intersection cameras to track their license plate. This was why her chosen route avoided traffic lights. The garage was important because of its roof. "He can't see us in here."

Mott watched Meredith's face closely, searching for any sign of disbelief.

"Okay," said Meredith. "Makes sense. You want to steal another car and drive that?"

"No, then we'd have a stolen car. The police might come after us too. All we have to do is take somebody's plates, then wait to leave until it's dark. We won't even use our headlights. That way we'll be invisible from above."

Mott said, "If you planned it this far, you should have planned a way to save my book."

Lyd rolled over onto her front, used her arms as a pillow. "I know," she said. "I'm sorry. I never thought he would come while we weren't in the room."

Meredith asked Mott if she would like to explore the garage. "I bet we can find some more signs of the end of the world."

Lyd said that was fine. She was experimenting with not moving.

Many cars in the ramp had been there for months. They had flat tires, broken windows, motionless passengers, or all of the above and more. Two floors up, Mott and Meredith found a foul-smelling camping tent, which had several buckets beside it, many boxes of energy drinks, and a television set connected by jumper cables to a car battery, which Mott suspected would never have worked.

Meredith opened her switchblade and showed it around to the abandoned cars. "Nobody better start nothin' with us. We're tough and mean as hell."

Mott flexed her muscles and laughed.

When they returned to home base, they found Lyd pouring out her emergency vodka bottle. It ran toward the wall overlooking the river and pooled there. She hurled the bottle out of the garage and into the river, perhaps unconsciously imitating what Meredith had done with her phone. She twisted the cap off her flask, took one last swallow, and tossed this as well.

It seemed that nightfall took forever, and even when it came, Lyd said they had to wait longer—until the world turned black.

.....

Lyd asked Meredith to drive again. "I have a terrible headache," she said. "I wouldn't be safe."

She allowed Meredith to use the headlights down to the bottom floor of the parking garage, which was illuminated solely by the abandoned attendant's booth at the exit. When Meredith switched off the headlights, most things in the world disappeared. The only other light was the pinkness of the sky itself, a reflection of the still-bright city.

The barrier arm at the exit was broken—someone had already forced their way through.

Lyd sat in the back seat, unbuckled so she could move freely and play lookout while Meredith wormed her way out of town. Mott wanted to hold someone's hand. Lyd had spent the past several hours studying a road atlas, memorizing the route they would take. They paused at each intersection and checked in all directions. Lyd avoided every stoplight that she could—cursing herself whenever they encountered one where she had expected a stop sign.

In this dark, every stray glint and glimmer demanded attention, no matter how small or how far. Not only streetlights, but the puddles that snagged their reflections. Stoplights and storefronts. Any lit window. Any TV in any home properly angled. Far-off cars. Wet pavement. Side-view mirrors. What the clouds had left bare of the moon. Mott felt as if she, the car, and everyone inside were falling upward. The determined calm of her mother's voice only furthered this sensation; when Lyd said "left" with such cold certainty, and all the little lights outside appeared to turn arbitrarily on their separate axes, it seemed impossible that anyone controlled anything. Surely the world did whatever it wanted.

As they neared the city's edge, they passed a home with two police cars and a moving truck parked at the curb. The cars were flashing their lights, smearing the street red and blue. A family bound by plastic zip ties around their wrists and ankles sat or lay down on their front lawn and watched the police carry stainless steel appliances, leather furniture, and other major purchases out of their home and load them into the truck, which would carry them to the infinite landfill-like lot where repossessions languished. A cop with a clipboard watched also, checking off items as they passed. Meredith drove steady. She held her breath too.

. . . . .

Mott, Lyd, and Meredith slept through the morning, parked at the edge of the lot of a Royse City convenience store. It should have been a three-hour journey, but the way that they drove it took five. Mott woke first. She wanted to wake Meredith for company, but this seemed inconsiderate, and furthermore perhaps impossible to manage without also waking Lyd, with whom she was still angry. So she waited.

"I decided to do it when I was fourteen," said Meredith, who appeared to still be sleeping. "But I was so small then. I wasn't just skinny, like now, but short too. Even with my knife, I could barely reach his throat. And Mom had such thick arms. I wasn't going to try anything if I wasn't sure it would work."

Now Lyd spoke, also asleep: "I didn't like parties, but I liked the feeling of being a person who went to parties. We would smoke and talk for hours. I didn't know yet that everything I said had been said better before by somebody smarter than me. It was so easy to talk then. I used to tell people I loved them just to make them feel happy. That was easy too."

Now Meredith spoke over Lyd: "I just honestly don't like kissing. Everything else is okay. People think you're bad or mean or weird if you don't want to kiss but you do want to do other stuff. It's not fair. It was my car. I bought the gas."

"I kept up with my homework pretty well," said Lyd. "Sometimes I forgot a small assignment, but the teachers always gave me an A anyway, because they knew I deserved it."

"I used to choke my boyfriend for practice."

"On the first day of class, I thought Laura was the best person I would ever know."

"But I'm basically a coward."

"I wanted to be just like her."

"I felt like I was no one."

"Afterward I followed her to her office."

"I don't know."

"She had a shelf that was nothing but copies of her own three books."

"I'm sorry."

"I said, 'You must be really proud.'"

"I don't remember."

"She said, 'Proud, but not happy.'"

"I'm sorry."

"Never happy."

AUGUST, LYD

LYD WOKE TO THE UNFORTUNATE DISCOVERY THAT THE CAR WAS not moving. The girls were perched cross-legged in the front seats, foreheads nearly touching, each holding a hand of five playing cards. Both tilted their hands so the other could see what they had. "Remember that three of a kind beats a pair, no matter what they are," said Meredith. "So you have your pair of aces, which is fine, but I have three fives. The fives take the pot, if we had one."

"So I wouldn't want to bet on that," said Mott.

"Right. You'd wanna fold."

"Where are we?" said Lyd. "Why'd we stop?" They were in a strip mall parking lot. There was a hearing aid store, a temp agency, a place that sold coffee and wine. One of the storefront windows was broken, entirely gone. Lyd's head felt like it had a hole in it too.

Meredith collected Mott's cards and shuffled them into the deck with her own. She said, "I had to stop because I don't know where we're going. You told me to take Exit 116, and I did, but I didn't know what to do after that, so I took the next off ramp I saw, and that's where we are. Wherever this is."

"Okay, so let's get back on the road. I'll tell you what to do next."

"Maybe you could tell us where we're going," said Meredith. "Then, if you need to sleep more, I could navigate for myself."

"I want to surprise Mott again. It was so much fun last time."

Meredith snorted. "No one actually likes surprises."

"Maybe you can give us a clue?" said Mott.

Lyd rubbed her aching head. "Let's try this. Our destination appears in my second book."

Mott sighed. "That would be a good excuse to read your book again, but we don't have a copy anymore. We left it in our room." Along with Mott's notepads.

"It's in the acknowledgments," said Lyd. "I bet you can remember."

Once they were back on the road, Mott recited Lyd's acknowledgments to herself until it put her to sleep. This left Lyd and Meredith alone in the car. They found they had nothing to say to each other. Meredith turned on the radio and tuned it to the clearest station she could find. "I hate country," she said, but left it on anyway.

"Keep the volume low," whispered Lyd. "Don't wake Mott."

Meredith turned it down until it was all but inaudible, but didn't turn it off, which felt like she must be making a point, but Lyd couldn't imagine what that point would be.

A road sign warned them of reduced speeds and road construction. Another sign on the horizon, a blinking arrow, signaled that the left lane would soon close. Then the traffic cones came into view. There were hundreds—the tall, skinny kind, with yellow reflectors fastened to their top ends. Almost all of these were fallen, overturned by other cars. Meredith tapped the brakes, carefully avoiding as many cones as she could.

Mott shifted in her seat, lolled her head to the other side. "I don't know," she murmured. "I don't remember. I was a baby. I'm sorry that I don't remember. I was stupid when I was little. I didn't know how to read. I wouldn't eat anything healthy. I fell down all the time."

Whatever the road crew had planned to do here, all they'd accomplished was ruin. Heavy machines languished on the median, where the tall grass slowly engulfed them.

"She used to quiz me when I finished a book," said Mott. "Who were the characters? What were the themes? I gave bad answers. She said I wasn't really reading, I was just looking at the pages. I cried because she was right. When I answered her questions correctly three books in a row, she stopped asking. And I was glad, because after she asked me her questions, if I answered wrong, I would remember that forever—what she'd asked, what I'd said, and all my mistakes. But if I got a question right, I forgot it instantly, and everything I'd said, and everything about the book, because I didn't need to know it anymore."

Meredith glanced over at Lyd inquisitively—who was the "she" that Mott was describing? Lyd shrugged as if to say, *Of course it's me.*

Later, when Mott woke, she declared that she knew where they were going. "I remembered! In your acknowledgments you mentioned Aunt Emily and Uncle Eugene. You thanked them for letting you borrow their 'wonderful and very peaceful cabin.' We're going to Michigan." As an aside to Meredith, she added: "They're not actually my aunt and uncle. We just call them that."

"That's right!" said Lyd. "Good guess. It's a great place to finish a novel and wait for November."

"Sounds nice," said Meredith. "Do they have cable TV?"

"They did before. Can I drive? I'm getting sleepy again."

They pulled over on the shoulder. Mott stayed in the back seat with Meredith.

"I thought you would sit up front with me," said Lyd. "But that's okay too, if you want."

Meredith and Mott resumed reviewing the rules of poker.

. . . . .

The last time Lyd went to the cabin, David drove her there. That meant they listened to his music and she slept through most of the ride.

David woke her five times, each one to see a tree. He would say, "You have to see this, honey. It's so old."

Or, "There's a beautiful grandmother here."

Or, "You can use this one in your book."

He would go around to her side and help her out of the car. They were parked just off the highway or they were on a narrow gravel road, or they were deep inside a wilderness or they were standing in a stranger's yard. He was holding her warm hand in his cold one.

He would ask what kind of tree it was. She didn't know about trees. Sometimes she felt he only asked her things she couldn't know. Sometimes she liked his pretty eyes.

"Isn't it something? Look at the bark. I love the way it sort of . . . puckers?"

She said that he loved anything that puckered.

"See that nest? It's a family."

It was hard to tell at this angle, but she believed the nest was empty.

The sun was streaming through the leaves and making dapple shadows on his face. Or the sun was gone down and the only lights left were those they brought with them, the car's.

If it was midday then they were in the stranger's yard and the stranger was there also, at the summit of his sloping driveway, washing the pavement with a hose, his thumb pressed against the opening to raise the pressure. Mulch chips and loose concrete pebbles rolled down with the water.

"How long has this tree been here?" said David.

The stranger said he didn't know. It came with the house. The lawn couldn't get enough light because of its shadow. It was hell to keep the grass healthy.

"No kidding. I'm sure that you could never cut it down, though. It's far too beautiful."

At night, in the woods, David pressed his ear to the trunk. "A stunning creature." He kissed it.

When they arrived at the cabin, Lyd asked David to stay in the car. She didn't want him coming in. He said that hurt his feelings. He said he wanted to stay with her at least through the night. "I already feel completely at home here," he said. "If you'd like I can show you around. Do you hear that stream? That's my favorite one. Let's go find it, I can show it to you."

As she and Mott and Meredith neared the cabin, Lyd caught herself missing David. It was almost autumn again. Some of the trees were already turning. The road became a dirt path. The air had total clarity. The rocks seemed to glitter. The sun was already setting. The sky was yellow where it could be seen. They came to a clearing.

"Is this the cabin?" said Mott. "It's huge."

In truth it was more like a house. There were, Lyd knew, three bedrooms inside, one office, and a kitchen, as well as a living room, library, and wine cellar. An AC unit attached to the side was audibly running.

Meredith said, "There's somebody's car here already."

"I see it," said Lyd.

"The lights are on inside," said Meredith.

"Yep. We might reasonably conclude that there's at least one person in the cabin."

"Aunt Emily and Uncle Eugene?" said Mott.

"Hope so," said Lyd. She switched off the car. She hadn't considered the possibility that Emily or Eugene might be here, but of course they would be. Anyone would choose to watch the world end from here who knew it existed. Lyd wondered for the first time if David might think the same thing—if he would come here looking for her, or already had. She had assumed it would be empty because it was not, to her thinking, a currently existing place. It belonged to the past, to the time that she had spent there.

Somebody opened the cabin's front door. The light behind them cast their shadow on the dirt outside, which had been trampled bare of any grass or underbrush.

"Is that her?" said Mott.

"Think so," said Lyd. "I can't quite see."

- - - - -

Emily's arms were harder than Lyd remembered. She might have taken up lifting weights since last they'd seen each other. Her face was also leaner—one might say *chiseled*—in a way that Lyd found slightly off-putting.

"It's so good to see you, and such a surprise," said Emily. "How long has it been? Mott, you're looking tremendous."

"Do you mean good, or big?" said Mott.

Emily laughed. "Both. Would you like a hug too?"

"Okay," said Mott.

Emily received Mott warmly. "You used to be so shy."

"I'm still shy sometimes. This is Meredith. We met her at college."

Meredith stood in the room's center, slowly turning. "Shit," she said. "This is awesome."

It was just like Lyd remembered. The kitchen, living room, and dining room were all one large, open space, subdivided by a table, an island, two sofas, end tables, three lamps, and the narrow vinyl strips that covered and tamped down their electric cords to prevent tripping, the floor all hardwood and softly shining. There were many paintings on the walls, all depicting natural subjects, each one its own size, a fragment—a branch or a nest or a rock or a stick bug—which made it difficult to find the windows.

"Meredith is almost eighteen," said Mott.

"My birthday's in three weeks."

"That's exciting," said Emily. "Eugene, do you want to say hello, or are you too busy?"

Eugene was seated in an easy chair in the room's corner, beneath one of the closed and curtained windows, with an open book in his lap. He looked older than Lyd remembered, had not aged as well as Emily. "It's been years," he said. "What a pleasant surprise."

Meredith said, "How much does a place like this cost?"

Lyd glared. "That's rude to ask," said Mott.

"A small fortune," said Emily. "Eugene's grandparents were wealthy. They passed the money on to his father, who saved and grew the wealth, and he passed it on to Eugene, who has squandered his inheritance on gifts for me."

Eugene laughed. "I guess I have."

"Emily, are you Black?" said Meredith. "I only ask 'cause I can't tell."

Emily made an incredulous sound, as if she had unexpectedly discovered something rare and precious. Lyd and Mott both glared this time. Eugene clicked his tongue.

"You would probably say that I'm mixed," said Emily. "I tend to say *biracial*. Thank you for getting that out in the open. It's best to be direct about these things."

"Sorry," said Lyd. "Sometimes she doesn't think before she speaks."

Meredith's face turned a deep red. She tried to hide her shame by closely examining some of the art on the wall.

"That's fine. Where are you all headed?" Emily tucked herself neatly into one side of a love seat and patted the cushion beside her, inviting Lyd to join her and relax.

For the moment, Lyd preferred to stand. "Here," she said. It came out like a belch, all hot and acid-tasting. "We were headed here. It isn't safe for us anywhere else."

Eugene nodded gravely. "These are dark times. Or so I imagine. We don't have TV, or Internet either. There's nothing nourishing in current events." He turned the page. "You're welcome to stay for a while."

"What he means is you're welcome to *stay*, period." Emily patted the love seat again. Lyd acquiesced and curled up beside her. The cushions were so soft they made her feel tired.

"What's for dinner?" said Meredith, who had apparently recovered. "Do you have string cheese?"

Emily said, "Check the fridge. You're welcome to eat whatever you find."

Mott approached the love seat and touched Lyd's arm with both her hands. "Can I see the room where you wrote when you were here before?"

"Of course you can," said Emily. "It hasn't changed at all."

"Never found another use for it," said Eugene. "I told Emily to make it her studio, but she prefers to paint in the room where she sleeps, even though the experts all advise against it."

"Have you been painting?" said Lyd.

Emily wrinkled her nose. "Technically."

"So I can see the room?" said Mott.

"Let's visit with it now," said Emily.

. . . . .

Lyd opened the door. There was only a desk, a window, a power outlet, and an office chair with a disintegrating afghan draped over the back and seat.

"Wow," said Mott. "I love it."

"I love it here too. It helped a lot to be alone. Your father and I were having a bad time."

"Where was I back then?" said Mott.

"I left you with David. I felt bad, but that was the only way I could get anything done."

Mott ventured into the room. She touched the afghan, the desk. "That's okay. I don't really have bad memories of Dad. And while you were here, you wrote a masterpiece."

"I wrote something, anyway."

Emily and Meredith watched from the doorway. The latter was snacking on a handful of lunch meat she'd found.

Mott said, "Aunt Emily? What do you want to definitely do before you die?"

Emily leaned against the door frame. "I'm not sure. I don't want to suffer or feel afraid. I think that I want to relax, be calm, and enjoy what there is to enjoy. And I think I want to paint something nice, a picture I can like without reservations."

"I was going to write a novel," said Mott. "My mom was going to read it and tell me if it was good, and if it was good enough to be published, and if it was then she might have shared it with her editor Gerrard, who might have told me whether he agreed that it could have been a real book if there were enough time. But my dad took the first half away when he almost caught us."

"Oh no. I'm sorry to hear that."

"That's okay. I made a decision. I'm giving up on writing anything before November. There's no point in trying anymore, and I always felt so bad while I was working, like sure that Mom was going to hate it. I'm going to spend the time I have left quietly enjoying nature, which I have never really tried before, and being a generous friend, which I also never tried."

Lyd said, "I would never hate your book. It hurts my feelings that you don't believe me. It makes me feel like you think I'm mean."

"You are a little mean," said Meredith. "Sometimes. You do know that, right?"

Now everybody glared at Meredith. "Oh," she said. "Okay. Got it." She backed away from the room. "I'm gonna go get some more turkey."

Emily said Mott should get a snack too. "Your mother and I will catch up."

"Oh. Oh! Yeah, okay. Thanks for letting us stay here!" She left too. Emily closed the door and took both of Lyd's hands. Emily's eyes were the same as they ever had been.

"You're mad at me," said Lyd.

"I'm confused. It's been years. Why didn't you call first? We would have liked some warning."

"David wants us to come home. We're hiding from him. He almost got us two days ago, and took Mott's book she was writing, and most of my money, and if I used a phone he would catch us for sure, and—"

Emily hugged her again. (She didn't seem to notice Lyd's gun, which was holstered in her waistband as always.) "Honey, I'm so sorry. Say no more. You're welcome to stay with us to the end. Of course you're welcome. And if he comes for you here, if he finds you somehow, we'll deal with him so you don't have to. I'll make him leave or strangle him or something. We won't let him touch you again." She paused. "You're pretty sure he doesn't know you're here?"

"He shouldn't know. I don't think he does. We've tried to be very careful."

"That's good. I'm sure you have. Can I ask who Meredith is?"

"Just Mott's weird friend. Mott wanted her to come along, I'm not even sure why, I should have said no. She's a distraction."

"A little distraction might not be the worst thing," said Emily.

Lyd pushed her face into Emily's hair and started to cry. "I don't want Mott to give up on her book."

Emily rubbed her back. (Lyd shifted carefully to avoid her finding the gun.) "She might change her mind."

"It's so beautiful here. Such a lovely place to write. Such a perfect place for November."

"I'm almost looking forward to it."

"Honestly," said Lyd, "me too."

AUGUST, MOTT

THE NEXT DAY, EMILY GAVE MOTT, LYD, AND MEREDITH WHAT SHE called a partial out-of-doors tour. The air was clear if slightly overwarm, the occasional breeze was refreshing, and the sunlight had a quality that made the world new. Mott savored all the crunch and snap beneath her shoes, the way everything shivered with being alive.

Emily occasionally pointed out a tree that she especially liked ("I tried to paint that one, but it didn't turn out"), a bird's nest, or a deer path, but mostly she and Lyd talked to each other, catching up on what they hadn't shared while they were estranged.

"I haven't talked to much of anyone since the divorce," said Lyd, "except for Mott, and for a little while my editor, back when he still gave a damn. I thought that when I split with David, maybe everything would change for me. I was so young when we got together." She tossed a rock as far into the trees as she could.

"Healing takes as long as it takes," said Emily. She rubbed Lyd's back. "If you needed years to get right with yourself after David, that's okay. If you never really do, that's fine. When somebody loses a leg, we don't judge them for not being able to run anymore. You don't have to get better. You can just be hurt for the rest of your life. Sometimes that's how it goes."

"Maybe," said Lyd. "I feel so pathetic sometimes."

Mott felt glad and calmed and comforted to hear her mother talk to another adult, to hear her supported by somebody else—even at the cost of hearing unlovely things about her father. Meredith sensed that Mott wanted to listen, and so did not speak, holding Mott's hand when Lyd wasn't looking, otherwise eating honeyed almonds from a small sandwich baggie she carried. Once, Mott wordlessly reached for the bag, and Meredith offered it, shaping it in her hand to better open the mouth. Mott took an almond and ate it. Somehow it all felt so easy.

They paused now on the bank of a small lake ringed by tall trees, with a wooden dock extending from its edge. Mott knelt to study her reflection in the water's surface. She was fascinated by how she had changed. Her eyes appeared much wiser now. She looked like a person who had seen some things—the kind of person who might have a book in her.

"Our tour ends here," said Emily. "I remember how much Mott loves swimming. The water is cold, but I like how the trees look reflected on it."

"It's nice and thoughtful of you to bring us here," said Lyd. "Maybe the girls would like to swim now."

"But I don't have either of my suits," said Mott. "I left them in our room in Houston."

"Me too," said Meredith. "I had a red-and-blue tankini."

"That's okay," said Emily. She touched the side of her nose. "It's just us chickens here."

"Huh?" said Meredith.

"She means that we're all girls," said Mott.

"Oh." Meredith flicked something off her finger and into the lake. "Okay, I guess. But no one look at me okay? I get shy if it's a girl because they judge."

"I promise," said Mott.

"Not a problem," said Lyd.

Mott and Meredith undressed with their backs to each other while Lyd and Emily walked the lake's edge, kicking pebbles into the water and watching the ripples. Mott covered her front with her arms. She turned around, saw that Meredith was doing the same. They blushed and looked away from each other. Mott walked to the little dock's end, dipped her toe. "Are there fish?"

"A few," said Emily. "They won't bite."

"Go on," said Lyd. "You'll have fun once you're in."

Meredith loped past Mott and cannonballed into the lake. The scars on Meredith's back, which Mott had only seen hints of before, were bright, long, and livid. Meredith surfaced, shoved her hair out of her face, and shouted, "So cold!"

"Don't worry," said Mott. "I'm coming." She cannonballed also, too close to Meredith; as she kicked back toward the surface, her heel struck her friend's leg twice, and she might have scratched her arm too.

"Jeez kid, be careful!"

"Sorry, sorry."

Lyd and Emily folded Mott and Meredith's clothes and held them in their laps. Mott couldn't hear their conversation anymore, but the tone of it was pleasant, gentle, and steady. Meredith told Mott to lead the way, and always swam behind her from then on, never letting her see her back again for the rest of the day. Whenever Mott glanced at the shore, she found that her mother was already looking at her.

After the swim, though Emily assured them that no one would see if they chose to air-dry as they walked back to the cabin, Meredith put on her clothes, which meant that she soaked them. Mott followed her example. Wet socks were the worst part. Upon returning home, they wrapped themselves in borrowed bathrobes, hung their clothes out to dry on a wire, and ate the best possible meal to have after a swim: several frozen pepperoni pizzas. Mott fell asleep in the love seat, and then again on the couch, this time in her mother's lap, with Emily holding her feet.

.....

In addition to their cabin, Eugene and Emily owned miles of surrounding land, and all the trees and rocks and water thereon, and rights to any minerals beneath, and while they did not own the animals that roamed there, they owned what the animals ate, as well as the animals' homes. They also had several neighbors, whom for the most part they never saw or heard, although they did sometimes find evidence of these other people: discarded plasticware, forgotten empty picnic baskets, or footprints on patches of earth that might plausibly belong to either party. "We all mostly keep to ourselves," said Emily. "We don't like each other."

There were three bedrooms in the cabin. Emily and Eugene slept in the master. Meredith got her own room, which she decorated with found objects, including a Rolling Stones poster from the sleeve of one of Eugene's records, a track-and-field trophy that Emily had won as a girl, and one of Emily's paintings, which depicted the silhouette of a dead rabbit hanging from an eagle's talons. Mott shared the remaining bedroom with her mother. The mattress, a queen, was just large enough for them to avoid touching, and this might be advisable given the heat, but most nights Lyd insisted on holding Mott or at least her arm.

On their second day in the cabin, Mott visited Eugene's library, which was the opposite of carefully curated. Biographies of history's great men were mixed with books about the lives of wild animals, which were shelved beside those about the import of certain early tanks, which were placed beneath a row of pamphlets on mysticism, cattycorner from the collected works of Charles Dickens, which were framed by a half-swallowed bottle of bourbon and three copies of *Uncle Tom's Cabin*, each in its own unique state of repair. Above those, a hardback 1990 library edition of *Little Women*, its cover a scaly burnt-orange fabric with the title inscribed in a typewriter font. Mott borrowed the book, found her approximate page, and started from there.

On the third day, Lyd sighted Mott with the book. She remarked on how this proved that it was possible to take up a novel again in its middle. "I bet that you could do the same with yours," she said. "Even if you don't remember where you were. You could start with the next chapter's beginning. Say you were at thirty thousand words. All you'd need to do is write thirty thousand more, and then you'd have a novel, even if it wasn't all in hand. You could describe the rest for me. I would listen closely."

But the truth was that Mott felt badly disoriented in *Little Women*, remembered few details of what she had already read, and had just decided that she would start over. Mott closed the book. She said, "I'm going outside. It's a lovely day."

The day was always lovely. Emily and Meredith joined Mott for frequent nature walks. Lyd sometimes came along, maintaining a respectful distance from the other three as if she had imposed on them. Emily carried an instant-print camera, which she used at most twice per outing. Mott suspected she was running low on film. Emily captured small birds, frothy water, rotting trees, large rocks and their shadows. "Maybe I can paint this," she would say. But if she did try, then Mott never saw the results. Soon Meredith asked if she could have a camera of her own. Emily hesitated briefly before going to her room and fetching a similar model in white.

It never occurred to Meredith that she should conserve film. Her favorite part of taking pictures was cupping her hand beneath the camera's print slot, waiting to see what it would extrude. She photographed animal scat, the tree line, her own image on the water, Mott (who resented being asked to pose), Emily (who flexed her biceps playfully), and the cars that sat outside the cabin, waiting to be needed. She tried a few times to photograph Lyd, but Lyd always covered her face with her hands. "No thank you," she said. "Really, no thanks."

A teenage boy made weekly grocery deliveries based on a list they'd provided the previous week. He drove a pickup truck and wore work boots, jean shorts, and tank tops. He reiterated during each delivery that payments were always in cash. "No checks," he would say. "I don't have an account."

He always had new, small cuts and bruises on his face, which went unacknowledged and unexplained. Meredith said he was cute.

Everyone was allowed to put whatever they wanted on the list, though not all that was asked for would come. Meredith requested string cheese and beef sticks and did receive both. Mott asked for grape soda, got strawberry instead. Lyd asked for Ibuprofen, received aspirin. Everyone wanted frozen pepperoni pizza, and they did receive it. Nobody asked for tuna, but four cans appeared in each week's delivery and on every receipt. Emily explained that she used to ask about these cans, and that every time the delivery boy had claimed it was a mistake, and he had seemed sincere, and she had asked him not to bring any more, seeing as tuna was not and never had been on her list. "I gave up on asking," she said. Tuna was the cost of doing business. They stacked the cans in a cupboard with no other food.

- - - - -

On their fourth day at the cabin, with less than one week remaining in August and then two months until the world's end, Lyd took Mott aside to share some good news. "I wanted you to be the first to know. I'm not going to drink anymore. I haven't since Houston."

"That's great," said Mott. "But I understand if you need to. I don't want you to have headaches or feel sad."

"I need to be here for you. I know that you're suffering. I know that you're lonely when I'm not all there."

"I'm less lonely now."

"I'm glad. Will you please do me a favor? If you see me start to slip, like pouring a drink, or asking someone else to get me one, please tell me so I can stop."

"I will, but you don't have to be perfect. I've been thinking. Maybe you're like the people who just sleep all the time since the November dream. We're all trying our best and we all have our limits. Maybe drinking's what you do instead of sleeping."

Lyd pushed her thumbs into the corners of her eyes. "Mott, my beautiful daughter, you are the only person I've ever known in this life who is actually sometimes too kind."

On the evening of their eighth day at the cabin, Lyd went to bed early, explaining that she had a headache. Mott and Meredith played cards with Emily. They gambled with buttons from Emily's late mother's collection, which were valued according to their subjective beauty as judged by each gambler, so that a vintage pearl-and-rhinestone flower button might be worth twice as much after Meredith (who found it very beautiful) won it from Emily (who said it was tacky). It occurred to Mott immediately that such a system was prone to corruption, but she was determined to be honest about her own feelings regarding each button, resisting the urge to inflate their value by professing false esteem. Meredith was slower on the uptake, but once she understood her opportunity she did take full advantage, cooing with delight at every won hobnail, shank, and fish eye, claiming that each was her favorite, so that she need only risk throwing one in the pot for every three buttons that Mott and Emily ventured. Then, at the end of the game, Meredith asked Emily if they would be allowed to keep their winnings.

Emily hesitated only briefly before saying that yes, the girls could keep her mother's buttons. "Why not? Maybe I can win them back before November."

When Lyd was not present, Emily drank wine. (Eugene drank beer and whiskey regardless, without comment or apology.) Meredith drank also. She tended to stay up too late or fall asleep too early, and often in the living room. That evening she collapsed on the love seat, abandoning a half-drunk glass of rosé, which Emily finished herself, explaining that wine stains were hell to get out. Emily circled the room, gathering empty glasses, and brought them to the sink. One glass fell from her hand and broke on the floor.

"Shoot. Don't get up, Mott. We don't want you cutting your feet." She went to find the broom. Mott sat in a soft chair and studied her button winnings. They looked like licorice candy and smelled like a jewelry box.

Emily swept the glass fragments into a central pile. "Tell me if you see any I miss."

"Mm-hmm," said Mott. But Emily didn't miss anything. She nudged the glass into a dustpan, emptied the fragments into an empty box of instant Spanish rice. This would stop them from cutting through the garbage bag. She threw the box away and sat down on the couch, where she had a sketch pad and pencil waiting. Mott pretended not to notice as Emily began to draw her.

"It was nice to see you visit the writing room, the day you arrived," said Emily. "You looked happy there."

"It was cool. I used to think about this place when I was little, imagine what it must be like. Honestly I pictured something a lot smaller."

Emily smiled. She flipped her sketch pad's page, started over. "Everybody did. Even me. When Eugene brought me here the first time, I was so angry with him."

Mott said, "I always wished that I could come here and write something too."

"For what it's worth, the whole reason your mom came here the first time was so she could work alone. If you liked the writing room with all of us in it, I think you'd like it better on your own." She sighed, made several frustrated scribbles, closed her sketch pad, set it down on her lap, then changed her mind and tucked it underneath the couch cushion. "Someday I will accept that I can't draw people for shit," she said. "Sorry for swearing."

. . . . .

Sometimes, when everything lined up just right, Mott and Meredith snuck out to sleep beneath the sky. Their friendship had so little time to justify what it had accidentally become—the final, culminating project of their lives. These nights were opportunities to make some quick progress.

Before sneaking out, Mott had to ensure that Lyd would sleep deeply, which often meant working extra hard to provide her with daughterly love and comfort while she was awake. On the night of the first late excursion, Mott rubbed her mother's back in soothing circles for more than an hour as Lyd tearfully apologized for abandoning Mott's book in Houston, for failing her as a mother, for not encouraging her to write more before the dream about November, and other things that Mott didn't fully understand. Mott told Lyd to breathe, and told her that it was okay, and told her to sleep, till Lyd closed her eyes. Eventually, Mott stopped rubbing her back. A little bit later, Mott tried rolling out of bed. When Lyd did not stir, Mott crept silently out of the room. Meredith was waiting for her in the writing room with two sleeping bags and backpacks full of useful things. Mott put on her jeans and shoes. They went together to the living room, where Uncle Eugene chewed his book. There was a zebra on the cover. Were he reading alphabetically, Eugene would be nearing the end.

"Have fun, girls," he said. "Be safe."

"I'll kill you if you tell Lyd," joked Meredith. Eugene didn't think it was funny.

Mott laughed enough for both of them. "Me too!"

The night was colder than she'd hoped. "Emily showed me a favorite spot," said Meredith.

They came to five clustered trees, whose trunks began quite close and grew apart, leaning outward like the five points of a star. This did not prevent their branches from mingling, weaving a loose canopy. The girls laid out their sleeping bags and crawled inside, zipping them up to their chins. Their noses itched.

Meredith said, "It's so quiet you can hear your own heart."

Mott listened.

"You can't hear it if I'm talking," said Meredith.

Mott laughed. "Maybe you should shut up then."

The girls weren't touching but they weren't avoiding touching. They said whatever they were thinking whenever they thought it.

Mott said, "I feel like I broke my mom's heart when I gave up on my writing."

"I feel like your mom is a little bit crazy."

"If she could stand to talk to Dad, I'd still have my book. Did your parents get along?"

"Before I killed them? Not really. Mom hated Dad and he hated her too. But neither one would leave the house, and neither could handle the mortgage alone, so they had to stay together. They took it out on me and my sister. I put up with it long as I could. I didn't like living with them, but I didn't know what I could do. I used to tell myself, 'Someday you'll get your GED and move out, get your own place, and you'll have a good time, you'll make new friends who love you, and you'll never see these people anymore.' But I couldn't say that after the November dream. If I wanted anything to ever happen, I had to get out of that house. That's why I killed them. Nobody believes that I did because everybody thinks I'm weak or not smart. But that's the whole point of having a knife. You don't have to be strong."

It was true that Mott had decided she didn't believe Meredith. She would never be friends with someone who could do a thing like that, so it stood to reason that Meredith couldn't have done it.

"Anyway," said Mott.

"I'm glad I met you."

"I'm glad too."

The next morning, they left their sleeping bags and backpacks in a pile behind the cabin. They pretended to return from an early nature walk. Lyd didn't ask many questions. She was reading one of Eugene's history books at the table, eating instant oatmeal with peach chunks and brown sugar. She made a point of telling Mott that her orange juice was not a screwdriver.

Emily collected the backpacks and sleeping bags, snuck them back to her room, and tucked them underneath the bed, where she was sure that Lyd would never see.

Mott went into the writing room, closed the door, and locked it.

There were notepads in the desk's middle drawer. There were some ballpoint pens. It was good to be alone here, just as Emily said.

SEPTEMBER, DAVID

IN THE CABIN'S COMFORT AND SECLUSION, LYD FORGOT FOR HOURS at a time to imagine what David was doing. It was difficult now to simulate his behavior—she had never known him to want something for so long without getting it. How would he spend what was left of his life if he never found her again? Could weed fill that many hours? She didn't know what he would do because none of it would matter, not even to him.

Lyd felt that she did know what he was eating. September would be a month of seeds, berries, nuts, gummi bears, and fruit snacks: small, manageable things he could ingest one piece at a time. He would never be full. The hunger would be a comfort. Food was something else to want—something he could always have.

.....

David searched the Internet for his wife's name. He ate a Craisin.

He read an old review of her debut novel. She was a startling new talent.

He read an essay that Lyd wrote about the year she spent watching her mother die. He found it excessively cold and cerebral. She didn't mention him once.

He ate a pineapple gummi bear. He rolled a joint. He looked at her social media profile. The last update was a photo of a broken cork on a paper plate. Thirteen people had "liked" the photo, including him. He read everything she'd ever posted. It wasn't much. She never mentioned him by name.

He logged into her account. No new private messages. He ate a sunflower seed.

He posted a photograph to her feed. It was the two of them when they were young. He was looking at her the way he used to. She was looking at the camera—smiling, yes, but also waiting for it to stop. This was when she liked to wear star earrings.

David wrote a post in her name. *I'm sorry,* it said. *Sometimes I don't know what I want.*

David checked in on his people. The unmarried Laotian journalist was cutting all his stories out of physical editions of his LA-based newspaper, preparing to make a collage. The teenage boy was drawing on himself again—this time flowers. When he was done he would post pictures of himself online and see if anyone liked him. The Chinese engineer was posting on an Internet forum devoted to the Zodiac killer. The unmarried Muslim man was texting with a woman on his dating app. They lived in the same city—the Muslim and the woman—but neither was willing to risk leaving home for a meeting. Today they were discussing hobbies.

David ate a Craisin. His assistant nudged a folder into the office under the door. Inside there were three pages of dictation:

> Alex. Thank you for everything that you do for me. I don't say that enough. [Coughing sounds.] There isn't much a man can depend on anymore. Not his wife. Not his children. There is no sense of obligation. Thank you for letting me hold

> your hand on our flight back from Houston. I know that was outside your comfort zone.

The assistant had written a note at the end of the paragraph, blue ink: *That's okay.*

His dictation continued:

> I'll leave my car keys in the kitchen, taped to the bottom of the silverware tray, so you can get them for yourself whenever you hear this. We need groceries again. They go through it all so quickly. We need eggs, milk, butter, like four kinds of bread, cream cheese, bagels,

The full list was two pages long. There were blue check marks beside each item, which David took to mean the food was bought. He glanced at the video feed that showed the kitchen, where someone he didn't recognize was making cookies, thumbing dough off a wooden spoon and onto a pan lined with parchment paper.

> Bring me the receipt afterward so I can see what it cost and I'll write you a check. Maybe we should take up a collection from the folks who live here. I'm a fortunate man, but I'm not made of money. Try passing a hat, see if you can get some cash.

There was a note beside this too, the same blue ink: *Sorry David. Honestly, I didn't try. The receipt is enclosed.*

- - - - -

David didn't know where to look for his girls anymore. He had checked every available camera in Houston, tried every functioning satellite with a relevant orbit. There were images of Lyd living with Mott, video clips of them drinking coffee outside or walking together, and these were thrilling to find in their own right, and he felt glad that his girls had enjoyed their time on campus, but he was sad he hadn't been there too, and none of this brought him any closer to finding them now.

He didn't know where to look for November ideas anymore either. Playing therapist with the police had seemed so promising at first. Clearly something was sending them nocturnal transmissions, but as they learned to dream lucidly per David's instructions, their dreams had become strange in a different, less useable way.

David reviewed what Sam had written in his most recent dream journal:

I finally did what you said. I was dreaming, and in the dream we were taking a test, an exam for getting promoted, but I couldn't read the questions, because the words kept changing. I thought, "Okay, this is it. I guess I'm dreaming." And I don't know if I did something wrong, but it didn't get more vivid or real like you said. Instead everything became more fake. I realized I was in a room I never saw before, it was sort of like a high school classroom, with those chair desks, and there were other guys hunched over, taking their tests, but they weren't ever turning the page. They just kept reading and marking the same questions. Everything felt like cardboard, even the people, and there weren't any lights on, but I could still see. There was a man at the head of the room, standing at the blackboard, he asked me to sit down. I brought my test to him to look at it, it was hard to remember I knew I was dreaming. I asked him what was wrong with my test. He said that there was nothing wrong. "It's just measuring who you are. We need to understand your progress." And I said, "This is a dream." And he said, "That's okay. You're in the right place." And I said, "This test isn't working." And he said, "It's a formative experience. The intent is pedagogical. Sit down." And I said, "I won't sit down, this is my dream." I had to look up "pedagogical" just now to spell it.

I decided I was going to fly away. There were rafters like a church, but there was no ceiling, and I thought I would be in the sky, but I was in space. I didn't want to be there. I couldn't see Earth anywhere, or anything I recognized, there were only stars in all colors, which looked cold. I couldn't find a way home. I floated through space for what felt like days, and I felt so embarrassed, like when you're lost in a big city where everybody else but you knows how to get around, and I didn't wake up until almost noon.

Are we sure this is a good idea? That it's going to help?

David wasn't sure that anything would help. He ate a Craisin.

He reviewed Rebecca's latest dream journal entry. She had dreamed essentially the same thing. It made him sick how similar they were—as if they were or were becoming the same person. Maybe the worst thing about surveillance was discovering that so many people had no actual secrets worth learning, were in fact exactly what they seemed to be from the outside. He didn't want to see them anymore. He didn't want to leave his house ever again, or at least until after the world didn't end. He resolved that his counselor alter ego—Peter Douglas Warford-Campbell, MS, LPC, ADC-II, CSAC—would fall ill, email all his patients, and instruct them to send him their continuing dream journals digitally while he received inpatient treatment at the Mayo Clinic. He would tell them not to expect many replies: *If I have a useful insight, I may call. Please continue the work in my absence. Take care of yourselves.*

He turned off his screens and slept without dreaming.

.....

Perhaps spurred by the recent influx of groceries, the beautiful young people threw their largest party yet. They invited dozens of friends, filling every floor of the house beyond its capacity, even the underutilized third. Rubber animal masks proliferated among them. Many wore the faces of cats, mandrills, pigeons, wolves, panda bears, and more. It might have been that these made them feel safe. It might have been that they were intended to make other people feel the way that those who wore them felt—as if anything might happen. They played music David didn't recognize, different songs in different rooms, with the volume turned up so everyone heard all of them. David hid in his office, watching through his screens as the celebrants danced in the hallways, used every bed, snapped glow sticks in half, shot bottle rockets out of open windows, consumed everything in the fridge, ate candy necklaces, moshed in the kitchen, and drooled and bled and came on one another.

David checked the camera that watched the backyard. The night was dark and clear. Alex was outside with Laverne, holding her by a leash, walking her along the fence. She kept glancing nervously at the house. She lifted her leg, but nothing came out. The assistant murmured calming things. He would give her as long as she needed.

David told himself the party would end quickly. It lasted two full days. He only left his office when he had to use the bathroom. There were always pills and powders on the sink and on the toilet's water tank, some familiar and some strange, all of which he sampled freely. He couldn't believe that the black pills he swallowed were working as intended. It seemed to him that no one would ever choose to feel this on purpose.

The children spilled wine everywhere, ashed cigarettes into cups, burned brownies, broke cabinet doors off their hinges, put a fist-sized hole in a second-floor wall, bled on sheets, lost three teeth, dropped crumbs, and left behind clothes, and left behind many small speakers with dead batteries. They drew on the walls and tracked mud in the house.

When the visitors were gone, the third floor was mostly empty again, and David felt more sober than he had in years, and older, and more alone.

He tossed all the little speakers in a trash bag and left them on the curb, where it might be weeks before the garbage people bothered visiting again. Alex swept and scrubbed the floor all afternoon. He ruined seven sponges, slicked every tile with bubbling spirals of soap foam. He worked on his knees, whisper-chanting "kill me kill me kill me kill me" to the rhythm of his work. Did he realize he was doing that?

.....

David woke in his own bed the next day. He had slept fourteen hours, and he felt exhausted. For the first time in months, he remembered his dream.

In the dream, he was a visitor in another man's home. It must have been years since he'd done that—since he'd visited with anyone. The home was vast, with ceilings as high as the nave of a church. On one wall there was a painting of the Earth as seen from orbit, and on another wall a painting of the solar system as seen from above, and on another wall a painting of God. Fruit trees grew in large planters in the corners of rooms.

The owner, a trustworthy man, was tuning his guitar. David wandered toward the sound. He found the man seated by the dining room table, guitar in his lap, twisting the tuning pegs, experimentally plucking the strings. No matter what he tried, the note he produced was the same.

The trustworthy man gestured for David to sit. David respected his host. There was a pitcher of clear, cold mountain water on the table, as well as two glasses. The man set his guitar aside, scooted closer, poured each glass full of water, and handed one to David. The glass looked empty.

"Why don't you sleep?" said the trustworthy man.

"I sleep," said David. He drank from the glass.

"You need to sleep. You need to dream. We don't know anything about you."

"I do dream," said David. "All the time I dream." He was desperate to be believed.

"We've been making a sculpture of you."

This was an incredible compliment. They were saying he was a good man if they were putting him in art.

"Would you like to see it?"

The trustworthy man removed a marble penis from his pocket and set it on the table. Not even the scrotum—only the shaft, terminating with a puckered foreskin on one end, the other end flat where it would attach to the hips. David wanted to hold it, but he felt that he wasn't allowed. "This is you," said the trustworthy man. "It's all we have. It isn't enough. We can't save you like this."

"I'm sorry," said David. He meant it.

"We need you to dream."

He promised he would, and in that moment he did believe he was being sincere. There was a tape recorder between them, next to the pitcher of water. The man refreshed their glasses. He asked David what his life was like growing up.

"I don't like to talk about it," said David, leaning toward the recorder. He talked about it for hours. The trustworthy man gave him more and more water.

SEPTEMBER, LYD

LYD DIDN'T PLAN TO SNEAK INTO EMILY'S ROOM. THE WAY IT HAPpened was that Mott, Meredith, and Emily went out for a hike. They invited her to come along, but she had a terrible headache, and furthermore believed she was not wanted—that Mott and Meredith were content as a pair, and that Emily found her draining and obnoxious. "Don't worry about me," she said. "Have fun." But she did want them to worry a little, to fuss over her for a minute, and ask if there was anything they could do. Instead they hugged her and went outside, discussing something they had seen the last time they went for a walk without Lyd: something that they called "the toad," but which Lyd did not believe was really a toad, based on the way that they said it, though she couldn't imagine what else it would be. The door seemed to slam shut behind them.

Eugene had fallen asleep in his library, reading from a book about the history of war on horseback, so now Lyd was alone. She could do anything she wanted so long as it was quiet and so long as it wasn't alcohol. Her head hurt too much to read. She poured herself a wineglass full of water and paced the cabin. She found that the door to the master bedroom had been left slightly open—the first time she'd seen it that way since arriving. Lyd had slept there when she stayed at the cabin before, whenever she wasn't working on her book or cooking her one daily meal. She found that she wanted to go inside.

Instead she started with Meredith's room. She reasoned that this would be more productive—she could check if Mott's friend was getting into anything she shouldn't. At least that was a reason for snooping.

Meredith's room was disappointingly identical to Lyd and Mott's. The bedding was the same. There was nothing underneath the bed. There was a small dresser, but the drawers were almost entirely empty. There were two empty wine bottles in the corner. There was a shoebox on the floor. Inside, on one end, all the buttons Meredith had won from Emily. On the other end, all her instant-print photographs. These were smeared, blurry, and full of Meredith's fingers, but Lyd found a few she could like: portraits of Mott, who smiled in a warm, unguarded way Lyd hadn't seen in some time. Lyd pocketed one of these, thought better, and put it back, now a little scuffed.

Lyd confirmed that Eugene was still asleep in his library, that everyone else was still in the woods, and returned to Emily's room. It was larger than Lyd remembered, with a series of picture windows that hadn't been there the last time she visited, all veiled by heavy brown drapes. There was a writing desk against the wall, loaded down with many books and several notepads. There were empty beer and wine bottles lined up against the wall beneath those windows, and crumpled paper pieces here and there under the desk. Across the room, on the opposite side of the king-sized bed, there was an easel with a bare canvas mounted on it, and beside that a stool, and on the stool a palette smeared with drying acrylics, and all around the easel and the stool there were variously colored dots on the hardwood floor. There were many other canvases in all sizes, some stacked and others propped against them, blank or hiding their faces if they were not blank. There were photos of people that Lyd didn't know on the walls, and there were none of her. There was a particular frame, the biggest in the room by far, hung in the corner, draped with a white sheet.

Lyd saw dry, dead leaves on the floor beside Eugene and Emily's bed. She got down on her knees and pulled out two wadded sleeping bags from under the bed. More leaves clung to both. Lyd understood immediately that the sleeping bags must be Mott and Meredith's, that they had been used during nighttime excursions, that these secret outings were why Mott seemed so tired all the time of late, and that Emily must also know, and Eugene must also know, and everyone had known but her. One hundred other details fell into place. Lyd understood that she was alone.

There had been dark pictures in Meredith's pile, which Lyd had interpreted as misfires, photos taken in the pocket or with the lens covered. She understood now that these were actually nighttime pictures. If Lyd looked at them again, knowing what she now knew, she might see her daughter's eyes.

Lyd shoved the sleeping bags back under the bed. She paced the cabin until she was so angry that she couldn't help falling asleep on the couch. She had tried not to hate Meredith. Honestly, she had tried.

.....

Lyd woke up still angry. Meredith stood over her, camera in hand. A square photograph lolled out of the slot on its front, not yet developed, currently gray.

"Nobody said you could do that," said Lyd, rubbing her eyes.

"You have to show me that when it's done," said Mott.

Meredith said, "Hey Lyd, you're kinda pretty for a mom." She gave Mott the picture.

"You don't have to tell people if they're attractive," said Mott. "They might not like it."

"Everyone likes compliments," said Meredith. "Even me!"

"We had a good walk," said Mott. "Did you have a nice, restful morning?"

Lyd rubbed her eyes. "Where's Emily?"

"Still outside," said Meredith.

"She's sketching," added Mott, who was watching color slowly infiltrate the photo of Lyd.

"We're going to my room," said Meredith. "We're making a collage out of my pictures."

Lyd went outside. Emily was sitting in a patch of soft grass, biting her lip, making fussy adjustments to a pencil drawing. Lyd peered over her shoulder. The drawing's subject was a person's open hand holding a flat, round rock. Lyd wanted to confront Emily about helping Meredith and Mott sneak out, but she found she had no words that were adequate to the task. Instead she sat beside her friend in the grass.

"Tomorrow is Meredith's birthday," said Emily. She smudged the pencil rock with her thumb, softening its shadow.

"Time flies," said Lyd. "Seems like just yesterday it was two days until her birthday."

Emily chuckled. "Mott and I have been planning a party. Eugene and I got her some new clothes, so she'll have more than one outfit. I thought we could say they were also from you."

"I don't want you to say that," said Lyd. "I can't help it, I don't like her."

"I know you don't," said Emily. "Believe me, I get it. She can be very teenage sometimes."

"I feel like Mott deserves a better friend."

Emily glanced up from her drawing. "Maybe. But Meredith's the friend she has. You should try not to be jealous. Mott loves you more than anyone or anything."

Lyd squeezed the highest point on the bridge of her own nose. "I want a drink so bad."

"Not to be an enabler, but it's okay if that's what you need."

Lyd shook her head. Emily set down her sketch pad and pencil, withdrew a small plastic bottle from her pocket—white, unlabeled, with a green childproof cap.

"I always carry these pills." She shook the bottle, made it rattle. "Eugene has some too. They make us feel safe. If things get too bad, in November or before, these mean we can die. Eugene did the research, got them from a doctor we know. It's going to be quick."

Lyd felt a fresh wave of guilt. She should have thought of this already, should have secured the same thing for herself and Mott.

"When I feel scared, I touch this bottle in my pocket. Someday I won't be able to make it all better, but I know that I can stop it getting worse."

Lyd imagined pushing a small, yellow pill past Mott's lips and telling her to swallow. Mott would do it if Lyd said.

"Point being, if you need some wine to get by, I'll pour you a glass. Nobody should blame anyone for needing what they need, and odds are you won't need your liver for long."

"Too kind," said Lyd. Her eyes stung. "Let's stick to water for now."

Emily showed her drawing to Lyd. She flipped to a blank page. She flipped back to the drawing. A flat, round stone in somebody's palm, or white, empty paper. "I'm not sure," said Emily. "Which one's better?"

- - - - -

They spent the next day celebrating Meredith. It began with Emily and Mott singing "Happy Birthday" to her while she ate sugar cereal, which had the unpleasant and likely intended effect of also waking Lyd, who crawled out of her nest of sheets and blankets, wedged her feet into borrowed slippers, and joined the festivities. Emily gave her a party hat.

Mott presented Meredith with a card that she had made herself. On the front there was a pencil tracing of a photograph that Lyd had never seen. In the picture, Mott and Meredith were up a tree—Meredith seated on a low, sturdy branch, feet dangling just beneath the frame, Mott standing barefoot on a higher, thinner branch, leaning against the trunk. Both looked down on the photographer, presumably Emily. In Mott's tracing, the girls' expressions were blank, with small circle eyes and no discernible mouths. Lyd suspected they were smiling. Meredith read the message in the card, wincing repeatedly from the pain of being cared for. Lyd expected her to pass the card around afterward for everyone's enjoyment, but she kept it to herself, slipping it inside its yellow envelope and thanking Mott profusely for her kindness, "even though I'm a dirtbag who used to shake your mom down for cash like some kind of bridge troll."

Mott kissed Meredith's cheek on tiptoes. Meredith blushed and pushed her away.

Emily gave Meredith her first present, a glossy paper bag that said it was from everyone. Inside the bag there were three sheets of blue tissue paper, many loose blue sequins, a pair of black jeans, and a heather gray T-shirt that said *ANGEL* in a white font on the chest. Beneath those was a pack of pastel underwear. Meredith immediately went to the bathroom and washed so she could try her clothes fresh. They fit perfectly. She turned a slow circle, letting Emily peel every label and scissor off each tag. She thanked everyone again. Emily said she was welcome, reminding her to thank Eugene whenever he woke up.

Next, apparently referring to a schedule that she had set with Emily, Mott declared that they would spend two or more hours listening to whatever music Meredith wanted. This was a special treat because Eugene and Lyd tended to monopolize the record player, preferring classic rock or jazz in his case and classical or opera in hers. While Meredith dug through Eugene's valuable collection of rare punk and noise, Emily revealed that she had gift bags for Mott and Lyd as well. "I know it's not your birthdays, but you need clothes too." These also claimed to be from everyone, and each contained an outfit chosen carefully for its recipient, in her correct size and good taste. Lyd repeated Meredith's performance, washing herself before trying her outfit, and then so did Mott.

They ate pretzel sticks and margarita cupcakes for lunch. (Emily promised the latter were nonalcoholic, but Lyd was convinced that she felt a buzzing, which made her want more.) When Eugene woke, everyone shouted "Thank you!" at him. He pretended not to know why, retiring to his library, where nobody would scream.

They played poker variations through the afternoon, gambling with Emily's mother's buttons. Every time somebody won a hand, Emily gave her a present: a new pair of socks, a bra, a winter hat, tights, a bathrobe, and so on, until each had a full week of clothes, including several unnecessities. When the games were done and all the gifts given, Meredith excused herself, went to her room, and returned with her hands in the shape of a bowl, chin trembling, eyes red. She tilted her hands and spilled many shining buttons onto the table. "Sorry. I knew I shouldn't ask for them."

"Of course you shouldn't have," said Lyd.

Meredith clenched her fists. "I said I was sorry. I know it was dumb."

"She didn't force me," said Emily. "Meredith asked nicely, and now she's nicely brought them back. Thank you for taking care of them."

"The fact remains," said Lyd, but she left it at that.

They ate frozen four-meat pizza. Dessert was strawberry cake. There were eighteen burning candles—Meredith counted before blowing them out.

Emily revealed the final gifts. "We know how Mott likes swimming," she said. There was a modest and elegant bathing suit in each bag. "They're the same brand as mine. Now we can all go to the lake without anyone feeling shy." They hadn't gone in since that first time. Meredith always refused.

Mott was practically vibrating with excitement. "Can we go tonight?"

"Of course not," said Lyd. It was already getting dark.

Emily said, "It's probably best to wait for tomorrow."

Mott scowled. "We don't have forever. Can we at least do a sleepover in Meredith's room?"

"You'll only sleep in late tomorrow," said Lyd, "which means less swimming time. But yes, you're allowed." The girls scampered off.

Lyd rubbed the fabric of her new shirt (one of seven) between her fingers. "How much did all this cost?"

Emily smiled, etching lovely, unfamiliar crow's-feet at the corners of her eyes. "It wasn't cheap. We'll probably all be dead in six weeks. It's not a problem."

"It's hard though, letting go of money."

"We've been learning to let go since the dream. The day after it happened, we made donations to all of our causes, the way we always said we would. That was most of it gone. Then, before we moved out here, we bought everything that we could imagine wanting before November. Booze, frozen foods, music, books for Eugene, paint and film for me, and every weird, indulgent purchase that we'd been putting off. I don't display it because I'm ashamed of owning it, but there's a painting by a major American artist, I don't want to say which one, in our bedroom. I keep it under a sheet because otherwise I would never sleep. I always wanted to own something like that. Now we're close to broke, or what feels like broke to me. But all we buy is groceries, electricity, and water. Blowing money is like practicing for dying. I feel a bit more ready every day."

.....

Lyd woke at midnight on the living room couch with a book on her face. She set this one on an end table, atop a stack of several others she had recently begun, which she would also never finish.

The lights were all off, but there was still enough to see by: the glow of the microwave's clock, the stove's clock, the coffee maker's clock and ready light, the light that meant the refrigerator was set to dispense ice cubes, and what the moon sent through the window.

There should be more noise in the cabin. Lyd snapped to a different kind of wakefulness—there should be noise coming from Meredith's room, where Mott was supposed to be sleeping over. Lyd crept down the hall and listened at the door. If they were really there, they would be giggling, whispering secrets, and hushing each other. There was nothing instead.

Lyd ran out the cabin's front door and down the path that led to the lake, only realizing several yards out that she was not wearing shoes. Damp seeped through her socks; mud clung, leaves gathered. Small rocks and twigs worried her feet. The air was mostly insect buzz and rustling branches. The moon was a delicate crescent, bright where it was not occluded. Two young girls were laughing somewhere far away. One shrieked.

Lyd crested a hill overlooking the lake, the water black like oil. There were a few stars in it. The girls were in their swimsuits, were standing at the lake's edge, were dipping their feet. They were lit by a kerosene lantern at rest on the shore. Their clothes and shoes were heaped nearby, weighed down with a small log. Meredith's switchblade would be in her pants pocket.

"God it's cold," said Meredith. Her voice carried well. Lyd drew closer, walking between the trees that lined the widening path that led to the shore, her feet turning blessedly numb.

The scars on Meredith's back shone where they were not covered by her new swimsuit.

"I'll go in if you will," said Mott. "We can do it. Let's be brave together."

They were in up to their knees. Lyd was nearly level with them, hovering at the tree line, planning what she would say when she made herself known. She watched them with one eye, closing the other, pressing that half of her face to a tree trunk to hide it, suppressing her own human symmetry. The girls were in up to their waists. No one could call herself a friend who led a little girl outside into the night and wilderness. No one could call herself a friend who would cause that little girl to swim unsupervised in the cold, dark water, who contrived to be alone with that little girl and a knife, who would separate mother and daughter, so that Mott was there in the lake with her friend, and here was Lyd outside, alone.

They were in up to their armpits now, so far away and so gone. Lyd wondered why she hadn't stopped them yet. She would be within her rights. It wasn't safe. They should wait to swim until tomorrow. Lyd also had a new swimsuit. She would go in too, would protect them. It would be warmer then.

"I think this lake is magic," said Meredith. "I think that when we're here, time is frozen."

"If it's stopped, then how are we moving?"

Now they were only shoulders and heads. Was Lyd ever going to stop them? Would she let them disappear?

"Time is what's frozen. Not us."

Mott said, "That doesn't make sense. Time's just a dimension. When we move through space, we also move through time."

"Don't be a show-off."

"I'm not trying to. Here, I'll explain it to you the way Mom taught me. Say a poem."

"I don't know any poems, just songs."

"Everybody knows one poem," said Mott. Lyd loved her for believing that.

Meredith closed her eyes. As she spoke, she metronomically tilted her head left and right. "Death is nothing at all. It doesn't count. I've only slipped away into the next room. Nothing has happened." Mott swayed in the water, patting its surface with one of her hands to count out a beat: one, two, three, splash.

"Everything remains exactly as it was. Call me by that old familiar name. Speak of me in the way that you do. Let my name be said as much as it was before, without a shadow of a ghost on it. Life means what it meant. It's the same and the same. I am waiting for you, waiting just a little while, somewhere very near, somewhere just around the corner. Nothing is lost. We're gonna laugh when we meet again."

Meredith opened her eyes and waited for Mott to say something. For an instant, maybe longer, Lyd saw what charmed her daughter in this girl.

"That was lovely," said Mott.

"I think I got most of it wrong. It's by a dude named Henry Holland or something."

"When you spoke, you felt your lips and tongue move." Mott closed the gap between them and touched Meredith's face, as Lyd had touched hers when she explained. "That was movement through space. You swayed with each beat of the poem. That was movement through space. But also, time passed while you spoke. That's movement through time."

"Okay. I get it."

"It's the same way when you breathe or your heart beats. So if time stopped, we'd die, or rather stop living."

"You'll see," said Meredith. "When we leave the lake, when we go back to the cabin, it's gonna be like we were only gone a minute. We can visit with your mom, and Emily and Eugene, and take food and stuff from the kitchen. We can spend a day with them sometimes, and make the time before November last for years. We'll be best friends, and have lots of fun, and we can swim all the time and get old together."

"At some point my mom wouldn't recognize me anymore," said Mott.

The girls were swimming away. Lyd could imagine their bodies under the surface, how they kicked and pushed. Meredith asked, "How long would it take you to hate me?"

"I wouldn't hate you ever," said Mott.

"You already hate me sometimes now. Like when I talk about the wrong things, or use the wrong word, or mispronounce. Or when I take too long with my turn in a game. Or when I'm drinking wine. Or sometimes even when I thought that we were having fun."

"I don't think that's true," said Mott, unpersuasive, voice shaking from the cold.

"You don't have to lie. One thing I know that you don't 'cause I'm older than you is it's okay to hate the people you love sometimes, as long as you don't rub their noses in it."

"I don't hate you, Meredith. I only get embarrassed."

Meredith lunged sideways toward Mott, bumping their heads together, and kissed her cheek. "It's nice of you to lie to me that way."

They were so small now. Lyd could only find them by the way the moon and stars rippled in their wake. "Let's run away together," said Meredith's voice.

Mott's voice laughed.

"I'm not kidding. Soon, whenever you're ready, let's go."

Mott didn't say anything.

"Emily will take care of your mom. They'll be fine without us. But we would be so happy. I'm so much better off without my parents. You'd be much better off without yours."

Lyd couldn't find them at all now.

"My mom would die," said Mott's voice.

"Maybe she'd write something about you."

"No. She would just die."

Lyd waited until the girls came back to the shore. As they rose from the water, becoming real again in the glow of their kerosene lantern, Lyd turned her back and started home. Clearly, they would survive the walk without her.

SEPTEMBER, MOTT

SEPTEMBER WAS HALF-OVER. THE WORLD HAD SIX WEEKS TO BE what it was.

A young girl woke early. For a moment, she was no one, blank and calm and only breathing. For lack of a better idea, she opened her eyes. This was her first mistake of the day. Mott remembered her name, what kind of person she was, and what would happen in November. Her mother lay beside her, speaking to her dreams.

"I used to say that it would be enough if I could have one book, just one, and if it had a nice cover, and if I looked smart and pretty in my author photo, and if there were even one good review, and just one letter from a reader who loved it, that would be enough, and I wouldn't need more. And I worked so hard, and never felt sure it would happen, and when I sold the book it didn't feel real, so I wasn't glad yet, but I assumed that I would be glad once it was in my hands and the world, and I would be happy, or happy enough, and it would be enough. So that took a year. Then it was in my hands, and there was one good review, and then there were more. I gave interviews and did readings. People wrote me nice letters. It should have been more than enough, but I wasn't happy. I never felt like it was real, like I had achieved anything. My life was still the same thing every day. I decided I needed to write and publish another. I had to show I could do it again."

Mott nudged her mother. "You're talking again."

Lyd opened her eyes just the slightest, then closed them tighter. She groaned and rubbed her own face. "Sorry, I keep having the same dream. There's a man with a notebook. We're on his deck outside his home, sitting at this plastic table. There's a pitcher of lemonade between us. He keeps topping up my glass, and I always thank him, but I never drink. He asks me things about my life. Whatever I say, he writes it down."

"Weird," said Mott. She had been having similar dreams. Hers took place in a small pizza parlor, in a booth with soft benches. The man across the table was the owner. She colored on her paper place mat (solving mazes, searching for words in a pizza-themed jumble, connecting some dots) while he asked about her life and she told him everything she could remember.

"I'm drenched," said Lyd. She dried her forehead with the blanket. "I feel disgusting."

"Sorry for waking you up. You can go back to sleep."

"What was I saying? Did I say something weird?"

"Nothing weird," said Mott. "It's fine."

Lyd rolled onto her side, facing the wall, taking most of the covers. Mott rubbed Lyd's back until she was sure she had gone back to sleep.

Mott slid out of bed, dressed in fresh clothes, and left as quietly as she could.

Nobody was up yet. Mott took two cans of sugar soda to the writing room. She slid out the desk's middle drawer, took out her current yellow legal pad, flipped back to the page where she had left off, and wrote a sentence she had planned the day before.

Two hours later, when she was done, Mott waited to leave the room till she heard her mother's voice, so she knew where Lyd was, and knew that she could go without it being seen where she had been.

Mott joined her mother at the breakfast table. Lyd was eating leftover grilled cheese. "Did you enjoy your walk?" she asked, apparently assuming Mott had been outside.

"Mm-hmm."

"Is it nice out?"

"Yes."

"Glad to hear it. You're welcome to have some grilled cheese by the way. How's Meredith?" Lyd studied Mott's face.

Mott didn't know what Lyd wanted. "Pretty much the same as ever?"

Lyd nodded as if Mott had said something profound—something that she would be mulling for days—and sipped from her orange juice. "That's our Meredith," she said. "I wish you would write."

.....

In Mott's novel, the mother graduated high school. She was not the valedictorian—her GPA had been too badly injured by the daughter when the daughter still wore her own body. Regardless, she was asked to give a speech. This was the latest in a long string of honors. She had been judged most likely to succeed, most likely to be famous, most likely to break a world record, most likely to get married first. She had appeared more than practically anyone else in the yearbook, had been gifted half a dozen bouquets in the last year alone, had been viciously bullied and smeared by the girl who was previously the most popular in their class, had dated the handsomest boys, had been voted prom queen. She had won the all-grades lip-synch contest, had sold the most cookies, had resuscitated a previously disfavored haircut—the bob—and built a circle of friends who swore they would care for one another forever, and probably meant it, despite their many differences in wealth, ability, beauty, and kindness.

The mother's graduation speech was about the necessity of hope in a world that often felt used up. She argued that her graduating class had a unique opportunity to rejuvenate each thing they touched—every institution, workplace, and home. They might be the first generation to live authentically. No one could stop them if they didn't want to be stopped. They were all beautiful, even the ones who were not beautiful in any conventional sense—indeed, especially them, because they had a special inner light.

And the daughter attended graduation in the mother's body. And she wore a hat to hide her thinning hair. And she wrapped herself in a polka-dot dress that she believed was slimming. And she chewed Tums to help her ulcer. And she regretted her decision not to use sunblock, as the light was relentless, and she feared she would develop melanoma. And the triteness of her mother's speech as spoken by her body made her squirm. To see herself speak these words was like watching a recording that had been made without her permission, only the recording was somehow also a fraud, in that it showed her doing things that she would never really do, indeed could not imagine doing.

The mother wore the daughter's body to college.

The daughter had planned to attend a state school of moderate standards and status. The mother had applied only to selective private universities with low student-to-instructor ratios. She qualified for some financial aid, but not enough. The daughter took out loans to cover the difference. The mother said it would be fine. "When we switch back," she said, "I'll have the debt and you'll have the degree."

But if they lived so far apart, how could they possibly switch back? And if they didn't, how would the daughter pay these bills? And assuming that the mother did learn something useful, if she leveraged this to get a good-paying or otherwise prestigious job, then how could the daughter learn what she needed to know to do the job when she resumed her body? Wouldn't she be fired? Wouldn't everyone hate her?

The daughter spent her weekends searching for the magic cave where they had swapped.

She called the mother every Thursday. Any more often than that and she would have seemed clingy. The mother assured her that everything would be fine. She said, "Unlike you, I've done this before."

"And now I never will," said the daughter.

She gave up on her diet. It was better eating candy with each meal.

One day she found a lump.

.....

On the third night of the third week of September, Mott snuck out of the bedroom with plans of working on her book. There was a light on in the living room; Eugene was in his soft chair reading. Mott asked what his book was. He checked the cover before answering. "Kurt Vonnegut," he said. "*Bluebeard*. It's about a painter. I think I read it before, but I didn't remember for sure. I want to be confident that I've read everything he wrote before I die."

"When you finish reading something, how does it feel?"

Eugene pushed his glasses up his nose. The lenses bent his eyelashes. "There used to be a sense that I was changed. After reading any halfway decent book, I felt both larger and smaller. Larger because I could see more and had more perspective. Smaller because you can't help feeling small when you see the world."

"And what's it like now?"

"I don't feel changed anymore. I feel swollen. No matter how broadly you read, there are limits to what you can learn. Any given person's only willing to see so much, and you see some part of it in everything, and once you've read enough, you have all the parts you'll ever have, and everything after will be repetition, like drawing Scrabble tiles from a bag. Not because there isn't more to know, but because you can't or won't see it."

"How come you keep reading?"

Eugene drank from a beer bottle. "I guess it's enough for me to know that the books are still great, even if I can't see it anymore. It's like jazz. I don't really like it, but I used to have these friends who loved it more than life. I can't access that joy for myself, but I listen to my records and I think about how my friends would feel if they could hear."

Mott had never heard Eugene talk for so long. His voice made her feel the late hour. He asked her whether she had been on her way to the writing room.

"Yeah. But I got tired. I might go back to bed."

"Don't let me get you down. It's good to write if you can."

"I feel like it's bad," said Mott. "It made my mom unhappy. It makes me sad too."

Eugene attempted to drink from his bottle again and found it was empty. "You have to spend your time on something." He asked her to bring him a beer from the fridge. She brought one and a bottle opener. "I've been lucky," he said. "I never had to work a job I didn't want. Emily loved me in spite of myself. People ignored my shortcomings. And then, at the end, you came out here and lived here with me. You're a good kid. If you finish your book, after your mother and Emily, if there's any time left, I'd like to read it too."

Mott blushed. "Thanks Eugene. You're a good fake uncle. But I don't think I'll finish in time." She went to the office, slid out the center drawer, and removed her legal pads. She flipped back to the place where she had left off. She had no idea what should happen next.

It was the fifth night of the third week in September. Emily declared it a game night. Everyone was required to play. Mott shuffled the deck and dealt out five cards for each player. The adults poured wine or beer or bourbon for themselves, including Lyd, who chose the latter. She gave Mott a can of strawberry soda. "Thank you," said Mott. "You're drinking tonight?"

"A little. I'm tired of feeling left out. And you said before that maybe I should."

Emily placed her mother's entire button collection in the center of the table in an open tackle box. The buttons were sorted into dozens of ice-cube-sized partitions by shape, style, material, color, and number of eyes. A substantial minority resembled flowers, leaves, or stars.

"Everyone take thirty buttons," said Emily. "Tonight they're all worth the same."

Meredith considered her cards. "Wow. These suck."

"Mine too," said Lyd. "Who dealt?"

Mott raised her hand. "I stacked the deck. You're all screwed."

Emily eventually took the hand and nine buttons with a straight. Next it was Lyd's turn to deal. She collected the cards, tapped their edges into place against the tabletop. She reached for her glass and found it was empty. "Can somebody get me another?"

"It's only been one hand," said Mott.

"The first drink goes down quick, 'cause that's when you're most thirsty," said Meredith. "I'll get it. Anybody else wanna be topped off?"

The other adults raised their hands. Lyd dealt while Meredith fetched liquor and circled the table, leaving each bottle behind with its user. The players studied their cards.

"Hey Meredith," said Lyd. "You realize it's cheating to peek at our cards, right?"

"I wasn't peeking. I didn't."

Lyd poured bourbon into her glass. It lifted her diminished ice cubes almost to the rim. "I saw you look at Mott's, and Eugene's too."

"You didn't," sulked Meredith. "I didn't see anything. Screw it, I fold."

Lyd tapped her own forehead. "She's folding because she knows one of you has a hand she can't beat. Because she looked at your cards."

"I'm folding because you're an asshole."

Eugene won the hand and seven buttons.

"You're a dishonest cheat, Meredith." Lyd leaned down and sipped from her glass until it did not threaten spilling.

Emily said, "Settle down."

"I'm settled," said Lyd. "It's just that she's so full of shit her nose is running."

"Mom, come on. You should pour that drink out down the drain right now."

"It's, uh, that bottle was pretty expensive," said Eugene. "I can finish it for you."

"I'm not angry with her because of some bourbon." Lyd tipped back her glass until it was gone. "I'm not even angry."

Meredith bet ten buttons on the next hand. Mott, Eugene, and Emily folded. Lyd called the bet. She said, "I'm going to lose." Meredith showed her hand: two pairs and a six.

"I know that you've been sneaking out with my daughter at night." Lyd fanned out her cards faceup: low numbers, mostly hearts. "Go ahead. The pot's all yours." Lyd shoved the heap of buttons across the table. Several slid off the edge and fell to the floor.

"Lyd, I see that your feelings are hurt," said Emily, "but you're going to feel ashamed of your behavior when you wake up tomorrow." She touched Lyd's shoulder. Lyd shrugged it off.

"Mom I'm sorry we snuck out. We just like to camp sometimes, and be alone so we can talk about our dumb kid stuff."

"I don't hold you responsible, Mott. I blame Emily and Eugene, who are supposed to be my friends, and I blame Meredith, who's old enough to know why you don't take thirteen-year-old girls into the woods alone."

"Mott is safe when she's with me," said Meredith. "I always have my knife." She took it from her pocket, set it on the table, made it spin. The blade was still inside the grip.

"That isn't what I meant," said Lyd. "What I'm saying is that you're a danger. You might take advantage."

"Put the knife away," said Emily. Eugene watched its spinning closely.

"I went through a similar phase with Emily when we were young," said Lyd.

Meredith grabbed at her knife, pressed it down, made it still. "Shut the fuck up."

"For years I wanted nothing more than for her to tell me I was pretty, smart, or good. And sometimes, every now and then, she did, which only made me want it more. Or maybe what I wanted was a kiss. Young people can be so excitable."

"I'm not gay!" shouted Meredith. She pressed the button on her knife that let the blade come out. It jumped a little on the table as that silver emerged. Eugene stared as if he might be able to make it retract by the force of his will.

"Nobody's saying you are," said Emily. "Though it would be fine if you were. Lyd's only saying that sometimes, especially when you're young, it's easy to confuse intense admiration with romantic love. And you admire Mott very much. Maybe, given the difference in your ages, it wasn't wise for me to let you two go out alone."

Mott covered her face with her shirt. "I wish I could die."

Meredith slammed her fist on the table; this made the knife jump again, made every full glass overflow. "You all better stop trying to make me feel bad. I'm a dangerous person. I told Lyd before and she didn't believe, but I really did kill my parents."

Lyd snorted. Emily squeezed Lyd's arm. "She told you she killed her parents?"

Lyd shrugged, reached for the bourbon bottle, and found Eugene had taken it away. "She says a lot of things."

Meredith drank what was left in her wineglass. "You should be nice and grateful to me. I'm the whole reason you're here in the first place."

"I'm supposed to get down on my knees and thank you because you helped drive us here?" said Lyd. "You all but begged to come along. You should be thanking Mott for putting up with you."

Meredith shook her head. "I mean you should thank me because I'm the one who called your weird, scary husband on you."

Lyd laughed, drumming on the tabletop with her fingertips. "Of fucking course you did. I should have known. Such a stupid thing to do, of course you did it."

"I didn't ask you to do that," said Mott, whispering because her throat was too tight. Nobody heard, or even seemed to care what she wanted.

Meredith jabbed in the air at Lyd with her knife. "I did it to save Mott. You were gonna keep her trapped with you in that ugly, puny room all the way to November, just so you could keep her to yourself."

"Fuck you."

Mott said, "Mom isn't like that," but she wasn't sure it was true.

"I called the tip line 'cause Mott said you would run if he found you, and 'cause I knew she would be happier running, and I even got you to take me with you so I could be her friend, because I'm not as dumb as you think." Meredith stabbed the table, but her knife wasn't sharp enough to truly pierce the wood, instead bouncing off at an awkward angle, gouging a six-inch dotted line across the surface and nearly slashing the back of her other hand.

"What do you think would have happened if we were in that room when David got there?" said Lyd.

Meredith hesitated. She had an answer ready but clearly wasn't sure it would fly. "That's why I got you to leave the dorm by telling you about the fire, so you would go see Mott's professor. I had a different plan, but when I heard the English building burnt down I knew that way was better. I was gonna spend the whole day keeping you away from the dorm if I had to. Or if you were there when he came, I would have said that you were somewhere else and then run and got you really fast. I had a hundred backup plans and ideas just in case—I figured everything out in my mind before I called."

Lyd pounded the table. "You were *lucky*. When David showed up, you told me yourself that he scared you, and that you took him right to our room because you couldn't think of a lie. You would have led him directly to us. Your plans were bullshit."

Meredith shook her head as if to clear it. "You think I'm dumb but I'm not. I even rescued Mott's king fish."

"But you didn't save her novel. Guess you didn't have a plan for that."

Meredith appealed to Mott, her face turning balloon red. "I didn't think of it till too late. The fish was easier. It wasn't fifty notepads."

Mott felt the loss of her novel again—the partial numbness of her hands and feet that had persisted for hours after she learned it was gone. "My book was important to me."

"I know," said Meredith. "You're important to me."

"Can you put your knife away? Mom'll shoot you if she thinks you might hurt me."

"You have a *gun*?" said Emily.

"I suppose we never explicitly said that guns and switchblades aren't allowed here," muttered Eugene. "I didn't think we had to."

"She's not gonna shoot me," said Meredith. "She just feels bad because she thinks you like me more than her, and because she thinks nobody really likes her, which maybe they don't, and because she feels all alone, which maybe she is, because she's being an absolute bitch."

"Don't call my mom that," said Mott. "I really like you both. Most of the time."

Lyd said, "Maybe nobody likes me, and maybe I am selfish and whatever else you want to say. And maybe I'm wrong, and you have nothing but the best of intentions with Mott, but the fact is I can't trust you if you're the one who called David. You have to realize that. You two will never, ever, *ever* be alone again."

Mott wanted to object, to stand up for her friend, but she had also been betrayed, and there had been moments—only a few, recently, in the woods—where she had felt an energy—a pressure—from Meredith that she couldn't explain. Maybe Lyd had named it. When a person wanted you to kiss them, how did that feel?

Meredith brandished her knife. "You can't do that. It's not up to you who Mott spends time with. I wasn't going to ever touch you Mott, I'm not like that, you're my friend. I promise I won't ever call David again or do anything like that. I don't even have a fucking phone, I gave mine up. Lyd's the one who wants too much."

Meredith stood and circled the table, stalking toward Lyd. Eugene and Emily sat rigid in their chairs. "You're the one who's ridiculous. You're the one who pushes everyone away all the time, moans and complains and scratches herself and berates me, and then you get all angry we don't always want to be around you. You're the one who won't let Mott say she loves you, and yet you demand that she only love you. You write this miserable book about how the world should end and then you get all sad and shitty when it does. You call it *Failure* and blame everyone else when it fails. You try to make Mott hate me, try to take everything for yourself, try to mess up everything when everybody was getting along. We just had my birthday party. It was great." Meredith loomed over Lyd, pointing at her with the knife. "I know that you hated my birthday."

"Close that knife before I count to three," said Lyd. She slowly moved her hand toward her gun's holster, not trying to hide the motion, only trying to stay calm.

"Get the fuck out!" shrieked Meredith. She stomped her foot. "You're not allowed to be alone with Mott anymore! You're the one who can't be trusted!"

"One," said Lyd.

"Don't hurt Meredith," sobbed Mott. Her mouth was full of spit. "Don't hurt my mom."

"She has to listen to me," said Meredith.

"Two." Lyd's hands were shaking. She was almost touching the gun.

"This is childish," said Eugene.

"Don't you fucking dare say three." Meredith leaned forward and touched the knife's broad side to the tip of Lyd's nose.

Lyd lunged, closed her teeth around Meredith's wrist, and pressed her gun to Meredith's gut.

The sound of Meredith's breathing. The way she strained to drink enough air, to keep hold of the knife. Lyd held on until Meredith dropped it.

SEPTEMBER, LYD

IT WAS AGREED THAT MEREDITH WOULD LEAVE. THIS WASN'T A LONG conversation. Emily and Eugene dictated the terms, speaking exclusively to each other while everyone listened. Meredith had to take Emily's car, they said. There were several fuel refills in the trunk, so that should be fine. She would leave the state and never come back. They would give her food, water, and cash enough to get by for a while. Nobody said explicitly that she would die alone when the end came, but it was understood by everyone present that this was all they expected of her, and Lyd felt that it was only fair and proper, seeing as the little shit had called David.

Lyd was getting everything she wanted, and so she knew enough to keep her peace. She rinsed her mouth with ginger ale and spit into the sink, mouthful after mouthful. She ran hot water to help it down the drain. It felt as if all the bourbon had left her body. That pleasant sleepiness was gone.

Meredith sat at the table, cradling her bitten arm and hissing. Emily lifted Meredith's knife from the floor and (after a moment of fumbling with the mechanism) closed the blade. She went to the front door, opened it, and hurled the knife into the woods.

"Awesome," grumbled Meredith. "Not like I needed that for self-defense or anything."

Mott crawled the floor, collecting Emily's fallen buttons. Lyd tried to scrub Meredith's blood off the table. The washcloth picked up some color, but nothing was cleaned in exchange.

Eugene called Meredith to the sink and cleaned her wound. He rinsed it until the water ran clear, dabbed it with disinfectant, and wrapped her wrist in gauze. "A bite will often get infected. Promise you'll drive directly to the nearest hospital. I can draw you a map."

Mott showed Emily the buttons she had found. "I think this is all of them."

"Thank you, honey. You can put them in the tackle box. I'll sort them later."

Mott put the buttons away and said she had to go to the bathroom.

Lyd gave up on cleaning the blood, threw her washcloth in the trash.

Meredith poured what was left of the wine they had uncorked and drank deeply. "You guys are all judging me because of my past, but I have a belief. From the moment she's born, every child has a right to kill her parents. That's how come everybody gets all worked up and scared when they get pregnant. They know the risk they're taking. If you didn't kill your parents, then that's just because they were nice, or anyway they never whipped and cut your back to pass the time. You don't get to look down on me just because you were lucky."

"Honestly, the parents thing, it doesn't bother me as much as the rest," said Lyd. She settled down into the living room love seat. Her body felt sore in unexpected places. She had been clenching all over. "I can't let you be around Mott if it's true, but I'm sure that they did deserve it. I've seen your back. My problem is we can't trust you. But that being said, I still need you to make me a promise."

Meredith shook her head. She didn't say anything.

"I need you not to tell David where we are, if he ever finds you. Now that you've met him, I think you know there's something wrong with him—that he would hurt me and Mott."

"I never wanted you to have to be with him," said Meredith. "I just wanted you to have to be with me. He's not gonna find me, but if he does, I won't tell him anything."

"Thank you," said Lyd. "Now let's work on getting you gone."

Emily emptied the refrigerator's meat and cheese drawer onto the counter, piling baggies of cold cuts and Swiss. "I'll put together a cooler. Take anything you want from your room."

"I want my blanket and pillows."

"Feel free. Do you have enough warm clothes? You can take some of mine."

"That's okay," said Meredith. "We're not the same size."

Meredith finished the wine. "One more thing," she said. "I want all the tuna the grocery boy brought. Every can."

"Okay," said Emily. "That's absolutely fine."

"Anything nobody wants belongs to the people that nobody wants." Meredith went to her room for the last time and slammed the door closed.

"Well," said Lyd. "That was something."

Mott marched up to Lyd and slugged her on the arm, glaring at her through overlong hair.

"Baby I'm sorry," said Lyd.

"Sure you are."

"She was being irresponsible with you. And she called your dad on us, and made us leave behind your novel."

"Maybe she didn't understand how bad it would be if he found us."

"If she couldn't figure that out from everything I did to keep us hidden, that just shows she doesn't care about other people. I tried to get along with her. I let her come along, and I didn't have to do that."

"I will keep liking Meredith until the world ends, even if sometimes she's bad."

"That's okay," said Lyd. "You're allowed to like whoever you want. You can even hate me if you think that will help. You just can't see her anymore."

Mott stomped away and tried to hurt a wall.

Emily started her car to confirm it still worked. She left it running so Meredith would understand it was time. There were two thick pillars of smoke rising from somewhere distant, tall enough and black enough to be visible above the tree line even at dusk. Meredith would be driving in that same direction, might have to see what made the smoke.

The girls carried a box of water bottles, the cooler full of sandwich makings, a tote bag overburdened with tuna cans, and all of Meredith's bed things out to the car, loading them into the back seat. The car still looked essentially empty. There was some clutter on the floorboard—a paper fast-food bag, pocket change, a few stale French fry ends. Mardi Gras beads hung from the rearview. Crumpled receipts and candy wrappers lined the cup holders. There were coffee stains on the passenger seat. Now this would be Meredith's home.

Mott said, "I thought it would be nicer."

"This is very nice," said Lyd. "It's kind of your aunt Emily to give Meredith her car."

Mott glared at her again.

"I'll just be over there," said Lyd. She pointed at the porch. Meredith waved her away.

Mott kicked a rock into the woods. "You actually killed your parents?" she asked, speaking low enough that Lyd barely heard.

Meredith gazed into Mott's eyes for a long time. She made a decision.

"Yeah. I didn't really use my knife though. I was too scared. I didn't want to see it happen. I didn't want to feel it. So I set the house on fire and watched long enough to make sure nobody got out. I think they both died in their sleep."

Mott considered this for a moment.

"They were really bad?"

"The worst."

Mott hugged Meredith, hiding her face from Lyd. "I'm sorry my mom bit you."

"I guess I had it coming."

"You shouldn't have told my dad about us. But she doesn't really hate you. She just loves me too much." Mott said this loud enough to be certain Lyd would hear.

"You sure that you don't wanna run away? We could be like those movie ladies who drive off the cliff."

Lyd's fist involuntarily clenched.

"No thank you," said Mott.

"No," said Meredith. "I guess not." She climbed into the car, swung her legs into place. The cuffs of her jeans rode up her calves, revealing that she wore no socks beneath her shoes. She pulled the door closed, adjusted the mirrors, and switched on the headlights, obscuring herself. She rolled down the window and leaned her head out. "Mott? Will you kiss my cheek?"

Mott did. There was a third smoke pillar in the distance now.

Meredith rolled up the window, aimed her car at the narrow gap in the trees that served as a road, and slowly drove away, becoming taillights and then nothing. If she ever looked back, Lyd didn't see.

.....

When they were back inside, Mott explained to Lyd and everyone that there was an empty bedroom now, and that she would therefore sleep alone from now on. Emily told her they didn't have any spare bedding for that particular mattress. Mott said she didn't mind if it was bare.

Emily tidied the glasses that were left on the table, rinsing and putting them away. "Actually," she said, "you'll have the cabin to yourselves until October. Eugene and I are going to borrow your car for a week. We have some last-minute end-of-life errands to run. Eugene's brother reached out, so we're going to visit with him, and we're going to see a concert."

"Henry Purcell," added Eugene.

"Lyd, when we get back, we're going to have a conversation. We didn't want to say in front of Meredith, because you and Mott were our friends first, but I don't know how we can live together anymore after what just happened."

Lyd paced back and forth along the wall, studying the many Emily paintings that hung there. Their little frames contained every shape of tree branch, and ordinary birds of common color. "If you make us go, David will find us again. He'll ruin our last month alive."

"I'm not saying that you definitely have to go," said Emily. "It's just that I don't know how you can stay, and I'm too angry with you right now to have a productive conversation about it. We're going to bed early so we can leave at sunup. Would you leave your car keys on the counter? That way we won't have to wake you."

"Sure," said Lyd. "I'll have to find them." She checked her empty pockets, though she knew there was no chance that she would have the keys on her, and only felt her holstered gun.

Emily and Eugene started toward their bedroom, but Mott was seated on the floor at the entrance to the hallway, legs crossed and arms folded. "I'm mad at my mom too, but you can't make her leave. She wrote a great book here. It was the best, most important thing that anybody ever did in this cabin."

Emily reached down as if to pet Mott's head, but then thought better of it. Instead she took Eugene's hand. "You don't know what we've done here," she said. "Even if that was how things worked, you can't know that we never did anything that was great or important the way a book is. Sometimes it seems like you both think that novels are the only beautiful things in the world. That's not the case. Everybody else doesn't secretly wish they could do what you do."

Mott curled inward as if she'd been kicked. She said, "I would miss you."

"I know," said Eugene. "We would miss you too. We just need to think. This is our home, and we should be able to peacefully enjoy it in the last weeks that we have alive."

"My mom is right that Dad will find us. I don't know all the reasons why, but Mom is really scared of him. She shouldn't have to live with somebody who scares her."

Lyd said, "That's what they're saying about me, Mott. They feel afraid of me. Get up off the floor, please. Let them go to bed."

Emily offered Mott a hand. Mott refused, leaning back to unfold her legs and then using the wall to help get upright. Having demonstrated this independence, she hugged Emily tight (chin twitching, lip bitten, eyes closed). "Be safe," she said. "Don't get lost. Come back soon."

"We will," said Emily. "And I'll be glad to know you're here waiting for us."

Emily glanced over her shoulder at Lyd, opened her mouth, and discovered she had nothing else to say. She shrugged, gave a weak smile, and went to bed, Eugene following behind.

Lyd offered Mott a hug also. Mott ignored her and went straight to what had been Meredith's room. Her bed would be bare, and she would have no pillow, but that didn't seem to concern her at all.

For the first time in months, Lyd knowingly slept the full night alone.

.....

Emily and Eugene went away before Lyd woke up. Emily left a Post-it note where the car keys had been. *Sorry,* it said. *Thank you. Let's forgive each other while we're apart, so we can be kind to each other when we're back together.*

There was a white pill bottle with a green childproof cap on the same counter. There was another note beside it. *There's one pill here for each of you, just in case something happens while we're gone or we don't come back. It's painless, or so I am told. XOXO Emily.*

Lyd pocketed the bottle. She folded the note and hid it beneath several items in the kitchen garbage can.

She opened the door to what had been Meredith's room, where Mott was sleeping with the light on, and watched her for a little while. Mott lay at the far edge of the bed, maybe touching the wall with her nose, arms wrapped around herself, breathing deeply.

Lyd said, "I feel like you're up."

Mott nodded, lightly thumping the wall with her forehead.

"Are you thirsty?"

"Yes ma'am."

"I'll get you a cup."

Lyd brought her orange juice. The cup was a collectible, depicting a green superhero. Lyd sat with Mott on the edge of the bed while Mott drank.

Lyd wiped a little juice from her daughter's cheek. "Are you mad at me?"

"Yes."

"I heard what Meredith said at the lake, when she asked you to run away."

"You followed us out there?" Mott was either too tired or too sad to be incredulous.

"I heard what you said about me, that I would die if you left."

Mott looked at the floor.

"You were right," said Lyd. "I would."

"Okay," said Mott. She looked down into her cup. "Good to know."

SEPTEMBER, MOTT

MOTT ATE BREAKFAST ALONE ON THE FIRST DAY OF THE LAST WEEK of September. Lyd slept in. The cabin was quiet and so were the woods.

Mott searched Meredith's room. Apart from one soda stain on the mattress, and the posters she'd hung on the walls, there was no evidence that Meredith ever lived there. Though she had left behind the shoebox that once held her many instant photographs, she had taken the pictures themselves—even the bad ones. This was partly Meredith being selfish, but it was also a punishment. Mott hadn't done anything to protect Meredith from Lyd, hadn't argued on her behalf, and so she would never see her again. Meredith, who had never given up on Mott, would be free to look at her friend whenever she wanted until the world's end.

It was nice though to think of being remembered.

Mott swam in the lake. She wondered about Emily and Eugene's neighbors, whom she had never seen. Were they lonely too? Did they have a plan for November? She put her head under, pretended to consider not coming back up.

Lyd was still asleep when Mott returned to the cabin. Mott ate a second bowl of cereal (emptying the last box that they had) and washed the dishes. She gathered dirty laundry, first in the room that used to be Meredith's and then in the room that was now only Lyd's. She threw it all in the washing machine. Lyd slept through this as well.

Mott made spaghetti. She burned the sauce where it touched the pan's sides, but most of it was still okay. She read a *Little Women* chapter. She was afraid to work on her book while her mother slept; when Lyd finally woke, the first thing she would do was find Mott, who still didn't want Lyd to know she was writing.

She played solitaire. She browsed Eugene's books. She went into the master bedroom and peeked at the painting that hung on the wall behind a white sheet. She didn't recognize the artist, could not read the signature, and could not discern what the painting depicted. It was quite green. There might be a face.

The garbage can beneath the writing desk was full of crumpled papers. She plucked one out, smoothed it flat against the floor. The paper was not lined, so the handwriting was badly disheveled, weirdly angled, drifting upward as it stumbled across the page.

> *Once upon a time, there was a boy with a gift. He could, by playing any instrument, remember the thoughts and feelings of the last person who played it, so long as he kept playing the song. He did not himself enjoy music, and so while he could skillfully perform on many instruments (the better to employ his gift), he had only ever learned one song: "Jesus Loves the Little Children." He could play it with equivalent fluency on guitar, on the piano, and*

The writing ended there, two-thirds of the way down the page. Someone, probably Eugene, had been trying to write a story. Mott crumpled the paper and smoothed out another:

The most important part of growing up is giving up on anything that you're not good at. I've always sucked at piano, but I can't give it up. When I play my song, the only song I know, on my dead, wealthy father's baby grand, I remember how he felt when he

It ended there. This was apparently the only story idea Eugene had.

The washing machine's buzzer sounded. Mott startled, left the room, and moved the laundry to the dryer. She visited her mother again. Lyd was still asleep. Mott touched her arm. "Mom? Are you going to get up? I made spaghetti."

Lyd rolled over, smiled warmly, and wrapped her arms tight around Mott. "Thank you so much for coming to get me."

"I burned the sauce a little," said Mott.

"That's okay. I'm sure it's fine. I'll get up now, just give me a minute, I'll take a shower. Thank you again. I'm glad we're together."

.....

The next day was much the same. Mott woke first, made toaster pastries for breakfast, dipped herself in the lake, tidied the cabin, went into the master bedroom, peeked at the painting under the sheet, and read another one of Eugene's failed beginnings. It was the same idea again. How long had he been trying? There must be at least a dozen crumpled pages in the bin.

She went to Lyd's room, knelt by her bed, touched her arm. "Mom?"

Just as she had done the day before, Lyd rolled over all bright-eyed and glad.

The next day, Mott accepted that Lyd would not get up without being asked, and woke her at nine in the morning.

Once Lyd was up, all she wanted to do was "enjoy her daughter's company," which mostly meant holding Mott on the sofa, listening to records together, discussing what to eat of the food that remained in the cabin, and talking endlessly about when would be the best time to go on a walk without ever actually going outside. She didn't drink. She had stopped wearing her gun. It lived now in her bedroom closet, on the high shelf, cradled by a green bath towel.

On the fourth day of the last week of September, after dinner and dessert, they sat together with no lights on. Mott said, "I was thinking about Dad again. Do you think he's still looking for us?"

"Yes," said Lyd. "I'm sure that he is."

"Maybe he found someone else. Or maybe he got too sad to try anymore and gave up."

"Maybe so," said Lyd. She stroked Mott's hair. "You do believe me when I tell you he's a bad man, right?"

Mott nudged her mother's hand away, put her hair back in its place. "Yes. Basically. But I still don't understand what he did that's so wrong."

"You're not old enough to know it all."

"Did he have an affair?"

"No."

"Did he hit you?"

"Less than I hit him."

"Is it his fault that sometimes you drink too much?"

Lyd snorted. "No, but I bet you he'd take credit if you asked."

She took Mott's hand and traced a braid around its knuckles. "Here's what I'll say. Your father says he doesn't believe in things like property or ownership. And the way that he talks, it's easy for people like me to buy in, because it sounds like he's saying we should share precious resources, or we should all develop beyond ego and recognize our oneness with the universe, or something like that. And maybe he does mean that too. But also, the way that he sees it, since there's no property and we are all one thing, nobody owns their own body, and no one has more right to their own person than anyone else."

Mott withdrew her hand from Lyd's. She didn't want to be touched anymore.

"For your father, if he wants to use another person's stuff, or even their body, he thinks he has the right to do that. And he doesn't always ask permission. And he doesn't always listen. Because he doesn't want to know about it if he hurts you. He just wants to do whatever he wants. He took pictures of me without my permission. He made embarrassing videos, where I would be naked or intimate with him or using the bathroom, things that I would never want anyone to see. Some of it I knew about, and some of it I even said was okay, but most of it I didn't. He promised he would stop a dozen times. He only let you and me live separately in our apartment for so long because we let him watch us through the webcam. I don't know what he'll do to me, or us, if we go back. But I know that we won't be safe. Not even for a month. And I know you want your book back, but let's be honest honey, you don't have time to finish writing it anymore. Even if you worked very hard every day, it's too late."

Mott pulled at a loose thread in the couch cushion, wrapping it around her finger as she worked. "How come you were okay with some of the pictures and videos?"

"It's not a rare thing for adult couples to do. Mostly they record themselves having sex. I didn't want to be unreasonable. But your dad decided that since I'd given him an inch, he could take a mile. And my point is he's like that with everything. If we went back and lived with him again, and if he pushed me the way he used to, I don't think that I could take it. I honestly think I would kill him."

"Oh," said Mott. "Like you almost did to Meredith."

Lyd slumped forward, nodded.

"So there are two people in the world you think that you would like to kill. But Dad's the only one who's bad, and not you. You think you're good, and I'm only safe with you." Mott lay back on the couch and pushed herself away from Lyd. The top of her head bumped the armrest.

Lyd sniffed. "I've always believed it's a form of emotional terrorism when a mother lets her daughter make her cry. Your grandma used to cry at me all the time."

"I'm mad you chased my friend away."

"I know. It's not fair to you how much I need you."

"You don't even let me say I love you. You just need me not to have anyone else."

Lyd punched the couch with both fists. Mott didn't flinch.

"When you use the word *need* you're explicitly acknowledging it's completely beyond my control," said Lyd. "And yet it's obvious that you blame me. I *need* food. I *need* air. I *need* you. Anything that anybody does to stay alive is self-defense. You're everything there is that's any good. I can't stop being the way that I am, that's impossible for anyone. You always want to say you love me. Well this is what you love. I need and I take and I eat you all up, everything about you, because you're the only thing that doesn't turn to ashes in my mouth."

Mott rolled off the couch and fell on the hard floor. She did this on purpose.

"Don't do that," said Lyd.

"But I *need* to," said Mott.

"What you need to do is write."

"You said I don't have time!"

"A real writer wouldn't let anything stop her."

Mott pushed herself up and stormed out of the room. She went to the office, yanked her yellow legal pads out of the desk, stomped back to the living room, and threw all that she had of her novel down at Lyd's feet as loud and as hard as she could. "I have been writing!" she said. "I needed to do it alone. You made it impossible. All I could think about was how disappointed you were going to be, and it was never fun with you around, and I was never happy."

Mott went to the kitchen and opened the fridge. There was nothing she wanted inside it. The grocery boy was days overdue. Her eyes settled on a large, plastic ketchup bottle. She loved ketchup. There were no foods to eat that needed any here.

Lyd picked up the legal pads, stacking them in what she surmised was their order. Mott peeked back over her shoulder to watch this—watched her mother read several sentences from each pad's top page. It was the most of Mott's book that Lyd had ever seen.

"I'm sorry," said Lyd. "I'm glad you've been writing. Have you been enjoying your work?"

Mott opened the freezer, found nothing there either. "A little," she said. "Not really."

"I know what you mean. No one likes needing things."

. . . . .

It was the fifth night of the last week of September. The sink was full of unwashed dishes, two light bulbs in the largest living room fixture were dead, and the AC had maybe stopped running. Lyd was listening to one of Eugene's records. Mott was sitting at Lyd's feet, failing to read. She kept having to start the page over. She sighed and set down her book.

"Mom? Can I stop reading *Little Women*?"

"How close are you to done?"

"I don't know. Pretty close. And I'm not saying it's bad. But it's not the best book in the world. That librarian promised. And I could have read so many other things in all the time I've wasted on this one, losing track of my place on the page, starting over, trying to read and just falling asleep. It's not what I wanted. And I've just been so disappointed." Mott hiccupped.

Lyd said, "Honey, it's okay. You're allowed to stop."

"I feel like it's too late to give up."

"Give it to me. I'll get rid of it for you. This is not the only copy in the world."

Mott lunged up onto the couch, hugging Lyd's arm. She was surprised to hear herself sobbing. "It's not fair what happens to Beth!"

Lyd held her, kissed her cheek, and hummed a calming song. She used her heel to nudge the book under the couch, where it would stay until November. Mott cried the way she used to do when she was small.

"Can I tell you something that I think you maybe already know?" said Lyd. "I haven't finished reading anything in years. When I start a book, I feel so excited, and then I get tired, and then I get scared. It's never what I want. What I'm scared of, I think, is it never will be—that I'll never read a book I love again, and never feel the way I used to feel."

"I'm sorry," said Mott. She had absolutely known. "My book might not make you feel that way either, you know."

Lyd rubbed Mott's back. "That's okay if it doesn't. I think I'm going to feel a whole new way."

SEPTEMBER, DAVID

DAVID CALLED A FAMILY MEETING. THE WAY HE DID THIS WAS HE SAT down on the floor in the center of the living room and rolled a dozen joints. He lit the first, breathed it in, closed his eyes, and waited. If the beautiful young people who lived in his home cared about him and wanted him to be happy, they would be moved to join him there, smoke with him, and listen to his heart.

He was halfway through his second joint when one of the young people found him. He heard their footsteps enter the room, stop, and leave again, and then he heard them climb the stairs. There was a series of knocks and murmured conversations on the second floor, and then a smaller number on the third. There was not, however, a clamor to reach him—nobody rushed back down.

David peeked when the first of them arrived. It was Alex. The sweet kid sat there cross-legged, mirroring David. Lately Alex had relaxed his dress code, often wearing pajama pants and flannel shirts where previously he would have insisted on a full suit. This was a positive step. It meant he felt at home. From the way that Alex looked at him, David wondered if there was something wrong. It had been a little while since David had showered, left his room, or eaten a full meal. Barely tolerable itches skittered all over his back and scalp.

A dozen of the other children joined them. David peeked again, this time suppressing a shudder of unease—every one of them wore a mask. There was a leopard, a horse, and an ape. There was also a boy with a vampire mask, which was the first Halloween monster that David had seen among them. Others at the edges of his vision were too blurry to make out. He decided to keep his eyes closed. It would be easier that way.

"Light up," he said. "Share with me." He allowed them some time to start smoking.

"You know that I love you all and want you to express yourselves freely," he said, nodding as he hoped they were nodding. "I'm aware that it's a stressful time to be alive right now. People in your other families probably believe the world is ending. That's what my other family thinks too." He nodded again and hoped they did too. "But the thing is that here is the thing. We've all been having lots of fun this last month, and I've enjoyed your parties, and I think your masks are great and very creative. It's like I'm living in an artsy horror film. But we've maybe gotten a little too wild. We've been messing up our house. And I've been thinking we should maybe try to tone it down a bit, because I expect to find my wife and daughter soon, and bring them here, and we'll all need to pitch in to make them feel loved and safe. You're intelligent, insightful people, so I bet that you know where I'm going with this."

David peeked again. Alex was bobbing his head in agreement. The other young people had pushed their masks up high enough to smoke, so that their human mouths were revealed, but they also retained their other, rubber mouths. He couldn't see their eyes at all.

"My point is that we have to keep the really wild stuff outside the house. If you need to break something, there are other places with things you can break. A lot of the homes around here are abandoned, so no one will mind. Does that seem okay, or does anybody have concerns that they would like to voice into the circle?"

No one said anything. David opened his eyes all the way. "If nobody argues with me or asks any questions, I won't believe we've really solved our problem."

The kid in the vampire mask snuffed his joint, pinching the burning end between his thumb and the bare tiled floor. He pulled the mask back down to cover his mouth. "It's fine, man," he said. "Whatever. It's your house."

"It's *our* house," corrected David. "We all get to use it. I'm only proposing that we agree as a community on some ground rules going forward, so we can all relax and know we're living in a mode conducive to our general collective happiness. Does that make sense?"

The kid in the vampire mask snorted. "Yeah, dude, we get it. It's fine, it's your house."

David reclined until he was lying down on the floor, hands folded under his head, looking at the ceiling, which had somehow been speckled with wine. "That's not what I'm saying. I'm not asserting ownership. Recently I've been dreaming again. In my dreams I'm in the home of a trustworthy man. You can tell he takes care of his things. Last night he told me that I'm running out of time to get serious and get ready. I'm taking this as a sign. Soon the universe will show me where Lyd and Mott are. We need to be mindful of how we are living together."

"Sure," said the vampire kid. "We'll trash some warehouses and whatever instead. We'll push some cars off some bridges. Got it."

"Thank you," said David. He wanted a nap. "Pass it on to anyone who isn't here."

- - - - -

David woke in his office, uncertain as to whether he had walked there himself or been somehow moved by his children. The day was half-over. It might be a different day.

He opened a new email from Rebecca, the pregnant police officer that he had pretended to counsel.

Hello Peter, it said, because she thought that was his name.

> I know that you won't write me back, and that's okay. I hope you haven't died yet in the Mayo Clinic, or that if you have died, that you didn't do it alone. Maybe you're married. My husband is up late every night playing video games. I want to be annoyed with him, but I don't know what to say he should do instead. He won't even talk about the baby anymore. I don't go to work most days. I stay home and stay in bed. That's what I'm writing you about. All my dreams are lucid now.
>
> I always recognize, even if I don't want to, that I'm dreaming, no matter what the dream's about. A man tells me to sit down at a table and I recognize he has no face and I know that I'm dreaming. My boss tells me to report to the public pool and I see that his badge is smooth, just a shape, and I know that I'm dreaming. A man pours me iced tea and I see there is no more in the glass than there was and no less in the pitcher and I know that I'm dreaming. When I realize that I'm dreaming, I always try to go inside myself and see my baby. And every time I end up in that same void, floating somewhere far away, I guess you'd call it outer space, among these stars of different colors, which I don't recognize, but which I think are always the same—they're becoming familiar.
>
> I don't know what it means. I don't think it means anything. The dream doesn't come from inside me, isn't mine. I blame the November people, God or whatever, but that makes me wonder where all my other dreams came from, like when I was young. I don't know that I ever wanted anything without the help of someone else, like advertisements or stories. If my baby were born, if there

were time for that to happen, I would never let them watch TV, or read books, or anything else that feels like a dream, until they had time to develop some wants of their own. Everyone thinks you're weird if you don't watch TV. You have different pictures in your head from everyone else. You want different things.

I hope that you're well. I hope that when the world ends, if it does, it all happens quickly. I don't want to have to sleep even once in November. I don't want to know what I would dream.

David deleted the email. There was nothing useful that he could say to Rebecca. She would solve or not solve her own problems. The world would take care of itself. Nobody ever got more than they were meant to have; nobody got less. He ate stray fragments of food off his desk. Whatever he was supposed to eat would be there, within reach. He closed his eyes and maybe slept a little more.

He checked in on his assigned suspicious persons—the ones that were, as far as he knew, still alive. If it was true that he was running out of time to prepare for Lyd and Mott and therefore happiness, he could only assume that the same was true of his people: that soon they would be happy too.

The white math teacher cowered in his classroom while students marauded through the high school, overturning chairs, ripping down flags, hurling basketballs in every direction, smashing computers, tearing up records. The math teacher had barricaded his door with his own desk, had turned off the lights, was trying to sleep on the floor despite all the clamor. He texted his wife to let her know he might not make it home. She replied wordlessly ten minutes later, attaching a selfie for him to look at while he waited to see what would happen. It was more than Lyd had done for David in months. David trusted that the teacher would survive.

The power in the unmarried Muslim man's home had gone out due to an irreversible, catastrophic failure at the Gulf Power

Company, which also meant that David's cameras in his home no longer worked. All that David had now was what the Muslim man's cell phone fed him, and its battery was running low. The Muslim man was chatting with the woman he had met through the app. Her power was out too. They wanted to be together, but they were still too afraid of going outside. David was confident that they would meet up somehow. All they had to do was wait for the universe to provide.

The Black math teacher was missing; David couldn't find her or any hint as to where she might be. Her husband assumed she would reappear shortly. He kept piling more laundry into the hamper, and yet every morning he appeared surprised when it was still full and not dealt with. David chose to believe that the teacher's husband was right, and that she would return tomorrow or another tomorrow.

His people were going through a rough patch, but they would be out of it soon. It was like the man in David's dream had said: get serious and get ready.

David's office door shifted in its frame. Alex leaned against it and whispered, "Are you up?"

"It isn't locked," said David. "Come on in."

Alex nudged the door open. He wore his suit, which had degraded considerably in the past month—stray threads, coffee stain on the shirt, lapels badly creased, loose and missing buttons. His shoes were missing their laces. "Your boss is here," he said. "He's in the kitchen."

David consulted his video feed of the kitchen. It was true. The house was otherwise largely empty—the kids must be wreaking havoc elsewhere as he had asked them to do. "I don't have a boss," he said.

"Okay," said Alex.

"There's a name above mine on the org chart. That's our relationship, Alex. He's above me on the org chart."

"Okay. Do you want to talk to him?"

"Sure. No reason not to."

"Would you like me to stall him a minute? Buy you some time to shower?"

"Nah, man. I'm fine as I am." David wore a gray bathrobe, blue thermal underwear, and red Christmas socks with trees on the ankles.

"There's sunflower seeds in your beard, sir, among other things."

"I'm fine, it's fine. He'll understand, he knows the score. They watch me while I work, and whatever else it is I do in here." David rubbed his beard until he was pretty sure most of the larger debris had fallen out. He tucked his hair behind his ears, sniffed himself, shrugged, and left his office.

There was a mop in the hallway, leaned against a door frame. The floor was wet and arguably clean.

David found the man who was above him on the org chart seated at the kitchen table, wearing a green suit, sipping a glass of club soda and ice, his face an image of magnanimity. There were many open chip bags on the table, leaning on one another like old friends. These held no interest for the visitor, who also appeared not to notice Laverne the dog sniffing his shoes.

"Hello," said the man above David. "Thank you for taking this meeting on such short notice. I know that we all have full plates and limited time."

He gestured at a chair. David sat as he did in the dream of the trustworthy stranger.

"I'm taking a management class," said the man above David. "One thing we learn is steady eye contact. I find this quite difficult, but notice I'm sincerely trying. Another thing we learn is how to motivate subordinates. Different people respond to different incentives."

David ate a stale potato chip.

"I have information on your wife and daughter. I'm willing to share it in exchange for one collegial, informal conversation on the subject of your recent work." He set down his glass on the ring of moisture that marked where it had been before.

"I need to know where they are," said David. "They're supposed to be with me." He started to sweat; he had less time to prepare for his girls than he'd thought.

"That can happen, David. First I want to talk about November."

David squeezed the bridge of his nose. "I don't know anything about that. Not really."

"You don't need to. I'm giving you permission to guess."

"Okay. My guess is it's a psyop. Nothing will happen in November except what we do to ourselves."

"That's conventional wisdom in the office. Give me something new. Make it up if you have to. Do you want to smoke a little marijuana? Would that make you feel more at home?"

"Thanks, but no thanks. Unless you'd like to share."

The man above David gestured to indicate polite but firm refusal.

"If you want me to say some stupid shit that isn't real, just sort of riff on my observations," said David, "I can do that. Like, if you just want to hear some crazy pot ideas."

"Whatever you need to do your best work."

David leaned back in his chair, bit a knuckle. "Okay. So here's what I think. They might be giving us instructions. The dream about November, they made it feel like a warning, but it was really a promise. It was designed to make us wonder, *How will I die? When will it happen? How long do I have to wait?* They made us want it."

"Who are 'they'?"

"Does that matter? It's working. You've noticed they send different kinds of dreams to different people. The uniformed types—police, soldiers—get special dreams with special orders. They'll probably be the enforcers. They've been told to lead us to the place where we die however we die. When they've finished with the rest of us, they'll probably shoot one another."

"Suppose that's all true. Why are lifeguards also having special dreams, and fishermen, and people who feed seals?"

"Maybe everyone is having special dreams. We notice the ones with bodies of water because of the November dream. We remember how it felt to drown. We don't see the other patterns because we don't know what to look for."

The man above David finished his club soda. He plucked the dwindling ice cubes from his glass and popped them into his mouth, crunching them between his teeth.

"You're doing well," he said. "Go ahead and roll one, David. Relax."

"Okay. You want a rum and Coke?"

"No thank you. Have one without me."

David did as he was told. His blood felt like syrup inside him. He needed to say something smart—one more thing that the man above him on the org chart would like.

"Have I told you about quantum physics?" said David.

"I've heard your monologue on the subject. It relies on a specious analogy, but it seems to make you happy."

The ice in David's glass touched his teeth. The cold stung. "Not very happy."

"Don't worry about impressing me, David. You only need to tell me who you think is sending us these dreams. Then I'll give you what I know about Lydia and little Mott. I just want your expert opinion. You may have noticed that I lack all intuition. I need you to loan me yours."

"You're going to think this is stupid, just like you think all my other ideas are stupid, which I hope you realize makes me reluctant to share them with you. But honestly, if it's anything at all, my best guess is that it's aliens and there's nothing we can do. They might do this kind of thing all the time. Maybe they already wiped out all the other aliens and that's why we think we're alone. I think they're aliens because of my analysis of images in the dreams, and because they don't know what hands feel like, and because of the way that police officers find themselves lost among strange stars whenever they try to dream lucidly, but most of all because of the apologizing woman. I think she may be an alien dissident. You can't trace her calls because they actually come from outer space. She is probably not a she. The aliens are like the government; they hate us and they need to keep us small. They need us to believe the lie that there is such a thing as death, that anything can ever end. The only part I can't explain is the dream where the trustworthy man asks so many questions. It makes no sense why they would want to learn more about people they've already decided to kill."

"Thank you, David," said the man above him. He didn't sound pleased. "That's enough."

David sulked. "You're disappointed. Even though you said it was fine if I just said some nonsense."

"Don't let that bother you." The man above David rinsed his glass, dried it, and returned it to the cupboard. "You've done your job, and for all I know your guess may be right. I'd hoped that you would say the dreams were caused by someone we could kill. Everybody at the office, me included, thinks it's China or Russia, whom we also cannot kill—not under the current regime. You should take some time off. Consider yourself free till November. I have to head back to the office. I'm going to send you two photos in thanks for your work. Refresh your email in five minutes. If it's not in your inbox, check spam."

.....

David refreshed his inbox maybe fifty times before the promised email appeared. There were two images attached. In the first, Lyd's car drove away from the camera, through a Chicago intersection with one working light. The license plate was not the same as it had been before, but David recognized the vehicle itself. The driver and the passenger were shadows, but the latter was far too large to be Mott—was probably a man. The pavement and the car were wet.

In the second picture, the car drove toward a camera on the same Chicago intersection's other side. The driver was Emily, Lyd's friend. The passenger was Eugene, Emily's husband, who was sleeping through the ride. The photos' metadata showed exactly where and when they had been taken, but the point was they were recent. Nothing else much mattered. David understood that Lyd had gone to see her friends at their so-called cabin, and must still be there now if they had her car. In fact, it seemed overwhelmingly likely that she planned to die there.

Enjoy your vacation, said the email.

> We wish you and your family the best. You can keep Alejandro. We don't have time to find something better for him. If we still exist in December, come down to the office. We'll talk.

David laughed so hard it made him light-headed. He sang the first verse of his favorite love song, then the chorus. He couldn't remember how the second verse went, so he sang the first again, louder. The unmarried Laotian journalist was singing also—classic disco, standing on his desk in his abandoned newsroom, joyfully tapping his feet. David felt at one with the universe, his desire at last realigned with the world's beating heart. Nothing ever really ended, and he never had to let go.

The flight to Michigan was all but empty. A man in the front row played a game on his tablet, trying to get the lowest possible score. There was a woman back in economy class who had been on the plane already when the other passengers boarded, and who hadn't moved or made any sounds since. There was a flight attendant who alternated between eating off the snack cart (offering nothing to anyone else) and checking the bathroom for troublemakers, though nobody but him had used it.

David told Alex (why had that email called him Alejandro?) to sit on the far side of the cabin so he wouldn't worry about being made to hold hands as they had done on their last flight together. The kid peered out his window and pressed the back of his hand to the glass, feeling whether it was warm or cold. David wondered how many flights he'd been on.

The pilot hummed over the PA. David tried to sleep. He wanted to tell the trustworthy man about everything—this moment and each moment leading up to it, and everything still to come. He wanted to tell somebody what was going to happen when he got Lyd home. She would be angry at first, but later she would come around. She would be afraid of him at first, but later she would remember how nice he could be. She would be depressed at first, but he would get her high.

They landed, rented a car, checked in at a hotel, went to bed early, woke in the small hours, and drove into the woods. David found it trivial to pick the cabin's lock.

The lights inside were off. David noted the row of empty shoes beside the doorway. He was wearing hiking boots with heavy treads, was tracking dirt into the cabin.

He was sucking on a strong mint. It was supposed to cover the smell of what he had smoked on the way.

Though it was almost nine, Lyd was asleep on the living room couch, hair covering much of her face, an open book on the floor where she must have dropped it. David knelt beside her and pointed his gun at her stomach, supporting his hand with the middle cushion. He motioned for Alex to go and find Mott.

David brushed some of Lyd's hair off her cheek. She wrinkled her nose but did not wake. She was still a sparkling thing in person, more so than any photograph or video could capture, though not so much as he remembered. Their time apart had diminished her. Alex emerged from a bedroom and did a hand signal that meant he'd found Mott.

"Go get her then," said David. Lyd stirred. He put his gun between her lower ribs. "Wake up." His lips curled into a smile, not because he thought it was appropriate but because he had to look like something. Lyd fought to keep her eyes closed. They fluttered, showing whites, then squeezed shut. She knew who it was and what was happening. She wanted to go back to sleep, maybe die there.

"I'm so happy I found you," said David. "I love you. I'm sorry I didn't bring flowers. You have to come home."

Lyd refused to open her eyes. "I don't want flowers," she said. "Please just go back to Virginia. Forget that you saw me. I want to stay here."

"I need you at home," said David. "Our daughter needs her father. You both need my protection. You need me."

"Bring me Mott," said Lyd. She opened her eyes and sat up. David followed her with his gun, digging it into her side, putting his free arm around her—he loved her, he needed to hold her. He called for Alex. The kid shuffled into the room, guiding Mott ahead of him by her shoulders. Her expression was a scream suppressed. David decided not to let that hurt his feelings. Children are naturally cruel; they lack all empathy.

"Mom? Is that Dad?"

"It's me," said David. "And that's my friend Alex. We came here to save you."

Lyd put her hands in David's hair, weaving her fingers in at the roots. She squeezed and pulled so hard that his scalp burned.

"Okay," she said. "We'll come with you. But there will be some conditions."

SEPTEMBER, MOTT

MOTT NOTED THAT THE YOUNG MAN HOLDING HER BY THE SHOULDERS had removed his shoes to come inside. They were by the front door, next to hers and her mother's—a pair of black-and-white tennis shoes, toes pressed to the walls. Her father had left his boots on. There were bits of dirt and dead leaves on the floor where he'd walked. Her mother had been right about what kind of man he was.

"You want to dictate conditions?" said David, in a reasonable-husband voice. He was kneeling like a suitor. He had his gun pressed to Lyd's belly; she had him by his hair. "Go on, love," he said. "Tell me how it's going to be."

"Mott and I will live with you until November, provided that you honor nine rules. If you refuse to honor them, either now or in the future, I will claw out your eyes."

Lyd's nine rules were as follows:

1. Mott will be allowed an office with a working lock, a writing desk, and unlimited supplies of legal pads and ballpoint pens.

2. Any rooms or hallways surrounding her office must be, whenever possible, both empty and silent.
3. On any given day, excepting bathroom breaks, Mott may not leave her office until she has written at least one thousand words.
4. Mott may not use pot, alcohol, or toxic substances of any kind. Not even if she asks.
5. Mott must occasionally eat a vegetable.
6. No one may touch Mott but Lyd.

(Here Alex let go of Mott's shoulders.)

7. Exception: David may hug or kiss Mott if he has Mott's permission.
8. No matter what happens, no matter what substances David provides, Lyd will not touch him, will not kiss him, will never fuck him, and David must never touch her, even if she says he can, or even if he thinks she might have said he can.
9. In the event that Rule #8 is broken, Lyd may at her discretion burn the house down, killing everyone inside.

"I have a rule too," said Mott.

"What's that?" said her father. He tried to turn his head to look at her, but Lyd squeezed his hair, kept him right where he was.

"Everyone has to be nice," said Mott. "Especially to me. Because I'm really tired. And I don't want to feel this way when I die."

"You're not going to die," said her father.

"Be nice to me anyway. And don't shoot Mom."

"I never would."

But he refused to holster his gun until Lyd's hands were bound and she had promised to behave. He tied the knot himself. He said what he used was called surgical tubing. "Don't you worry, Mott. It doesn't hurt."

Alex searched Lyd's pockets. He found a small, white, plastic bottle with a green childproof cap. He shook the bottle and it rattled. David took it from Alex, opened it with some effort, and tossed the cap aside. He emptied it into his hand. There were two pills, both an unreal shade of yellow. "These what I think they are?"

Lyd briefly met Mott's eyes. "Probably."

David patted Mott's shoulder, stroked her hair. "You're lucky that I found you when I did. I'll tell you why when you're older."

"Can I get my king fish and notebooks?" asked Mott.

"Yes," said Lyd. "You can."

.....

Mott's father's car was a rental, a silver sedan. Mott's mother had to ride in the back seat, and Alex had to ride beside her. There had to be a gun on her at all times. David made sure that Mott was buckled in like it was something he did every day.

Mott checked her mother's face in the rearview. There was nothing to stop Lyd from speaking; she chose to be silent. Mott's legal pads were on Lyd's lap.

Her father asked what her fish was called.

"He doesn't have a name. He's just a king fish."

They took the same dirt road that they had driven to come here, and which Meredith, Emily, and Eugene had taken to leave. It occurred to Mott that she didn't believe anyone would come back. Not her friend, not herself, and not her mother, but not Emily or Eugene either. Something would waylay them. There would be some disaster. They would not die where they wanted to die. No one was allowed to have what they wanted, apart from possibly her father.

.....

They left the rental car still running in a place they weren't supposed to; nobody cared. The airport was pretty much empty. Men in suits slept on the floor, empty coffee cups balanced on their chests. Soldiers in fatigues ate ice cream, bought duty-free cell phones, tossed playing cards into mixing bowls. Mott's father carried her notepads with ostentatious care. Screens throughout the airport cycled advertisements: 33 DAYS TILL THE END OF THE WORLD. HAVE YOU TOLD YOUR MOTHER YOU LOVE HER? DON'T LET EXORBITANT LONG-DISTANCE FEES GET BETWEEN YOU. 33 DAYS TILL THE END OF THE WORLD. HOW MANY TIMES HAVE YOU AND YOUR PARTNER MADE LOVE? TALK TO YOUR DOCTOR ABOUT YOUR ERECTILE DYSFUNCTION. IT'S JUST 33 DAYS UNTIL EVERYONE DIES. WHEN WAS YOUR LAST VACATION? GET AWAY FOR A STAY ON THE BEACH. YOU HAVE JUST 33 DAYS TO REFINANCE YOUR MORTGAGE. YOU HAVE TO TRY THIS ICE CREAM BEFORE THE END. LOSE THOSE LAST FIVE POUNDS BEFORE NOVEMBER. DON'T DIE UNEMPLOYED: OUR AGENCY CAN FIND YOU TEMPORARY, FLEXIBLE WORK. YOU HAVE 33 DAYS TO FIND LOVE. These screens were failing, cracked and smudged with finger grease, pixels out of step, one ad behind, so that the photographs and slogans blended, becoming a slurry of yearning, lonely, hungry, eager people, the solutions that would complete them, and the number 33.

Mott's family waited ninety minutes at the gate. David asked her if she wanted beef jerky. She said she did not. He asked if she wanted a personal pizza. She did not. Would she drink some water if he brought her a bottle? Yes, sure, fine. He brought her a bottle.

The desk lady said they could board. Mott didn't need a ticket. What she had to do was to hold her father's hand. Lyd was still bound and nobody asked. They flew first class. The other passengers—there were six, all mutual strangers—had to stay behind the curtain.

"Have you flown before?" asked Mott's father.

"Two times when I was little. I don't remember what it was like."

He tucked her hair behind her ear like he knew where she wanted it.

"You have to take the window seat. It's a beautiful country up there. There's a height where everything makes sense. The people disappear first. Then you're above the towers. Then, like a kaleidoscope, everything shifts into place and becomes rectangles. Not because that's how the world works but because that's the shape we buy and sell it in. The lines are weirdly clear. I guess you won't see what I mean, though. It's dark out. But we'll reach a certain level, it's different for everyone, where the city is nothing but lights. And that always makes sense."

The air pressed on her ears, but it couldn't get in. She watched for the lights. It wasn't anything like what she expected. There were broad, deep patches of darkness, gaps in the city—gone swaths.

"It's been a rough year," said her father. "Things aren't like they used to be. Even small cities were blinding before. They called it light pollution."

The air pushed inside. It stung and it itched all at once. She closed the window.

They landed in Virginia. The air wanted out of her ears now. She could not hear her father's voice. Her mother still was not speaking. There were soldiers here also. They were also eating ice cream, buying whiskey duty-free, and playing a game with a gun.

Her father's car smelled like he smelled. There was hardly any traffic on the way to David's home. That had seemed normal in Michigan, but in Virginia the absence was smothering—so many parking lots empty, so many dark windows, and most driveways clotted with too many cars, and each home mute despite all the people who must be inside. In David's neighborhood, several houses were extensively damaged: broken windows, ruined doors, walls sprayed with obscene graffiti, two overturned cars, and one house fully burnt down, a pile of rubble and nothing on a concrete slab foundation. David made no effort to explain. He said, "That won't happen to us."

David's home was unharmed and in fact very nice. There were four sedans, two minivans, one motorcycle, three scooters, and four bicycles parked outside his house or abandoned in the large, neglected yard, which was a swirl of mud and sand, sparse grass, weeds and wildflowers. There were tire tracks, dog prints, Frisbees, hula hoops, and fully yellowed Polaroids abandoned to the sun. "The kids wrecked my lawn," he said. "Now I can't decide how to fix it. I wanted pretty flowers. But I also want sandcastles too."

There was rock music playing in the house—too loud by far. David went in ahead with Lyd and made the music stop, then waved in Mott and Alex. There were many footsteps overhead: young people hiding in their rooms.

The kitchen counters were stained yellow and brown from turmeric and garam masala. There were crayons and construction paper on the floor, mismatched shoes, half-full chip bags, and battered sci-fi paperbacks with green breasts on their covers. The couch was missing all its cushions. Lyd's surgical tubing lay cut and coiled on the table, a bread knife beside it. She was rubbing her wrists. David hunched over said table rolling a joint. Mott had seen him do the same at least one hundred times before, but she hadn't thought about it in so long, had forgotten he smoked anything.

"Make my little girl an office, Alex," said David. "My wife and I have to talk."

He lit the joint. Lyd plucked it from his lip and took a drag. Mott had forgotten all about that too. Lyd put the joint back on his lip. "Come here," she said to Mott. "Let me hug you."

"I don't feel safe." Mott went to her mother but did not open her arms, which were occupied with her king fish.

"You aren't. I'm not either." Lyd rubbed her back. "But I'll take care of you the best I can, because that's my job. Your job is to finish your book."

"You're entirely safe," said her father. "We run a tight ship."

"There's cocaine on your coffee table," said Mott.

"You don't know what cocaine is." David glanced at the coffee table. "And it's there because I let it be, because it's no big deal."

"Did you bring the other half of Mott's book here?" said Lyd. "When you visited our dorm room?"

"If you mean the yellow notepads, then yeah, we did for sure."

Mott felt a relief so violent that it was more like falling.

"Wait," said Lyd. "You took the notepads, Mott's book, but you didn't read them at all?"

David was puzzled by the question. "Should I have? Did you want me to? Why would I do that?"

"I can't believe you," said Lyd.

Mott was glad he hadn't read her unfinished work, that he hadn't gotten there before Lyd, but it was unfathomable to her that he had no such desire—indeed, the thought had obviously never crossed his mind.

David redirected the conversation to a subject he found more comfortable and relevant. "We also brought your other books from the dorm, and your clothes. We want you to feel welcome and cozy and glad to be home."

"How very kind of you," said Lyd. "So considerate."

"Alex, I asked you already to take Mott upstairs. And give her the notebooks, please. I think they're in my bedroom, on the dresser."

Alex escorted Mott up the stairs and down the hall to what would be her office. For now it was a nearly empty bedroom: air mattress, one pillow, no blanket, inspirational cat poster, an opened box of Band-Aids. "I won't let anybody hurt you," said Alex. He ruffled her hair. She glared at him, but he didn't notice. He left and came back with the notepads. Mott sorted them into their correct order and flipped through their pages, confirming everything was where it should be. Alex left the room a second time and closed the door behind him.

Mott screamed and threw her king fish at the door, then collected him and kissed his head and said that she was sorry.

Lyd's rules would be mostly followed. Their family's new routine would take one week to form—a skin of normalcy that draped the days.

OCTOBER, MOTT

WEDNESDAY AND SEVEN HUNDRED WORDS. MONDAY WOULD BE Mott's birthday. She would be fourteen. There was a bottle of peach water on the corner of her desk. Half-empty, once bubbly, gone flat. There was another behind it, and behind that one another. Her father, hearing she'd emptied the first bottle, had sent Alex to the store with forty dollars and a pistol. "Buy what they have left," he'd said. "And I want some pretzels. Not the pretzel-shaped pretzels. The sticks." The pistol was for self-defense. Alex probably wouldn't have to kill for peach water, but he would have to not die long enough to bring it home. Mott did not like peaches. What she wanted was grape soda. If she asked her father for what he didn't know she liked, it would hurt his tender feelings. Wednesday and seven hundred words.

A crunchy guitar riff drifted down the hall. She wrinkled her nose. There were also voices. They were just this side of audible. It was impossible to think.

Nobody ever said "Wednesday" correctly. It drove her up the wall.

If the world would end November first, then there were only three Wednesdays left.

She tapped the chewed end of her pen on her yellow legal pad. It flecked a little spit across her words.

In Mott's novel, the daughter was mostly recovered from her mastectomy. She felt that she should mourn the taken breast, but in fact she was glad. The mother's body was now more like the daughter's body was before they'd swapped. She prayed that she would get a second lump so she could have the other breast removed. She researched the world's most carcinogenic foods. The state of the science was such that everything edible was correlated with at least one kind of cancer, so she had to buy a little bit of all of it, like building Noah's ark for groceries. The haul took weeks to eat. She prioritized what would otherwise spoil.

Somebody knocked on Mott's door. "Lunch."

Mott said he could come in. It was Alex. Someone had sewn fresh buttons onto his suit; these should have been black, but were instead a dark blue, and the difference was not subtle. He held a tray. The plate was crayon-green plastic. "Pancakes," he said, in case she was blind. "There's syrup. David didn't know what kind you liked, so there's three flavors."

"Thank you." Mott set the tray on the desk between her legal pad and king fish.

Alex felt his clothes. He rubbed the tired fabric of his jacket's hem between his thumb and forefinger.

He remembered where he was and asked Mott how the day's work was coming.

"Seven hundred words so far," said Mott.

"That's great. You're nearly there already and it's lunch."

"Late lunch. It's almost four." She pointed at her wall clock.

"Shoot." Alex rubbed his temples. "Time flies." He coughed. He smelled like her father. "Sorry. I'll let you get back to it."

She drizzled her pancakes with maple.

In Mott's novel, the daughter watched TV alone. She tried cross-stitch but did not have the patience. The mother called her for the first time in months. "There's someone I want you to meet. Everything is happening so quickly. I wish that I could always feel this way."

Mott finished her pancakes. If she could see the sun, it would be setting already.

.....

Friday night and nine hundred words. Nine hundred words but she needed one thousand. Monday she would have her birthday party. She would get nothing done that day. Her father had declared it: she was not allowed to work on her birthday. She would have to eat cake and play games. She told him that she wanted pizza. "Of course," he said. But he would forget. If she did not write one thousand words per day then she would die having accomplished nothing. So today it had to be twelve hundred words. And tomorrow, and Sunday, and Tuesday, and Wednesday, to make up for Monday. Nine hundred words but she needed twelve hundred.

There were two people running up and down the hall, a boy and a girl. They were laughing and teasing each other and probably falling in love. The girl was probably beautiful and probably didn't have enough clothes. No one in Mott's father's home believed in wearing what they should. Their feet shook the floor. Mott sat cross-legged on her chair to feel what they did less.

Somebody hit the wall. "I'm going to put it in you!" said the girl. The boy giggled. They both giggled. Somebody hit the wall with their whole body. There were kissing sounds.

In Mott's novel, the daughter was meeting her mother's boyfriend. He was eating what she'd made for dinner, pretending to love every bite. The mother said he was a sociology PhD. He studied how different kinds of people managed death. He claimed that no one whose household income was less than fifteen thousand per annum had ever been to or taken part in a funeral. He claimed the very poor mourned differently, and sometimes not at all.

Mott wrote a long paragraph about the daughter sneaking through her dark house late at night to peek at the mother and her boyfriend. The daughter kept banging her shins on things that weren't where they should be. She nearly fell down the stairs. Every time she made or heard or thought she heard a sound, she froze, and listened to the night, waiting to see if she was found out. But no one ever caught her. But she never found the room. Though she had lived there all her life, the house was not like she remembered. She woke up on the couch in a nightgown, an afghan thrown over her legs, and it was a quarter past ten, the day already half-gone. Her mother's boyfriend sat in a rocking chair, reading a book that wasn't his. The daughter pretended to sleep, watching him through squinted eyes. Disgustingly, his lips moved as he read.

The daughter referred to herself in third person. She could not remember her age, nor her mother's. She asked, "When is her birthday?" And the mother gave the day but not the year. The daughter asked, "How old is she?" How old, and how far gone?

Someone turned up the music downstairs. It was "Monster Mash" again. Her father's borrowed children shout-sang along.

There were slapping sounds in the hall. The girl was laughing uproariously, but the boy was not amused. There was a scuffle—then a deep, yucky grunt.

Mott kissed her king fish's cheek. She opened her door, which was against the rules. She wanted to shout at the boy and the girl. If they wouldn't be quiet, then she couldn't work.

But the boy was throwing up onto the wall. He wore a rubber wolfman mask, its mouth pushed up to his nose. He clutched his bare stomach—his only clothes were black basketball shorts and orange socks. The girl wore bloody panties and a blue bikini top. Her mask was Frankenstein's creature. She laughed and laughed. The white paint on her toenails was chipped. She pushed her mask up far enough to kiss the boy's shoulder. He shrugged it off. She kissed his other shoulder. He elbowed her gut. She spit on the wall. Someone downstairs dropped a glass.

"You have to stop!" said Mott. "I'm trying to write!"

Someone turned up "Monster Mash" even louder. The boy and the girl regarded her through their masks. Both were kneeling from the pain the other caused. She wore more clothes than they did, so she ought to be in charge.

The boy barked at her and the girl made a sound like a corpse. The boy barked again and the girl also barked. Mott closed her door as they started to charge. They beat the door and laughed and talked as if she couldn't hear about how cute she was, how funny.

In Mott's novel, the daughter found what seemed to be the magic cave. She lit a torch and went inside.

.....

Sunday night and twelve hundred words. Mott took down her princess calendar from the wall. The calendar was a gift from her father. In the October picture, the princesses were all dressed up for Halloween. Each one pretended to be a different princess. The one that lived in the desert was dressed like the one who lived in the sea. The one who wore provocative dresses now wore the bridal gown of the princess who was always about to get married. The chaste bride princess now wore a little black number and blushed.

Mott listened at her door and counted to ten before she opened it. There was no one in the hall tonight. The carpet had new spots since last she'd left her room to use the toilet, bloodstains and cigarette burns. There was hard candy stuck to the floor.

Mott walked down the stairs toward a mass of party voices. There was psychedelic guitar music. The living room was full of half-costumed boys and girls. They were dressed as zoo animals, as witches in cheerleader skirts, ghosts in skimpy sheets, naked zombies, women drowned in bathing suits. They felt each other's bodies.

The walls were hung with fake spiderwebs, and these jeweled

with rubber spiders, gummi worms, little action figures, and crawling army men.

Alex was among the dancing, drinking, smoking, sweating horde. Everybody wiped their dirty hands on his jacket. He laughed every time. A ghost blew her nose on his shoulder. He reached to flick it off, but the ghost slapped his hand. He made himself laugh.

David's massive dog stood in a corner, rubbing its butt on the wall. It breathed and twitched and waited, and licked its lips and nose, which were already licked raw.

Mott found her parents in the kitchen. There was her father mixing a drink in a glass that Lyd held. There was her mother waiting and already drunk. Mott could tell from the way that she stood with one foot on the other. David rolled a joint.

Lyd saw Mott and her princess calendar. She set down her drink on the counter and pushed it with the backs of her fingers until it was partly hidden by a box of water crackers. She held out her arms in a way that said it would be Mott's job to close the distance. Mott looked down at her feet as she walked, watching for broken glass.

"Mom, I did twelve hundred words."

"That's wonderful baby. You get a gold star."

Lyd set the calendar on the counter. She searched her pockets for the stickers.

"They're on the table," said Mott. Between two glass baking dishes full of three- and five-layer dip.

Lyd ventured to retrieve them. David's other children showed their respect by ignoring her and not touching. David lit his joint and breathed it in. He said, "You feel okay to be down here, honey? It's kind of a rough scene tonight. The kids are scared about November. I said they could blow off some steam."

"It looks like Halloween."

Her father closed his eyes and let the smoke leak out of him. "If you believe, incorrectly, that the world will end on the first of November, then you believe that Halloween will be our last day together on Earth. They're facing their fears. I told them it was okay."

Lyd knelt beside Mott with the calendar and the stickers. She peeled a gold star from the sheet. "Twelve hundred words, you said?"

"Mm-hmm."

Lyd applied the star to the day's date. It was Mott's third gold in a row. The two before that were silver. "You're doing so well. You're working so hard." Lyd kissed Mott's cheek. Her breath stung Mott's nostrils. Mott wished that Lyd had asked permission.

"You should go back upstairs. Leave the light on when you go to bed so I can find you."

Lyd used Mott's shoulders to boost herself to standing.

"Why do you squat to talk to me when I'm almost five feet tall?"

"I don't know, honey."

"Why are you drinking instead of running away?"

"Honey," said Lyd. "This is working."

Mott's father said, "You have to live with both of your parents. You don't know what it's like out there. I'm protecting you from coyotes and lonely men." He put his hand on the small of Lyd's back. She relaxed into his body, pressed her side to his side, let her head rest on his shoulder. Mott felt dizzy. She should be happy. Her parents were back together. Her mother was relaxing in a way that Mott had never seen.

Mott would later realize that her own shocked expression must have been what woke Lyd, who now turned all rigid, elbowed David in his side, and hurled what was left of her drink against the wall, shattering the glass. She shouted, "No!"

David stumbled to the table for support, put his hand in the five-layer dip.

Now everyone with a glass threw theirs at a wall, and the walls were all dented and stained, and the record had run out of music. Lyd said, "We agreed on my rules." She tilted toward her husband, who was licking five-layer dip off his hand, and punched him in his jaw, so he bit his finger bloody and fell down.

He lay on his back and kicked to keep her away. She circled him and waited for her chance.

"Don't touch her!" he shouted. Alex (smeared and spat upon and armed and dangerous) backed off.

Lyd pinned one of David's legs, trapping the cuff of his pants beneath her heel. She knelt on his chest and tried to get her hands around his neck.

Mott said, "Mom? Can you stop?"

Lyd glared over her shoulder. She was not absent from her eyes, was not lost in some red haze. She knew what she was doing.

"I love you, Lydia," said David, straining to get out the words despite the weight of her on his chest. "You love me too. I'm so glad you've come home." He gasped as Lyd stood up off him. "You're a little blue planet orbiting my sun. You've turned away from my warmth, but you'll come back around. You are, despite yourself, a good woman. You're the bowl of ice cream and the dollar that bought it. I'm sorry that I broke the rules."

Lyd walked to the cabinets, took one of the few remaining glasses, and made herself another drink. She said, "You'll be good?"

David said, "I'll be good."

Lyd said, "Go to bed, Mott. I'll follow you soon."

The party resumed. Those in bare feet took a break to find their socks and shoes.

. . . . .

Monday morning and no words. Fourteen years old felt the same as thirteen. There was no peace in her. She did not feel smarter, more informed, more generous, or calmer or better or kind. She was no less afraid nor alone. She kissed her mother's arm, which held her. The comforter felt cold today.

Monday morning and no words. She was not allowed to write. This had sounded like a great idea when her father proposed it, and better still when her mother agreed.

Mott whispered her own name and climbed out of bed. It was colder in the open air.

"Happy birthday," said Lyd.

"I'm going to take a shower."

Mott collected her birthday outfit, which she had chosen with her mother the previous night. It was her best jeans, a pink shirt with white stripes, her yellow cardigan, and her mother's flower necklace.

The hallway's carpets and padding had all been torn out, exposing the cold plywood subflooring beneath. The wood was badly stained in several places where some spill had seeped through.

The walls had been thoroughly scrubbed. This did not make them clean, and now their paint was patchy, with bald spots and thin circles. But it helped.

The bathroom was also improved. It had been Mott's least favorite part of the house—the much-abused toilet and surrounding tiles more yellow than white, the tub ringed with filth, and the small trash can overstuffed with used tissues, fast-food and condom wrappers, expired toothbrushes, newspaper pages, and other. Someone always left the sink running. Someone usually plugged the toilet. Someone often flushed it anyway and let it overflow. Whatever the long-term structural implications of that water, the short-term problems were much easier to address. Someone had thoroughly mopped the room. Someone had cleaned the rings out of the tub. Someone had made the toilet look new and ministered to the surrounding yellow tiles. The smell of vinegar hung on the air, pungent and pleasing.

Mott showered, dried, and put on her outfit. Lyd was still in bed. Mott told her the shower was free.

The glass downstairs was all swept up. The tiles and counters were as clean as they could be. It smelled like vinegar here also. Her father's dog slept in the living room. Her father, who wore a gray T-shirt that said PEACE on the chest in white letters, was finishing a load of dishes. There were water spots all down his front and his forehead was dewy with sweat. His jaw was bruised and swollen on the right side, where Lyd had hit him.

"Did you sleep okay, honey?"

"I slept fine."

"No bad dreams?"

"I don't remember."

"Just so you know, I sent everybody out for the day. I gave them some money. They're supposed to go bowling, get ice cream, see a movie, whatever they want. It's just me and you and your mother, and Alex."

"Why Alex?"

"He helps me. He helped me clean last night and this morning. You should thank him when you see him. Right now he's napping."

"Okay," said Mott, but she didn't mean it.

Her father pulled a chair from the table to the sink. He patted the seat. "Hop on up, little apple. I'm going to cut your hair."

"I like it this way. I want to see how long I can grow it."

David smiled. "Because you really think you're going to die."

Mott nodded.

"You don't want to die itchy, my love. Please let your father do you this kindness. I've already assembled my tools." He gestured to a small array of scissors, combs, shampoos, and other, less familiar items. "Let me *practice* my *art*, pretty girl." He tickled her sides. "Let me make you *fab*."

Mott laughed in a way that made her feel unlike herself. She mounted the chair. Her father wrapped a bedsheet around her and safety pinned it closed in the back. "Don't want to get hair on your clothes. Now tell me, is there some particular young starlet whose hair you admire?"

He rubbed her shoulders while she thought.

"I don't like how anyone looks," she said. "Or maybe I just don't remember."

"That's no problem. I can already see your loveliest you." He let the sink run into his palm until the temperature was what he wanted. "Close your eyes. Tip back your head." He guided her into the water. "Hold yourself still for a second." He squirted shampoo into his hand, then lathered and applied it to her scalp. "You're a beautiful girl."

"No, I'm not."

"If that makes you feel better. I don't feel beautiful either. Not since I was a young man." He kissed her forehead. He rinsed her clean and helped her sit upright.

Mott opened her eyes. Lyd stood cross-armed by the table, her own hair still damp from the shower. "Did you give him permission?"

"I think so," said Mott.

David dried her hair. "Maybe your mom will let me do hers next. She used to love this. I trimmed her every month for years."

"No thank you."

"But you miss it." He made the first cut. A thick lock of Mott's hair landed on her sheet.

"I miss something," said Lyd. "But it isn't you cutting my ear."

He cut so much it made Mott want to cry.

He swept up all of it and showed her the dustpan full of her frizz and coils. "Do you want this? I could bag it for you."

"Just put it in the trash, Dad."

"There are indigenous tribes who believe our hair stores all our memories and dreams. They never cut or trim anything for fear of forgetting themselves. Of course, they still bite their fingernails when they're nervous. Some things are universal."

He dumped the hair into a zippered plastic bag. "Hold on to this," he said. "I've never regretted keeping any part of myself."

"How do I look?"

He showed her a mirror, holding it close enough that she could only see herself in pieces.

"You're perfect," said her mother. Her father agreed.

And from a certain angle, yes. Why not. There was a kind of brightness in her eyes.

The pizza came at lunchtime. Mott had been sure her father would forget. There were various combinations of pepperoni, sausage, ham, and pineapple. There was even dessert pizza, with icing and brown sugar crumbles, chocolate chips and peanut butter cups.

Lyd grumbled about fat and sugar. David laughed and kissed her cheek. "If you're going to die, you might as well live!" She flicked his forehead but did not throw her glass, did not punch or tackle him.

Alex ate pizza too—cheese only. He said he wanted to try an ethical diet, free of cruelty and flesh. (David said there was no such diet, that nothing was cruelty-free.)

David gave Mott her gift. It was a small box, red paper and white ribbon, her name handwritten on the label, and beside her name a heart. Inside the wrapping and the box was an elegant dip pen suitable for calligraphy and everyday use. There were also six interchangeable nibs, which varied in their shape and function.

"Those are from your mother," said David.

"Your father is lying. He wouldn't let me leave the house to choose your gift, wouldn't loan me a laptop for shopping online."

"Well they were your idea."

"I would have never chosen those."

"Let me be nice to you."

Lyd smiled. "I'd like to, but you don't know how."

There was also a four-pack of small jars of India ink. "You can use it for your book," said David. "Won't that be nice? I know it must suck using cheap ballpoint pens."

Mott thanked her father, her mother, and Alex, who had retrieved her gifts from the store.

Her father's other children came home throughout the afternoon and evening, returning in pairs and trios. Many still wore their Halloween masks. Some came with bloody knuckles and radiant bruises. They ate what was left of the pizza.

Come nightfall, Mott's father served three chocolate cakes—almost enough for everyone in the house. Mott blew out three sets of candles. Each time the same wish: *Please God let me finish my novel.*

Monday night and fourteen years. They were all that she would ever have. It wasn't enough. It was all too much. The whole house singing "Happy Birthday" with voices strong and clear, even through their rubber masks.

OCTOBER, LYD

THEIR FIRST DAY IN HIS HOME, DAVID SHOWED THEM WHERE THEY were allowed to be and where they were not. "We share everything here. You can use the kitchen freely, but I'll ask you not to touch the knives. If you need a lime cut, ask for help.

"Don't go in my office. You wouldn't like it. Frankly I don't like it either.

"And here's the master bedroom. Your clothes are in our dresser or our closet as appropriate. Make sure to thank Alex for helping with that. I want you to feel that this is your home now. This is your family. Laverne is your dog."

Lyd said, "I won't be sleeping in this room."

"That's fine," said David. "You can sleep wherever you want. Just please don't try to leave. You would take my heart with you. There are cameras and other useful systems here. This is the only place you're truly safe, where I can keep an eye on you."

He said Mott's things were also in a dresser, which would be moved to her new office. Many of the books that they had left behind were packed in boxes. If they wanted he would buy some shelves, but he felt the books should stay in their boxes. He didn't want his loves to be overwhelmed with clutter. "This is a chance to start over." But it was also a homecoming. "You're finally back where you belong. In the end you'll be a better wife to me for all the time we spent apart, and I'll be a better husband and father. I'm ready to love all of you for what you are. When November comes and we're still alive, I think you'll be glad to be here."

He rolled himself a joint. He rolled himself a joint. If not in that moment precisely, and if not just a minute before, then in another soon thereafter: he rolled himself a joint.

He sent Mott to bed. The kid that he called Alex would guard her bedroom door. "Of course she is my hostage. If you need to see it in those terms to act rationally."

Lyd demanded that she be allowed to share a room with her daughter. "She can't sleep without me," she lied. David said that was fine.

"Do you still prefer whiskey?"

"I don't prefer that you pour anything for me."

"Will you drink it if I do?"

Lyd looked at her bare feet and the dead skin that had accrued thereon. (Shoes were not allowed.)

"I'll pour you a whiskey. If you want a little water in it, stomp once. If you'd like some bitters, stomp twice."

She said, "You can bring me the bottle."

A vision of her body lying still. Her dead body lifeless on the ground. Her dead body and its open, sightless eyes. Her dead body and no breathing. Her dead body and no one to dig the hole. Her dead body like it always was. Lyd closing her eyes and her dead body opening its. Lyd's last heartbeat. Lyd's last breath. Lyd's dead body and the air moving through it as the air moves through a conch.

She drank. "This arrangement is stable so long as Mott keeps writing. If you let her finish, we'll stay. If you don't interrupt her, and you leave her alone while she's working, I'll spend time with you. And when she's done you have to let me read it."

David said, "Of course you can. Just promise not to forget me while you're reading."

David's head was rolling on his shoulders. It was whatever day it was, another. They were listening to jazz. He said, "You've never trusted me to love our daughter."

"You don't know about girls. You only like women."

"I do like women." Smoke leaked from every hole in his head. He passed his joint to Lyd. "I want to kiss you."

"No," said Lyd.

"Can I hold you in my lap?"

"Absolutely not."

"We could dance. You used to like that."

"You can on your own if you want." She passed back the joint.

David studied her face and breathed in the smoke, struggling to discern whether she would actually like to see him dance. Lyd wondered if he even remembered the times he had done that for her when they were young—the moments he'd been high or drunk enough to leap at such suggestions, forgetting his masculine self-consciousness long enough to lift his hands above his head and spin.

"You just want to make me look like an asshole," he said. "If I did it, you would laugh."

She laughed. "I would never."

David slid his butt forward and lay back in his seat—a large, soft chair only moderately damaged by the young people who lived with him—until he was nearly horizontal. "Someday when this is over, after November, when the world hasn't ended, you'll ask me to fuck you," he said.

"Sure I will," said Lyd. It was better for everybody for now if he believed that. Soon afterward he fell asleep. Lyd made herself a drink—not her first of the day, not her first of that hour. How her stomach burned in October. How wretched were her eyes.

Her dead body. Her dead body in this home. Her dead body's bones when the home was become dust. Her dead body feeling nothing. Her dead body never writing. Her dead body never writing. Her dead body numbly holding Mott's. Lyd's dead body's always-open eyes.

He held her close, and for a moment she let him. It was a party. Mott wanted her gold star. Everyone was dressed up like an animal or a monster. She pressed her warmth to his. He didn't have to be strong to get what he wanted. It also worked if she was weak.

She realized what she had allowed—what she was allowing. She screamed. She broke her glass. Everyone broke all the glass. She punched him, knocked him down, tried to get her hands around his neck. Mott was afraid. If Lyd killed David, Mott wouldn't finish her book. Mott asked her to stop. David said he was sorry, said that he loved her, and promised that he would be good. She sent Mott to bed.

Lyd asked David for permission to wear shoes just for the rest of the evening given all the fragments of glass on the floor. He said, "Maybe you should of thought of that before you broke yours." The bruise was showing on his jaw already. He told her she could wear a second pair of socks. "Go up to our bedroom and get one of your thick winter pairs from the dresser," he said. "I won't follow." His tone implied that this was a mercy and a kindness on his part.

Lyd wove between and past gawking kids in rubber masks, went to David's bedroom, locked the door behind her. Most of her clothes were still here; David allowed her to store a couple outfits at a time in Mott's room, requiring her to come back to the master bedroom to replace them, so that she had to see the bed that they could be sharing and the negligees he'd bought in anticipation of having her again—these hanging in the walk-in closet, among her ordinary shirts—and so she had to smell the incense he burned there to make the air musky and sweet, and so there was always a moment where she had to fear he might come in and try to force the issue.

She chose fluffy purple socks and sat on the foot of the bed so she could watch the door as she put them on. It was difficult for her to pull them fully over the pair she was already wearing. Her right hand ached from punching David. Both hands, in fact, were shaking.

Lyd's dead body's broken hands. Her dead body under snow. Her dead body in the flood. Her dead body and how the wind will change her bones. Smooth and polished. Sandblasted to a tear-shaped wafer the size of a hand. Curved like a hand. Like a lens. Like the first cup. A hand was the first cup. Lyd's dead body without Lyd.

Mott dipped her pen in the India ink. Its nib came out entirely black. She tapped it on the little jar's lip. This knocked several flecks free—some went into the jar, some ruined Mott's shirt. It was the cute one with the star, one of her favorites. Lyd thought how Mott would never find another shirt like that. She thought how David ruined everything.

Mott growled. She tapped the nib again. This time went better, but the ink was still too much. The paper wrinkled where it touched, already so damp it threatened to tear.

"What do you want to wear on the last day?" asked Lyd.

Mott stared at her. "I hadn't thought about it."

"I'd like to wear a sweater so I don't get cold."

"I guess I'd like to wear something pretty, like a dress. But we don't have any dresses. I want to wear my violet shirt, my cool jeans, and the belt with the little gemstones."

"I'm sorry, I'm distracting you. I'll leave." If she left the room, then David would expect her to keep him company. He always knew when she was alone—she tried not to think about why.

"Don't go." Mott dipped her pen too deep. She held it over the jar and let the excess drip.

"Honey, you don't have to use that just because it's from your father."

"It's a bad gift, I know. But it's the best he ever gave me."

Somehow this made Lyd need to cry. She went out to the hallway, did it there, bare feet on the bare plywood subflooring, which was already ruined—stained and molding. But it would last two weeks. Two weeks was all that anybody needed. David would be watching her cry through his cameras. He would come to her soon, would test to see if he could take advantage.

Lyd's dead body in two weeks. Two weeks until her body.

When she picked up the phone, David answered. There wasn't even any dial tone.

David sometimes let her watch the news. There was a story about the high cost of gas. There was a story about a doctor who was euthanizing all her patients. There was a story about a war that Lyd did not remember. It was apparently going quite well. There was a story about how the fake David—the handsome, mustached actor—was moving on with his life. Lyd asked the real one what that meant. "What happened to Linda and Margot? The fake me and fake Mott? Didn't he find them?"

"You didn't hear?" said David. He twisted a bit of his beard. "They died. It was a tragic accident. Done in by a gas leak, if I recall correctly."

The fake David was weeping on-screen. The manic quality had returned to his acting, the pleasure of performance. He was showing his full range. "I guess I'll be alone when it happens," he said. "I keep making too much food for dinner."

There was a story about teenagers who walked out of school to protest November. They reminded their elders to vote in the coming election. There was a story about the final presidential debate. Both candidates agreed with the global consensus that the world would likely end in November, and that Election Day itself would therefore never come to pass. One emphasized the importance of early voting. "I may never have the privilege of leading you," she said. "But you can still make your voice heard. Cast a ballot while you're able. Get out there and show the void what America's made of."

Her opponent said that voting was a waste of precious time. "But if you gotta do it, vote for me. Practice acceptance. Look the end in the eye. Give it to me because I want it more. Give it to me because I'm not pretending it's more than it is. Let it go."

There was a story about roving youths in Halloween costumes

and animal masks. They overturned cars, set fire to houses and fast-food restaurants, smashed windows, put pipe bombs in mailboxes, threw bricks into traffic, dropped TVs off bridges, sprayed Silly String on the homeless, openly molested children, and fucked in the streets. They shat wherever they went. They cut themselves and each other. They bled into rivers and pissed on the walls. They were destroying everything in Virginia, except for DC, where there were too many soldiers and police. They wore rubber masks and zombie makeup, cat suits and fake muscles, bright wigs and presidents' faces. The anchor noted that the police officially refused to deal with these problems, being occupied already with assorted asset seizures. They advised that it was safest to dress up as a monster when and if you left your home, and best not to go anywhere at all.

David called a family meeting. Mott was exempt, as she didn't yet have one thousand words for the day. He told Lyd to roll him a joint. It was easier to comply than to argue.

"We share everything in this house," said David. "Even the things we're not proud of. So I need you to tell me the truth. Are you the ones they're talking about on the news? Are you out there setting fires, killing people, touching children?"

He crossed his arms and waited for an answer. Most of his kids were dressed much as the news described, to the extent that they were dressed at all. Most of them had recent cuts on their bodies—little nicks and long gashes.

"That's not us," said a boy with plastic vampire teeth, every word deformed. "Those are other people. They're bad kids. When we see them while we're out, which sometimes we do, we encourage them to stop marauding. It's fun and healthy to get rowdy, that's natural."

"That's natural," echoed several boys and girls.

"But it's bad to cross the line, and we know that, and we tell these other people, which by the way they aren't all kids, I see a lot of older people out there too. The man who burned down the McDonald's was like fifty. But the point is, even though it might be exciting to break shit, there's a line. And when we go out, we don't cross that line."

"Then take out your vampire teeth and give them to me." David held out his hand.

"I don't even live here, man."

"It's his house," said the kid that David called Alex. Today he wore paint-stained cargo shorts and a faded baseball jersey.

"It's his house," echoed several other boys and girls, but they didn't mean the same thing.

The vampire kid showed his teeth. They were the pale green that means glow in the dark.

David lowered his hand. "Just don't burn my house down, okay? My family lives here."

The kids shuffled up the stairs or out the door. David called Laverne to him and petted her and scratched behind her ears. "They're good kids," he said. "They're going through something right now."

"They'll be done soon enough," said Lyd. It was only ten days till the end.

"I hope that you'll start thinking soon about how to go on living when the world doesn't stop spinning in November," said David. His smirk implied he knew what she would have to do, how she would have to change.

Lyd's dead body feeding worms. The worms dried up and dying on the pavement. The universe devoid of life. So many burning suns and no one making love.

She asked "Alex" where he'd put the books that were left behind in the apartment when she and Mott ran away. He was startled by direct address. "Oh," he said. "I think—oh right—I put them in the garage. It says BOOKS on the boxes in permanent marker. They're kind of hard to find though. I'll go out and get them for you."

"Maybe you can just show me where they are?"

"Sure. By the way, my name is actually Alejandro."

"And I'm Lyd, not Lydia." She shook his hand.

"I know." He scratched his face beside his eye. "I'm sorry about when I pointed the gun at you. You're safer here than you were out there."

"Let's go get the books."

She didn't know what she was looking for until she found them. They were first-edition copies of her novels. Two hardbacks and one paper. That had been a disappointment at the time—the transition, which signaled that her publisher no longer believed she would sell, which meant they would spend less on promoting her, which meant they would prove themselves right. But her third book did have the best cover art. It was a picture of the universe. There were all these stars. Earth was on it toward the bottom left—a small blue circle, nothing special.

She took her books to the kitchen, put a kettle on, and forgot it. She read the first book in five hours. She set it aside. She turned on a light. She started the second.

David had walked through the room several times, never speaking. (He was the one who took the kettle off the burner after a full five minutes of whistling.) Now he sat beside her at the table. "Is this fun for you?" he said.

"It hurts so much."

"Did you know you've been crying?"

Lyd felt her cheeks. He was right.

"I didn't know."

"What's wrong?"

Now she bawled, body shuddering like a machine coming unstuck.

"I should have written another."

"Honey, I'm so sorry. I could have told you that."

"It could have been beautiful." She hiccupped. "I was so close to getting it right."

David put his hand on her hand. She let it be where it was.

"Now there's no time," she sobbed.

"I know, honey." He lifted her hand, kissed her knuckles.

"Don't push your luck David."

He held her hand a little longer, too firmly, digging his thumb into her palm in a way that forced her fingers to curl, almost making a fist. He looked pointedly into her eyes—he was going to keep pushing his luck. If he was right about November, if they really did live past it, he would eventually leave her without any choice but to knock him down and squeeze his throat again.

Lyd's dead body's calm. Lyd's dead body's peace. Lyd dead and gone thank God. Lyd nobody, thank God.

.....

"I'm finished," said Mott. "One thousand crappy words. Can I have a sticker?"

"Of course you can, baby." Lyd peeled a gold star and put it on the day. One week left in October.

"I wish I spent more time with you today Mom. I wish we played a game or went outside. I wish that you would read a book to me."

"We can play something now if you want. I'm sure somebody has a deck of cards. There are hours still left in the day."

"I wish we did fun things together all the time."

"There's nothing we can do that will make you glad to die, my love."

"I wish that Meredith were here."

"I'm sorry that she can't be."

"I wish that you weren't drunk."

"I'll read to you now if you want."

"Can I sit on your lap?"

"Go pick a book. I'll prep my lap."

.....

Lyd opened her eyes. She sprawled on the living room floor. She did not remember lying down. The floor was sprinkled with tortilla chips, popcorn kernels, and M&M's candies.

The party was outside now. She could see it through the windows. There were David's children, and there was the fire they built.

They drummed on pots, buckets, and bowls, on dictionaries and drums. She glimpsed David several times among them—their young bodies always parting around him so that he was never touched. He must know on some level that he was not loved.

Lyd closed the blinds and turned off the lights. She scraped her feet clean on the edge of a stair step stripped of its carpet.

She crawled into bed beside beautiful Mott, wormed her way under the blankets.

She held her daughter. Mott pretended not to wake.

Lyd's dead body numb and blind. Lyd's dead body holding Mott's dead body. Mott's dead body cold as dirt. Lyd's dead body doesn't care.

OCTOBER, DAVID

THERE WERE THREE KINDS OF HOURS IN DAVID'S OCTOBER. THE first kind was sleep. He didn't live this kind often, and rarely received the full benefit, as he was almost always high, drunk, both, or—in the case of one evening—concussed. When he slept, he did so in his office, sometimes on the floor and sometimes in his chair, precariously slumped, lit by monitor glow: images of other people sleeping, including his wife and daughter without him. Watching other people sleep felt in some ways more restful than doing it himself, and so he often chose to do that instead.

The second and best kind of hour was time spent with Lyd—sharing meals, making drinks, listening to music, blowing smoke at each other, doing nothing in particular, arguing about the past. David had somehow forgotten that he not only loved but actually liked her, liked just being in a room with her, even if they weren't talking or touching, even if she said she hated him. It was disappointing that she didn't want to be his wife, that she refused every offer of intimacy and support, but there would be time to fix all of that after the world didn't end. She would need something new to do with her time. Mott would have to go back to school. Maybe they could try to get pregnant again. Would he rather have a boy or a girl? Each option had a lot to recommend it. A son would love him more, but he would better love a daughter. The universe would do what it would do, and this, whatever it was, would be perfect. If Lyd's eggs weren't working anymore, that was fine because they could adopt. The love in any household expands geometrically with every family member added. There were, despite David's best efforts, still several empty rooms on his third floor.

The third kind of hour was time spent awake without Lyd. David used much of this time to watch her through his cameras. He watched her talk and cuddle with Mott, each exuding a warmth that he had never felt directed toward himself. He watched her sit on the toilet for long stretches, not using it for the most part, only hiding there from him and from everyone else. He watched her change and shower. He watched her in the master bedroom, glancing nervously over her shoulder as she picked out clothes for today and the next day. He watched her interact with his young and beautiful houseguests in those rare moments where she could not avoid being with them alone; there was an unmistakable terror in her of their masks and nakedness, a revulsion at their bruises and bleeding and reek, and he understood why—it frightened him too, in moments of weakness. If things ever went too far with them, then certainly he would protect her, certainly he would be able, but the children were a helpful reminder for her of the dangers of life without David's shelter. It was important that Lyd should never feel, until she learned to love again, entirely safe.

He reviewed footage of the hours that they were together—Lyd and himself—in the various rooms of his house, searching for proof that she found him more charming than she would admit, that he was already winning her over, and there was always ample evidence. He called Alex into the room and gestured at the screen, seeking confirmation. "Her face is softening, don't you think? Look at her eyes." "She doesn't want to hit me so much when I talk anymore." "Look at this week, now look at last week." "We're making real progress." She had even smiled for him twice. "By March, we could be renewing our vows." Love was not a choice that anyone made for themselves. It was something that happened to them.

David also used these hours to watch other girls who lived in his home. It was hard to tell them apart and remember their names given that some of their masks were the same and sometimes they traded their masks. He had changed his mind about sleeping with them. Now it sounded like a great idea. Since Lyd's return, and since she had demonstrated that she really would at least attempt to kill him if he touched her any way she did not want, he'd made unsubtle passes at several of the more approachable young women (two masked and one maskless), and each pretended not to hear or understand. That hurt his feelings but that was okay. They were young and beautiful and barbarous; they couldn't help themselves. He was fully committed to Lyd anyway. He should never have divorced her in the first place—nobody can undo a knot the brute heart tied. He was so sick of her face at the time. The way she looked at him like she knew what he was, like he'd been catalogued and pinned down under glass, so she didn't have to listen when he spoke, or think about him when he wasn't there. She had no idea what he was or could be. A man can change. All you have to do to know that is look at the news. Men are changing all the time. They are learning and growing each day.

David trimmed his beard and no one noticed.

David wanted comfort. He searched for Laverne the dog but could not find her even with his cameras. He was too ashamed to ask Alex where she had gone.

.....

Though he was officially on vacation, David continued checking in on his assigned suspicious persons. He still believed in them and their potential happiness.

It was true that the white math teacher had been pummeled to death by his students, but that was okay because now David watched the widow instead. He hadn't noticed before how pretty she was. Most days she drove down to Sandy Point State Park and combed the beach with a metal detector, posting photos of her best finds to social media (coins, cans, bottle caps, bracelets, umbrellas, shells). Chesapeake Bay looked beautiful this time of year, especially the sunsets. When November was not the end of the world, he would visit with her. There was so much that he could say about her husband. Maybe she would come and live with him in his house, up on the too-quiet third floor—she could bring a whole crateful of treasures. She could be a friend like a sister to Lyd.

It was true also that the unmarried Laotian journalist lived now in his otherwise abandoned newsroom, subsisting on the contents of snack machines on his floor and other floors, washing himself daily with a kitchen sink and dish soap, writing down the story of his life in something like the AP style, emailing each day's work product to one person or another who had wronged him or been kind. That was okay because when the world did not end in November he would have a memoir to submit for publication, and the memoir might even get to be a movie—owing to several thrilling chapters on the journalist's years as a war correspondent—and the journalist might even get to play himself. Then he would be glad that all of this had happened. David would introduce himself and they would eat lunch somewhere nice and might become friends. The journalist could then, if he wanted, move into David's third floor.

It was true that the Black math teacher had reappeared one day just as her husband expected, that she had done the laundry that he piled in her absence, that she had given up on drafting suicide notes in the morning, and that now she only watched TV or sat motionless whenever possible, waiting for nothing or nothingness, and that she refused to say where she had been. It was also true that the laundry was accumulating again, that she ate too little, and that David had never had an opportunity to read one of those suicide notes in its entirety, despite their obvious intelligence value, so that now he could not know what would need to change after the world did not end for her to be happy. He only felt sure that whatever was needed would happen. She could come and live with him too, and so could the husband, and they could help look after Mott.

It was true that the white teenage boy had found his father's gun and shot himself dead in the front yard of his maternal grandparents' former home (sold two years prior to cover the costs of the grandmother's funeral and six months of the grandfather's nursing home care). That was okay because it was okay to make one mistake. It was fine for the boy to be dead because it meant his suffering was over. When the world did not end, the boy's parents would come home and mourn him. David would write them a letter. They could maybe move in if they wanted. They would have to show that they were capable of better. Maybe he and Lyd could teach them.

The unmarried Muslim man, now living with his brother, was waiting for a call from the woman that he'd met online. He texted hourly at minimum, asking if she was okay, if she needed anything at all, if she still wanted to meet. She was alive, she was fine, but she'd stopped replying. When the world did not end in November, David planned to find this woman and demand she justify herself and her disinterest. Maybe she would think better of it. Maybe she would marry the Muslim.

One day, while David happened to be watching, the unmarried Muslim man received a call from an out-of-state number that neither he nor David recognized.

"Hello?" said the Muslim, his voice cracking from the effort of not getting his hopes up.

"I'm sorry," said the apologizing woman.

"That's okay! Don't worry about it, that's fine!"

"Lo siento," she continued. "Je suis désolée. Jeg beklager. Es tut mir leid."

"I, I can't tell what you're saying."

"Prosti menya. Maf kijiye."

"You're not her, are you."

"Duìbuqǐ. Gomenasai."

The Muslim had nothing to say in response, but he wasn't hanging up.

David joined the call. "You are forgiven," he said. "Estás perdonado. Vous êtes pardonné." It was true that he believed he might be speaking to an alien. "Du er tilgitt. Ich vergebe dich." And it was true that he believed, when he was honest with himself, that there was every chance the source of this voice, whatever it was, wherever they were, really would end the world in November, or change it so much that it might as well end. "Ya proshchayu tebya. Koi baat nahi." That was okay because it had to be okay. "Yuán liàng nǐ. Yurushite ageru." The world is one more thing that just happens to people.

The apologizing woman let David speak uninterrupted. His pronunciation was poor, and he was only reading from a list, but he gave it his best. He thought that maybe this would help.

She spoke again when he was done. "I'm sorry," she said.

"You are forgiven," said David.

"Lo siento."

"Estás perdonado."

"Je suis désolée."

"Vous êtes pardonné."

And so on like that. The unmarried Muslim man listened, saying nothing, for nearly an hour before his phone died. He never charged it again, and so he was lost too.

. . . . .

David dreamed of the home of the trustworthy man. He approached the table. The man was not waiting for him. On the table there were five actual-sized marble sculptures: David's penis, which he had seen in a previous dream; his hip bones, but not the typically attendant flesh; his nose; his right hand, each finger fully extended, a neutral position; and his left thumb and pointer finger, with no other part of the left hand.

The trustworthy man peeked into the dining room from the hall. He was effortlessly carrying an extension ladder on his shoulder. He would use it to get someplace high.

"This isn't enough," said the man. He pointed at the table and its marble spread. "We can't help you."

David matched his hand to the left thumb and finger.

He would never dream again.

OCTOBER, MOTT

TUESDAY AND TWO THOUSAND WORDS TO GO. FIVE DAYS UNTIL NOvember. David knocked on Mott's office door. "Girls! I made breakfast and found my guitar."

Mott kissed her mother's cheek. Lyd refused to open her eyes. "If we eat the breakfast, do we have to listen to you play guitar?"

"You could always plug your ears." David plucked a sour note.

The kitchen counter was covered with skillets and frying pans, all loaded with fried eggs, potatoes, bacon, sausage, and hash. There were also jugs of orange juice, pink lemonade, milk, and two tall cartons of ready-made mimosa. "You can have whatever you want," said David. "But I did build you plates to start." The plates were waiting on the table, generously overburdened with shining fried things. He had poured Mott a tall glass of milk. He had poured Lyd an orange juice or a mimosa. He allowed himself only water.

"Thank you Dad," said Mott, between bites. "It's really good."

"You're welcome, dear." His guitar lay across his lap. He played an open chord. "Honey, do you like it?"

Lyd said, "Needs salt. But otherwise nice." She drank her orange juice or mimosa.

David's other children wandered downstairs or in the front door. They lifted their masks, sniffed the air. They made plates for themselves. They sat on the couches, tile floor, soiled rug. They bled where they rested and chewed far too loud.

"Dad?" said Mott. Which appeared to startle Lyd badly—that Mott would use the tone of an inquiring child, a little girl about to ask permission from her father.

"Daughter?" said David, delighted.

"Do you have any cell phone chargers? Or can Alex get me one?"

"His name is Alejandro, honey," said Lyd. "Why do you need a charger?"

"I'd like to play my puzzle games, like the one with the fish."

"Five days left to live, and you want to play with your phone?"

"It helps me relax. If I relax I can finish my book. It doesn't help me relax when you talk about *D-E-A-T-H*."

David played another open chord. "Honey, I'll get you a charger. Just tell me what kind you need. I'm sure these kids have one. You know we share everything here."

Mott's phone was slow to wake, having been left off and unused for five months. Mott wrote while it charged. She only did two hundred words. She didn't want to finish yet. When the phone had enough power, she locked her office door and tucked her blankets under it to keep the sound inside. There were two names on her contact list. She called the second.

A boy picked up. "Hello? Who's this?"

Mott held back a happy laugh. "Is this Malik's brother?"

"It's Malik. My brother gave me his phone. He doesn't believe in it anymore."

"Malik! It's me, it's Mott. Is this a bad time?"

"Mott! No, it's fine. I'm not busy. I guess I should warn you the phone's almost dead."

"That's okay. I shouldn't talk long. Did you see a lot of historical things on your trip?"

"We only did that for a little while. I don't think I learned very much. Then my dad got sick. We've been at the hospital since."

"Oh no! I'm so sorry."

"It's okay. He was in a lot of pain at first, but the doctors here are some of the best. We're in Cleveland. They can't fix him but they made it stop hurting. He'll last until the first, which means he'll get to see whatever happens then I guess."

Mott didn't know what to say.

"Sorry Mott. You didn't need to know all that. You probably called to get cheered up. How's it going with your people?"

"Bad, but that's normal for them. My mom and dad got back together kind of. They completely hate each other."

"That sucks. You still boss of the whole middle school?"

"I left two days after you did. They were making the bad kids watch movies all day."

"Yuck. Way to teach."

Mott laughed. "I know! They're so lazy. I got in trouble, so I stopped going. Now I'm writing a book."

"Like a novel?"

"Yeah. Not a real one. It won't ever be published."

"Sure, but that's really cool. You're doing your dream. I always figured you would, but once we knew about November it felt like nobody wanted to do anything anymore. It sounds like you've got a good thing going. I haven't used my time so well."

"You're with your family. You're taking care of your dad. I'm not taking care of anybody. Everyone looks out for me."

"My mom kind of left. My brother did too. So it's just me and Dad, and he sleeps eighteen hours a day. When he's awake, all he wants to do is drink water. You have to hold a sponge over his mouth, drip it in. I spend a lot of time with the nurses, playing cards and dice, hanging out."

"I'm almost done with the book. I have to write eighteen hundred words. I just wanted to tell somebody who would get excited. And I thought, *Malik will know how special this is.* You were always really nice to me."

"I always wanted to tell you how pretty you are."

Mott laughed again. "You were a good friend. But I didn't know you were my friend. I don't always listen."

"You were special to me."

There was a plaintive beep on Malik's end of the line. "Shit," he said. "It's dying."

"I'm sorry. You don't have your charger?"

"I'm not at the hospital right now. I was getting a gift for someone. Man. I'd like to talk to you some more. Where are you now?"

"Virginia. Near DC. My dad's house."

"That's not so far from Cleveland. I could swing that."

"Malik?"

"Sorry. Nothing."

"Thank you for listening."

His phone beeped again.

He said, "Can I be honest with you about something? I always thought we'd get married someday. I know that's irrational, it's just something I believed. But I haven't thought about you in a while. I had to let you go. I felt so stupid for giving you my brother's number instead of getting yours. I was trying to be cool, make you come to me. Hearing your voice again, it makes me feel like I want to live."

"I, um. That's very nice of you."

"I can drive Dad's car. It's in the hospital parking garage. They'll let me take it because I know everyone here. I could come see you tomorrow. We could be together when it happens. Or maybe just a day. I don't know."

"Um," said Mott.

"I don't want to die alone, Mott. I don't think you do either."

She considered hanging up. "I'm not alone, Malik. I have my mom and even sort of my dad."

"That's not what I mean."

"I know it isn't. But I don't have time for what you mean. I'm an author."

His phone beeped again. "I'm sorry, I never thought to ask—do you like boys?"

"I don't know what I like. Maybe not anybody. I've decided not to think about it. I used to have a lot of ideas about what growing up would be like. I used to know who I was gonna be. But I don't get to do that now. I never get to be me."

Malik's phone beeped. "Sorry that I made it weird."

"You should go. Your phone's dying."

"Do you think we would have maybe ever gotten married? If it weren't for November?" His phone beeped again. "I promise I'll believe you if you lie."

"I'm sorry. Go be with your dad."

She ended the call and turned off her phone.

- - - - -

Tuesday night and one thousand words left. She hadn't wanted any lunch after David's big breakfast, had wanted dinner and skipped anyway. Now her stomach fizzed and grouched.

Lyd let herself in. She carried a plated poppy-seed bagel and a can of sugar soda. Mott pretended not to care about the food, not because she was ungrateful but because she was an artist. Lyd opened the can and set it down beside Mott's legal pad. "Not done yet?"

"Nope."

"But you still want to finish tonight."

"If I do we can go for a picnic tomorrow. We can make Dad take us to a park. It can be my retirement party. When I'm done with this book, I never have to work another day."

Lyd kissed the top of Mott's head. "It's too dangerous to go outside. The kids only behave when they're inside this house. They'd hurt us. Your father can't keep us safe."

"Okay, but I want to celebrate. I want to have a party."

"We can't have a party. The kids will get worked up. They'll hurt us."

"Then I want a present. I want you to get me something really fun."

"If I give you something fun, they'll take it."

"Will you at least be very happy when I finish it?"

Lyd laughed. "Yes I will."

"And will you stop drinking so you can read it sober?"

"I already did, love."

Mott smiled. "How's the headache?"

Lyd lay down in their bed, made an angel in the sheets. "Truly incredible."

"Is anything good going to happen when I finish?"

"Something good will happen for me. I'll get to read it."

"Will something good happen for me?"

"No, you'll be in agony. All you'll be able to think about is everything you got wrong. You'll watch my face for some particular reaction, but I'll never be able to give you what you want."

"So why did I do this?"

"Because you would be sorry if you didn't."

Mott drank deeply of her sugar soda. "That's dumb."

"The world is dumb, honey. That's why they're shutting it down." Lyd covered her own face with a pillow.

Mott wrote a sentence of middling quality. Tuesday night and nine hundred ninety-five words.

In Mott's novel, the mother found her daughter in the deepest chamber of the magic cave. The walls glowed all around them with variously colored lichens. The dead dinosaurs watched them through hollow eye sockets. The mother knelt, holding the daughter's head in her lap. She still wore the daughter's body. The daughter still wore the mother's.

"I think I'm dying," said the daughter.

"You stayed here too long," said the mother. "You needed your medicine."

"I wanted you to come with me."

"I know."

"I wanted to trade back."

"I'm sorry."

"I miss my body so much. I miss being your daughter."

"I miss being your mom."

"You don't miss your body."

"No." The mother stroked the daughter's hair—her own hair, her own body's. "I hated living there."

"Can we try to go back one more time?"

"We can try."

"Hold me please. My spine is totally ruined."

"Okay."

"I hurt so much all the time."

"I'm sorry. I know."

And the mother held her daughter. And they slept together in the cave, lit by the lichens, protected by the bones. But the mother did not dream.

And when she woke, her daughter was dead—the mother's body was dead.

The mother rocked that lifeless body in her arms for several minutes. But the body was already cold.

She used her feet to push it into a small pool of water, which was dark and bottomless.

The mother's body vanished.

The mother felt glad in her heart that it was not she who had died.

She left the cave alone.

- - - - -

Mott threw her hands up in the air. "I'm finished!" she shouted. "I'm done!"

But Lyd did not stir.

Mott said, "Sixty thousand words and change!" She held her hands up and wiggled her fingers. "I'm all ink-stained!" It was even on her elbows and shirt.

Lyd rolled over in a way that meant she was disturbed but not awake. Her body was ten percent sweat.

"That's okay," said Mott. "I can celebrate with Dad."

She gathered all the legal pads that were her novel and turned off the light.

She found her father downstairs. He was seated on the couch with Alejandro and a girl in a plastic ski mask. They were listening to slow jazz. David played along on his guitar, which lay flat across his lap and Alejandro's. David's playing was improved. He must have found a chord. All three on the couch were taking turns smoking, tapping their ash onto the floor. The girl threaded the joint through one of her mask's mouth holes.

"Little Mottle!" said David. "Pretty girl. What'd you bring us? Some business papers?"

"Not business. Something really special."

He was only half listening. He plucked each guitar string, testing their sounds. He played his chord.

The girl asked Mott what the special thing was. She passed the joint to David.

"I want my dad to ask me what again."

"Okay," said David. "I'm asking. Consider yourself asked."

He passed the joint to Alejandro. Mott waited for his focus. His head was only loosely attached to his body, and his face was all lit orange. Someone outside had sparked a fire.

Mott held the yellow legal pads over her head like a trophy. She shouted, "It's my novel!"

Her father played his chord. "Oh," he said. "Hey. That's really cool."

The girl also said it was cool. She said, "I always thought that I would write a book about my life. I bet it's hard."

Mott said, "It's really hard."

Alejandro said, "You're like a genius, aren't you. I was in the gifted program, but there's no such thing as a gifted adult. You grow up, it's all about your job. Nobody even asks your IQ."

"You want to celebrate?" said David.

"It's one hundred thirty-five," said Alejandro. "That's well above average."

"Yeah!" said Mott. "I want to celebrate!"

He handed her the stubby joint. "Go ahead and finish it off. I'll get another one started."

Mott turned the joint in her hand, holding the stack of legal pads against herself with her other arm. She had become so accustomed to the smell that now it was impossible to find among the others in her father's home. She could smell the guitar more than she could smell the pot.

She sucked the smoke inside, coughed it up, and swallowed more.

Alejandro said, "When you're an adult, you're on your own. You can't ask for help. I wish I'd done everything different."

"You'll get it right next time," said the girl. "We never do anything once."

David's other children were growing their bonfire out in the yard. It must be at least six feet tall. Mott could see them through the window. They had Laverne with them—she faced away from the fire, toward the empty street, pulling her leash taut, keeping still. The boy who held her leash wore a wolf mask.

Mott blew a thin ribbon of smoke. Her mouth tasted awful. She didn't feel different.

"I'm a novelist!" she said. "I did it!"

"That's really great." David gave her the new joint he'd made. He took the other away, pinched it out, and dropped it on the floor.

"I shouldn't have any more."

"Go on, honey. You did your big thing. Now you can relax. Nobody wants to die sober."

Mott didn't feel different at all. Not that she could tell at all. She was fine.

"When I was a kid, my favorite thing was being sick," said the girl on the couch. "My mom would stay home from work just to take care of me. We would watch cartoons and eat cereal without milk. We mixed up all the cereals we had in one of those punch bowls, the fruit kind and chocolate, cinnamon, whatever."

The record had run out of music again.

"Are you proud of me, David?" said Alejandro. "Do you think that I'm good?"

"No one's good," said the girl. "But when I'm high, I can be friends with anyone."

"Stop crying, Mott," said David. But she wasn't at all. She didn't feel different. And he didn't know. He didn't even know about the fire that his other children had built.

David pulled Mott close, tweaked her chin. "You're not smiling," he said. "Don't you dare smile. Mottle, you listen to me, now don't you dare smile. I know that you won't. You're not smiling. You're not smiling! You're not smiling!"

Mott tried so hard not to smile, but she couldn't stop her face from doing what it wanted.

David took the joint from her and used it. "You're not laughing!" He kissed her nose. "You're not laughing! Don't you laugh! Don't you dare laugh. You're not going to laugh, I know you won't, you're much too serious for that, and much too sad from writing your big, miserable novel. No daughter of mine would ever laugh, would she? Don't laugh, Mott! Wait! Stop! I beg you! Please! Don't! Laugh!"

But she couldn't help it. The sound began as a belch. It came out so hard that it hurt. She dropped her novel on the floor. Her body was shaking all over.

Outside, Laverne barked, yelped pitifully at her shock collar's punishment, then barked and yelped again, as she struggled to flee David's children. The wolf-masked boy yanked at her leash with both arms, jerking her close; she snarled and bit his hand. He couldn't help letting go. Mott needed to stop laughing. Laverne was gone and David didn't know.

A girl with a white sheet over her head pointed at the house, and all the young people outside turned to look where she pointed, and in through the window at David and Mott. They walked (or stalked or crept or crawled) toward the house.

OCTOBER, LYD

LYD THUNDERED DOWN THE STAIRS, PULLED A LONG KNIFE FROM the block in the kitchen, and put herself between her daughter and the front door, holding Mott's king fish under her arm.

"You're not allowed to have a knife," said David. He searched himself for his gun.

David's other children knocked the front door off its hinges. A crush of Halloween bodies crowded the entrance, lit from behind by their fire and lit from within the home by its lights. The boy with the vampire teeth shouted, "Monster mash!"

The other children overturned the kitchen table and chairs.

The boy shouted, "Monster mash!"

The other children pulled the dishes out of the cupboards and hurled them on the floor. They opened the cereal boxes and shook them out. They opened every liquid in the fridge and poured these on one another. Mott pressed herself to Lyd's side, hugging her notepads. Lyd stayed as still as she could, squeezing the grip of her knife.

The boy shouted something not a word. The other children

pressed themselves against the walls and beat them with their palms. There was no rhythm, no restraint; the upper floors rattled and groaned. They made craters in the shapes of their hands. Where the walls were already damaged by previous nights, they put their hands through.

The boy with the vampire teeth stepped too close to Lyd. She reached out with the knife to show him what a better distance was, and barked at him, and he obeyed.

The vampire lifted Alejandro from the couch by his hair, grasped him by the shoulder too, and showed the room his neck. He bared his plastic teeth and his real ones. The plastic glowed its sickly green. "Let's spare him November," he said.

"Wait!" said David. He leapt to his feet and smashed his guitar on the floor. It took four swings to do the job. Then all that was left in his hand was the fretboard, the strings tied to their tuning pegs, and the bridge, which hung from the strings. "Wait!"

The boy let go of Alejandro, who stumbled back and fell onto the couch beside the girl in the ski mask. She was keeping still like Lyd and Mott.

"Would you listen to me for once in your lives?" shouted David. "Do you want to die assholes? I've been telling you since the dream, there isn't going to be a November. Not like you think. Every one of you will still be alive in December, and everything will start getting better. But if you break my fucking house, there won't be anywhere to keep you warm. And if you kill my buddy Alejandro, I won't care what happens to you. He's such a nice kid! Meanwhile, you've all been hideous, ungrateful shits. You're going to be so embarrassed when none of you die."

The boy with the vampire teeth smirked. All the other children stood at the room's edges and in the hallways and stairwell, some of them struck dumb by David's shameful display, others sniggering at him.

"Why do you live here if you don't want to listen to me?" shouted David. "Why come into my home if you don't love me? My daughter is crying because you're all jerks. Get the fuck out, I told you the rule, we only have one anymore. You're not supposed to trash my place! Look what you've done to my walls! Where do you think you're sleeping tonight? You've totaled every home on the block!"

David searched himself for his gun. It wasn't in his pockets, tucked into his belt, holstered underneath his shirt, or anywhere in reach. The kids were closing in around him, clicking their teeth. The boy with the vampire teeth said, "Maybe it's time we spared David."

The front door was clear now. Everyone was crowding David. Lyd got low, locked eyes with Mott, put a hand on her shoulder. She whispered, "Do you have your whole book?"

Mott nodded. She held all her notepads as close as she could.

"Okay," said Lyd. "Here's your king fish. Count to five, catch your breath, and then run. Go straight out the door and get as far away as you can. Keep your book close. I'll be right behind you, okay?"

"Okay," said Mott. Her whole body shivered once. "I'll go straight out the door."

"One," said Lyd.

"Two," said Mott. She breathed the rest—*Three, four, five*—and then bolted.

Lyd put her back to the door and held out her knife, showing anyone who might consider pursuing Mott that this was not permitted. David saw Mott leave, but he couldn't possibly follow. His other children wrapped their arms around his arms and legs and waist. The boy with the vampire teeth put his hands over David's eyes from behind. The other children pushed their masks up to their noses, so that they had their rubber mouths and their real ones. Tenderly at first, they mouthed David's skin. He was shaking. Alejandro buried his face in the lap of the girl in the ski mask, who still hadn't moved.

Then David's children used their teeth. They bit him through his clothes, and on his bare arms and hands. The boy with the vampire teeth removed his hands from David's eyes. David looked down at his children, looked across the room at Lyd, and screamed.

Satisfied that no one would follow, Lyd ran out the door.

.....

There hadn't been time enough for Lyd to tell Mott where to go, so now she had to guess where her daughter would be. The fire outside David's house was consuming the front yard. Though it could not burn the dirt or sand, it could make something of the grass and other living things. Its tongues were also licking David's home.

The street on which David lived was a ruin. His children or some other cult of this final Halloween had knocked down or wounded every wall, destroyed every car. Even now, in this dark, the street was well lit by what spilled from the seams of these homes, electricity and fire. Water sprayed from ruptured pipes. Lyd looked for a good hiding place where Mott might be cowering, but there were none that looked safe. She tried to think like her daughter. Mott could only move so fast with her novel, her king fish, and her socks.

The road continued left at least one mile. Lyd could see no motion there but fire. To her right, the road was wrapped around a corner. Mott would understand instinctively that turning the corner was safer than taking the straight road.

There were more and different screams in David's home. Lyd forced herself to run. She bled from her bare feet.

There around the corner was her daughter, crouched behind a car flipped on its side. Mott held all her notebooks and her king fish, and hid from a man playing zombie.

The man wore corpse makeup and rubber wounds. His teeth were half-gone or more likely half-blacked. He wore a pin-striped suit. He made a spectacle of himself stumbling down the road, all hisses and gurgles and moans. There was an undeniable lilt in his gait, a whimsy to the way he advanced, lunging with the right loafer and dragging his left like an anchor.

Lyd went to her daughter and bent to kiss her head. Mott hugged her leg viciously.

"That's okay," said Lyd. "Let go."

The zombie, seeing Lyd, sped his limping, raising his arms and making them stiff—reaching for her.

She opened his palm with the knife. He hissed and stumbled backward, sucked the wound.

"I've made it this far without killing someone," said Lyd. "Don't take that from me."

The zombie turned and ran as quick as he could. Lyd took some of Mott's novel in her free hand. She led her daughter to the nearest gutted house that did not burn. They searched inside for shoes and backpacks.

By now the screams in David's home were audible at any distance. And elsewhere it was much the same.

They found not shoes but slippers. They walked into the thickest night, away from any light or sound, through small forests, across the outskirts of some golf course—not the fenced part but the lush grass that surrounded—and through a neighborhood apparently abandoned, to the deepest circle of its nested cul-de-sacs, where there was no power, where most cars were gone, where any other person living was huddled in some silent corner of a room without windows. Lyd chose a home for them that looked like nothing special. She tried the doors until she found one left unlocked.

The fridge was all but empty. What remained was rotten. There were cans of green beans and pie filling in the cupboards. There were many photos on the walls. It was too dark to see their faces.

Mother and daughter slept together underneath the largest bed.

OCTOBER, LYD

MORNINGS BEFORE THE SUN WAS FULLY RISEN, LYD SCAVENGED IN the other homes.

Afternoons she read her daughter's novel.

Mott asked her often how she liked it.

"I love it," said Lyd.

Mott often asked why.

Lyd said she loved the characters. She loved how scary it was. She loved many of the sentences. She loved how strange the premise was. She loved the way that Mott tried so hard to be cruel. She loved how Mott was only ever actually kind.

Mott called her mother a liar. She made her say it all again.

.....

Under ordinary circumstances, Lyd could have read a book this brief in a day. But there were many complicating problems. The first was Mott's handwriting. It only grew worse as the novel progressed. And there were often missing words—things that Mott had thought she wrote, but never did. Lyd often pointed to a certain line. "What does this say here?" Or, more painful still for Mott, "What did you mean to write?"

And Lyd had to forage daily for water, leaving Mott alone beneath the largest bed, kitchen knife clutched in one hand, king fish in the other.

And Lyd was racked by painful headaches, which sometimes would not let her read.

And whenever Lyd laughed or even smiled, Mott interrupted to ask why.

"You're really funny, baby."

It wasn't supposed to be funny.

"Funny's good, I promise. I always wished I could be funny."

Mott smiled. "Mom. Your books are hilarious."

And Lyd needed frequent breaks to look at her daughter.

Mott blushed. "Mom, you need to keep reading."

"Every time I look at you there's a part of me wondering if it's going to be the last time that I get to see you. It really hurts to look away."

"I love you."

"I love you."

"I love you."

And Lyd could only read when there was daylight. When night fell, there was nothing else to do but hold each other underneath the bed.

- - - - -

Though she knew he was most likely dead, Lyd couldn't help thinking of David. She imagined him living.

He wouldn't go far from his house's ashes. She imagined him nesting in a makeshift tent that Alejandro pitched in the backyard, built from sticks and blankets gathered from the neighborhood's remains. His arms and hands were wrapped with many yards of gauze bound by strips of painter's tape, his lower half ensconced in a puffy sleeping bag. He lay on the ground, head and upper back elevated by a stack of pillows in mismatched cases. There were water bottles piled on the ground, soda cans, and candy bars. Alejandro sat beside him, legs folded, cradling a bowl of water.

Alejandro put the bowl to David's lips. He said, "Drink."

David coughed and in so doing fouled the water. Alejandro sighed and poured it out.

"She left me again," said David. "She left me to die."

Alejandro opened a fresh water bottle, poured it into the bowl. "You're not dead yet, sir."

"You're a good son," said David.

His face was nothing like it used to be. Lyd could not imagine how it would look now.

Lyd saw Alejandro put the bowl to David's lips again. "Drink."

- - - - -

Lyd and Mott debated which can of pie filling to eat for dessert.

"I don't like cherry," said Mott. "It's gross and really bad."

"You only think you don't like cherry," said Lyd. "You haven't tried it since you were a little girl."

"I want the pumpkin."

"That's your favorite. We'll have it tomorrow. Let's be brave and try the cherry."

She opened the can. They ate with little spoons.

Mott wore a preemptive stink face for three bites. "It's bitter," she said. The corners of her mouth kept twitching.

"You like it," said Lyd.

Mott couldn't hold in the laughter.

"It's so good!"

It was light enough to see the family photos on the walls now. They showed a mother, a father, two daughters, a cat, two grandparents, one Christmas tree, one kindergarten graduation, one veteran grandfather, one day at the zoo, one water park trip, one day learning how to ride a bike, one daughter caring for a little boy doll.

"They seem nice," said Mott.

"You've been a wonderful family to me," said Lyd. "I never needed more."

Mott fed her mother a spoonful of cherry.

- - - - -

And on the final day it rained.

Lyd laid down the last legal pad.

"I can't talk about it anymore," said Mott. "Just tell me did you love it."

Lyd nodded. She pulled Mott into her lap.

"And do you think it could be published?"

Lyd scratched Mott's back in circles.

"I think you would have published something wonderful someday."

"Thank you, Mom."

"I'm sorry about everything I ever did to hurt you, Mott."

There was a feeling in her chest like the high point of the roller coaster—like the instant before the first fall.

"Are you ready, Mott?"

"I'm not ready."

"Lie with me and let me look at you until November."

"Mom, I think. I think I'd rather go outside."

Poised to fall.

"It's raining, Mott."

"We can share the umbrella."

Mott led her to the door. She unlocked all its locks. She began to turn the knob.

Lyd jerked her hand free of Mott's hand. "I'm scared."

"Don't you want to see what happens?"

NOVEMBER

LYD OPENED HER EYES.

The rain fell through her body and each body.

The rain filled her with the glow of being kind.

She held her daughter's hand. Her daughter also filled with this good rain.

There was hardly any point in moving.

A policeman appeared in the rain. He looked like someone they could trust.

"Ma'am," said the policeman, "we need to do our work."

"Mott will help us," said Lyd.

Mott said, "I'll clean my room."

He led them to his car.

Mott had her king fish. She didn't have her book. There was nothing to be done.

All the windows were rolled down to let the rain in. It pooled around their feet and cooled them while he drove. The clouds above were vast and purple, backlit as if by many little suns. Gentle, shifting rays of light shone down through them on everything, and every color was changed.

Lyd and Mott and their policeman saw many other police cars, and trucks and vans of other providence, some unknowable number, traveling in all directions, containing other families, sometimes just a single person. Their windows were also rolled down. They were also filled with peace. Nobody waved.

Lyd held her daughter's hand. They crossed bridges. They rolled past empty fields and disused cities.

They didn't need the radio.

. . . . .

They were in the old apartment. They had taken all its best things when they left, and David had taken the second-best things, so nearly all that what was left was clutter, garbage, and mess.

All the clothes that no one wanted, the books that would never be finished or even begun.

All the coffee rings on stiff paper towels.

Empty canola oil bottles.

All the crumbs swept under the oven, candle wax on the counter.

The carpet-thick layer of dust on the ceiling fan's blades.

All the balled-up tissues in the bathroom waste bin, cardboard tubes.

Dead batteries in a disposable bowl.

The broken mug behind the faucet, all its shards dropped inside it.

Rotten pennies in the couch. Lyd's computer on the table.

All the nicks and stray pencil marks on the walls.

The policeman said, "Please make it clean."

They folded their clothes and put them away.

They sorted their books onto the shelves, by genre and by alphabet.

Lyd scrubbed the counters.

Mott did the dishes.

"This is good," said the policeman.

Mott folded the linens.

Lyd peeled every famous figure and building that she'd ever glued to the wall.

She scrubbed all the glue from the wall.

She pulled the clock free from the window.

Mott hummed a song.

And all the families cleaned all their homes.

Each had their own police officer or uniformed person, who oversaw and praised their work. These were trustworthy people. They knew what was right.

There were footsteps in the halls of the apartment building—people taking out the trash, taking laundry to the machines. When any two people crossed paths, they smiled and nodded. Neither quite looked at the other. There was a fascinating something inside each person, a thought in the stomach, which made it difficult to lift their eyes.

The sound of the rainfall made everything sleepy.

It made being inside feel so good and so warm.

The policeman said, "This is good. Thank you."

Lyd picked up the floor in her bedroom.

She dusted the nightstand.

She changed the bulb.

There was a second Lyd asleep in her bed.

The second Lyd lay naked on top of the blanket. She looked exactly like the first Lyd—the one who was looking at her.

She reminded Lyd of many things that she had forgotten about her own body, and showed her some things she had never quite seen. There were so many lines on the soles of her feet.

She looked cold, so Lyd tucked her in. Her skin felt smooth as polished marble.

The first Lyd was kneeling to look at the second.

The policeman came into the room to spot-check her work. He smiled. "You probably want to know who that is."

Lyd could barely feel her hands. She could barely want anything. She said, "Who?"

"That's the next and better you. The ones who sent the dream are helping us. They're replacing everyone with a new person. It's our job to make the world ready."

Lyd adjusted the blanket that covered the next, better her. There was a tenderness for this person in Lyd that she had never found for herself.

"It's not our fault," said the policeman. "We're basically good. It's our bodies. They're inadequate."

Mott was with them now. She was also looking at the other Lyd.

"We only have so much energy in us. We have limited empathy, limited love. We can only remember so many faces. When we run out of room, we forget someone we used to know. It's our hardware. Cooked in."

He tapped his forehead, which made a wooden sound.

"The creators wanted us to struggle so we could be beautiful, poignant, and inspiring, but we're supposed to succeed, and we just can't. Not while we're like what we are. They tried to find another way. There was nothing they could do to fix us. Soon we'll move on. The new bodies will do better. They'll be kinder than us. They'll be adequate. They'll love one another. They'll know how. They'll care about everyone. When we're gone, they'll be happy."

There was a sound like rushing water in Lyd's ears.

Mott kissed the next Lyd on the cheek, glancing at the first afterward to check if this had been okay. It was fine.

Mott went to clean her room.

"The dream of the attentive listener," said Lyd. "We told him everything." She was still kneeling.

The policeman nodded. "That's how the creators made the new us. We told them what we were and wanted to be. The next me won't hurt anyone. I asked specifically."

"My friends were going to kill themselves. Emily and her husband. They wouldn't want this."

"They won't have to do this," said the policeman. "The ones who sent the dream gave us time to decide for ourselves. Anyone who chose to die, their judgment will be trusted, and they won't be made again, and they won't have to suffer. Any institution, any structure, any living thing that chose to end, will really end. And all the rest have chosen life, and they've been made again as better bodies, and what the bodies do will all be better."

Lyd couldn't think. She gazed upon the new Lyd's face and waited for a thought to come. This other Lyd's lips were pursed as if she was thinking right now—as if she was mildly worried.

The policeman put his hand on her shoulder. "After everything that happened, everything we suffered, all the fear," he said. He squeezed her shoulder in a way that meant she had done well. "Anyone who's living now, they've made their choice. They wanted to live."

Lyd left the room—scrambling on her knees at first, and then on her feet.

She scrubbed the toilets.

She mopped the vinyl flooring.

She deleted every file on her computer and cleared out her Internet cache.

She recycled the coupons and all of her accumulated bills.

Several family photo albums were still in the apartment. These would be mostly pictures of Mott; there would also be a little Lyd and David. There would be a few of Lyd's parents and brother.

Lyd made sure each album was neatly placed on the bookshelf where it should be. There was no time for flipping through their pages. The policeman would never permit it.

Lyd went into Mott's room.

Where Mott had tucked in the next Mott's body, which lay on the bottom bunk.

Mott knelt watching her better self sleep.

And Lyd thought how beautiful they were, her daughters.

And Lyd wondered how this other Mott would be when she woke up, and when she grew.

Would she ever write another novel? Was that something that good people did?

Would she ever fall in love?

She imagined the love the other Lyd would feel for this next Mott.

There was nobody better than her daughter.

How could anybody love Mott more?

There was no such thing as more love or less. There was only love or its absence.

Lyd stomped into her living room, which was also her kitchen.

The policeman had opened the window. He cupped his ear and listened to the rain.

Lyd pulled a knife from the drawer for sharp things. "No one is better than her."

The policeman put his arm out the window, moved his fingers in the rain. "Ma'am," he said, "I need you to be calm. Let's step outside a moment. That'll cool us all right off."

She could feel her hands again. She could feel her whole body. All the kindness had left her. She put the knife in his chest.

"Ma'am," said the policeman. He fell on his back.

Lyd raced back to Mott's bedroom. She said, "Honey listen to your mother now. I need you to take off your clothes."

Mott, still kneeling bedside, considered her as if from a great distance.

"Stand up," said Lyd. She helped her daughter stand. "Raise your arms." She pulled off Mott's shirt, struggling especially to get it past her head. She yanked down her pants and underwear. "Lift your feet."

Mott would not lift her feet. "Goddamn it." Lyd had to do it for her, one foot at a time. She had to remove Mott's socks herself.

"Get in the bed now."

Mott looked at the bed. She looked at her second self.

"Get in the bed!"

"Mom, I don't want to."

"Use the top bunk."

"Mom, I want to be with you."

"Get in the top bunk," said Lyd. She pushed her daughter toward the ladder. "You're too big now honey, I can't lift you."

"Mom, I don't want to!"

"You have to go to bed!" screamed Lyd. She closed the bedroom door and locked it. "They're going to send another!"

Mott regarded her mother with some hazy version of fear. She climbed the ladder and crawled into bed.

"Now you have to sleep," said Lyd.

"I don't think I can," sniffled Mott. "It's cold. I'm scared."

"Then just pretend you're dead."

Mott closed her eyes.

"Stay like that until I come for you. Okay?"

She knew she never would. The other, better Lyd would be the lucky one.

Lyd put the king fish on Mott's tummy. She said, "I hope that you know you're amazing to me."

Mott shook her head, eyes still closed. She hugged the fish.

"It's true. Even if you never write another book. Whatever you do, however you change, you'll still be my favorite person."

Mott said, "I'm going to try to dream about you."

"I'll try too."

And Lyd cried. And Mott was quiet. Lyd wouldn't hear her voice again.

Lyd knelt beside the bottom bunk and kissed her other daughter's cheek.

Which was cold as an apple at first. It warmed quickly.

"Wake up, sleepyhead."

The better Mott opened her eyes. They were beautiful and bright. There was some spark in them that Lyd had never seen before. "Mommy?" said this Mott. "It's too early."

"I know it is," said Lyd. "We have to get out of bed and get dressed."

"There's no school today," said this Mott.

"It's a chore day," said Lyd. "You need to help your mother clean."

This Mott stretched and yawned. She moved so easily. There was no terror in her body. There was no knowledge of November, and nothing unkind. There was no Mott. "Okay," she said. She sat up, swung her legs out of bed, yawned again.

"Put these on please."

"But they're yesterday's clothes. They're on the floor."

"Am I your mother or am I a stranger?"

"You're my mother, of course." This Mott put on her clothes. She didn't need Lyd's help at all. She kissed Lyd's cheek. "Who's that in my top bunk?"

Lyd kissed this Mott's cheek again. "Somebody you would be lucky to know. But we have to work now."

They set to cleaning what was left. This Mott hummed as she worked. Lyd could not help but admire her diligence.

Another policeman identical to the first came into the apartment, pulled the knife from his duplicate's chest, and rinsed it under cold water. The water ran a pale red down the drain. "I'm sorry I upset you, ma'am. That was thoughtless, what I said. Thank you and your daughter both for your efforts on behalf of the next world. I'm sorry for all that I bled on your floor. Let me help you get that stain."

- - - - -

When everything was as it should be, the policeman thanked them again. He said, "Now please get your swimsuits."

He said, "You won't need a towel."

The rain had stopped and the sun was setting again. Clouds were mostly ordinary gray. The air smelled fresh. There was—everywhere—the slightest radio crackle.

There were no worms on the pavement. There were no birdsongs.

Nobody was using a car anywhere.

No one was buying anything. No one was watching TV.

Everyone in the world was out on the streets. They were all walking together. Lyd held this Mott's hand. No one wore a rubber mask. They carried backpacks, duffels, or grocery bags with their swimsuits inside. Laughing children stomped in puddles. Every family was led by its own policeman or soldier or postman or other uniformed guide, and every alone person. Some of the uniformed people looked just like one another. Lyd saw several copies of her own policeman.

Strange shapes floated in the sky, angles of light, which twisted and changed if anyone focused on them, so that it was impossible to really see them. They were like the ghosts that light bulbs leave on eyelids. They were like the corners of a room without the room.

"Watchers," said Lyd's policeman, pointing at these shapes. "They'll tell everyone how good we were today."

The watchers were large and quite far away, or they were close and quite small.

The policeman led Lyd and this Mott to the YMCA. Not everyone was going to the Y, but many other families were as well, or were already there.

"I'll meet you at the pool," he said, and opened the door to the men's locker room. The usual sounds escaped—boys' laughter, a blow dryer, lockers slammed closed—and there was the smell of chlorine. There was a set of stairs behind the door, just as there was behind the door to the ladies' locker room. He began his descent, trusting them to do the same.

Some small part of Lyd still had the energy to think of running away. The feeling in her hands was mostly gone again. Her body was becoming kind. And if she resisted, then they—the policemen, the soldiers, the postal service, the watching impossible shapes, or some other entity—would surely find her. And if they did, they might inspect the Mott beside her. And if they did, they might know what she had done.

"Come on," said Mott. "Let's go swimming!"

"Sorry honey. You're right."

They went down the stairs holding hands.

. . . . .

And in the ladies' locker room it was much as it had always been. The girls on their periods changed behind curtains—sometimes alone, sometimes with their mothers. The old women sighed as they took off their bras and hung them in lockers. The teenagers compared bodies in whispers both flirtatious and ashamed. They shared benches and stools. Some folded their clothes very neatly. Some heaped it all at their locker's bottom.

Mott put on her blue one-piece with the white frill around its waist.

Lyd slipped into her two-piece, dark blue, and felt her own stomach, and wished she had eaten.

"Mom," said Mott, "you're really beautiful."

"Thank you honey. You are too."

"I'm not," said Mott. She smiled. "I wish people wouldn't get so anxious about it."

"I'm sorry," said Lyd.

"That's okay."

They rinsed themselves in the showers, joining other women and girls. There were no stalls nor dividers; everyone was together, a little more than arm's length from each other. Lyd watched her daughter wash. It was hard to look at her, impossible to look away. The faucets all ran far too hot or cold, so they didn't linger.

They climbed the small staircase that led up to the indoor pool. (The outdoor was closed due to weather.) A sign on the wall forbade running and food.

. . . . .

The pool was lit with soft blue lights.

Children ran despite the sign, and some fathers had smuggled in potato chips or beers. The lifeguards turned a blind eye.

No one was really swimming in the pool, though some of the little kids did dip their hands to splash each other, and some people did sit on the edge, slowly kicking their feet in the water. Mostly they sat dry in their bathing suits, waiting on the folding chairs like patio furniture, in some cases shivering from the cold, in some cases holding each other.

Some conversed and some watched the divers. Some chattered their teeth.

This Mott was pressed tight against Lyd, both clinging and shaking. Lyd held her with one arm. She fought the urge to push her away.

About once per minute, the lifeguard on the high chair blew his whistle, called a name. The person who was called lined up behind the diving board, where they waited for their turn to jump. There was no saying who would be called next. The lifeguard was not using the alphabet, was not calling families together. If he had a system, then it was his own.

"Mom," said this Mott, "can you hold me with both arms? I'm getting really cold."

"I'm sorry," said Lyd. She hugged this Mott close.

When a diver went under—however they fell, classic form or cannonball—they never came up.

The water teemed with dark indistinct shapes, shadows, figures or unlikely folds. It was not infinitely deep, but would hold what it was given.

The lifeguard blew his whistle. He called Mott.

"Sorry Mom. It's my turn." She shrugged off Lyd's arms.

"That's okay," said Lyd. "Be careful, love."

Mott gave her a smile. She went to the diving board. There were three other people already in line.

Lyd tried to remember some part of her Mott's book. She tried to remember one line.

There had been so many nearly perfect things inside Mott's book that she would never have another chance to read.

She wished her Mott were with her now.
Soon, and sooner now, Lyd would be called from her seat.
Now this Mott climbed the ladder.
This Mott walked the trembling white board.
She waved at Lyd to make sure she was watching.
This Mott took two steps and leapt.
Lyd studied the ripples until they were gone.

ACKNOWLEDGMENTS

THANK YOU TO TRACY FOR YEARS OF LOVE, SUPPORT, AND ADVICE, and for always being my first and best reader.

Thank you to my mother, Mary, for everything. Thank you to Laura and Alex for being my siblings, reading my work, and always being kind to me.

Thank you to my agent, Monika Woods, who did so much to make this book what it is now. This wouldn't exist without her.

Thank you to my editor, Gabriella Doob, whose belief in this book means the world to me, and whose editorial judgment I quickly learned to trust completely. I have loved working with her.

Thank you to everyone at Ecco: Elizabeth Yaffe, who designed a jacket that feels like a dream; Angela Boutin, who designed an interior that makes the words real; Christina Polizoto, this book's production editor, who made it all happen; and Sonya Cheuse and Meghan Deans, for their publicity and marketing direction. Thank you also to the folks who provided copyediting, who answer phones and manage calendars, who vacuum the floors and keep the lights on.

"Death Is Nothing at All" was written by Henry Scott Holland; I apologize to him for Meredith's mangling his words and forgetting a part of his name.

Thank you to Shaun Hamill and Rebekah Harrelson, who spent a lot of time with me and Tracy when I felt worst about this book and its chances.

Love and gratitude to everyone in my Iowa City circles—the folks at game night, taco night, video game night, and the D&D crew. You helped make life bearable in the years my chemicals were at their most imbalanced.

Thank you to my friends in the Discord. Thank you to every reader who sent me a kind note between books. Thank you to the students at my day job, who are a constant source of life. Thank you to River, Elise Pizzi, Carly Nichols, Bill Watts, Christopher Backley, and Brett Ortler, who taught me new ways of saying I'm sorry. Thank you to the folks at Butler and New Mexico State.

My grandmother and grandfather, Helga and Mike Meginnis, died between the time I wrote the first draft of this book and the day it was sent to the printer. In my grandmother's case it was sudden, unexpected, and basically normal; in my grandfather's case, he died during the height of the pandemic, more or less alone, in a hospice. I could have visited him, no one would have stopped me, but I was afraid. I can't say that I wrote this for them—I tried as best I could to keep them from reading my fiction, as I was certain they wouldn't have liked it—but I want to say here that I loved them and that they are missed.